NOT YOU AGAIN

NOT YOU AGAIN

A Novel

INGRID PIERCE

alcove
press

This is a work of fiction. All of the names, characters, organizations, places, and events portrayed in this novel are either products of the author's imagination or are used fictitiously. Any resemblance to real or actual events, locales, or persons, living or dead, is entirely coincidental.

Published in the United States by Alcove Press, an imprint of The Quick Brown Fox & Company LLC.

Alcove Press and its logo are trademarks of The Quick Brown Fox & Company LLC.

Library of Congress Catalog-in-Publication data available upon request.

ISBN (paperback): 978-1-63910-813-8
ISBN (ebook): 978-1-63910-814-5

Cover design by Dawn Cooper

Printed in the United States.

www.alcovepress.com

Alcove Press
34 West 27th St., 10th Floor
New York, NY 10001

First Edition: July 2024

10 9 8 7 6 5 4 3 2 1

To the ones who stayed.

MARCH

CHAPTER ONE
ANDIE

I spend way too much time underneath brides' skirts.

It's humid and scratchy under here as I search for the source of the mysterious ripping sound among layers and layers of tulle. When I find the culprit, I dig through my sparkly clutch on the tile floor between my legs for a needle and thread.

I'm getting too damn old for this. My knees ache, nothing between them and ceramic tile except the layer of chiffon from my own skirts. My bodice bites into the skin under my arms as I shift my weight forward to work on the tear.

Just as I have the needle lined up to spear the edges of the tulle together, the bride shifts her weight in her stilettos. The needle misses its mark and stabs directly into my fingertip. I let out a curse, sucking my finger into my mouth.

"Bonnie," my best friend's voice says soothingly outside my tulle prison, "I need you to hold still while Andie works, okay?"

"Sorry." She shifts her weight again. Bonnie Mae is the oldest daughter to Beau Davenport and the heiress to a biscuits and gravy empire. I wish I was kidding. She saw my designs on TikTok and had to have me design her perfect wedding dress. "I didn't ruin anything, did I?"

Heidi makes a show of raising her voice so I can hear her clearly underneath all these skirts. "What's the prognosis, Andie?"

I remove my aching finger from my lips and reply from under Bonnie's skirts, "You tore three of the tulle underlays."

Bonnie swears, but I send a silent thanks to whoever is up there listening that she hadn't torn the hem of the overlay she'd insisted on being beaded with Swarovski crystals.

No matter how many times I explain to a bride that wearing a couture dress means that it's all handsewn and takes time to perfect, they always, *always* want a last-minute change. As charming as Bonnie is, she's no exception to the rule. I was in my studio until three in the morning for a solid week trying to get this hem right after she made the last-minute request.

She did the damage to the underlayers during photographs after the ceremony. So here I am, babysitting both bride and dress for the night. When a bride pays ten thousand dollars for a handmade dress, they expect the highest level of service. That includes an onsite seamstress, and as my business consists of me, myself, and I, I often find myself on my knees under skirts as I take care of any dress emergencies that come up.

The rest of the wedding emergencies are up to Heidi to solve. As one of Atlanta's most sought-after wedding planners, she can whisk away any and all wedding day mischief with a swipe on the tablet I know she has tucked into her Balenciaga bag.

Right now, Heidi's holding Bonnie still while I finish up with the tulle. The toes of her Jimmy Choos peek from underneath the front of Bonnie's skirts.

I finish whipstitching the last layer of tulle closed and sever the thread with my teeth before tucking everything back into my bag. I bite back a groan as I maneuver out from under the skirts as gracefully as I can manage in my floor-length gown. Part of being a personal seamstress at one of these weddings is that I absolutely cannot look like I'm here as staff.

I smooth Bonnie's skirts back down, double- and triple-checking for any damage to the top layer of the design. If she has a single bead or crystal missing, it's my job to notice and to fix it immediately. If she loves her dress and experience enough, she'll recommend me to her dearest friends when it comes time for them to get married.

And with a little luck, I might stay in business.

Determining nothing else is awry, I grip the marble counter in the bathroom and hoist myself off the ground, straightening my own dress as I stand.

I toss my clutch on the counter and tell Bonnie, "Good as new."

"Shit, you don't think we spent too much time in here, do you?" Bonnie asks in her southern drawl, pulling a flask from her skirt pocket. I never design a wedding dress without pockets, because there's no earthly reason why not.

Heidi gives me a wry look over Bonnie's shoulder as she takes a swig of whatever's in her flask. Southern brides are all smiles and hospitality, but you can always count on bourbon being nearby. "It's your day," Heidi tells her as she recaps the flask. "You will take the time you need. Besides, I made sure the band started up during cocktail hour. I doubt anyone's noticed how long we've been in here."

Bonnie tucks the flask back into her pocket and takes a deep breath, shaking out her shoulders on the exhale. Getting her game face on.

Heidi grips her upper arms. "You look beautiful, and your dress is perfect. Your groom is waiting outside the ballroom for your grand entrance, okay?"

Bonnie nods and gives us both a smile before swooshing away in her gown.

As soon as the heavy bathroom door closes behind her, both Heidi and I slouch our shoulders and lean on the counter. She smooths a stray hair into her perfect French twist and hands me my drink. It's just club soda with a wedge of lime in it—we're working, after all—but I'm grateful anyway.

"For someone who doesn't believe in love, you sure do make some fairy-tale dresses." Heidi clinks the rim of her glass to mine before taking a sip.

I cover a scoff with a sip of my drink. I feel relief in my raw fingertips and chafed palms at the coolness of the glass. It's soothing and goddamn necessary, because I just know that beaded hem is too heavy. It'll get caught underfoot soon enough, and we'll be back here with me trying to pull everything back together.

If only holding my business together was as simple as fixing a hem.

Heidi sets her drink down and rummages through her own bag. "Did Clover Callaway change her mind?"

"No." I press the cool glass to my forehead. "Apparently her fiancé sleeping with the maid of honor is not only cliché but unforgivable." And a huge blow to my finances.

Atlanta Ballet's prima ballerina Clover canceled her order after local gossip blogs caught wind of the scandal.

"Damn." Heidi knows the lurch that cancellation left me in. "Have you made much progress with your designs for Fashion Week?"

I shake my head. My designer's block has arrived like a bridesmaid to a karaoke bachelorette—loud and eternally off-key. The timing is the actual worst, as it's my first year showing in Atlanta Fashion Week, and I wiped out my bank account purchasing materials to create my line, counting on the payout for the delivery of Clover's dress. And now it will never come. "My muse is a fickle bitch."

Heidi snorts and pulls out a Band-Aid. She gestures for my hand and finds the fingertip I stabbed earlier. We've been friends since we met at a bridal expo five years ago. She had a burgeoning wedding planning business, and I wasn't much more than a seamstress at the time, working with a large bridal chain to alter dresses. But as her business took off, I struck out on my own—so came the benefit of sharing clients and providing for things they didn't know they needed yet.

In five years, I went from working for a bridal house for a pittance to designing my own dresses. Until the future Mr. Callaway sampled the maid of honor before the ceremony, I was on a roll, landing some of Atlanta's elite brides. Now wedding season is here, and I cleared my calendar for Clover, whose dress is now moot. If I can't seduce my muse in time to wow investors at Fashion Week, my once-sparkling business will be underwater before the next wedding season.

"Please, tell me your week has been better than mine," I say as Heidi finishes wrapping my finger in the Band-Aid.

"As a matter of fact," her lips curl into a devious grin, "I had a *very* interesting week."

"Don't leave me hanging." I shift in my heels. My heart aches to be back in my studio, barefoot, in an old Georgia State T-shirt, eating lo mein and sketching designs on my tablet. As if I'll magically break through my designer's block and use all the time I blocked for Clover's dress to design something so innovative, investors will have no choice but to line up for a piece of Andrea Dresser Designs.

Right.

"A scout from Optimax came by my office." Heidi's fingers fly over her phone in response to it buzzing on the counter. When I raise a questioning brow, she waves it off. "Crystal's got it under control."

God, I need an assistant like Crystal. And a miracle.

"Are they going to shoot some sort of wedding planning series or something?" The publicity alone would be a great opportunity for her.

She shakes her head and takes another sip of her drink. "I know you're, like, living under a rock in that studio, but—"

"It's a *nice* rock." I roll my eyes. I have a wall of windows that shows Atlanta's glittering skyline from sunset to sunrise. And I would know because I've been up until two AM every night this week trying to beat my muse into submission.

"You live where you work," Heidi scolds. She's right. My bedroom is in the loft above the studio where I meet brides and make gowns. "You know how I feel about that."

"I like the commute." I smirk. She has to drive in Atlanta rush hour to get to her downtown offices; I just have to go downstairs. And it keeps my living expenses at rock bottom.

"Whatever." She waves it off. "I know that if it's not in a bridal magazine or on BrideTok, you don't see it."

I don't react to the dig. Mostly because it's true.

"Optimax is the one that owns the Vibe channel," she explains, letting our bickering drop. "They're filming the next season of *First Look at Forever* here in Atlanta."

My brows draw together in confusion. I don't own a TV, so I'm not quite sure what show she's talking about. I *do* practically live under a rock. Between designing gowns, attending the weddings as personal seamstress to the brides, and trying to design an entire separate line to show at Fashion Week, there's not much room left in my life for anything else.

"It's that show where matchmakers arrange marriages?" She raises a brow at me.

I shake my head. It still isn't ringing a bell. "Why were they at your offices?"

"They need someone to plan the weddings this season." She shrugs like it isn't a big deal to be recruited by TV producers.

"How many?" I'm already doing math in my head.

"Three to six. All on the same day."

My jaw drops. Heidi is some kind of organization wizard and multitasking goddess, but six weddings *in one day*?

She laughs at my incredulousness. "I think you should meet the producers."

I scoff, tapping one of my fingers nervously against my glass. As much as I need the paycheck, it's not like I could design up to six dresses for brides I haven't even met yet, make them to my level of perfection, then babysit them all on the same day while brides drank too much and tore their hems on stilettos and spilled wine on their bodices.

Could I?

"I meant as a candidate for matchmaking," Heidi scolds.

My breath catches at the idea. "How strong is that drink?"

She laughs again, taking another sip. "Do you know the premise of the show?"

"I live under a rock, remember?"

"Perfect strangers marry, then they have eight weeks together to decide: stay together or walk away."

"Why in the hell would I do that to myself?" I already know marriage is never on my to-do list, let alone in front of a TV audience. And especially not if all it's bound to do is crash and burn. My mom's been married enough times; I know exactly how this will play out.

"Because if you choose to divorce at the end, the show pays you a hundred grand for your trouble." She sips on her drink and shrugs one shoulder. "Each."

"A hundred grand?" I ask quietly. That would cover the materials I purchased for Fashion Week, pay for the models, and then some. I might not even *need* an investor right away. "But why would anyone stay married if you get paid to divorce?"

Heidi leans closer, raising her eyebrows like she knows a big, juicy secret. "It's hidden in the contracts. Listed under *payment for damages.*" She leans back against the counter and shrugs. "They let me speak with some brides from last season, and one of them let it slip. Apparently, the show has six figures set aside for each cast member, just in case. It's probably to avoid a lawsuit or something."

I frown.

"I'm just saying, it's there if you want it. I know how you feel about business loans."

I bring my glass to my lips to help swallow the bitter pill of my mother's unfilled promise to invest in my business. It went out the window with her last marriage. A six-figure paycheck that I can get myself sounds appealing. Eventually I mumble, "It's an option."

Heidi gives me a perfunctory nod. "You're a catch; they'd definitely cast you. And we both know you're not going to *fall in love.*"

It's true, but something behind my rib cage twists at the cool statement of fact. No way in hell am I going to tie myself to a person for life. It's only license for them to take what they want, then cast you out when they're done with you.

I'm fine on my own.

Or I will be when I finally get through my designer's block and come up with a theme that's new and interesting, or even just a little unexpected at this point. Fashion Week looms like an omen in the not-so-distant future. I murmur into my glass, "A hundred grand."

Heidi snorts and rolls her eyes. "Think about it, okay? At the very least you get an all-expense-paid vacation, and God knows you need one of those."

She whisks out the bathroom door, leaving me to ruminate.

CHAPTER TWO
KIT

The rotting wooden steps to the front door groan under my feet, and I make a mental note to send a handyman out to repair them. The paint on the exterior of the single-wide manufactured home needs some love, too. I'm not surprised. It's been a while since I've been back, and I knew my mom was in no state to take care of the house when I left.

The screen outer door squeals on its hinges, and guilt gnaws at my guts. It's something my dad would have taken care of if he was still around. I clear the knot of emotion from my throat; I'll oil them before I leave. It's the least I can do. It takes a moment for my knock on the front door to be answered. I breathe in the cool late March air; the weather is much nicer in northern Georgia than it is in New York City this time of year.

"The prodigal son returns!" Mom answers the door in a house dress and slippers, readers dangling around her neck from a chain with dragonflies on it. "Come in, come in."

"You look . . . good." I offer her a smile that wobbles at the edges. The linoleum in the tiny kitchen is the same as it was my entire childhood, though now it's yellowing with age and peeling away from the dusty pink cabinet edges.

"How many times have I told you, you never have to knock?" She closes the door behind us and shuffles into the living room. "You grew up here; it's your own home."

I wince, gripping the back of my neck, and say to my feet, "Mom, I haven't lived here in over a decade."

She tuts. "It will always be your home, Kit."

How can she say that so easily? She'd had me young—she and Dad were only nineteen—and married when my mom was still pregnant. It made for a hard life. My dad tried his best, but we'd never had money. The walls of this place still echo with the late-night conversations they didn't think I heard. The ones where they had to choose between cable and a new jacket for me. They always chose me. But when Dad died, I couldn't choose her.

Mom's already marching to the kitchen. "You better be staying for dinner."

"Of course." I shove my hand through my hair, mussed from the redeye from New York, and that was a mere twenty-four hours after the flight from Paris. I haven't shaved in almost four days, and Mom reaches up to pat the stubble on my cheek. I give her a weary smile, the vise around my lungs loosening an iota.

"I'm glad you're home, kid."

"Me too." I've been a tangle of nerves since she told me she had to have her operation. I put in for a transfer to Atlanta as soon as I heard. Someone needs to take care of her, and I'll be damned if I'm not here for her. I can do better now, stay this time.

I take my messenger bag off my shoulder and flip it open. "I've been looking into some home health nurses to be here when I can't." I pull out a stack of tabbed brochures and flop them down onto the small dining table. "I'm still planning on coming by every Wednesday for dinner, like we planned, but—"

She scowls at me. "I can't afford a nurse, Kit."

I swallow. "But I can." Thanks to her guidance, I managed a scholarship for undergrad, and a fellowship for grad school. Now I work for an international resort chain and have the bank account to match.

She breaks eye contact and shakes her head, mumbling under her breath. "You should be living your life," she finally tells me as she wanders to a drawer in the kitchen. "Building a career."

"I've done that," I say softly. I'm not a billionaire, but I make enough to send her groceries every week. Enough that I cover her medical bills for all the testing she's been through, and enough to cover what comes after her mastectomy. Including a home health nurse and any experimental drugs she may need if the approved ones don't help.

She waves me off. "Making friends, putting down roots."

I frown. Because I travel to wherever my company needs me, I haven't had to put down roots. They pay for my accommodations wherever I end up, so I haven't had to buy a home or rent an apartment in years. It frees up money to take care of her, so I'm okay with not having a permanent home.

"Finding a partner?" She raises a brow and pulls out a stack of paper from the drawer she yanked open. She closes it with a bump of her hip and drops her document on top of the home health brochures.

"I'm fine on my own, I promise," I insist. I've had girlfriends; I know how to date. It's just not something I have room for in my life right now. Not with a new assignment and her surgery looming.

She jabs a finger at the document she just dropped. "You may be grown, but I'm still your mother."

My eyes dart to hers. I can't remember the last time she pulled the Mom Card. She used to do it all the time before Dad died. She was broken beyond repair when I departed. It still keeps me up at night, knowing I should have stayed. I should have done better.

"You need a partner," she says firmly, tilting her chin to look me in the eyes. "Someone to be there for you and make new memories with."

I bite my tongue. She gave up everything for Dad, and he left her behind to clean up the mess. That's the thing about partners, isn't it? Till death do us part?

But the spark in her eyes makes me so happy I could cry. She jabs at the papers again.

I sigh and pick them up. "What is this?"

She smirks, and I'm stunned by the glimpse of who she was before. "There's a show filming in Atlanta. That's an application."

I flip through the pages. The show films from mid-July to mid-September, then airs several months later. "I have a job."

"It's a matchmaking show."

There's a determined set to her mouth, a seriousness to her gaze.

"I'm not going to be around forever, Kit." Her words are soft, angling right between my ribs and straight into my heart, too tender for its own good. "And I want to see you settled before I go."

"The doctors said you'd—"

She shakes her head once, firmly, as if she doesn't want to hear it. "I don't care what they say. You need someone in your life to be there for you."

I clench my jaw as something in me long dormant wakes up. A distant memory rises to the surface: two bodies tangled in a tiny dorm room bed, a murmured *I love you*, and the promise of a future we never saw.

The long-suppressed echo of hurt gains a pulse, like it's alive and breathing again. My gaze falls to the teetering pile of paperbacks on the end table by the worn-out sofa.

Mom always has stacks of thrifted books scattered around the house. Most are romances, and growing up I read quite a few. It was nice to read about people finding the kind of love that was strong enough to last forever. They gave me hope. That hope was tangible years ago, just before it sifted through my fingers like sand. Out of time.

I swallow, looking at the application in my hands. I'm being melodramatic, thinking for even a second that love will solve everything. Mom still has her surgery in front of her, and the results may be devastating. In any case, the heroes in all those books were the ones who saved the day. No one is going to save *me*.

"You're a good man," she says, growing serious. "You deserve to find someone who appreciates you like I do."

"You show your appreciation by returning all the checks I sent to pay off your mortgage." After she sent the last one back in shreds, I finally gave up. All I want to do is take care of her after I failed so miserably at it the last time. But she won't give me the chance.

"Kit." She puts a hand on her hip, like she used to when she was about to ground me when I was a teenager. "I need you to worry less about me and more about yourself."

All I've done since I left is worry about myself. My phone rings on the table. Without thinking, I take a step toward it, but Mom's sharp gaze stops me in my tracks. My fingers twitch as I fight the urge to reach for it.

The caller ID says it's one of my bosses. Anxiety gnaws at me. My job pays so well because they need me constantly available. All the time. And after the move I pulled to ensure I got placement in Atlanta, the calls have increased tenfold.

Mom holds her glare.

I groan and pace into the living room until my phone goes silent. I pause to look at the Sears family photo with all of us she still has hanging over the sofa, shame washing over me. It really is remarkable how much I look like him. Staring at the photo, I murmur, "I do enough for me, Mom."

"I'll make you a deal." Mom's voice carries a bit of playfulness to it.

I slowly turn to face her and quirk a brow. "What kind of deal?"

"Fill out the application. Turn it in." She tosses me a pen.

"And?" What on earth is she up to?

"And I will accept the help of a home nurse of your choosing without complaint."

I scoff. "That's it?" Applying to this stupid show doesn't mean I'll get picked. In fact, the odds are I won't. I could even fill it out with some bogus information just to seal the deal.

"And don't even think of being dishonest when you answer those questions," she warns. When I give her a placating look, she snorts. "I raised you, remember?"

I finger the pages of the application and frown. What harm could it do, really? She's only asked me to apply. I don't have to actually find someone or fall in love or even be *on* the show. And, in the end, there's nothing I wouldn't do to make sure she never had to worry about anything ever again.

"Fine." I raise my hands in surrender, a smile tugging at my lips. "I'll fill it out. And I'm setting up interviews for nurses starting tomorrow."

JULY

CHAPTER THREE
ANDIE

The giant mahogany doors to the conference room-turned-wedding venue send my heart racing. All at once my dress is too tight, the room is too hot, my heels are pinching my toes, and all I want to do is *run*.

"I hope he's handsome." My mom hooks her arm in mine. When I told her I was getting married to a complete stranger on television, she was delighted. Like, she actually leaped out of her chair, spilled her wine, and tackle-hugged me, saying she thought I was going to be alone forever.

It didn't inspire much confidence, really.

"I'd rather he not be a dick," I mutter as I shift in my heels. I can put up with a lot for eight weeks if it means I'll pocket that hundred thousand dollars at the end, but I'd at least like to be treated with some respect. In any case, I know he's handsome.

Heidi has been scurrying around the venue, preparing for three weddings today. She hired an extra assistant and enlisted a gaggle of the show's interns to help wrangle the details. After shoving some champagne in my face in the dressing room an hour ago, she disappeared, only to send me a text that simply said, *Technically I can't tell you, but your groom is hot AF.*

"Stop slouching," my mom scolds. "A bride never slouches."

I roll my eyes. She would know. She's been married five times. I can't fault her for it. She never finished a degree or had a career of her own, but she always made sure we had a roof over our heads and food in our stomachs. I'm well aware of how much she sacrificed for that. With a sigh, I straighten my spine.

"So," I say casually as cameras move around us, capturing several angles of the pre-wedding moments, "Jim seems nice."

My mom smiles, her blush showing even through the professional makeup. She swipes a salt-and-pepper curl out of her eyes and says, "He is a very nice man."

She wandered in with Jim early this morning. I knew she met someone—the ink on her most recent divorce papers had dried a month ago—but I hadn't met him yet. Jim strolled up in jeans and a T-shirt this morning, just under six feet tall, with a wide smile and wavy hair that had gone gray. He has a soft jawline and eyes that sparkled with laughter. He carried my mom's garment bag. I'm still not sure why, but that feels so *different* from the other men I barely called my stepfathers.

"Where did you say you met him?" I ask as a producer approaches.

Her reply is soft. Girlish and demure. "The dry cleaner."

Before I get a chance to ask more about it—normally she finds them at a high-class bar or a country club—the producer is telling the cameras closest to us what to capture. The room goes silent, and one of the matchmakers approaches, a cameraman on her heels.

"All right, Andie." The show's host Petra grips my free hand in both of hers. It's supposed to be a comforting gesture, but it feels more like a vise. The bodice of my dress feels infinitesimally tighter, and I struggle to take in a breath.

Petra is turned so the cameras can catch her lithe form in the best light, a broad smile on her face. Her pale pink dress shimmers in the sunlight coming in the windows of this anteroom.

The morning was a furious blur of action. I was poked and prodded while producers asked me questions from behind the camera.

How are you feeling?

Who do you think the matchmakers paired you with?

What if he's shorter than you? Or bald?

Are you getting cold feet?

I mumbled perfunctory answers until my mom turned up with Jim.

And it all boiled down to this moment. Right now.

Petra squeezes my hands and asks the question that plugs the name of the show, "Are you ready for your first look at forever?"

Forever is for suckers. I'm here to get mine and get out. But I flash a grin I hope looks equal parts glamorous and demure. "I suppose I have to be."

Behind me, a PA says into her earpiece, "Cue music."

I take a deep breath and squeeze my bouquet even tighter, my pulse bounding in my ears.

The doors open, and I see my groom at the altar, his back turned. Well, if I'm going to marry someone on TV who I've never met, at least he's got a great ass. He turns to greet me, a half grin hooking the corner of his pretty mouth.

My heart stops.

Oh. Fuck. No.

FIRST LOOK AT FOREVER
SEASON THREE
EPISODE ONE

PETRA ASHLING:
First Look at Forever attempts what modern dating fails to do: finding people their perfect match. We use extensive interviews and questionnaires used by organizations like the CIA to determine long-term compatibility. With such a high success rate, *First Look at Forever* is changing the dating landscape forever.

This season, we scoured our pool of applicants and found three couples our experts—a marriage counselor and a sociologist—believe can go the distance. The catch? The first time our couples will meet is at the altar, where they'll be legally married.

JAMIE:
I'm ready to get married.

KENDRA:
I want to find my perfect match.

KIT:
I hope I find a partner I can grow with.

LESLIE:
It's time to make room for the great love of my life.

PATRICK:
I want that connection I've been searching for.

ANDIE:
I'm as ready as I'm ever going to be.

PETRA ASHLING:
The stakes are high as our couples sign on for the commitment of a lifetime. After eight weeks, they'll have to decide if they want to stay married to the love of their life or choose to divorce.

CHAPTER FOUR

KIT

"Do you, Andrea Dresser, take this man Christopher Watson to be your lawfully wedded husband?"

As the officiant rambles on with traditional wedding vows about a wife *obeying* her husband and blah, blah, blah, all I can think is, *The matchmakers set me up with Andie fucking Dresser.*

I honestly thought I'd never see her again.

I swallow the lump in my throat and desperately wish I could turn back time.

She's beautiful. Of course she is.

The last ten years have loved her in the way I wasn't able to. Her dark hair is curled and tucked back from her face, leaving her bright hazel eyes exposed. I can't meet them yet. Not until I've cataloged the curve of her cheekbone or the dip of her cupid's bow. The spray of freckles across her cheeks. The only sign she's aged at all are the faint lines on the outside corners of her eyes—they betray a life of hearty laughter and smiles. She's been happy.

I selfishly wish for more signs she missed me. *We* were happy before life ripped us apart.

On the officiant's orders, I pick up her hands. She flinches like my touch hurts. The hope that blossomed in my chest as she walked down the aisle wilts.

She doesn't want this. It's in her grimace, the way her back is ramrod straight, the tiny line deepening between her dark brows.

In this moment, I'm grateful Mom isn't here. She was over the moon to hear the application I completed for our bargain had resulted in a match for me. But just this morning she was so sick from the chemo that she couldn't stand, let alone participate in a reality TV wedding where filming would last hours upon tedious hours. It took me, the home nurse, and three of her doctors to convince her she truly couldn't be here today.

If my match lasted beyond filming, I promised her I would happily partake in a vow renewal with all the bells and whistles so she could be there.

Now, with Andie so close, looking like a scared animal ready to bolt, I know I'll have to tell Mom her hopes that I've found my soulmate are dashed. I'll have to find some way to stop her from watching this season on TV. I don't know if I can bear sitting through each episode with her asking me why Andie and I couldn't just work it out.

The officiant clears his throat. My attention snaps to him, staring at me. Shit.

"Repeat after me," he says again, calmly. I nod, and he continues. "With this ring, I thee wed."

The words come from my lips, hollow and unfeeling. With shaking fingers, I slide the delicate gold ring onto Andie's left hand. And dammit, my own fingers linger on hers, betraying the ache that never really left me. I swallow and let her go.

She repeats the ritual, claiming me with a broad gold band. Her hands tremble with the motion, her mouth set in a determined line. Like she'll get through this by sheer force of will. This time I don't let go, catching her hands in mine.

"You may now kiss the bride!" The officiant beams, as though he can't feel the way the earth just stopped spinning underneath our feet.

I can only stare at Andie's hands in mine. Despite my hands being much larger, she's always had the ability to make me feel . . . small. The way you feel standing on the edge of the Grand Canyon. Like as heavy as your problems weigh on your shoulders, they are so insignificant in the presence of a natural phenomenon.

I take in a sharp breath when I realize we've both stopped shaking, now that we're connected. Almost like we're better off this way, reaching for each other.

"Cut!" A producer swoops in and whisper-yells at us, "What's wrong? What's happening?"

Andie flinches, and I tighten my grip on her hands. It's the only thing that keeps me from baring my teeth at the producer, like some kind of rabid bear.

"Oh, I, um . . ." Andie looks at the producer, then at me. Intentionally, I soften my gaze and muster the courage to meet hers. Her lips part, but no words come out. I tilt my head in a silent question: *Are you okay?*

"Why didn't you kiss her?" the producer asks, the veneer of calm not even close to masking her frustration. I'm three seconds from growling at her for pushing us like this. Andie is scared, for fuck's sake. She looks like she's seen a ghost. Like she's being forced to *marry* one.

Andie sets her jaw and tilts her chin up a tick. I let out a soft puff of laughter. She returns it with a glare.

How could I forget? This woman's stubborn pride is the eighth wonder of the world.

I wouldn't dare tell the producer to back off because Andie is clearly terrified and regretting everything that brought her here. To me.

But I can give Andie the option to back out.

I clear my throat and shift my weight on my feet. She's still holding my hands like they're a lifeline, and that gives me a fraction of peace. It may be all I get.

"I'm sorry," I finally say to the producer. Then I swallow, mesmerized with the way Andie's gaze drops to my throat. I squeeze her hands until she meets my eyes. "Do you want . . . I mean . . . is it okay if I kiss you?"

She hesitates, and my heart drops to the floorboards. The weight of my wedding band is fresh, and goddamn if it doesn't feel like an anchor. I want her to feel it too. To take this leap into the unknown with me. Because for a split second, I understand we'll never get this chance again. We fucked it all up last time. This time we can make it right. If she'll join me.

Quietly, she answers, "Yeah. It's okay."

My heart soars.

The producer lets out a heavy sigh and claps her hands together. "Okay. We're gonna go again."

She scurries off behind the cameras and shouts, "Action!"

Andie smiles up at me, looking ever the nervous bride. Her hands flex in mine, and I know it's too small a gesture for the cameras to have captured. That was for me alone. Hope blooms once more in my chest.

The officiant beams and says like it's the first time, "You may now kiss the bride!"

I lean in, dropping her hands so I can slide mine to her neck and cradle her head. Fuck the cameras, it's just us now. When my lips are a breath away, I say so low I know our mics won't be able to pick it up, "You look beautiful."

Then our lips connect, and I'm lost. This should be stiff, clinical. But she smells exactly the same. The memories hit me like an avalanche, abundant and aching and fresh. I can't breathe.

Right now, I'm not in this room at all. I'm in an auditorium on campus, playing a shitty movie I can't even remember, because I learned the shape of her body all the way through it. I'm in her dorm, and she's stealing my pencil, hiding it so I can't finish my calculus homework until I kiss her senseless. I'm pulling her into my room, rain-soaked and sobbing because her mom was going through a divorce, erasing her tears with my mouth.

Blown away by the pure force of her, my lips slide slowly on hers, coaxing her forward.

We're in this together. You jump, I jump.

Then, just as I'm ready to open my mouth to take the kiss deeper, she pulls away, opening her lips just far enough to scrape her teeth across my bottom lip.

My eyes fly open, my entire body *awake.*

I blink and take in a deep breath like I didn't just have a religious experience.

I swallow and let the cheers in the room wash over me. Married. Me. Legally fucking married. To Andie Dresser.

Somehow, that kiss turned back time.

CHAPTER FIVE

ANDIE

After the ceremony, we're whisked away to a "private" room at the country club lined with windows overlooking the rolling green hills outside. Even if the cameras weren't here, we'd still be in a fishbowl. Country club members in polo shirts and visors golf outside with a perfect view of this catastrophe.

I tap on my flute filled with warm, flat champagne to hide the hammering of my heart against my rib cage. The matchmakers paired me with Kit Watson. The man who broke my heart clean in two a decade ago.

Suddenly this whole in-it-for-the-money idea feels dangerous.

"So," I clear my throat and say delicately, "it's nice to meet you, Christopher."

He tilts his head in question, his lips pulling into a frown. I can't believe I kissed him. Like, really *kissed him*. And he kissed me back. With purpose. "Everyone calls me Kit." He says my name gently. "Andie."

I swallow and give my head a subtle shake. If the producers discover that we not only know each other, but already had a relationship—however long ago—my chance at one hundred thousand dollars is dead in the water. I look into my champagne glass and redirect the conversation to the things we should be talking about.

What we do for a living—he's an architect, I make wedding dresses.

Do we have any siblings—only children, the both of us.

What part of the city do we live in—him, lavish Buckhead, and me, bustling Midtown.

Where we went for school—Georgia State, of course. Where we met.

All I can think as I sip my champagne is how much I hate this. I can't help thinking it's all things about him I should already know. Like it was wrong for us to have been apart all this time.

Which is absolute bullshit, considering the way we ended things.

Out of nowhere, Kit tilts his head and asks, "Are you all right?"

"I'm fine." I steel my spine and focus on the way my heels pinch my toes.

He shakes his head. "I can always tell when you—"

"Kit," I warn. If he outs us right now and ruins my shot at that money, I might murder him.

He lets out a laugh that falls flat, scrubbing his fingers against his jaw. He's close enough I can smell his aftershave. Citrus, cedar, sandalwood. It's a more adult version of him, and I want to nuzzle into his neck to breathe him in.

Of all the men in Atlanta, why the hell did it have to be him? He's not even supposed to be here; I heard years ago from an acquaintance that he'd surfaced in Manhattan.

"What brings you here?" I ask abruptly. After a nervous glance at the cameraman behind Kit, I rearrange my face to look demure. Polite. Kit is supposed to be a stranger, after all.

He sucks in a breath and levels his gaze on me. "To the show or—?"

"Atlanta." My champagne glass clunks down on the table as I shift on my feet in frustration. "Why are you in Atlanta?"

"Because I live here?" He gives the cameras a sidelong glance, setting his glass down, too.

"Right." I scoff.

He turns to face me fully, squaring up for a fight, then deadpans, "Andie, if you say this town isn't big enough for the both of us—"

A frustrated sound somewhere between a whine and a grunt leaves my mouth, and I can't help myself. I stomp my foot. He's under my skin after only five minutes. How the hell am I supposed to make it eight whole weeks?

The producer behind him watches in amusement, brows raised.

"I need some air." I down the rest of my champagne, pick up the skirts on my off-the-rack gown and march out the door.

My heels sink into the soft country club grass, but I don't stop. Calves burning, I glance over my shoulder. Kit's closer behind than I expected. He eyes the curves of my hips with a deep frown on his face. The camera crew is on our heels, ready to catch more of this disastrous reunion.

There are so many words that want to claw their way out of my chest—most of them made of four letters—and I don't know where to start.

But he does.

"What brings *you* here?" he blurts out as I stop to lean against a white oak, shoulders slouching. The crew hustles to get a clear shot, forming a semicircle around us on the lawn.

"To find love, obviously." I flick his question away with my hand. It's a lie, of course. I'm here for the divorce money in eight weeks. I suppose I should be grateful I landed the one man I can guarantee I'll walk away from.

He gestures to the crew around us. "Maybe we should tell the producers we've—"

I glare at him. It's a look that says *don't you dare.* If he outs our past relationship right now, I'll—

"I don't see how we can hide it."

"Kit," I say through my teeth. "Shut. Up."

"Andie," the producer behind Kit interjects, "have you met Kit before?"

Without removing my glare from Kit, I bite out, "Yes."

"Was he a coworker or a roommate or—?"

"We dated." Kit says it calmly, matter of fact, slipping his hands into his pockets. "In college. Only for a couple months. Ancient history."

My jaw drops. I can't believe he just equated our relationship to *nothing*. As if it hadn't changed us both. Or maybe that was just me.

"Right, Andie?" He leans forward just enough to feel like he's looming over me.

My mouth flaps open and closed like a fish. Four-letter words flash through my short-circuiting brain in seventy-two point, sans-serif font. Underlined. In bold.

"Right." I force my lips to curl into a smile. "Old news. Practically strangers anymore."

Kit's mouth tilts in a half grin, brutal in its familiarity.

Heart in my throat, I look at the producer in the middle of the semicircle. "Is that going to be a problem?"

We signed the papers. A prenup and an NDA. The marriage license and the contract with the network; the phrase Heidi mentioned was there, sure enough. They wouldn't make it all null and void right now, would they?

The producer—tall and blond—smiles and shakes her head. "This is unexpected, but I think it will make for great television. Luke and Mia had met before last season, and fans loved them. We'll work on the storyline."

Great. The fear of losing my shot at the money evaporates, leaving behind a very different kind of discomfort. Instead of being released from the show, they'll use the second-chance angle to paint some story of finding our first love again.

My stomach lurches at the idea. I curl my fingers against the lace on my bodice, trying to stop my spiraling thoughts. Kit just made this infinitely harder.

We're both in this now. The only way out is through. Eight weeks. I can do this.

I could use some bourbon right about now. Why doesn't this damn dress have pockets?

"Still in, sweetheart?" Kit plants a hand on the tree trunk next to me, settling into a perfect lean.

I take a deep breath. "Why not? The matchmakers saw something here, didn't they?"

"They must have," he murmurs to the ground. I take a moment to study him. Time has treated him well—it really is unfair. He's always been an attractive man, but I've never seen him in a suit. His body has filled out, no longer lean and wiry. His tux stretches across his broad shoulders, strong enough to carry whatever is weighing him down. His brown hair is shorter, and he has a tiny streak of gray at his right temple. When did that happen?

He looks up, and my eyes dart away like I wasn't just drinking him in. "I'm in Atlanta because I work for an international resort company," he says, answering my question from earlier. "I'm here to supervise the construction of a new property."

"The Colonnade?"

He nods to confirm it. "That's the one."

I whisper a curse into the breeze that blows through. That resort is going to be one of the hottest new wedding spots in town. Which means I'll be there, looking at the walls, knowing he had a part in them. Heidi showed me drawings of the domed hothouse they're building, so they can host luxurious garden weddings year-round, no longer beholden to the weather. I stared at the drawing in rapt wonder—the geometry was as beautiful as it was functional. I immediately sat down to sketch a dress inspired by it.

The lump in my throat becomes impossible to ignore as it hits me: Kit designed the dome. I should have known it was his.

There's no escaping him. There never has been.

And now we're bound together in a legal marriage for the next eight weeks. With cameras following us everywhere.

His gentle question invades my thoughts. "It's hot out here; do you want to go back inside?"

I hate the way he asked that question. The way it feels like an intimate inquiry, like he has access to every dark corner of my soul. He doesn't know me now, and he doesn't deserve to. Steeling myself, I push off the trunk of the oak and give him a mocking, saccharine smile. "Sounds great. I'm parched."

His wedding ring glints in the sunlight as he drags a hand through his hair, leaving the style off kilter when he lets go. He pushes off the tree and holds an arm out for me to take.

I offer him a perfunctory nod and straighten my skirts. This man will not see me look a mess. When I slip my arm in his, I mutter, "I can walk fine on my own, thank you."

His jaw clenches, tension making itself known across his brow. "Yes, but what kind of man would I be to walk away from the supposed love of my life?"

I trip over my skirt, and he catches me, making sure I'm steady on my feet. I refuse to look at him as we stroll back to the building, bracing myself to dance and take wedding photos, like nothing is amiss.

FIRST LOOK AT FOREVER
CASTING INTERVIEW: ANDREA “ANDIE” DRESSER
SEASON THREE: ATLANTA

PRODUCER:
So why do you want to be on the show?

ANDIE:
I’ve been relying on myself for a long time. It would be nice to have someone to lean on sometimes, you know? I mean, I have friends, but this would be . . . different.

PRODUCER:
Do you think you’re ready to be married?

ANDIE:
I don’t think it’s a question of readiness. I wasn’t ready to drop out of college to help my mom after her divorce, but it helped make me who I am now. I think marriage is another challenge I can rise to.

PRODUCER:
You say it like it’s a game to be won.

ANDIE:
No, not really. Just like . . . it’s the next step in my life. The next level. I think I’m ready to take it on.

FIRST LOOK AT FOREVER
CASTING INTERVIEW: CHRISTOPHER "KIT" WATSON
SEASON THREE: ATLANTA

PRODUCER:
Have you ever been in love before?

KIT:
Once. A long time ago.

PRODUCER:
Never after that?

KIT:
No. Every other relationship sort of paled in comparison. Then my life got busy, and I haven't had time.

PRODUCER:
What makes you think getting married sight unseen will change that?

KIT:
I'm open to it. I don't think I should base my entire future on old ghosts. My life is more stable than it used to be. So am I. I'm ready and willing to be the partner someone can rely on.

CHAPTER SIX
KIT

It's too damn weird having cameras in the honeymoon suite. I know they'll leave soon, but hotel rooms are a place I generally associate with privacy and quiet. Right now, the producer is crammed into a corner of the room with a cameraman named Steve tripping over suitcases trying to get the right shot.

Andie's hands are balled into fists, her fancy hairstyle—twisted and pinned, curled and sculpted—frizzing around the edges, when she announces she's going to get changed into pajamas.

"Why don't you ask her if she needs help out of her wedding dress?" Cassidy, our assigned producer, prods me as Andie steps out of the bedroom, beelining toward the bathroom.

I fight the urge to roll my eyes, asking with gritted teeth, "Do you need me to help you get out of your dress?"

She shoots me a glare over her bare shoulder. I know that look; I *remember* that look. If the cameras weren't here, she'd have flipped me off for suggesting she needed my help with anything. Ever.

I press my fingers to the bridge of my nose and close my eyes. If the cameras weren't here, she wouldn't be either. This is so beyond fucked; I have no idea what to do. Signing on to marry a stranger and then spend the next eight weeks being filmed up to twelve hours a day suddenly seems like the dumbest idea I've ever had. I'm just lucky they'll let me keep working. My bosses don't need to know what I've gotten myself into.

"Let me know if that changes, sweetheart," I mutter around the lump in my throat that tells me I somehow fucked everything up beyond repair. I shouldn't have been so sharp with her earlier, but she hit me below the belt.

"Not likely, honey," Andie scoffs and picks up her skirt to disappear behind the bathroom door.

After the latch clicks, I shrug out of my suit jacket, taking care to hang it up in the closet. I know we're only here for one night before we jet away on our honeymoon to . . . somewhere tropical, I guess. But I'm used to taking care of the few things that belong to me.

I shoot Cassidy a look. "You're not going to film me undressing, are you?"

"Of course not." She taps Steve on the shoulder and nods her head toward the living room portion of the hotel suite.

I quickly do the math in my head: I turned up at this country club to film having drinks with the other two grooms this season—Jamie and Patrick—at nine in the morning. I made it through that, confessionals, a ceremony, more confessionals, then a farce of a reception I'm sure they'll edit into something that looks like we're falling in love already.

It's now after ten at night.

I read that damn contract through and through. I've met my minimum hours of filming requirement for the day, and I'd be surprised if Andie hadn't. One look at the producer and cameraman assigned to us tells me they're dead on their feet too. For as long as we've been filming, I know they've been here longer and will have more to do even after our day is done.

Clearing my throat, I tell Cassidy, "I don't think you're going to miss anything if you decide to leave."

"We're not supposed to leave until you're ready for bed." She yawns anyway.

I offer her a pleasant smile, the one I use to charm board members. Sometimes women at a bar. One that I know wouldn't do a thing to win Andie over, anyway. "You've been watching us for the last several hours; do you really think we're going to do more than avoid each other tonight?"

She snorts. Steve too. "No. I suppose not. But we can't leave until you two are in bed."

I undo the knot in my tie, chuckling in a way that says I don't care if Andie talks to me one way or another tonight. It's easy enough to ignore the bile climbing up my throat at the thought. "Why don't we just call it a night? You both must be exhausted, and we've got a travel day ahead of us tomorrow."

Cassidy hesitates. Steve says nothing but meets her gaze. She clenches her jaw, and he tilts his head, communicating something only they know. But with the way his eyes go soft as her shoulders slouch, I've got a few guesses.

I don't know much about Andie now, but I know something about being raised by a fiercely independent and driven woman. Trying to talk her out of the notion that she could get everything on her list done *today* was a regular part of caring for her. Steve looks like he knows this game too.

My attention focused on my cufflinks, I ask casually, "How long have you two been together?"

Stever's soft laughter doesn't cover Cassidy's gasp. I glance up and catch them lost in their silent conversation again.

Finally, Cassidy sighs and clicks off her headset, sliding it off her head. Steve knocks his headphones off his head too, removing his camera from his shoulder with a grunt as he turns it off. "Six years."

I smile. "That's a long time."

"Best six years of my life, man." Steve says it without irony or expectation. "She hated me at first too."

Cassidy rolls her eyes. Just to show she's not giving up, she says, "This is all very sweet, but I mean it. We need footage of you two getting ready for bed. Together."

"Of course." I nod my agreement, setting my cufflinks aside. With a smile, I offer, "If you need shots of us brushing our teeth together or whatever, I'll see if I can't talk her into it in the morning, eh?"

Cassidy shoots me a look I don't dare cross. Steve slips his headphones back on and hoists the camera back on his shoulder.

I close my eyes and take a deep breath. Andie's in the bathroom and hasn't made a single noise since she got in there.

She may not be happy to be legally married to me, of all people, but I'm still a fucking gentleman. Most of the time. I work the buttons on my shirt loose as I make my way back to the bathroom door. I knock gently on it with one knuckle.

When I don't hear a reply, I say, "We need some footage of us getting ready for bed."

A rustle of fabric is the only sign that she's still alive in there, but she doesn't come out.

"Please, Andie."

No answer.

I sigh. She'll come out of there when she wants to. She always did everything when she wanted to, how she wanted to, holding onto control of her situation until her knuckles were white.

I duck around the corner in the bedroom to tug off my shirt and hang it up, then my pants. A quick glance at the door says she's not coming out right this second, so I slip off my socks and boxer briefs too. I'd like to shower before bed, but I'm not dumb enough to tell Andie that while she's in there. So I find a clean pair of underwear and a pair of sweats and pull them on. I've just slid on a T-shirt when I hear the latch on the bathroom door click.

I stand, looking over my shoulder. As the door opens wider, I turn to face Andie. The camera on Steve's shoulder gives a mechanical whir as he frames the shot.

She's still in her wedding dress, full makeup, hair twisted and curled and pinned within an inch of its life. There's something poetic in me being completely undone and her looking like some sort of fairy-tale princess.

Quietly, she says, "I, um, need some help. With the buttons."

I don't gloat, even though I probably should. It would be safer to keep that wall between us. Instead, I nod, gesturing with my left hand for her to turn around. My wedding ring feels at once completely foreign and just right. I clench my hand into a fist as I close the space between us, doing my damnedest to ignore Steve and Cassidy mere feet away.

There's about a million tiny pearl buttons running down her spine from just below her shoulder blades all the way over the round curve of her ass. I've been with enough women to know she's probably wearing shape-wear underneath, not sexy lingerie.

That knowledge doesn't stop my mouth from going dry as I reach for the first button with shaking hands. At least she's turned around so she can't see me.

"Thank you," she whispers. Her arms are crossed over the bodice of her dress, and her eyes are on an unknowable spot on the carpet in front of her.

Two buttons. Three. "Any time."

Four, five, six. "You were kind to my mom, too."

"She cares about you," I murmur. Seven through ten. We never met each other's parents the first time; our relationship was four months of heat punctuated by laughter. The thought of how we were still warms me through.

She takes a deep breath and shakes her head, dangly earrings brushing her bare neck. "I'm sorry your parents weren't here."

I freeze, button fifteen in my hands.

Before I can speak, she says softly, "I noticed the seats were empty. I just . . . don't know much about your family."

I clear my throat. My fingers resume my work on the buttons, and I give her the barest sliver of information. "My mom . . . couldn't make it."

"Oh." The word is soft. Loaded. She probably thinks my mom doesn't approve of me being on the show, marrying a complete stranger. The truth is far from it.

Button twenty slips free where Andie's waist dips into the curve of her ass. I swallow. The back of her dress is open enough now she can probably handle it from here. My fingers move lower to button twenty-one.

It's the closest to a real conversation I've had with her in ten fucking years. I'll be damned if I just walk away now. She seems like she's done talking, though. So there's nothing left for me to do but to stare at the skin that's making itself known on her back. She's got freckles there too. The urge to trace them like constellations—like I used to—slams into me, and I let out a heavy sigh.

My breath skims down her back and she shivers, goose bumps rising on her exposed skin. Also making itself known are all the places the dress has been digging into her body.

There's a spot just above her right hip that's raw enough it looks like it's bleeding. An unwieldy frustration slams into me so suddenly I flinch—why didn't she say anything? I could have helped her with this earlier. Could have snuck away and loosened her dress or found a way to pad that spot or—

I close my eyes and take a shaking breath through my nose.

Andie looks over her shoulder, eyes wide and tired and apprehensive. "What?"

I slip the last button through its eyelet and run my finger down one of the red marks from her dress. "You should have told me you were hurting."

Her eyes grow cold, shuttered. I somehow said exactly the wrong thing, undoing any progress we just made. Holding her bodice up with one arm and fisting her skirt in the other, she huffs, "I can take it from here."

She used to go soft for me, warm and pliant in my arms, trusting me to keep her safe. Now all I get is her gleaming armor, reflecting all my mistakes back at me.

Steve and Cassidy stick around while we brush our teeth and wash our faces. Andie climbs into the big bed with me just long enough to hear the latch close behind them when they finally leave.

Andie throws off the comforter, mumbling, "I'll sleep on the couch."

I don't argue with her. Not because I won't gladly take the couch, but rather because I know she's too far gone to change her mind now anyway.

Only when she turns out the light in the living room do I turn out my light too.

I should have kept my mouth shut about the marks on her back. She'd never liked to hear she was human. In her mind, she's some sort of warrior who can handle anything. In a way, I suppose she is. She hadn't run screaming from me at the altar today, even when I gave her the option. Rubbing my hand over my mouth, I can't fight a smile—her stubborn pride might be exactly what I need.

CHAPTER SEVEN
ANDIE

The alarm on my phone is a scream out of hell, slicing into the nightmare that I married Kit fucking Watson in front of friends and family. When I fall off the couch, smacking the coffee table in a desperate attempt to turn the damn thing off, I know it's all real.

I mutter a curse as I untangle my legs from the blanket I found in the closet last night. My phone isn't where I left it. Instead, it's screeching from the desk across the room. Just as I push off the floor, Kit wanders out of the bedroom.

My brain screeches to a halt. He's in a towel, fresh out of the shower. My mouth goes dry as he reaches for my phone to turn the alarm off.

When did he turn into such a . . . specimen? In college he'd been tall and thin. Gangly. The man in front of me clearly spends some time at the gym. He isn't perfectly cut like some kind of unrealistic fitness model either. His muscles swell under his skin in a perfect display of strength and nonchalance. Like he actually cares about being fit instead of how he looks.

Well.

I swallow the lump in my throat.

My eyes fall to his chest. That's new—the smattering of hair over his pecs, the line marching down his toned stomach until it disappears below the too-tiny hotel towel. With effort, I avoid gaping at the glimpse of toned thigh making itself known where the towel edges don't quite meet up.

By the time my gaze makes it back to his, I realize too late he's been perusing my body too. I feel naked despite my tank top and satin shorts. I haven't been to the gym in ages, and I've been surviving off coffee and takeout. I know I don't look like I did when I was younger.

I clear my throat as I remember I don't give a shit what he thinks of my body, because we are one hundred percent not going to go there. Ever. "Did you move my phone?"

He shrugs, running his left hand through his still-damp hair. He's still wearing his wedding ring. Somehow, I thought he'd have chucked it out the window by now. "I was up early, and it wasn't plugged in when I left. Figured you'd want a full charge."

"When you left?" I narrow my eyes. I didn't hear him come through here at all. I cross my arms over my chest when I realize that means he saw me sleeping. Something about it feels too damn intimate when I can't say the same about him.

He doesn't answer right away, instead plucking a to-go cup from the coffee shop downstairs off the mini-fridge and offering it to me. "I hope you still take it with cream, no sugar."

I can't help but curl the warm cup against my chest, trying to shield my sucker of a heart that wants to swoon. He remembers how I take my coffee.

And he let you sleep on the couch.

"Where'd you go this morning?" I take a swig of the liquid gold inside the cup. My hair must look like a rat's nest after tossing and turning all night; I tuck a stray strand behind my ear.

He turns back to the bedroom and waves off my question. "Couldn't sleep. Went for a run."

I follow him into the bedroom, my brow furrowed. It's been a decade, so I'm a little rusty when it comes to his intonation, but that didn't sound like the whole truth. Before I have the chance to push him for more—we're married now, after all, I deserve the truth—I stop in my tracks, staring at the door to the closet.

"You hung up my dress," I say so softly I doubt he hears it.

But he does hear it. He gives me a sheepish smile as he lifts a hand to grip the back of his neck. "It's . . . a nice dress. I saw it on the floor this morning and . . ."

He trails off, looking at the garment in question, hanger hooked over the closet door. I slid out of it before making myself comfortable on the couch and left it in a heap on the carpet. It doesn't matter. It's just a dress, right? My world is made of tulle and lace and chiffon. One dress doesn't mean anything.

Especially not when I picked it out of a preselected lineup of dresses, presented to me in a slide show. Just like my ring and the bouquet. This entire marriage is one giant business transaction, for fuck's sake.

And yet here I am, sliding the hem of the chiffon skirt through my fingers. There's a grass stain from when we took our wedding photos on the lawn, and the bright green smudge is an imperfection that tells a whole story.

A story of how I loved Kit years ago, before we fell apart. A story of how I built myself back up without him, piece by precarious piece. A tale of how we somehow stumbled into each other's lives by sheer accident. Or maybe fate. The little stain is the visible reminder of how he dipped me low for a photo, his arms around me like he won't let me go this time. Not now that he's found me again.

It's an empty promise, I know.

"Maybe there's something more interesting on a different channel." His voice is right behind me.

I spin around, surprised he's so close. Quickly, I set my lips into a line. "Like another reality show where you can ruin someone else's life?"

The sparkle in Kit's eyes dulls and his teasing grin falls flat. He clears his throat and states, matter-of-fact, "The producers will be here soon. Bathroom's all yours."

I wince when I think about what the producers will think if they find out I slept on the couch. That'll make a fun segment in an episode, huh? And while I know they'll spin a story no matter what we do, I do not want them finding out the truth.

Nobody needs to know how broken this man left me all those years ago. Least of all Kit.

"Right," I say, pulling myself together. "They'll probably want some shots of us eating breakfast in bed. Talking or whatever."

"Or whatever," he repeats. Humor twinkles in his eyes again, and his voice is all gravel and sin. He didn't even have to try to make those two words sound absolutely filthy.

I roll my eyes, if only to keep from staring at him.

He sighs, shifting on his feet. "Andie, before the cameras get here, can we . . . talk about what happened? Before?"

I have *not* had enough coffee for this. My hand curls into a fist at my side and I take a deep breath before saying as calmly as I can, "We dated. It ended. We were young and stupid and it doesn't . . . it doesn't matter."

He frowns, deep lines appearing between his brows. "Of course it matters. You never gave me a chance to—"

"It doesn't matter," I repeat, too loudly in the hotel room. My words ricochet off the drywall and fall softly on the plush carpet between our bare feet.

Kit watches me, his gaze intense. I feel like an ant underneath a magnifying glass. I tug at the hem of my tank top and try to keep my hands from shaking. He left. When he came back, I said we were done. End of story. *Why* won't change anything, and I'm not looking to fix the pieces of me he broke. I patched them together myself, with my bare hands, and I can't risk ripping old wounds open. Not when I have so much to *do*.

He opens his mouth to speak but is interrupted by a knock on the door. I clear my throat. "That'll be the producers. I'm going to shower." Before Kit can stop me, I lock myself in the bathroom, and I climb into the shower before I can determine where the wetness on my cheeks is coming from.

* * *

The airport is unbelievably busy. Or maybe it's not. I wouldn't know.

Despite my dreams of traveling far and wide when I was younger, I've never even made it onto a plane. My heart kicks up a few beats per minute as I walk up to the ticket counter with Kit. The attendant takes one look at us and beams.

It takes everything in me not to roll my eyes. The producers made all the couples wear matching T-shirts. Jamie and Leslie are the next counter over in white ones that simply say, *We're on our honeymoon!* Somehow, Kit and I got stuck with bright orange ones. His says *She's my sweet potato.* Mine reads *I yam.* Both are hashtagged with Just Married, and we haven't been able to have a single normal interaction since we left our room this morning.

I picked at breakfast in bed on camera. It was a delicious spread of Belgian waffles, eggs Benedict, and enough fruit to make an extravagant centerpiece, but trying to fake a smile as producers prompted conversation from Kit and me made me lose my appetite. I'm paying for it now—my stomach is a gnawing pit in the center of my abdomen, and based on what the producers told us, we won't have time to eat before we get on the plane.

Kit smiles as he hands over his passport. It's in decent shape, but the pages have clearly been used and used well. And it's one of the thicker ones, with more pages that I read about when I was applying for my first-ever passport mere weeks ago. I'm embarrassed to hand over my little book, so crisp and new.

Kit eyes it with a frown as the attendant opens it to check my name and the spine actually cracks. "First international trip?" he asks me, an eyebrow raised.

I give him a smile that feels more like a grimace. "You didn't know I was a virgin?"

Kit nearly chokes, turning a shade of red that clashes with the orange of our shirts. He smooths his hair back and accepts his passport from the attendant as she says, "Have a nice trip to Costa Rica, and congratulations on your marriage."

He offers a weak smile, handing over his bag so she can tag it and toss it on the conveyor belt behind her. The attendant turns her attention to me, handing over my documents with a bright smile. "There you go, Mrs. Watson. Hope you enjoy your flight!"

I open my mouth to correct her—my passport clearly says my name is still Andrea Dresser—but Kit cups my elbow and steers me away, saying a polite goodbye to the attendant. Fuming, I wrench my arm from his grip and follow the crowd to security.

Steve and Cassidy are smack dab in the middle of the line that's about three miles long. Cassidy leans into Steve, his arm thrown over her shoulders while they watch a video on her phone to endure the wait. I bite my lip to hold in a wistful sigh. My life is filled with grand displays of love in glittering gowns under fairy lights, but it's these small ones I crave. They're sacred in their secrecy; something only these two people know.

When I stop at the end of the line, lost in my thoughts, Kit shakes his head, literally *tsking* me.

Hungry and tired and aching from a night spent sleeping on a creaky couch, I curl my hands into fists and demand, "*What?*"

"Come on." He nods his head toward another line—much shorter—that's roped off with a sign declaring *First Class, Diamond and Platinum Members*. When I hesitate, he gives me an amused smile. "If we wait here, you'll either murder someone or eat me for brunch."

I bite my tongue. My body is very interested in the idea of having him for brunch, just maybe not in the way he meant. I sigh, muttering a "fine" as I follow him into the other line.

The security guard at the podium takes Kit's passport and some sort of silver credit card. I hand over my brand-spanking-new passport and plane ticket. While the guard examines my plane ticket that clearly has us flying coach, Kit tells him, "Her reward card hasn't arrived in the mail yet because we decided to elope—just couldn't wait another moment, you know?—but we're excited to be on our honeymoon. Aren't we, sweet potato?"

I look up at him, stunned into silence. The guard glances between us for a moment before his gaze falls to our shirts. A smile stretches across his face. Biting back a curse, I tell Kit through gritted teeth, "I sure yam, honey."

Kit's eyes light up with laughter. My stomach growls. The security guard beams as he hands over our documents. "Congratulations, Mr. and Mrs. Watson. Have a safe trip."

Goddammit.

Once we're through the metal detectors, I shove past Kit, muttering something under my breath I'm glad the cameras aren't here to catch. "Our gate is over there," Kit nudges me in the correct direction. "Sit. I'll get you something to eat."

CHAPTER EIGHT
KIT

The espresso machine behind the counter hisses, drowning out the conversations around me and erasing the overhead announcement. The airport coffee shop is packed to the gills with businesspeople on their way to God knows where. A sigh escapes me when I realize, had I not forced the transfer to Atlanta, I could be on my way to Spain or Australia or Italy right now.

None of those options compares to the adventure I embarked on yesterday.

I can see Andie by our gate, leaning against a wall, trying to escape conversation with a chatty woman next to her who must have found out we were on our honeymoon.

The show made us wear these stupid T-shirts in matching colors, so there's no escaping the congratulations as we flee the country.

Andie slouched in the van all the way to the airport, her sunglasses perched on her nose. She curled up in the fetal position against the window, attempting to get more sleep, probably. If the other couples weren't with us, I'd have teased her relentlessly about choosing to sleep on the couch.

But seeing her in her satin shorts and tank top this morning was a sight that went straight to my cock. She's filled out in all the right places. Her hips are more pronounced, and even under clothes I could see the soft curve of her belly, where before there was only skin and bones.

She looks so much softer than she acts, which feels like a secret only I know. She's incredibly tender underneath the scales and claws and growls and glares. When she wants to be, she's so brutally soft, it knocks the wind out of me. Or at least it had back then. Maybe her body is the only gentle thing about her now; we've both changed.

I frown at my shoes.

How's that spot on her hip that looked raw last night? She hasn't complained about it, but it must be black and blue by now. And we're about to cram into tiny airplane seats for a few hours. Do I have any Advil in my messenger bag? I might have time to grab some if I—

The barista yells my name and I flinch out of my brooding thoughts. I collect my coffee and the brown paper bag she slides across the counter.

I head back to the gate, making a beeline to rescue Andie from the chatty woman, but I'm intercepted by one of the other grooms, who pats the empty seat next to him. With a glance at Andie—she hasn't even noticed I'm back—I take the seat.

"Is it just me, or was it iceberg city between you two on the bus this morning?" Patrick doesn't waste any time.

I bide my time with a sip of coffee so hot it scalds my tongue and makes my eyes water. The waters between Andie and me are frigid, to say the least. They're choppy and filled with the flotsam and jetsam of our previous crash and burn.

By the time things had settled down enough at home for me to get my head on straight, I was delinquent on my phone bill and couldn't pay to turn it back on. Strung out on adrenaline and grief, I didn't have the forethought to bring my laptop with me, so I hadn't emailed her either. When I was finally able to turn my phone back on, there was a voice mail from her, confirming all my worst fears.

We were done. Forever.

We need to fucking talk. She needs to know why I left, that it had nothing to do with her or the stupid fight we had right before my world fell apart. But she doesn't want to hear it. Won't even let me finish my damn sentence.

Not now, and not then, either. When I finally found her, her roommate wouldn't let me in. Called me all sorts of names on her behalf. I did catch a glimpse of Andie on the couch just before the door slammed in my face. She was . . . *broken*.

That image has been burned in my brain for a whole decade, along with all the things I wish I'd told her earlier.

I don't know what our plan is going forward, to get through the next eight weeks. I feel like the universe personally handed me a get out of jail free card, and I'd be an idiot not to cash it in. Surely eight weeks is enough to convince Andie I'm sorry, to show her the truth.

What we shared for those few months was unforgettable, even a decade in the past.

Patrick nudges me with his elbow. "What did you do?"

I swallow the bile climbing up my throat. "Nothing. She's just . . . going to be a tough nut to crack, I think."

Patrick nods, looking toward his bride, Kendra, who's headed our way, coffees in hand. His face softens. I've never seen anyone truly *light up* before, but Patrick does. "If the matchmakers did for you what they've done for me, Andie will be worth the effort, man."

* * *

Once in the air, Andie won't stop fidgeting. She's clearly doing everything she can to avoid touching me, but we're packed into this plane like sardines. Calmly, I ask, "Is your hip bothering you?"

"What?" Her brows furrow as she finally looks at me like she's surprised I'm here.

"That spot on your hip looked raw last night," I remind her. "You're clearly uncomfortable now. Is it bothering you?"

She lets out a heavy sigh and flops into her seat. "No. I mean yes, but no."

I can't help the snort of laughter that comes from me.

"I'm—" She pauses, frowning at the seat back in front of her. Then she shakes her head and mutters something to herself under her breath.

Finally, her foot bouncing on the carpet, she tells me, "I didn't know I'd have to turn off my phone."

I frown. Her passport told me she's never flown internationally. That comment tells me she's never flown at all. "You really are a virgin, aren't you?"

She lifts her thumb to her lips to chew on it, shooting me a sarcastic look. "I had to hand over some business stuff while we're away. I just hate not knowing what's going on."

An amused smile tugs at my lips. There's that control I remember. "You're welcome to use my phone. It's got international service if you need to check on something when we land."

She looks at me, lips parting gently. Her eyes skate over my face, and for a split second, I think she's going to do something bizarre like *thank me*. Instead, her brows draw together, and she gives me a firm shake of her head. "It's fine. It'll be fine."

I nod. She said those words like she's trying to convince herself rather than me. Distraction it is, then.

She doesn't want to talk about the past, so the present is what's left. I dip my head to speak with her more privately. Her hair tickles my nose. "Maybe it's a good time to talk about what we want the next eight weeks to look like."

She takes in a sharp breath as her leg slides against mine. God bless coach—it's the only time she's likely to touch me, it seems. Breathily, she says, "Seven weeks and five days."

"Andie," I scold in a low voice. I plop the paper bag from the coffee shop into her lap. "You should have eaten more at breakfast."

"You didn't eat at all," she counters.

"Not a breakfast person." I shrug. It's the truth, but also it's a bold-face lie. I don't eat breakfast because I remember what it's like to go hungry. The gnawing ache in my stomach, the dizzy spells, the brain fog. I don't want to forget that feeling. It motivates me on difficult days.

As Andie peers into the bag to see the croissant I got her, I try again. "It would help if I knew why you signed up for the show."

"I told you"—she tears off a chunk of pastry—"I'm trying to find love."

I can't help it. I chuckle. It earns me a glare. I lift a hand in surrender and counter, "You told me once you never wanted to get married." In fact, she doubled down on it the night she showed up on my doorstep in tears after her mom told her she was getting a divorce. *Marriage is just another way to force women into a life of servitude because some fictional woman ate a fucking apple.*

Andie bides her time with another bite of croissant. Her fingernails are painted a delicate pink. Flakes of pastry cling to them, and I want to lick them off. I swallow to chase away the image coming to life in my head.

"Andie," I say gently, "why did you jump through all the hoops to be on the show?" If she went through every interview and background check I did, she wants this. In some way, shape, or form, she wants this.

It's just *me* she didn't plan on.

She fingers the edge of the pastry bag, pressing her lips into a frown. She glances to the row in front of us, where Patrick and Kendra are seated. Both have their headphones on. Andie chews the inside of her cheek for a moment, contemplating.

When I think she's never going to show her hand, she shrugs and admits, "I need the money."

My brow furrows. "What money?"

Andie looks at me like I'm stupid. "At the end of filming, if we choose divorce on decision day, we get a hundred grand each."

"No, we don't."

She rolls her eyes. "It's in the contract as payment for damages."

It takes a moment for her words to sink in. Cold seeps into my chest as I sit still as a stone. Here I've been thinking we can connect again, maybe have a chance to start over, and she's been planning on divorce since she put her name on the application. No matter who she got stuck with. Hell, it shouldn't feel so goddamn *personal.* But it does. Oh, it does.

Slowly, I ask, "What do you need the money for?"

She can't be in massive debt or a fortune hunter—the show screened those contestants out with all their flaming hoops. For better or worse, the producers were actually trying to make good matches. Which raised the question—what did they see on our applications that made us special?

Andie looks out the airplane window for a moment. When she turns back to me, her eyes have a determined set to them. "I told you yesterday, I'm a dressmaker."

I nod. I don't dare speak, for fear she'll reconsider telling me anything. Dressmaking wasn't on her radar when we were in college; she was after a business degree at the time. What changed?

She toys with a loose thread on the seat. "I, um, have a spot at Fashion Week in October, and if I can attract some investors, I—"

She bites off the end of her sentence and shakes her head. "You don't need to hear all this."

But I do. I need to understand what makes Andie tick. To know what she dreams of accomplishing. It's a piece of her, and I'm greedy for it like a dog desperate for scraps from the dining table. I nudge her with my elbow. "Tell me."

She eats the last bit of her croissant and begins licking the crumbs off her fingertips. I bite back a groan, curling my hand into a fist on the narrow airplane armrest. She crumples the pastry bag into a neat little ball, then rubs it between her palms. Her lip is going to go as raw as her hip with the way she's chewing on it.

With a little line between her brows, she tells me, "A lot happened after we—"

I feel her words lodge in my own throat, sticky and hot. I hold my breath, waiting for what she'll say next.

She looks at the floor. "I wasn't able to finish my degree."

The air in my lungs comes out in a rush.

She waves it off with a wry snort. "Don't flatter yourself. There were a lot of things going on."

Of which my leaving her was one. I swallow, guilt gnawing at my insides.

With a determined set to her jaw, she meets my gaze. "I built my business from the ground up. With my bare hands." She holds them in front of her, palms up.

Another look at them shows me what I felt yesterday at the altar—calluses on her fingertips, dry and chafing everywhere else. The manicure she got before the wedding probably helped, but it wouldn't make up for years of difficult manual labor.

"If I can get investors"—she curls her hands into fists and rests them on her thighs—"it's a gateway to a more secure income that won't rely on the whims of a single bride or internet review. Right now, it's feast or famine."

I want to tell her I understand, that she's a goddamn force of nature to build that on her own. But I don't want her to think I'm bullshitting her, so I keep my mouth shut. A flight attendant comes by with a drink cart. I ask for another coffee, and Andie gets a club soda.

After we've both indulged in the beverages, Andie asks, "And why did you sign up for the show? Somehow, I doubt it was to fall in love."

She spits out the word like it disgusts her. I suppose that's fair. She did tell me she loved me all those years ago. We were half asleep. I never returned the sentiment, frozen by what it would mean. Love was big, love was permanent. Love was *terrifying*. Even more so when I learned how much love could wreck you when it was gone.

That fight over what she said—or rather, how I reacted to it—feels so stupid now.

Slowly, in a measured tone, I say, "I don't know about love. But I do want to find a wife."

She tilts her head in question. "What does that even mean?"

"I've spent a lot of time building my career, securing myself financially." I shrug. Knowing Mom's prognosis, I want her to see me settled. Soon. It's the only thing I can remember her actually asking me for in the last several years. "It's time to find a partner, and dating takes time I don't have."

Andie scoffs, looking out the airplane window. "Well. With an attitude like that, I can't see why you haven't found your match yet."

After this conversation, the only thing I'm sure of is that neither of us planned on each other being at the altar on wedding day. Would I be this invested in the outcome if it was anyone else?

Andie picks up the DSLR camera Cassidy slipped us to film some footage on the plane. She holds it up with the lens facing us, then shoots me a look. "Act like you like me for five seconds, okay?"

It's my turn to roll my eyes. But then she rests her head on my shoulder, and my heart stutters in my chest. She taps the button to record.

"We're on our way to Costa Rica!" She smiles into the camera.

I can't help it; I smile too. I reach up to pat her cheek, teasing, "Ready to spend forever with me, sweet potato?"

She shoots me a glare. "Can you pick another pet name?"

"But you *are* sweet." I pinch her cheek for emphasis.

She lifts her head to rest the point of her chin on my shoulder. "Sweetie is right there."

"It's so generic." I flick away the suggestion. "You, sweet potato, are one of a kind."

She playfully sticks her tongue out, and I laugh. She smiles too, wrinkling her nose. It's enough. For now, it's enough. She stops recording and tucks the camera back into her purse under the seat.

With a sigh, settling back into her own space, Andie says, "I need that money, Kit." She sounds so earnest, so raw, my heart is ready to sacrifice everything if it will make her happy.

I can't help myself—I brush a hair out of her face and cup her chin. She really is something else.

When I stare at her gently parted lips for a second too long, she whispers, "Maybe you should save that for the cameras."

My hand falls from her like I've been burned. "Touching you?" I ask, because surely she can't mean *caring* about her, like I can turn that function on and off at will.

"Yeah," she looks at my hand on the armrest. "It's safest, don't you think?"

To keep her safe from me, or the other way around? Who are we protecting? I frown. "So we—what?—put on a show for the cameras, then? Then part ways amicably in eight weeks?"

Her eyes light up at the idea. I hate it. She sits a little straighter in her seat. "We can say we became good friends and just couldn't see ourselves married. Whatever. Don't worry, I won't fall in love with you."

Bitter, I brush the idea away with my hand, like it doesn't matter. "Fine."

As much as I hate the idea that I'll have to let her go again, I suppose it's penance for the last time. This time we'll do it on her terms; I owe her that. But every stupid hope I had of us somehow rekindling what we had in college just dove straight off the airplane wing and into the Caribbean.

CHAPTER NINE
ANDIE

Kit and I wait outside the room we'll be staying in for the duration of our honeymoon while Cassidy and Steve set up inside. They want a shot of us entering the room and smiling about the resort. I'm sure they paid a fortune to be featured on the show.

I twist the plastic band around my wrist—it'll allow us unlimited food and beverages on the property—and lean against the wall. Kit is examining the silver number on the door with such intense interest, I don't dare interrupt.

He's been put off since I pulled out the camera on the plane.

On my TikToks, I show the process of designing and constructing a dress. I leave out the parts where I'm staring at the designs, wondering if they're any good. Or the parts where I'm shoving takeout in my mouth at midnight because I'm up against a deadline. What I show is real. It's just not the whole story.

I can't imagine this show is any different.

That means we'll need footage of us smiling and playing along, even though we already know where it ends.

"Okay, we're ready!" Cassidy's voice comes from the other side of the door.

Kit lets out a heavy sigh, and I use my card to unlock the door. We wheel our suitcases inside, smiles plastered on our faces despite the tiredness leeching from our bones.

My smile falters as I take in the room. One room, as in: this is not a suite. A giant king-sized bed is dressed in white linens, and the hotel staff scattered rose petals in the shape of a heart on the duvet. I swallow the lump in my throat. There's no couch in here. Just a couple of uncomfortable-looking chairs next to a small dining table by the doors to the balcony.

I'd suggest Kit can sleep in the bathtub, but it's a moot point. Aside from the cameras following our every move, the bathtub is smack dab in the middle of the fucking room. There's a bottle of champagne in a bucket of ice on the ledge surrounding the tub.

Next to it is a plate of chocolate-covered strawberries and a handwritten welcome note addressed to Mr. and Mrs. Watson.

Kit sees it too, and lets out a snort of amusement. "Looks like they didn't get the pet name memo."

My lips pull into a smile as he picks up the note and pulls a pen from his messenger bag. He takes the cap off with his teeth, and it's all I can do to tear my gaze away. Looking at his hands isn't any safer, unfortunately. He deftly crosses out our names and writes in his confident block lettering *Mr. and Mrs. Sweet Potato.*

He replaces the note on the bathtub ledge and recaps his pen, a satisfied smile on his face. I find myself smiling at him, still.

God, I'm tired.

"It's late," Cassidy begins another one of her leading questions, and I know we've been silent for too long. "Don't you two want to get ready for bed?"

Kit clears his throat. "Which side of the bed do you want, sweet potato?"

I shoot him a look and heave my suitcase onto the bench at the foot of the bed. Kit follows suit, and soon we've both ducked into the bathroom at intervals to change into pajamas and brush our teeth. Not the romantic evening Cassidy wanted for us, I imagine.

By the time I emerge from the bathroom, Kit has already removed the rose petals from the bed and slid under the comforter, scrolling through his phone.

"Guess I'm sleeping on the right," I say, forcing too much brightness into my voice.

Kit sets his phone face down on the nightstand. "You do enjoy being right, if I remember correctly."

I narrow my eyes. He laughs when I yank the comforter back hard enough that it exposes his legs. Thank God he's wearing a T-shirt and sweatpants. I'm not ready for a full flash of thigh like I got this morning. A woman can only take so much before she does something decidedly stupid.

When I pull the comforter up to cover my own bare legs, Kit catches my hand in his. He turns it over, brushing his thumb over my palm. I yank it out of his grip and give him a scowl.

He rolls his eyes and slides out of bed. "I'll be right back."

After he disappears into the bathroom, I hear the faucet running. There's some more clatters and shuffling. The mattress shifts under his weight when he returns, and he dumps his haul on top of the comforter: hotel-provided lotion, a small bottle of ibuprofen, a bath towel, and, still clutched in his fist, a hand towel.

He sits cross-legged on the bed, facing me. "Hands, Andie."

I scowl.

He rolls his eyes. "Jesus. I'm not going to hurt you."

My eyes slide to Cassidy and Steve, watching our every move. With a heavy sigh, I turn to face him, holding out my hands.

He turns them over, then frowns. "This looks like it hurts."

"It does." I punctuate it with a shrug. This is just what it's like to work with my hands. Sometimes they hurt.

Kit slides my wedding band off and sets it aside. He wraps both my hands in the wet towel. It's warm, a contrast to the cool air-conditioned room. Goose bumps climb over my arms, and my nipples stand at attention. I shift on the mattress, hoping to readjust my shirt so no one notices.

Then he squeezes my hands in the towel, and I can't help the groan that escapes me. I can't remember the last time I was touched like this. It's so delicious, I want to drown in it.

Kit laughs. "If I didn't know any better, sweet potato, I'd say you like that."

"Shut up," I mumble, flexing my fingers in his hands.

He removes the towel. Without looking me in the eye, he asks, "How do they get to be like this?"

"I work with delicate fabrics in colors that show every single speck of dirt. I have to wash my hands a lot to make sure I don't ruin anything."

His eyes meet mine, and I swallow a gasp. The look is intense—like he's trying to look right through me. I expect a probing question about our past, but he only says, "You said you're showing at Fashion Week."

I nod.

When it's clear I've lost my capacity for speech, he picks up the lotion. He starts working it into my skin, and I groan again, my eyes falling closed. Kit chuckles as he kneads the heel of my palm.

Cassidy clears her throat and asks, "You two dated in college, right? How did you meet?"

I shake my head. "We really don't need to talk about—"

"An art class." Kit answers without hesitation. He stays focused on my hands as he explains. "We were both late, so we got stuck at the front. She dropped a pencil; I picked it up. When I handed it back to her, she just stared at me like she couldn't believe I was a real person."

I snort my disapproval. "Right. Because you were such a beautiful man, I was stunned into silence."

He begins to work on my other hand, a smile playing at his lips. "You looked at me like that this morning too. Some things never change, do they, sweet potato?"

When I use my newly free hand to flip him off, he laughs wholeheartedly, throwing his head back. "Whatever," I mumble. "I caught you looking, too."

He nods, a smile still on his face. "Did it occur to you that I meant for you to catch me?"

Another round of goose bumps tingles across my skin. Kit's hands slow on mine, and his thumb rests across the pulse point on my wrist. It feels like time stops in this moment. We're alone and the world is ours.

But we've been quiet too long again. Cassidy pipes up from the corner of the room, "Do you feel like you've changed since then?"

Kit clears his throat and shifts on the bed. "She's still stubborn as ever."

"And he's still an arrogant ass."

"I still have to make sure she eats, or she gets mean."

"He still thinks I can't function without his help."

His eyes meet mine, and he drops his teasing tone. "You've always been like this."

I narrow my eyes. "Like what?"

"A force of nature." He drops my hands and wipes his hands off on one of the towels.

I bite my tongue, afraid to say something I'll regret. He's talking like he still has feelings for me. That's a dangerous game to play, especially when he knows why I'm here. I clear my throat and say, "We've both changed. It's been a long time."

"It has," he agrees. His chest rises and falls with a deep breath, then his lips part to say more. I'm afraid of what will come out of his mouth. It will be too honest, I know it.

He leans forward, bringing our faces closer together. I hold my breath. If he touches me now, I don't know that I have the strength to say no. Just as he lifts his hand from the comforter, a shrill ringtone starts up in the corner of the room.

We flinch apart.

Steve mumbles an apology as he lowers the camera from his shoulder and digs in his pocket for his phone, avoiding Cassidy's glare all the while.

Kit closes his eyes and slowly shakes his head, as if he's coming out of a trance. My heart rattles in my rib cage like I'd just completed the hundred-meter dash. I suck in a breath and don't miss the way Kit opens his eyes in time to see the rise and fall of my chest.

Cassidy curses under her breath. "That's enough for tonight. I think we got what we needed."

My shoulders sag with relief. We're silent as we unclip our mics to hand them off to Steve and receive our missive for morning filming from Cassidy.

Kit follows them to the door and deadbolts it behind them. He flicks off the lamps on the way back to the bed. I lean against the headboard while he tidies up. After returning the supplies to the bathroom, he picks my wedding ring up off the comforter.

He holds it between us. "You did well today. For a virgin, I mean."

I snatch the ring from his fingers with a scowl. As I examine it in the lamplight, I tell him, "I think maybe we should stick to the present from now on. We don't need to rehash the past."

He climbs back into bed and leans against the headboard too. "What if I want to?"

"What difference will it make?" I frown at the ring in my hand. "What's done is done. Ancient history, right?"

"Practically strangers anymore." He echoes what I said yesterday, though his tone is flat. He turns away from me, clicking off the lamp on his bedside table. "Goodnight, Andie."

I don't reply, choosing to set my wedding ring on the nightstand. I pick up a pen and hotel paper and begin to sketch a new dress.

CHAPTER TEN
ANDIE

"Andie," Cassidy says, stirring me from my sketchbook on our hotel room balcony. I've been trying to get the lines on this dress right for the last hour, and trying to *not* think about how if I can't present something unique at Fashion Week, I may have to start working as a seamstress again.

"Yeah?" I reply, tapping the tip of my pencil on the sketch paper, as if beating it into submission will help the lines flow better. After Kit's attention to my hands last night, the design came pouring out. I had to capture it before I fell asleep. But ten hours without a touch that intimate, and my muse left the building. There's no way I'm going to ask him to do it again—how humiliating would that be?

"You've got to go join the group by the pool," she tells me firmly, like my mom may have told me to finish my homework before hanging out with my friends. If my mom ever did that sort of thing.

I sigh. I thought the cameras would just follow us around as we did things, but it seems I get told where to go and when.

One hundred thousand dollars.

"Kit's already down there."

Of course he is. I force a smile and close my sketchbook before I stand.

"Andie." Cassidy stops me as I head to the door.

"What?" I just barely cover the annoyance in my voice.

"Maybe wear something less . . ." She gestures at my outfit.

I look down at my terry cloth pants and cotton tank. It's a comfortable outfit, and I'm on vacation.

At my hesitation, Cassidy explains, "I know you've already married him, but maybe trying to look good for him isn't a bad thing."

I mutter a curse under my breath and duck into the bathroom to change. When I emerge in a red bikini and a long, flowing skirt I made myself—with pockets, of course—Cassidy gives me a wide grin. "That'll do."

She clips the pack to my waistband and attaches the mic to my bikini strap over my heart. When she's satisfied, we make our way down to the pool to drink cocktails and have our conversation directed by the producers on the sidelines.

What I find when I get there, however, is Jamie in a Hawaiian shirt and swim trunks, assembling what appears to be a giant game of Jenga. The tower is as tall as he is.

"Hey, Andie"—Kendra waves me over with a megawatt grin—"you made it!"

Kit rounds the corner of the pool—on his way back from the bar, with a beer in his hand—and stumbles over his feet when he sees me. He recovers with a lighthearted chuckle, and I register that he's not wearing a shirt. I swallow as he approaches, my heart clanging against my rib cage so hard I'm surprised Steve isn't flinching at the noise.

When Kit is close enough that I could run my fingers along the tan line right above the waistband of his shorts—not that I'm thinking about doing it—he reaches out and plucks at my bikini strap right below my collarbone. My lips fall open in a gasp. I suppose I should have expected it with how he's been teasing me, but that touch was *playful.*

His skin barely brushed mine, but my nipples tighten. I cross my arms over my chest to hide them from the cameras.

A sly grin crosses his face. "You look beautiful."

My tongue darts out to wet my lips, and his gaze follows it like his life depends on it. "Thanks. You look . . . comfortable."

He laughs good-naturedly, and I can't take my eyes off the muscles in his throat. "It's a comfortable kind of day."

An image of our limbs tangled in bed overtakes me so fast I swallow to push it down. Back to the depths of hell.

"We're about to start a game. Can I get you something to drink?" He plucks my bikini strap again. Alcohol. Right. That's probably why he's so relaxed.

I can see Cassidy out of the corner of my eyes, so I give Kit a smile. "Can I share yours? If you don't mind, I mean."

"What's mine is yours," he says with a twinkle in his eyes. It's not fair how good-looking he is, truly. He's only gotten better with age, a veritable god standing in front of me.

I take the beer when he offers and bring it to my lips. His brown eyes darken as I take a slow drink. It's crisp and bitter on my tongue. I hold out the glass so he can take it back. With his free hand, using his thumb, he wipes a bit of foam off the corner of my mouth.

I expect him to wipe it on his shorts, maybe, or shake it off in the sun. But no. He brings that thumb to his mouth and makes a point of licking the foam off, never once breaking eye contact with me. My cheeks burn and my nipples go hard again. My body can't decide if I'm hot or cold.

That was a dick move.

"Quit flirting and come show us what you're made of," Patrick booms, adjusting his backward baseball cap on his head.

I take a step back from Kit and clear my throat. He gives me one last smirk before turning to the game. "I'll tell you a secret." His fingers brush my lower back. "I'm a Jenga champion."

I snort, rolling my eyes.

"I mean it." He nudges me with his elbow. "In grad school, a bunch of us from my architecture program would get together to see who could stop the tower from falling. I'm undefeated."

The spark in his eyes reminds me of the Kit I used to know, and it makes my heart ache. I reach to rub away the pain but get scolded by Cassidy for messing up the microphone. She ducks in to readjust it. When she's back out of frame, I tell Kit, "Don't let me down, then. I don't like to lose."

He gives me a smile that says he knows. He never forgot my competitive streak. This really is unfair.

"Let's do this thing!" Patrick whoops, sending Kendra into a fit of giggles. I already have them pegged for the losers; we haven't even started and they're already unfocused.

Jamie steps up to the tower to go first, testing the blocks by tapping. Kit asks him, "Is Leslie going to join us?"

Jamie presses his lips together in a grimace and shakes his head. He pulls an easy block from the middle, only a few rows down from the top. "He says he's not feeling well. Something he ate." Jamie places the block on top of the tower with a look that says he doesn't think Leslie is actually sick.

My heart lurches against my rib cage. Jamie and Leslie had been full of heart eyes since the wedding day. If they're having trouble already, Kit and I don't stand a chance.

Which is a good thing. Right.

We all take our turns for the first rounds without incident. By round three, Kit leans over and whispers, "Find an easy block on the right, then place it on the left up top. And push, don't pull."

I walk toward the tower, ignoring the shiver at how filthy *push, don't pull* sounds coming out of Kit's mouth when he's focused. With his instructions, my next few turns go smoothly. On one of his, he pulls a move I've never seen before: bracing the tower with his forearm as he shimmies a block free. It gives me too long to look at the map of veins under his skin, to admire the sun filtering through the hair on his arm. It's downright erotic, and we're in public. On camera, for fuck's sake.

On Kendra's next turn, the tower almost tumbles. We all wait for it to settle with bated breath. Who knew a game of Jenga could be so intense?

Kit. Kit clearly did. While Jamie works another block loose, Kit murmurs in my ear, "Hinge one of the side blocks out. Find a smaller one."

His warm breath unfurls over the skin of my neck, falling down my collarbone. It's a surprisingly intimate gesture. When I look over my shoulder to see if he's *trying* to be so sensual, his eyes are locked on the tower and a frown pulls at his mouth. Strategy for the game, that's all his whispers are.

I shake it off as I approach the tower, testing blocks. It takes a while to find a good one, poolside. Okay. Go time.

I bite my lip and move ever so slowly to tug the block from the tower. I sew thousands of minuscule beads onto delicate fabrics, my hands are as steady as they come. Call me Captain Fine Motor Skills.

The group holds their breaths along with me, including Kit. I've absorbed his quiet guidance the entire game, and this time it's definitely going to pay off.

The block catches and I let it go. The tower sways as Kendra squeals, clasping her hands in front of her chest. Kit doesn't say anything, but I can feel him behind me, watching intensely. His gaze makes my skin vibrate with electricity, and I shake out my hands to rid them of the sensation before I try again.

The wood is rough against the pads of my fingers, and I use the friction to gently pull. One deep breath at a time.

The block is stubborn, so I give it a small shimmy back and forth. The tower sways over my head again, and I redouble my focus. It's just a little physics problem, that's all. Slow and steady wins the race.

I let out a breath when I manage to free enough of the block to regrip. As I give it a gentle tug, the whole tower quivers, leaning further over me.

Fuck. No.

The blocks reach their tipping point, and I cover my head to keep from getting clobbered.

Before I can catch my breath, an arm wraps around my waist and pulls me backward. I gasp at the collision of my back into Kit's warm, naked chest. He grunts as our legs tangle from the momentum.

Suddenly we've reached *our* tipping point, and his grip on me gets tighter as we fall backward. My stomach plummets with the give into gravity, and I brace for a landing on the warm pool deck, gritting my teeth.

But it never comes. Instead, it's a tidal wave of chlorinated water as Kit breaks our fall into the pool. For a moment I can't breathe and the world is upside down. A block tumbles through the water and smacks me on the shoulder. It's not enough to hurt, but definitely enough to shock me into swallowing a mouthful of water.

Kit's hands are rough on my waist, pushing me to the surface. I burst out of the water and gasp for air. I'm sputtering and choking out what I swallowed when Kit pops up next to me.

Cassidy is swearing in the background, barking at a junior producer. "Fuck, the mics!"

But that all fades into the background as Kit hooks an arm around my waist and pulls me into him, using his other hand to push my water-laden hair out of my face. Fingers lingering on my cheek, he asks, "You okay?"

"No." I shake my head. "That tower shouldn't have fallen over. I chose the right bock to—"

Kit throws his head back and *laughs.* His skin glides along mine underwater and the vibrations of his guffaws hit me square between the legs.

Frustrated with the betrayal of my body, I splash him. "Dammit, Kit, this isn't funny; we should have won!"

He wipes the water from his face and gives me an ear-splitting grin. "I told you to *push.*"

Am I hallucinating or did our hips rock together ever so slightly underwater? I don't have time to hash it out logically. Cassidy and the junior producer appear at the edge of the pool begging us to climb out. "These aren't the waterproof mics!" she wails in despair, a grimace etching into her features.

As we climb out of the pool and wrap ourselves in towels, Cassidy bemoans the loss of these mics because the water's shorted them out. Steve puts his camera aside for a moment, his hand moving in slow circles across her back. I can't look away from the gesture. Yearning threatens to split my rib cage wide open right here for everyone to see. Kit listens intently as Cassidy works through the problem out loud, Steve comforting her all the while. The waterproof mics are apparently charging for our mysterious rainforest activity tomorrow, which means Kit and I are mic-free for a few hours.

Freedom.

I smile. He meets my grin by throwing another towel over my head and scrubbing it in my wet hair. I'm smacking him away before I recognize the sound of his hearty laughter twining its way around my beating heart.

Just when I think I'll be able to return to my sketchbook on the balcony of our room, fully charged and buzzing with Kit's touch, Cassidy claps her hands. "New plan: talking heads. Go upstairs and get cute. You have five minutes while we set up the boom mic. Get ready to answer some questions. Individually."

I bite back a groan and steal a glance at Kit, whose mood looks equally dampened by the news. My heart squeezes in my chest. For a few blissful moments, Kit managed to make me forget about anything but right now. The gnawing guilt over the designs I should be working on rushes in, settling heavy on my shoulders. I school my face into a blank expression and shrug, telling Kit flatly, "Dibs on the shower."

His look is blank too, though his tone is defeated. "All yours."

FIRST LOOK AT FOREVER
SEASON THREE
EPISODE TWO

PRODUCER:
It looked like you were having fun with Kit by the pool today.

ANDIE:
Um. I ended up nearly drowning. So.

PRODUCER:
Your chemistry together is pretty amazing.

ANDIE:
[frowns]

PRODUCER:
Is it possible you still have feelings for him after all this time?

ANDIE:
I don't—I can't—what?

FIRST LOOK AT FOREVER
SEASON THREE
EPISODE TWO

PRODUCER:
It seems like you're relaxing around each other.

KIT:
I think so, yeah. It's good to see her loosen up a bit, have some fun.

PRODUCER:
Does it frustrate you that you have to work so hard to get her there?

KIT:
Not really. She's always been like this. Andie may take some things too seriously, and she's pretty closed off, but I think that makes those moments like today better, doesn't it? She doesn't hand out her joy to just anyone. I like being the one to earn it.

PRODUCER:
Do you think you may still have feelings for her?

KIT:
Of course I do. You don't meet a woman like Andie and walk away unchanged, you know?

CHAPTER ELEVEN
KIT

"Come on, Andie," I say over my shoulder as I drag her down a well-worn path in the Costa Rican jungle. Her hand is in mine, if only because the cameras are hot on our heels as we head out to the adventure course sponsored by the resort.

After the way she felt against me in the pool yesterday—all soft curves and gentle heat—I'll take any excuse to touch her. It makes me feel *awake.*

"Kit," she whines, "where are we going?"

"Getting you out of your head." My reply is clipped, more frustrated than it should be.

She stayed up drawing until late last night, only slipping into bed after I was asleep. I woke up to her curled into a ball on the far edge of the mattress, like she'd turn to stone if she so much as brushed her foot against mine.

It didn't make a person feel great, is what I'm saying.

We woke up to the little gold envelope that told us what we were going to be doing today.

Now here we are, in a dripping sauna of a rainforest, surrounded by cameras. My shirt sticks to my back and Andie's dark waves are going limp. It reminds me of a night we got caught in the rain.

My memory of undergrad is fuzzy in a lot of places, but my time with Andie stands out in sharp relief. We scurried under tree branches in Piedmont Park, huddling together until we forgot about the weather entirely, distracted by each other's bodies.

I stumble over a tree root, lost in the memory.

Andie wrenches her hand from mine as we draw to a halt outside a small portable trailer in the middle of the jungle. Attendants come out and have us step into harnesses, tugging us this way and that as they explain the rules for our safety. When we get a second to catch our breath, Andie hastily gathers her hair into a messy knot at the nape of her neck, just in time for one of the zipline attendants to plop a helmet on her head.

I'm mid-chuckle when I receive the same treatment. I make quick work of the chin strap while Andie struggles with hers. I'm not sure she's ever put on a helmet before. She's not really an outdoorsy type, last I checked. Save that night in the rain, where her nails scraped their memory into my skin. As if I could ever forget.

My fingers twitch at my sides, and fuck it—we're on camera, so I can touch her. I'll use that advantage every time, for as long as I have it. Knowing the cameras are going to be dissecting our every move—along with a TV audience—I close the distance between us and swat her hands away from the mess she's making. "You really can't survive without me, can you?"

She scowls, but drops her hands at her sides, balled into fists. "Amazing I'm still alive, then."

"A miracle." I say dryly. "Don't worry, I'm here now."

She flips me off, and I don't bother hiding my smile.

Andie looks at the wire between the trees, far above our heads. Her lip catches in her teeth and her foot taps a speedy rhythm on the forest floor.

A producer signals for one of us to say something, and Andie lets out a frustrated sigh.

I scoot one foot close enough to touch hers and ask, "What's wrong?"

Her foot stills against mine. "Why didn't we get surfing lessons or something?" she mumbles, crossing her arms over her chest. She squeezes her eyes shut while I untangle a knot she's somehow managed to tie in the chin strap by the buckle.

It would be easier to take the helmet off to wrangle this thing, but if she's saying she'd prefer hours of sand and saltwater, I know something's bothering her.

"You afraid of heights, sweet potato?" If there's one thing that can distract Andie, it's the insinuation she can't do something, especially if she's afraid to do it.

One time, in college, she volunteered to go onstage with one of those insufferable improv groups, simply because I teased her about being quiet that evening.

Now, her eyes fly open and meet mine. I fight a smug smile—her look is all fire and frustration, her hazel eyes bright and focused in the sunlight streaming through the tree branches. I can feel her vibrating with barely contained energy.

The freckles splattered across her nose and cheeks are on full display. The flush on her cheeks doesn't even begin to obscure them. Instead of makeup, she's been slathering her face in sunscreen every morning. I doubt it has anything to do with me, and everything to do with the humidity and relentless sunshine. But I like that she lets me see her like this. Undone, just a little.

Finally, she huffs her answer. "What does it matter?"

The knot loosens and I pull the buckle through the loop I've freed up. I take my time straightening out both straps, my fingers dangerously close to her skin. Brow furrowed at the buckle on the helmet, I answer, "Why wouldn't my wife's fear of heights matter?"

That earns me another death glare.

I can't help it. The corner of my mouth tugs into a half smile. Her eyes dart to the ladder that's bolted to the tree next to us. It leads up to the platform we'll be throwing ourselves off of. She's terrified, if the pulse in her neck is anything to go by.

"We don't have to do this," I say gently, without a hint of sarcasm. As much as I enjoy pushing her buttons, I don't want her to be terrified. That's different. I want her annoyed, frustrated, and ready to conquer what's in front of her to prove she can. Not scared for her life.

"I'm not afraid," she states firmly, setting her jaw. "There's a bunch of experts here, and they inspect the lines every morning to make sure they're in good condition, and we'll have a safety harness on, and—"

I clip the buckle into place and tug on the strap until it's snug against her chin. I can't help myself—I brush my thumb along the corner of her jaw, as if I can make her loosen her gritted teeth.

She doesn't. But her breath catches, and I let it be enough, my hand falling away from her skin. Our eyes meet in a split second of understanding, like no time has passed between us at all.

"Just because it's logical to be calm doesn't mean you can't be afraid." My voice is so low, a breeze through the jungle nearly carries it away. "You don't have to do this. I'll even tell them I'm the one that's scared."

Andie's eyes flash with emotion, raw and pleading. It feels like I finally see a glimpse of how she became who she is now: fear and pride mixing to create an addictive cocktail of *hope*.

Her eyelashes flutter downward, stealing away the taste. The moment is gone, like it never existed. I swallow, ignoring the stab of pain at the loss. We used to spend hours talking, never once hiding from each other.

"Shockingly enough," she says tartly, "I don't need you to save me."

Our moment is gone as attendants guide us to the tree we'll climb to get to the first platform. I let Andie start her ascent first, following behind her. I don't let the cameras see how delighted I am to have an excuse to stare at her ass, like some kind of animal. But I don't hesitate to use my hand to cup her buttocks when it's time to boost her up to the final platform. She glares at me over her shoulder, breathless. From the height or from my touch, I'll never know.

"Who's going first?" the attendant asks, a sparkle in his eyes. This is clearly his favorite part, pushing people over the edge.

Andie stares at the handles he's wrangled, chewing on her lip.

I clear my throat and step forward. "Me," I tell the attendant. Then I turn to Andie and give her a lighthearted smirk. "That way I can catch you on the other side."

She scoffs, rolling her eyes. But she can't hide the way her shoulders loosen just a bit as the attendant begins attaching me to the safety line, tugging on every strap and buckle to make sure I'm secure.

"Any last words?" I ask, reaching for the handles.

She gives me a playful smile, pure devious delight in her eyes. "Can I have your special edition Montblanc drafting pencil if you die?"

I lean back until my harness catches my weight. She only wants me for my four-hundred-dollar mechanical pencil, and I can't bring myself to care. "How do you know I have one?"

Her cheeks turn pink as she ducks her head to look at our feet. "You were sketching the morning after we got here."

I swallow. She was drinking her coffee on the balcony, and I hastily sketched her image on hotel paper, desperate to hold the moment in the palm of my hand. For some reason a photo just wouldn't do. My hands needed to touch her in any way they could. The human form was never one of my strong suits, but I captured her likeness well enough that I folded the paper up and tucked it in my bag for safekeeping.

I didn't know she saw me at work. Something warm turns over in my stomach, and if I sit with it for too long, I'll feel things I know I'll regret. "What's mine is yours," I tell her with a genuine smile. Her bright eyes lift to mine, and I add for good measure, "See you on the other side, Mrs. Watson."

She flips me off as I take the leap, laughing.

CHAPTER TWELVE
ANDIE

My stomach drops as Kit's feet leave the platform. Some baser instinct screams that I can't lose him, and I hold my breath.

The feeling doesn't subside until he pumps one fist in the air and lets out a triumphant yell. The air comes out of my lungs in a whoosh as he smiles. His arms are doing a lot of work, showing off the muscle and sinew beneath his skin. Sunlight casts them into dips and shadows. Suddenly I miss their heaviness around me, how safe he always made me feel.

His feet hit the destination platform with a firm thud, and he stands. Smiling as he chats with the attendant on the platform, he turns to look at me. I tug on my helmet strap as they pull the handles back up to me.

Kit puts his hands on his hips and beams. My knees wobble. A dangerous thing to do on a platform this high off the ground.

I make the mistake of looking down.

My head spins, and I clench my teeth. I grip the railing so hard my hands hurt as I close my eyes and attempt to take in a deep breath. Images of everything that can go wrong flash across my eyelids.

It's not the height that terrifies me; it's the falling.

Kit's voice jerks me out of my spiraling thoughts. "Andie, if you jump, I'll *give* you that damn pencil!" Everyone around us chuckles.

My eyes fly open to see him smiling. He looks so much like the Kit I used to know, my heart squeezes in my chest. He always knew how to reach me through my brooding.

And I'll be damned if I let him know how much it affects me now. I glare at him, though he's probably too far away to discern it. I haven't needed him in almost a decade; I've taken all kinds of leaps without him. This is just one more, really.

I grip the handles of the zip line and shake myself out, hopping up and down a little. Kit grins wider, as if he takes pride in me facing this.

Ignoring the fluttering in my chest, I take a step back.

Kit's smile falters. It feels a lot like being at the altar again, watching his thoughts play out across his face. Delight gives way to apprehension, which gives way to fear.

His shoulders heave with a breath as I jump. I squeal when my feet leave the platform, and I force myself to keep my eyes wide open instead of shutting the world out.

My breath leaves my lungs in a whoosh.

Kit whoops, jumping on the platform. Adrenaline spikes through my veins.

I rush toward him through the canopy of tropical leaves, looking like an answered prayer in the golden sunshine. I smile, thrilled by the leap, the speed, the freedom of letting go.

Kit doesn't cede the edge of the platform, instead opening his strong arms and widening his stance. My eyes go wide as I realize he's not teasing.

"Kit, what are you doing??" I squeal. My core aches as I try to turn my body, as if I can stop my momentum.

It's no use.

I crash into him with an unseemly grunt, and he wraps his arms around me as he staggers back to absorb the hit. I squeeze my eyes shut, terrified of the fall. We stop moving with a jolt, Kit swearing with the impact.

Then it all slows down. Kit's back is flat against the tree trunk, and he's breathing hard. He readjusts his grip on me, pulling my legs around his waist. His fingers sink into the bare flesh of my thighs. I press my palms into the bark on either side of his head, my body shaking with breaths too big for my lungs.

"Andie," he says in a low voice, just for the two of us, "you did it."

I force my eyes open so I can see the light in his. The sunlight turns them caramel underneath thick eyelashes. I lick my lips. "I can't believe you caught me."

His smile crinkles the corners of his eyes. "I told you I would."

"You're not hurt, are you?"

"No." As if to emphasize his point, his hands slide ever closer to my ass. One of his fingers dips under the hem of my shorts.

My traitorous hand leaves the tree to rest on his bulging biceps. I gasp when our skin meets—he's trembling. Not because he's struggling to hold me, though. He hasn't moved since I plastered him to the tree trunk.

"I'm proud of you." His smile gives way to a serious look, his eyes falling to my mouth.

My hand slides from his biceps to his chest, where his heart rages against my palm.

Gravity pulls my face toward his, ready to cross every line I put in place to keep myself safe.

The truth of the matter is, even though I'm at a standstill, I'm still falling.

When our mouths are close enough that Kit's warm breath skims across my lips, the plastic of our helmets clacks together. Stunned, my eyes find his. Then he laughs. It's open and full and vibrating between my legs.

To cover the wave of heat that just rocketed through me, I snort out a laugh too. Remembering where we are and what we're doing—namely that we're filming a reality TV show—I attempt a joke for levity. "Is that a Montblanc in your pocket or are you just happy to see me?"

Kit laughs harder, throwing his head back so his helmet scrapes against the tree trunk. It exposes the lines of his neck, and heat slices through me anew. His fingers dig into my thighs with a delicious bite. If there wasn't a camera crew, I'd be shamelessly grinding against him any second now.

Kit gives my ass a playful swat, ducking his head to press his lips to my cheek. With a sound that's half grunt, half frustrated growl, he puts me down. His hands hold me close, so every bit of my body slides against every bit of his. The hem of my shirt creeps up when it catches on his fingers.

He meets my gaze with the intensity of the tropical sun as he slowly, deliberately pulls the hem of my shirt back down. When we step apart, I'm shocked by how cold I feel. My whole body wants to tuck back into his, where the world is quiet and still.

Kit breaks the spell with a pat on my helmet, shooting me a knowing look. "You did good, sweet potato."

FIRST LOOK AT FOREVER
SEASON THREE
EPISODE FOUR

PRODUCER:
What happened between you two earlier? On the zip line course?

KIT:
[smiling] She jumped.

PRODUCER:
Was she not going to?

KIT:
She's afraid of heights.

PRODUCER:
But you talked her into it.

KIT:
[shrugs] We made a deal.

PRODUCER:
Right, the pencil. Do you feel any closer to Andie now than you did a few days ago?

KIT:
I think . . . it's hard for her to trust me.

PRODUCER:
Do you have any plans right now?

KIT:
[heavy sigh] I have no idea what to do. Anyone got any ideas?
[Crew laughing off camera]

FIRST LOOK AT FOREVER
SEASON THREE
EPISODE FOUR

PRODUCER:
Do you want to tell me what happened between you and Kit after zip lining?

ANDIE:
Nothing, really.

PRODUCER:
Did you get your pencil?

ANDIE:
[narrows her eyes] I can't tell if you're trying to make it a euphemism, but yes, he kept his end of the deal.

PRODUCER:
Do you think there's a chance you could fall in love?

ANDIE:
Again? [frowns] I . . . don't know.

PRODUCER:
So you were in love with him before.

ANDIE:
Sometimes I think it was love. Sometimes I think he was who was there when I needed to lean on someone.

PRODUCER:
Is there a difference?

ANDIE:
[stares contemplatively in the distance]

CHAPTER THIRTEEN

KIT

When we arrive at the resort's dance studio, Patrick and Kendra are already leaning against the far wall. I'm still not sure whose idea it was to take a group salsa dancing class, but the cameras are placed strategically around the room already, so they don't catch their own reflection in the mirrors. I'm in slacks and a button-down, and Andie is wearing one of her flowing skirts and a loose silk sleeveless blouse. It's more or less her uniform, and I love the way the fabric shows hints of the body she's hiding underneath.

However, we look overdressed next to Patrick and Kendra's gym shorts and tank tops. I've never been to a dance class, so I'm not really sure what the dress code is. When Leslie strolls in also wearing slacks and a button-down, I take a deep breath. Jamie is in bright shorts and a Hawaiian shirt. His smile matches the burst of sunshine on his chest.

"I'm so glad you were all down for this idea." He gives everyone a kiss on each cheek.

"We wouldn't do it for anyone else," Andie says when it's her turn.

"I figured it would be nice to work up an appetite before our last honeymoon dinner." Jamie very nearly skips back to Leslie, who's standing on the sidelines with his hands in his pockets.

The salsa instructor strolls in with a megawatt smile. She's the shortest one here, with her hair pulled back into a ponytail.

She asks us about our dance experience, then tells us to pair up.

I turn to Andie, and she slides into an awkward dance frame with me. My hand on her waist, her hands on my chest. It's the closest we've been since I caught her on the zip line course yesterday.

"No, no, no!" The instructor comes by to gently pull us apart. "This is *salsa*, not a waltz."

She arranges us into the proper position: standing a few feet apart with both of Andie's hands in mine. Before long, we're stepping back and forth in tandem while salsa music blares in the background.

"So," I say when I notice a camera specifically trained on us, "is this more or less terrifying than jumping out of a tree?"

Andie snorts. "I think more."

"Me too." I stumble over my own feet, which makes Andie shuffle back too quickly. Her legs get tangled in her skirts, and she gasps. I lunge forward to grab her around the waist.

It's the studio wall that finally stops our chaotic stumble. I press my hand to the stucco next to Andie's head.

I let out a breath and mutter, "Well, that was embarrassing."

Andie barks out a laugh, tossing her head back and exposing her throat. I'm mesmerized, swallowing the urge to press my lips to the underside of her chin. It doesn't take long for me to realize my thigh is between her legs, and all at once it's too much.

I push myself off the wall and brush off my hands just as Patrick booms, "Get a room!"

"We're just taking steps," Jamie teases. "You know, like *walking*."

I drag a hand down my face as Andie shakes with giggles. Though my face is burning with embarrassment, I smile at her joy. It's the lightest I've seen her since our wedding.

She takes the hand I offer, still beaming. I love the sparkle in her eyes and the pink that's showing high on her cheeks. "Definitely more dangerous than zip lining."

"Should have brought our helmets." I gently tap her forehead with my index finger. Her eyes cross a little, which makes me laugh. "Sorry I suck at walking."

She sighs, her shoulders heaving. "I guess we have to try again, don't we?"

We resume our spot on the dance floor. "I know you won't let us eat until we're the best salsa dancers in this room."

"True," she says, bending down. Before I can ask what she's doing, she grabs the hem of her long skirt and stands, tucking it into her waistband.

It flashes the bare skin of one of her legs, and the finished effect makes her look like a pirate woman at a Renaissance festival. Especially when she puts her hands on her hips and her cheeks puff out with a deep breath.

"Let's go again, Watson." Her mouth is in a determined line. I offer my hands without hesitation. When she slides her fingers against mine, I can't help but give her a squeeze and a confident smile.

"Once you master this, we can work on a lean." The instructor circles back to us. She watches us, clapping out a beat and counting until we can do the basic steps without much thought. "But first, honey," she says to Andie, "you need to learn to follow his lead. You can't both lead, or you'll end up on your asses again."

Andie puffs out a breath. "Why do I have to follow?"

"Because sometimes it's good to let him do the work. It gives you a break."

Andie steels her jaw, stubborn as ever.

"Stop thinking so hard," the instructor says to Andie as she watches us. "It's his turn to do the thinking. You just go with it. Trust him."

Andie shakes out her arms mid-step, takes a deep breath, then settles back into our pace. Back and forth. Back and forth.

"Better." The instructor nods her approval. "Better."

For the lean, the instructor has us stand side by side, Andie's right hand in my left. I watch her as our arms extend and she prepares to spin toward me. Her hair is frizzing at the edges, and her chest is now pink from the exercise. It has me thinking of how she used to look after another kind of aerobic activity.

My mind is so far gone that she presses her hip to mine, and I flinch. Her body against mine jolts me back to the present moment, and

I forget what I'm supposed to do next. So I just stare at her—her face so close to mine I can see the way her irises change from caramel brown at the center to gray-green at the edges.

Even more stunning than her eyes—she doesn't pull away. Instead, her eyes are on my mouth, her warm breath skimming over my neck and creeping down the collar of my shirt. It's all I can do to keep my eyes on her face as I feel the rise and fall of her chest.

"Get a room!" Patrick booms again.

I give him a sidelong glance as Andie steps away from me. The left side of my body is cold in her absence. She smooths her hand down her ponytail and shakes out her arms.

"That was a good spin," the instructor tells us. Then to me, "Do it again. This time, lunge, señor, okay?" She claps her hands together and I flinch at the noise.

This time, when Andie presses against my side, I lunge and relish the pull in my thigh. While we're suspended in the pose, Andie asks, "What are you thinking about?"

"Nothing." My answer is impulsive and one hundred percent a lie.

"Bullshit." Andie calls it like she sees it. "You're doing that thing with your mouth."

"What thing?"

"You know, the thing." She presses her lips together, then pulls them to one side. "You've always done it when something's on your mind. So come on, spill."

I shake my head. "You don't want to hear it."

"I asked." She gives me some of the strongest side-eye I've ever witnessed.

I sigh, pushing us both back to standing upright. I don't let go of her hand and force myself to look her in the eyes. "I was thinking . . . you look beautiful. Like this."

"Like . . . frustrated?"

"No." I shift on my feet. "I mean, yes. When you're focused, trying to get something right. You light up."

She rolls her eyes. "Okay. Then I must look like a maglight from being around you twenty-four seven."

I tilt my head and step closer. "Sweet potato, are you saying you're trying to get this marriage right?"

"Oh my God." She playfully shoves my chest. I let it be enough for now.

Our conversation stalls until we're learning a dip. She waits until I'm fully supporting her weight in a lunge before she says, "Okay. I have a question."

"And you think now is the time to ask it?" Honestly, I'm amazed that I haven't dropped her since we couldn't even manage stepping without making a mess of things.

"It's relevant."

"Okay." I raise a brow, curious about what she could possibly think is relevant right now.

She blows a breath out, making the hair that's fallen into her face flutter. "How in the hell do you get away with having thighs like this?"

I laugh, losing my grip on her. I pull us to standing, my hands still splayed across her back. "Are you *offended* by my legs?"

"It's not fair." She looks over my shoulder. The muscles in her throat work as she swallows.

"That's a long way to go to say you're attracted to me."

Her eyes snap back to mine. "What? Where the hell did you get that from?"

She puts her hands on my chest and pushes.

I let her go. "And you're pissed off about it."

"Pissed off about you making assumptions, yes."

"Why else would you ask about my thighs?"

"He's got great thighs," Jamie says as he hangs halfway upside down from Leslie's arms. "It's okay to be affected by those babies."

"I'm not—I can't believe you think—"

Patrick spins Kendra out. "My dude does not skip leg day."

I cover my mouth to hold in laughter. Andie stands there, mouth hanging open. She glances around the room, realizing all eyes—and cameras—are on her. The salsa music still pulses in the background. To Cassidy she asks, "Do you have an opinion about his thighs too?"

Steve pipes up. "Kit's got salsa thighs."

When she glares at me, I shrug. "You started it."

"I started nothing."

"Just admit you like my thighs, sweet potato."

She shakes her head.

"I said nice things about you."

"You called me a maglight."

"You called yourself a maglight."

"Fine." She curls her hands into fists at her side, then looks around the room again. Very quietly, she says, "I like your thighs."

Cassidy can't fight the smile on her face. "Andie, the mic didn't pick that up. Can you say it louder?"

Andie mutters something indecent under her breath. She closes her eyes and takes a deep breath. Then she looks me square in the eyes and yells above the music, "Kit Watson has thighs that should be illegal, okay?!"

Everyone in the studio cheers, including the crew. I take a bow.

Andie rolls her eyes. "Screw all of you. I need a drink."

CHAPTER FOURTEEN
ANDIE

After our dance class, cameras are waiting on the restaurant patio overlooking the water. Kendra and Patrick are already at the table, touching and clearly enamored with each other. Kit takes a seat, and I take the chair next to him as directed by the producers. Our distance stands out in stark contrast to the display in front of us.

All of us have loosened up from physical activity. It's most noticeable on Kit, who's rolled his sleeves up to his elbows and let his hair run wild. I catch myself smiling at him when he isn't looking. Quickly, I look at the table instead, shaking my head. It must be the magical atmosphere the show created here on the beach.

Leslie and Jamie join us, the strain between them palpable. Despite the awkwardness, we get by on small talk about the weather and how beautiful the view is until cocktails grace our table.

"I heard a rumor that you two already knew each other," Kendra says as she sips on her fruity drink.

I suppose I should have seen that coming. Unwilling to answer, I sip on my cocktail too.

Kit clearly has no such qualms. He leans forward, resting his forearms on the tabletop. "That's true. We dated in college."

"No way." Jamie leans forward in his seat, eyes wide with delight. "Was it serious?"

"Jamie"—Leslie shakes his head—"you can't just ask people questions like that."

Jamie appears chastened, slouching in his seat.

"It's okay," Kit says, waving it off. "We dated for a couple of months."

"Four." I reach for a chip from the communal bowl. "It was four months."

Kit nods, a sparkle in his eyes. "That's right."

"Did you love each other then?" Kendra asks as she snuggles into Patrick, a wistful smile on her face.

Kit looks at me while I chew slowly, hoping everyone will forget this topic of conversation. I did love him. I told him I did. And he couldn't say it back. It shouldn't still hurt this much, but it does.

I swallow my food. "It didn't work out. It's not often that two twenty-one-year-olds make it, you know?"

Patrick nods. "But you found each other. Professional matchmakers think you're going to make it now. That has to count for something."

"Maybe." I shrug, refusing to look at Kit. Instead, I turn to Kendra. "You look exhausted. Having fun?"

Kendra and Patrick smile at each other. "We are. We went horseback riding on the beach yesterday."

"That sounds amazing." My smile is genuine this time. Just because this experiment is a joke for Kit and me doesn't mean everyone else can't get what they want. "We should have done that instead."

"You'd still have to wear a helmet." Kit scoops some guacamole onto a chip.

I stick my tongue out at him, and he nearly chokes on his food trying not to laugh. He swallows, brushing the crumbs off his hands. "We went zip lining."

"Now *that* sounds like fun." Jamie lights up once more. "Was it scary?"

"Terrifying." I give an exaggerated shiver in the balmy air. "Why do people think jumping off high things is fun?"

"I don't like any sport where both of my feet aren't firmly on the ground." Leslie raises his glass in a mock toast.

Jamie stirs his drink with the little paper umbrella that came with it. "We all need to get out of our comfort zones now and again."

Leslie purses his lips and sets his glass down with a frown.

"I agree," I say, trying to deflect whatever tension is between them. "However, there's ways to do it that don't involve flinging yourself out of a tree."

"But she did it." Kit beams. "She's never been one to back down from a challenge." He sprawls his arm across the back of my chair, and I'm not sure what to do.

The move is possessive, and it sounds like he actually meant what he said. Our eyes meet, and for a split second, it feels like we're twenty-one again. I open my mouth to say something—I'm not sure what—when everyone's attention turns to the deck.

I clear my throat, tearing my gaze away from Kit.

"Hello, couples!" Petra waves with both hands as she approaches. Her perfectly made up face and slightly too formal sundress make her seem like she's on a stage instead of at a casual resort restaurant. "I hope you've all been enjoying your time in Costa Rica."

We all raise our glasses. Kendra and Jamie cheer enthusiastically, shimmying in their seats. I giggle at their display; it's impossible not to smile around people who are so infectiously joyful. Patrick laughs. Kit snorts. Leslie attempts a smile, though it looks more like a grimace.

"Most of you met for the first time at the altar as strangers." She looks around the table, making eye contact with each one of us. It's all I can do to not squirm in my seat as if I've been caught texting during class. It feels like there's an important subtext that only I'm missing. "All of you have spent this time getting to know each other. But you can't stay in paradise forever.

"Tomorrow, you'll go back to your real lives, only this time, you'll be with your new spouses." Petra smiles her pageant smile. "We've set up apartments for you in the same complex so you can begin your new lives on neutral ground. In addition, Dr. Shaw and Dr. Leon will be meeting with you when you return so you can discuss anything that came up during your honeymoon."

My smile becomes forced as I clench my teeth together. The last thing I want to do is sit down for a couples therapy session with Kit. It doesn't matter if we fix any problems we may have; we're going to go our separate ways in a few weeks anyway.

"This honeymoon is just the beginning." Petra looks at all of us once more. "You had your first look at forever at the altar one week ago. Now you have seven more weeks to decide to stay together or walk away from what could be the love of your life."

FIRST LOOK AT FOREVER
SEASON THREE
EPISODE FIVE

PETRA ASHLING:
Our couples got to know each other on their honeymoon, but now it's back to real life.

DR. LAUREN SHAW:
It's easy to fall in love when you're in paradise, but living together day-to-day can present challenges for even the most stable couples.

DR. KENNETH LEON:
Living together also provides a new level of intimacy. Our couples will learn up close about their partner's likes and dislikes and learn to negotiate the problems that pop up during a normal day.

DR. LAUREN SHAW:
These are the building blocks for our couples to create happy, fulfilling lives together.

CHAPTER FIFTEEN
ANDIE

"Good morning, my newly married bestie!" Heidi's voice fills my loft. She's carrying two giant iced coffees in her hands, and I've never been more excited to see her.

"Oh, thank God." I stand from where I was leaning over my workbench. My back aches from the flight home and sleeping on the very edge of another hotel bed. "You brought caffeine."

She plops my coffee down on the edge of the table, far enough away from my pattern that the condensation won't bleed into the bodice I'm translating to paper. I'm hoping to have at least one new design pieced together by the end of the day. Structurally, anyway. The devil is in the details. Making this bodice sparkle with a spray of beads to mimic how Kit's fingers felt on my bare skin is a challenge for another day.

Heidi pulls up a stool and tucks some of her blond hair away from her face. "How was your trip?"

I reach for the iced coffee. After a cool sip slides its way down my throat, I answer, "Tropical. Pools, dinner on the beach, zip lining, salsa dancing. That kind of thing."

Heidi narrows her eyes. "Zip lining? *You* did something . . . fun?"

"I know how to have fun." I flip her off with my free hand. The memory of Kit catching me and throwing his head back in laughter is still fresh. My skin turns to gooseflesh, and I scrunch my toes in my shoes. Warmth rises in my chest, like I'm back in the tropical sun and not surrounded by bolts of fabric that only remind me of my business misstep and the pittance in my expense account.

Heidi scoffs. "And Kit? Does the rest of him look like his face?"

I snort. "What does that mean?"

"Come on, Andie. That man is gorgeous. Tell me the rest of him lived up to the hype."

"Why would I know what the rest of him looks like?" I pick up my scissors again. I have to finish cutting the edge of this piece before I can move on. And I definitely don't want to think about Kit shirtless. Catching me as we both fell into the pool, skin sliding on skin.

"Because you were on your *honeymoon*." Heidi's voice is frustrated, like when she's arguing with the caterers about where to put the chafing dishes.

I stay quiet as I focus on the pattern piece. It needs to be perfect; I can't afford to waste any fabric if I want to keep the lights on. I mutter a curse under my breath, directed at Kit, who isn't even here to hear it.

There's only twelve weeks left to perfect an entire line of dresses that will determine the fate of my business. Which would maybe be enough if I didn't also have to film a reality show at the same time. Cassidy slipped me a production schedule for the week, and while I can still work, I have to spend plenty of time with Kit on camera, too.

I'm never going to sleep again.

"You *do* know what couples do on their honeymoon, don't you?" Heidi teases, taking a sip of her coffee.

I roll my eyes. "Those couples usually meet before they're at the altar."

"You're telling me you have that man with a dream of a body, and you haven't made good on it yet?" Heidi picks up a scrap of muslin on my workbench and runs it through her fingers.

I shrug, biting my lip as I concentrate on keeping the line I'm cutting straight. "It didn't feel right."

Heidi frowns. I avoid most of the intensity by simply not looking at her, focusing all my attention on the pattern in front of me.

"Is he nice to you?" A serious tone weighs down her voice.

"He's very respectful." Too respectful, honestly. Treating me like I'll break if he makes one wrong move. Kit has kept his emotions on a tight leash since the wedding day, and I miss the raw side of him I used to know. Maybe he's completely tamed it.

When I look up, her brow is furrowed in concern. Once I finish my cut, I lean on the table and sigh. "Listen. There's something you should know about Kit."

Heidi's eyes go wide. "He doesn't have, like, a second family in a different state, does he?"

"No." I take a sip of coffee.

"Does he have a sex dungeon?"

I snort. "Heidi, really?"

"Because that never works like it does in books." She shrugs.

"No." I shake my head. "Well . . . I haven't seen his place yet, but I'm ninety-nine percent sure he doesn't have a sex dungeon."

"It's always the ones you'd never expect."

"Trust me." I scrub my hands down my face. "Kit and I have dated before."

"*What?*" Heidi smacks her hands on my workbench, leaning forward with the appropriate amount of shock.

It's my turn to shrug. "It was a long time ago."

"What did the producers say when they found out?"

"They think it'll make for good TV."

"Oh." She sits up and primly smooths her skirt. "Well. Are you *sure* about the sex dungeon?"

I give her a look. "I'm sure."

"Damn." She wrinkles her nose. "That could have been fun."

I toss another strip of scrap muslin at her.

"I guess . . ." Heidi hesitates, tying the strip of muslin into a knot and pulling it tight. "Can you see yourself falling in love with him?" Her intonation lifts at the end, and her eyes are locked on me, ready to catch any slip in my façade.

I scoff to cover the way my heart lunges against my rib cage. Kit was so easy to love, the first time. He was open and honest and passionate and ambitious and attentive and—

I thought I saw a glimpse of that man during our salsa lesson, but now I'm not so sure. Maybe none of it was true in the first place. I don't know anymore.

"No." My fingers fuss with a pin that's rolling around on the table. "I don't think I'll be falling in love with him."

"Good," she says with finality, bringing her palms to the table with a smack. "Then your divorce money is safe."

I swallow. I'm not sure how I momentarily forgot why I was willing to marry a stranger in the first place. This is why my heart isn't in charge of things around here.

"But Andie." Heidi's eyes twinkle with something mischievous. "You don't have to be in love with him to treat yourself to a little dose of fun, if you catch my drift."

My thin wedding band suddenly feels as heavy as an anvil, and I rest my shaking hand on the table. Could I enjoy sex with Kit without letting him into the softer parts of me, the ones he'd left broken and bruised the last time? We were always good together in bed. But then, maybe sex with him had always been good because I didn't feel like I had to hide from him.

I give my head one firm shake. "That's what vibrators are for." I make a mental note to stealthily pack one to bring to the shared apartment we were moving into later today. Just because I wouldn't be having sex with Kit didn't mean I couldn't *think* about having sex with him. And if he kept wandering around in towels like he did in hotel rooms, well. A girl can only hold out for so long before she needs to take care of a few things.

Heidi snorts. "You can show him how to use one."

"How to use one what?" Kit's voice startles me. I flinch so hard I knock my scissors to the floor with a clatter that only punctuates the silence that follows.

He's in slacks and a button-down, a leather messenger bag slung across his chest. Every bit the business casual catalog model. I forgot he was going to meet me here for filming. When I see the camera crew behind him, a part of me winds tighter.

I blush a little when I realize he's holding a couple of iced coffees too.

Choosing to ignore that I haven't answered his question, he gives me a half grin. "You didn't sleep much last night, so I thought you could use this." He raises one iced coffee in a mock toast. "But it seems you're fine without me."

Heidi looks him up and down, a playful grin on her face. Cassidy takes the moment to clip a mic to me. When Kit sets the coffees on the workbench next to her, she says, "Hi, I'm Heidi."

"The wedding planner." He shakes her hand. "I remember."

I fasten one of my pincushions around my wrist and drag the painstakingly cut butcher paper bodice pieces over to the nearest dress form. As I stab the first pin into the form along one of my tape lines, I tell Kit casually, "Heidi's my best friend."

"And business buddy," Heidi adds cheerily.

I nod, informing Kit, "We share clients sometimes."

"Ah, so the show is *rigged*."

I turn to look at him so quickly I tear the pattern I was so careful with earlier. A chunk falls to the ground at my feet. He already knows I'm on the show for the money, and if the producers think we somehow rigged the match, I can kiss that money goodbye.

When I tentatively meet his gaze, there's a sparkle of humor in his eyes. I let out a puff of laughter. He's kidding. Of course he is. If the game was rigged, I definitely wouldn't have paired myself with the only man I've ever loved and lost.

I swallow, picking the pattern piece off the ground. To reduce the chance of any more pattern casualties, I grab the dress form by the hips and scoot it closer to my workbench.

Kit jumps into action. He's around the back of the dress form, his fingers brushing mine as he grips the waist. I shiver.

"Let me help you," he grumbles over the dress form's shoulder.

"I don't need your help, Kit."

I can't handle the tender look in his eyes, so I grunt as I tug on the dress form again. "It's amazing how I've done this without you for years."

"For fuck's sake, Andie." Kit moves around the form and bumps me aside with his hip. "Do you ever *stop*?"

Heidi snorts from her spot on the bench. "No. She doesn't."

"Kit," I complain when he dodges my attempt to get to the form.

He swears under his breath, but his voice is frustratingly calm. "Where do you want it?"

I can't formulate an answer. My brain pops and fizzles out. I'm frustrated with him, but he is perfectly content with my mood.

I contemplate trying to move another heavy object, just to see what he'll do.

"Do you want to fight about this now or later?" he asks, an eyebrow raised.

Heidi's purse scrapes over the surface of the workbench as she stands. "And that's my cue to go. Play nice, you two."

Before I can beg her to stay and act as a buffer, her Louboutins click right out the door.

Kit lets out a grunt, and I turn my attention back to him. His lips are turned down in a frown, his brows lowered over his eyes. He's quietly pissed. Great.

The muscles in his throat work. He closes his eyes for a moment and takes a deep breath in through his nose. When he lets it out, his body relaxes just a little. He opens his eyes and rubs his jaw. "Do you need a ride to your place, or do you have a car here?"

My brows pull together. As I stare at him, baffled by his question, his fingers sink into the dress form, forming little shadowed dents in the sunlight. I feel them digging into my own flesh like it was just yesterday that I had him undone as he drove into—

Damn Heidi and her sex dungeon talk.

My lips part to say something I shouldn't, then he relaxes his hands and runs one through his hair again. The moment is gone. I shake my head. "My place is here."

"What?" He looks around, like he's not sure how he got here.

I roll my eyes and take stock of the place too. Aside from a small kitchenette on the far end of the apartment, it's mostly dress mannequins and bolts of fabric shimmering in the light. A tall hanging rack at the far end of the room is heavy with bagged-up gowns. There's a dark blue velvet couch near some of the dress forms, and some stools around my workbench, also draped with fabric. But there's no TV or area rugs or houseplants or any other signs that someone actually lives here.

It works for me. I make fancy dresses, but I don't have expensive tastes.

One dress form has muslin pieces pinned halfway around it, some draping all the way to the floor. Kit's mouth tugs into a half grin when his eyes fall on my drafting table. It's scattered with torn-out magazine pages, sketches of dresses, and fabric swatches. Right. He's an architect, so he probably has a drafting table with a ruler and a protractor lined up like little soldiers ready for their battle with physics.

He wanders over to the wall of windows overlooking the Atlanta skyline. Instead of taking in the view, he's looking at the window frames, even tapping a knuckle against the narrow strips of brick in between them. I don't know whether to be flattered or annoyed that he doesn't seem to trust the integrity of the building. I *do* know that he looks like a god in the golden hour sunlight as it wraps around his face and body. I bite the inside of my cheek to keep my thoughts from getting carried away.

His question startles me. "Where do you sleep?"

I scoff, happy he's brought us back to reality. "Mostly I don't. But when I'm lucky enough, my bedroom's up there."

I gesture to a set of warehouse-style stainless steel steps leading up to a loft above the tiny kitchen.

"Is this also where you meet clients?" He shoves his sleeves up his forearms. I bite the inside of my cheek harder.

My hands need something to do other than tingle with the need to touch him, so I reach for the coffee he brought me. "It's easier to sleep where I work. I don't waste time on a commute."

He frowns. I divert my gaze, because I don't care what he thinks of my sleeping situation. Do I?

His shoes land in thuds on the hardwood as he strolls to a bolt of fabric leaning against the green couch across the room. I follow like some kind of tether ties us and we can't stray too far from each other.

I fight the urge to ask him to practice our salsa dancing, if only to break through whatever awkward wall is suddenly between us. Instead, I tell him, "Burano lace. From Italy."

He looks over his shoulder, the lace between his fingers, and I cross my arms over my chest.

Focus on the lace, Andie, not the godlike man in front of you.

I can feel his eyes wandering over me and get the impression he can see every last piece of my thoughts. Hopefully he can't see the financial dread snaking its way around my throat every waking moment.

"Five hundred dollars per yard." I shake my head, a small smile tugging at my lips at my own foolishness. "I shouldn't have spent the money, but I couldn't stop myself from loving it."

Kit drops the lace like it burned him. He shoves his hands into his pockets and clenches his jaw. Pissed again. But *why*?

Kit clears his throat and moves the topic away from the expensive fabric. "How many dresses do you make in a year?"

"About ten. If I'm lucky," I admit, though it feels like it should be more. I scratch the base of my sloppy topknot, afraid to meet his gaze. Ten dresses a year doesn't sound like much when he creates whole-ass campuses of buildings.

He lets out a low whistle, eyeing the rack of gowns in progress. "That's a lot of work, Andie."

My eyes fly to his. Is he teasing me? "You design entire resorts, Kit."

He shakes his head, his hair catching the sunlight just so. "I create the blueprints and do the math. Check in during certain stages. You do everything from the blueprint to the interior design, all on your own, with each unique design taking months to complete. Your project management skills must be out of this world."

My lips part in shock. He actually . . . respects my work? On something as frivolous as a dress that will only be worn *once*? In thirty seconds, he's shown more understanding about the complexity of my job than brides I work with for *months*. I don't know what to say, so I don't say anything at all.

Kit meanders to a dress form draped in muslin. Taking in the design from the hem to the bodice, he asks, "How much do you charge for a dress?"

I don't want to answer that question. He'll think it's way too much, and that I'm silly for asking for it. Any respect he just found for me will dissipate into thin air. I chew on my lip and move to toss my empty coffee cup into the stainless steel trash can by the fridge before answering, "Enough."

"Just like my thighs are average, eh?" He shoots me a half grin over his shoulder as he turns back to the wall of windows.

"Oh my God, you will never let that go, will you?" I roll my eyes but can't fight a smile, glad our rapport isn't completely gone.

"Never, sweet potato." His smile grows brighter. "Never."

CHAPTER SIXTEEN
KIT

After wandering awkwardly through our show-provided, already furnished apartment, I heave Andie's bag onto the bed in the only bedroom. The apartment is maybe six hundred square feet, with modern finishes and some city views. It's definitely a little cramped with Cassidy and Steve in here too.

I'm still processing how Andie lives where she works, and all I could think as we packed up her few belongings from her loft was that I wonder if she gets cold in the winter. Those windows were older, and I bet when the wind picks up her whole studio is drafty.

Then that fucking Italian lace. The way she'd looked at it—fondly, admiring. *Smitten.* Being jealous of a scrap of lace wasn't on my bingo card for today, but here I am.

Andie begins sorting the clothes she's brought from her place. She lives where she works. It's sparsely decorated and lacking basic comfort. And I noticed as we packed up her outfits from the tiny IKEA wardrobe in her bedroom that none of her own clothes had designer labels on them. Or labels at all, actually.

I put her toiletries on the counter in the bathroom for her to sort out later. When I return to the bedroom, I lean against the closet door and ask, "Andie, do you make all your own clothes?"

She snorts and waves it off. “Not *all* my clothes.”

I give her a stern look. Everything in her life is streamlined as an arrow, pointing straight at her goals. Making her own clothes must be another cost-saving measure.

She rolls her eyes at me and stuffs some shirts in a dresser drawer. “I like dresses and skirts with pockets. They’re harder to find than you think. I don’t make anything special.”

Fucking *pockets*. I’ve never seen anyone deny their own genius with the excuse of *pockets* before. Does she not understand how special she is? Before I can argue my point, there’s a knock at our door. Cassidy suggests I answer it, which means she knows who’s on the other side.

I open the door for Dr. Kenneth Leon, one of the show’s hosts and therapists. He’s in a sharp suit with a polka dot bow tie, and his smile is blinding. “Hi, Kit.” He shakes my hand firmly and comes into the apartment. Cassidy has wrangled Andie from the bedroom and asks us both to sit on the couch in the living room.

Dr. Leon takes the uncomfortable-looking chair by the window. He tugs on his lapels before saying, “It’s good to see you both. It’s been a while, hasn’t it?”

“Since our interviews, I think.” Andie nods, folding her hands in her lap. Both Dr. Leon and Dr. Shaw had interviewed us individually, almost a month ago now, before they made their final picks for the show.

Dr. Leon leans his elbow on the arm of the chair and gives us both a curious look. Sunlight glints on the lenses of his gold wire-rimmed glasses. Finally, he says, “Before I ask about the honeymoon, I heard that you two aren’t strangers at all.”

“It’s been ten years since I saw him,” Andie says with a sweet smile. “We might as well be strangers. Right?” She looks at me for confirmation.

I shrug. Despite the way I told her our past was ancient history, all our moments together keep flooding back. It’s a tidal wave I can’t outrun.

“But you dated each other; is that right?” Dr. Leon frowns.

“We did,” I confirm it. “For a few months.”

"Why did it end the first time?" He rests his chin on his fist, ready to wait us out.

I look at Andie, and surprise flashes in her eyes. I clear my throat and tell Dr. Leon, "A lot of things happened at once."

Andie adds, "We were twenty-one. Kids. How often do those relationships work out, you know?"

Dr. Leon nods sagely. "That's true, but for you to form a lasting, deep connection now, you're going to need to make peace with your past together."

"Ten years apart isn't peaceful?" Andie asks, her voice teasing. She's trying to keep things light, but I don't miss her pulse pounding in her throat.

"You *are* here for the right reasons, aren't you?" Dr. Leon won't let her get away with it.

"I don't understand." I lean forward with my elbows on my knees. "Are you suggesting that we . . . planned this?"

"People have done wilder things to be on TV, son." Dr. Leon shrugs.

I can't help but let out a puff of laughter.

"What's so funny?" Andie asks, her brows drawing together.

"I'm here because my mom asked me to give it a shot." I shake my head and press my thumb against my lip. I watch Andie to gauge her reaction. She frowns. "She was diagnosed with breast cancer and knew I would do anything to make her happy. She said she wanted to see me settled and gave me the application for the show."

"That's sweet, I guess." Andie wrinkles her nose. "You must be really close with her."

"I am." I nod.

"Andie, why are you here?" Dr. Leon asks.

She looks at her hands in her lap and stays quiet. I know why she's here, because she told me. But she's not about to tell Dr. Leon that she's here for the divorce money that's hidden in the show's contract. Someone's phone buzzes in their pocket, but it's ignored.

"Andie?"

"I think"—she spins her wedding ring around her finger—"despite everything I've experienced, I do want to believe that love exists. The forever kind."

I swallow. I want to believe she means that.

"Are you concerned that we've paired you with someone you've already dated?"

"Of course I am." She sighs and runs her hand through her hair. "Kit and I failed at this once already. I'm not sure what you saw in us that makes us a match."

Dr. Leon smiles. "I suppose that's for you both to figure out along the way. You may already have a guess based on how your relationship went the first time."

I look at the ring on my finger.

"Kit, what drew you to Andie the first time you dated?"

My eyebrows shoot up, surprised he asked. I clear my throat. "Um. She's beautiful, obviously." I gesture vaguely in her direction. "But I think my favorite thing about her is how she held space for me to dream bigger at a time in my life when I was barely getting by."

Andie's gaze softens as she looks at me, her lips parting. I don't think I ever articulated that feeling when we were together, if only because I only recently was able to parse it into words. "It's true," I assure her.

"Andie, what drew you to Kit ten years ago?"

"Aside from his thighs?" she quips, and I can't help but laugh.

Dr. Leon chuckles too. "You know what I'm asking."

Andie takes a deep breath. "Back then he felt . . . so steady. My life had always been chaotic, and Kit felt like the calm in the storm. When he left so suddenly, I realized maybe I'd been wrong."

I frown. "You know why I left." I yelled it to her through the crack in the door while her roommate blocked me from coming in.

"Why did you leave?" Dr. Leon asks gently.

"My dad passed," I tell him, but keep my eyes on Andie. "I got the call in the middle of the night and took the first bus home. It took me a few weeks to get my head on straight enough to get back to school and find Andie."

Andie shakes her head. "You were gone before then."

"What do you mean?" Dr. Leon asks.

She pauses, picking at one of her cuticles. Finally, she says quietly, "He wasn't ready for a relationship. So he checked out."

"Is that true, Kit?" Dr. Leon frowns at me.

My mouth goes dry. I remember the night Andie told me she loved me. We were half asleep. She'd spent hours crying on my chest because her mom was going through a divorce.

I drag my hands down my face and echo what we've already said ten times over. "We were twenty-one. I had no idea what I was doing."

Dr. Leon nods. "I suppose the question now is: are you both going to be able to put that piece of your past behind you and start fresh as adults?"

"I'd like to," I say truthfully. How many times have I wished we could go back and do it differently?

"Andie?"

She looks me over, then turns her gaze on Dr. Leon. "I'll try."

"That's all we ask." Dr. Leon shifts in the chair and flashes his smile. "Now, let's hear about the honeymoon."

CHAPTER SEVENTEEN

ANDIE

The next morning is a blur. I didn't sleep well—on the edge of our shared bed, awake long after the cameras left, my mind replaying how I told Kit I loved him ten years ago, and he couldn't say it back. I told Dr. Leon I'd try to move past it, but I'm not sure I can.

I'm a zombie as we go through the motions of getting ready, tiptoeing around each other and the camera crew in this tiny apartment. We're going to Kit's place before we head to work, and I'm already mourning the lost time to work on my dresses.

Kit hands me a cup of coffee in the kitchen. I mumble my thanks and lean against the counter. Mid-sip, I notice the drawing on the fridge. It's got the logo of the resort we stayed in last week on it. The pencil strokes create the image of a woman holding a coffee mug. She's barefoot and staring into the distance. Her hair twists in the wind, and the look on her face is serene. Gentle.

"What's that?" I ask, nodding at the fridge.

He shrugs, stirring cream into his coffee. "It's what you saw me drawing the other day."

"Oh." I look at it again. "Is that . . . ?"

"You?" Kit gives me a smile over his shoulder. "Yes, sweet potato. That's you."

I bring my mug to my lips so I don't have to reply. The knowledge that this is how he sees me throbs in my chest. The woman in that drawing isn't closed off or unapproachable at all.

"If you hate it, we can take it down," Kit offers as he sips on his coffee.

"No, don't," I say before thinking it through. I clear my throat and say in a more measured tone, "Leave it. You've always been a talented artist."

"That was dangerously close to a compliment."

I roll my eyes. "I like your thighs and you can draw nice pictures. Don't let it go to your head."

Kit laughs. "Are you ready to head to my place?"

"Born ready." I raise my coffee mug in a mock toast. The truth is, I'm a little terrified to see his place. He's so pulled together these days, I truly wonder what his life is like behind closed doors. I finish my coffee and grab my purse. "Quick question before we go."

"What's that?" Kit chugs the rest of his coffee.

"You don't have a sex dungeon, do you?"

Kit chokes on his coffee, spraying some on the counter. He takes a moment to recover, pounding his chest with his fist. "*What?*"

"I'll take it that's a no."

"Jesus Christ, Andie." Kit rinses his mug in the sink, then wets a paper towel to wipe his face after that coffee mishap. "No. I don't have a *sex dungeon.*"

"Just checking." I shrug and slip out the door.

* * *

By the time the camera crew has us mic'd up outside the door to Kit's suite at the Colonnade, I'm bouncing from one foot to the other.

He leans against the door, arms crossed over his chest, watching me with an amused smile on his face. "Excited about something, sweet potato?"

"I want to see your fortress of solitude." I clap my hands. It makes him laugh.

"You will, but first I need you to understand something."

I stop bouncing. "You said you didn't have a sex dungeon. How bad could it be?"

He rolls his eyes. "I mean it. Are you listening?"

I take a deep breath and nod. "Listening."

"I've told you I travel for work." He pauses until I nod. "The Colonnade sends me where they need me. Because I'm usually supervising construction—sometimes new and sometimes remodeling—I stay there for a while. They need me on site around the clock, so they let me live in one of their suites."

I look at the collar of his shirt. It's pilling around the fold, and it makes me wonder how long he's had it.

"Andie?"

"Yeah. You live in hotels. Got it." I force a smile. Something about his worn clothing and this fancy resort aren't fitting together. I'm hoping seeing inside will help fill in some blanks.

He sighs. "I don't own a house or a condo or property of any kind. Even my car is a rental I'll use while I'm here, on the Colonnade's dime."

"Why are you telling me all of this?" I meet his gaze.

He pulls out the key card for the room. "I just . . . don't want you to get the wrong impression, that's all."

"I already know you're no lord of dance." I smile, hoping he'll just relax.

He gives me a look and scans the keycard. I step in the open door and take it all in. The entryway is marble—I note the crystal chandelier above our heads—and the suite opens up into a large living room. There are dark hardwood floors covered in luxurious Persian rugs. Leather couches. I can't help it: I run my hand along one of the cushions. It's smooth as butter.

I groan dramatically.

"What's wrong?" he asks, his hands in his pockets.

"You didn't tell me you were Scrooge McDuck."

He tilts his head in question. "What are you talking about?"

I point down the hallway off the living room. "If you tell me there isn't a swimming pool full of money behind one of those doors, I'll be disappointed."

"No swimming pool." He shakes his head, an exasperated smile on his face. "Did you listen to anything I said earlier?"

"No sex dungeon, yeah, I got it." I brush past him on my way out of the living room.

When I see the dining room—a huge solid wood table large enough to seat ten people—I pause, all jokes lost.

All at once, the stench of stale French fries from the dollar menu at McDonald's hits me, along with the sound of radio static and my thighs burning on a scalding, cracked leather bench seat as my mother studies a map, looking for the nearest country club.

I swallow the bile rising in my throat, remembering how she had designer dresses in the trunk, leftovers from the marriage she left behind, when I was only fourteen. How she wore one later, looking elegant even without the diamonds we had to sell so we could eat. How she mingled and flirted and—if she wasn't lucky—would sneak out with some hors d'oeuvres for me. And if she was lucky? She went home on a wealthy man's arm in hopes she could make him fall in love, marry her, and he could take care of us for a while.

It's probably why seeing Kit's place feels like I'm going to break out in hives. The jokes are really there to distract myself from how this is so close to everything I didn't want for myself. It's why I hand sew beads and hems until my fingers crack and bleed. My life will be mine and no one else's.

Kit's hand on the small of my back startles me back to the present, as does his question. "What's wrong?"

"Nothing." I shake my head and force a smile. "What do you want to take with us?"

His lips tilt into a half grin as he watches me invade his space. "Not much."

That makes sense, based on what he told me at the door. I wander down a short hallway and step into what appears to be his office. He's got a laptop open on a heavy wooden desk, screen dark, and a neat stack of brochures on the side table beside an actual wingback chair. He leans in the doorway, blocking the camera from entering. Steve raises the lens over Kit's shoulder to film me anyway.

I run my finger over one of the piped seams on the chair, then pick up a heavy crystal paperweight from his desk. "Wow."

"What's wow?"

I lean on his desk, tossing the paperweight between my hands. "You've achieved everything you ever wanted, haven't you?"

"I mean, now that I know a sex dungeon is a possibility . . ." His eyes twinkle with laughter.

I roll my eyes. "You told me you wanted a life like this. Don't you remember?"

"And you wanted to visit Paris. I remember." He nods. "I'm comfortable. But I'm not in Forbes, or anything."

"Sure. Whatever you say, Mr. McDuck. I'm glad one of us accomplished what we wanted." I push off his desk, and my eyes fall to the brochures on the table by the chair. I expect them to be related to the Colonnade, research he'd do on other properties or something.

Confused by the one on top, I push it aside to see the one below it. My brow furrows as I nudge that one aside, too. They're all brochures for assisted living and hospice, flagged with sticky notes.

My eyes fly to Kit in the doorway. I don't dare ask him about them now. Not when his eyes have gotten a shade darker as I looked through them. He hasn't told me the whole truth about his mom, apparently.

I swallow the lump in my throat and ignore the way my heart becomes so heavy I can barely breathe. In a casual move, I place the paperweight over the title of the brochure on top, so the camera can't see it if Steve wanders in here.

"Should we start with your closet?" I ask, my voice too hoarse for my liking. The lump in my throat wants to climb out as a sob. I didn't expect a ridiculously lavish penthouse to stir up so much emotion in me today. Especially when there's so little of Kit here. I'm sure he could tell a lot about me from visiting my loft. I can't piece together anything about him from this suite.

Kit pushes off the doorframe and continues down the hallway. "Sorry there's no swimming pool of money."

"With a diving board," I add, grateful he gave me a way to get back to a lighter topic.

"Of course." He shoots me a look over his shoulder. "What's the point of a pool full of money if you can't dive into it?"

When I follow him into the room at the end of the hallway, I gasp. It's a grand room—a modern four-post king bed, made up with way too many pillows and a comforter with shimmering gold filigree embroidered on it. There's a separate sitting area made of the same buttery furniture as the living room.

I stare at the bed, biting my lip. When I tuck my hands into my skirt pockets, Kit snorts a laugh. "Go on. I know you want to."

"I couldn't." I shake my head. But I'm bouncing on the balls of my feet.

"The opportunity expires in three . . . two . . ."

I squeal with delight and run across the room, launching myself onto the mound of pillows. Kit's laughter chases away the fear that the camera might have gotten a flash of my underwear as I jumped.

I nestle deeper into the pillows, until I can pretend the cameras aren't here at all. The mattress dips when Kit joins me, digging his way to me through the mess.

"Are you sure we have to live in that little apartment?" I ask when his nose is inches from mine. His brown eyes are bright with laughter, and it's almost like we've traveled back in time to a dorm room night at Georgia State.

"That's the deal, yeah?" He smiles, his eyes crinkling at the corners. "For richer or poorer, remember?"

"I prefer richer." Ignoring the flicker of doubt in his eyes, I scoop up one of the down-filled pillows, squeeze it against my chest, and bury my face in it. "Can we at least take a pillow?"

Kit laughs, tugging the pillow away from my face. "They belong to the Colonnade, remember?"

"There's so many pillows," I complain. "They won't even notice one missing."

"You're in this place for three seconds and you're already a pillow snob."

I grab a smaller throw pillow and whack him with it. He's unbothered. Rude. "I'm in my thirties. A good pillow is worth its weight in gold."

"Maybe I'll get you a nice pillow for Christmas." He shrugs, like it's no big deal to think we'll still be together after the cameras are long gone.

When I'm silent for too long, he slides off the bed and offers me a hand to get up too. But I don't miss how he sneaks one of the Colonnade's pillows into the bag we take home. Or how he hangs his mere three suits in one corner of the closet, careful not to take up too much space.

CHAPTER EIGHTEEN

KIT

I smile as I pull into the dirt driveway in front of my mom's place Wednesday evening. It's been a long few days since we returned to Atlanta. Catching up at work after a week away, plus being filmed every time I come home, and moving into a tiny apartment with Andie—I'm exhausted. I'm looking forward to a regular dinner where I don't have to be Perfect Husband Kit for a couple of hours.

As I walk up the steps, I note that the landscapers I sent to clean up the yard did some great work. I'll add them to the list of companies I can trust to take care of things when I'm halfway across the world. My steps slow as I approach the door. Living in a new country doesn't sound as exciting as it used to, for some reason. Probably because I know my mom is still struggling with her health. Once she's on the mend, I'll want to travel for work again, I'm positive.

She answers almost as soon as I knock, a broad smile across her face, despite the exhaustion hovering just behind her eyes. "Welcome back, Kit." She grips my arm as I cross the threshold. "I hope you're okay with some casserole; I didn't have the energy for much else."

"Casserole is perfect." I bow to kiss the top of her bald head and let her lean on me on our way to the couch. She seems so much frailer than I know her to be. The doctors warned me this wouldn't be easy—for either of us—but I'm not sure what to do with this version of the woman who raised me.

I clear my throat and say, "I was thinking—what if we took that trip to Paris?" Talking about it with Andie has my mind spinning on all the things I haven't done, even when they were right in front of me. It's like she shook open the curtains on the periphery of my tunnel vision and asked me to look out the window, for fuck's sake.

"I can't travel right now." Mom waves it off.

"But when you're done with chemo and radiation," I counter. "We'll go. We'll do everything we planned, and anything else you want. Spend the summer exploring Europe, maybe."

She tilts her head to study me like a specimen. "You can't take all that time off work, can you?"

"I—" I want to say that of course I can, but I don't know if that's true. I never ask for time off. Hell, I told my job I had a lead on a property in Costa Rica, so I wasn't on my honeymoon, really. I was scouting the potential investment. And I've been at work since seven this morning, trying to catch up from the single week I was gone. Every email I missed was a notch on the vise strapped around my chest, cinching tighter every day. A simple reminder that if I fail at this job and they let me go, the life I've built is moot.

The oven timer beeps, and I gesture to my mom to sit while I take care of it. It only takes a few minutes to turn off the oven and serve us up a couple of plates of a noodle casserole where most of the ingredients probably came out of a can. It will taste like home, I'm sure of it. Mom refuses help to the small table, teetering into her seat with a heavy sigh.

I push some food on my plate, my mind back at my penthouse at the Colonnade. That large dining table I never use and never invite her to sit at. The world-renowned meals we have the option to eat, but for some reason I never thought of it until Andie was standing in my space, looking at it like it *hurt* her.

"What do you think?" I ask, spearing some green beans along with an egg noodle. "About Paris, I mean?"

She gives me a long look across the small table. "Is there a reason why you're not telling me about your new wife?"

I choke on my food, reaching for my glass of water. A few gulps do the trick, and I take in a deep breath as I slouch in my chair. Thank God there are no cameras here to witness this conversation. "What do you want to know?"

"Everything, Kit." She pushes her food around but doesn't take a bite. "I want to know everything about the woman who's stolen your heart."

I bite my tongue to keep from correcting her—our hearts are definitely not involved. Andie has made that perfectly clear. I'm grateful I never told Mom about Andie when we dated the first time. Four fast and fiery months that went up in smoke; at least Mom didn't have to witness that destruction too. After swallowing another bit of food, I try to answer. "Her name is Andie. Brown hair, hazel eyes, about your height."

Mom snorts. "I mean who is she as a person?"

"She's determined." I scoop up another bite of casserole. "Proud. Stubborn."

"Sounds like a good match for you, then." Mom takes a sip of water, and I eye her shaking hand carefully as it returns the glass to the table.

"What does that mean?" I mumble around a mouthful of food.

"Kit, you and I both know how you get when you're faced with a problem."

I bide my time chewing, then chasing it all down with a swig of water. "How's that?"

"You've never been able to sit with it." She pins me with her stare. It's too perceptive. Even now, despite how much I want to prove her wrong, my body revs like it needs to run. "You need someone stubborn to keep you in the room long enough to work it out."

"I'm sorry." The words tumble from my mouth, and still I want to flee the table. Will I ever feel okay with my decision to leave? "I should have stayed with you when you needed me."

She waves it off. "You were young and didn't know how to handle it."

My foot bounces under the table and my eyes dart to the front door.

"You can stop running, Kit." She reaches a hand across the small table and grips my wrist.

I don't know how to explain the storm of emotions swirling in my chest, or the thoughts clattering in my head. How sitting here at this table without my dad still makes me feel so lost. Leaving was the only way to outrun the grief crushing me from all sides—my dad no longer with us and my mom slipping away in front of my eyes, grief eating away at her. Running was the only way I could breathe.

I frown at a pea that's rolled to the edge of my plate, thinking of Andie yanking open those curtains again. My foot stills under the table.

"When do I get to meet her?" Mom asks, a smile tugging at her lips and a sparkle in her eyes. It's a ray of sunlight peeking through the storm of drugs that rob her of her energy, and part of me is ready to call Andie right now and tell her to come over if it means it will make my mom feel better.

But that light in my Mom's eyes will flicker out again if she sees Andie and me together and sees the truth—we're not in love. And we won't be falling, either.

I stuff another forkful of food into my mouth. "I don't know. She's really busy. Works late a lot." It's a half-truth. Andie is incredibly busy, but Cassidy already asked me to pick a date for the "meeting the parents" episode with my mom. She said she needs to scout locations and get filming releases beforehand. I told her I'd ask Mom, but I can't bring myself to ask her to allow the chaos that is *First Look at Forever* into her life. Not when she needs peace and quiet.

"Doing what?" Mom puts down her fork and gives up the pretense of eating. My heart sustains a tiny, paper cut–thin tear.

"She runs her own business." I set my fork down too. My appetite is evaporating by the second. "Making wedding dresses."

"Can I see?" That spark in my mom's eyes is impossible to say no to, so I pull out my phone and google Andie's website. I haven't looked at it yet, mostly because I haven't had the time, but now that it's in front of me, I'm greedy for it.

It's not pink. I don't know why I expected it to be pink. Andie isn't a pink kind of person, anyway. Instead, the website is variations on sunshiny yellows with a clean, modern font and photos of some of her designs. I pass my phone to my mom and let her poke around.

"She's showing at Atlanta Fashion Week," I say, just to keep from snatching my phone back to look at the website again. It's a piece of her, and I don't know what to do with it.

"What does that mean?" Mom taps on the phone screen.

I scrub my knuckles along my five o'clock shadow and admit, "I'm not sure. She hasn't told me much about it, but she's always working on new designs after I've gone to bed."

Mom makes a noncommittal noise, and I make a mental note to look up what it takes to show at Fashion Week.

"She's beautiful, Kit."

My eyes snap to Mom, who's smiling at my phone screen. I know she hasn't opened my photos, because I haven't taken any of Andie. The only image I have of her is the one I drew on hotel paper and hung on our fridge.

Mom turns the screen toward me, and it's like a kick to the chest. She's pulled up the site's About page, and right there is a picture of Andie at her workstation, focused on the task at hand.

She's in a white T-shirt and long, electric blue pleated skirt. One she no doubt made for herself; is that skirt hanging in our closet at home? The spray of freckles across her face is gorgeous, even in a photo. Her hair is dangling over her shoulder in a haphazard braid, some glasses perched on top of her head. Her lips are in the shape of a round vowel as she's pointing to her tablet, nested in a cloud of white, shimmery fabric, like she's talking to someone just out of frame. A bride perhaps.

It's Andie in her element, and it's stunning to witness in this still. What would it be like to experience in person?

"Yes," I croak, reaching for my water, "she is."

Mom turns off the screen and sets my phone down in the middle of the table. "Is she good to you?"

I rest my hand on the table and stare at my wedding band. It's not that Andie has been awful to me, it's that she won't let *me* be good to *her*. I swallow and admit to my mom, "She won't let me in, and I don't know what to do."

Mom nods sagely, then slowly stands, leaning heavily on the table. She picks up her plate and gives me a determined look. "Don't forget you need to let her in, too."

CHAPTER NINETEEN
ANDIE

It's been a long day at work, and I'm not in the mood to film. But Cassidy clips on my mic in the apartment complex parking garage and follows me to the clubhouse, where a group cooking class awaits.

There's a full studio setup in the clubhouse kitchen—lights and boom mics and cameras set up to get several angles. It's not only Cassidy and Steve in the wings, but the producers and camera people assigned to the other couples too.

And Kit got out of it. Somehow, he doesn't have to be here. After our meeting with Dr. Leon, when Cassidy gave us our schedule for the coming weeks, Kit said he had to have dinner with his mom tonight. He did reveal that his mom was sick and fighting cancer, so the production team said this event was okay to miss.

It's not fair, really.

I could have had dinner with his mom, too. But then I guess the cameras would have followed, and since she wasn't at our wedding, I'm assuming the cameras are what she's trying to avoid.

"Hey, Andie." Jamie greets me with a smile. "Long day?"

"The longest." He hands me a red apron, and I slip it over my head.

"I don't remember you saying," Leslie pipes up from behind Jamie, "what it is you do for work."

I do my best to smile. I've been designing dresses professionally for years now, but it still feels fraudulent to call myself a designer. "I, um, design wedding dresses."

"Oh my God." Kendra bounces over from the other end of the kitchen. "Are you the same Andie from the TikToks?"

"I like sharing my process." I shrug, heat rising in my cheeks.

"It's so interesting to see all that goes into making a dress." Kendra opens a bottle of wine and tips it in offering to all of us. "I had no idea all those things had to happen behind the scenes."

"I used to design menswear," Jamie says as Kendra fills his wine glass. "Back in the day, you know. As a hobby, I mean."

"Oh?" I'm surprised to meet someone else who understands being a creative who works with their hands all the time. "What do you do now?"

He shrugs. "Not much right now. Some freelance writing here and there."

"He's trying to figure out what he wants to be when he grows up." Leslie ties his apron on. The look he gives Jamie is incredibly long-suffering considering we've all only been together for about ten days.

Jamie's eyes lose a touch of their sparkle. Instead of responding, he sips on his wine.

"Hey, me too, man." Patrick offers Jamie a fist bump. "How the hell are we supposed to know what we want to do when there's so much out there?"

"I thought you were a firefighter." I narrow my eyes at him.

"For now, yeah." He secures his apron, too. "But eventually my body isn't going to be able to do that anymore. Where's Kit?"

"Dinner with his mom." I wave it off and take a sip of my wine. "He'll join us later." I think. I hope. He'd better. At least this wine is good. I can already feel its warmth leaching into my sore muscles.

A man with tattoos up and down both arms strolls in and announces he's worked as a private chef for celebrities and athletes for a decade, and tonight he's going to teach us how to make pizza. I'm glad it's nothing too complicated, especially since I'm on my own.

Getting the dough to come together is easy enough. So is bringing the tomatoes and seasonings to a simmer on the stove. It's when it's time to begin shaping dough that it gets difficult.

While I'm struggling with how much memory my dough has—I can't get it flat enough and wish I could use an iron on it like I do with stubborn fabric—a metal pan clatters to the floor on Jamie and Leslie's side of the kitchen.

All eyes turn to them. A dough blob stretches off the edge of the counter, and one of the pendulum lights above the island swings back and forth. Leslie buries his face in his hands while Jamie shrugs sheepishly. "I thought I'd try throwing it?"

I want to laugh, but Leslie frowns, his hands balled into fists.

"You hurt?" Patrick asks him.

He slowly shakes his head and looks at Jamie, furious. "No, I just—for once, can you take something seriously?"

Jamie's smile melts into a grimace. "Would it kill you to have some *fun* for once?"

"You ruined your pizza and made a mess of this kitchen that isn't even yours."

"The kitchen will clean, and it's pizza, not life and death. Relax."

Leslie closes his eyes and takes a deep breath. "I think I will relax. At home." He forces a smile for the rest of us and offers, "Enjoy."

After a cameraman follows him out the door, I check on Jamie. He gives me a small smile. "It's fine. I'm fine."

I squat down with him to help scrape the pizza dough off the floor. "I'm sorry. He shouldn't talk to you like that."

Jamie sniffs, making a point to hide his face so the camera can't see him cry. "I'm trying so hard to get to know him, and nothing I do is right."

This experience is an uphill climb for all of us, apparently. "Is he always like this?"

"No." He shakes his head and plops a handful of dough onto the metal pan that fell. "When we're alone, no cameras around, he's so . . . gentle. And kind."

I nod. "It's stressful to get married to someone you've never met and then be on camera all the time."

Jamie laughs. "Yeah. Yeah, it is."

"Do you want to help with my pizza since I'm solo anyway?"

He smiles. "That'd be fun."

I smile in return. As wild as the experience of this show is, I'm glad I'm at the very least not doing it alone.

By the time our pizza hits the oven, it's a misshapen lump of dough with some sauce on it, but I'm proud of the work. I remove my apron and excuse myself to go to the bathroom. My hands are covered in flour and dough bits, and the rest of me is sticky with sweat from hovering over hot pots and ovens. Cassidy flicks off my mic before I duck into the ladies' room in the clubhouse.

After splashing my face with cool water and sniffing my shirt to make sure I don't smell like yeast, I stare at my reflection. The woman looking back is tired, dark smudges under her eyes.

I open the bathroom door and lean on the frame. Cassidy waits patiently in the hall. "How do you do it?" I ask her.

She tilts her head. "Do what?"

"Work full-time and keep a house clean and eat and"—I gesture at the clubhouse kitchen, where Steve and the army of producers and equipment wait for us to return—"keep a relationship going?"

Cassidy shrugs, watching Steve frame a shot of the pizza in the oven. "Our place is a mess and we've been living off gas station food. While we're filming, something has to give. There just aren't enough hours in the day."

"What about each other?"

She smiles. "We're lucky. We get to work together."

I look at my shoes. There's a splotch of marinara on my right toe. "I don't think I'm cut out for this."

"You did great with the pizza." She waves it off.

"No, I mean"—I shift on my feet—"the relationship part."

"It's new. Give it time." She studies me and twists the cord for her headphones around one finger. "Listen—this is my third season filming the show, and I can tell you, if you're worried about how to make it work, it's a good thing. It's the ones who don't think they need to try that are in trouble."

I nod, not sure what to say to that. Making it work shouldn't be what I want, right?

"Some days that's all it's about. Trying, I mean." She gives me a small smile. "Show up. Try. Repeat. Some days are hard. Hardly any are perfect. But the good ones always follow as long as you keep showing up."

I frown. Things were so easy with Kit the first time, but we really only made it a few months. Where would we be now if I didn't expect everything to be easy with him forever? What if I let him in the door when he showed up after his absence, and what if I'd forgiven him for not being able to tell me he loved me too? I rub my forehead with my palm, shaking my head. I can *what if* myself to death, and it won't change where we are now.

"Look who's here." Cassidy nods toward the kitchen.

Kit strolls in, his shirt unbuttoned at the top, sleeves rolled to his elbows. It's a look I've come to appreciate on him. A look that says he's worked his ass off and now he's coming undone at the seams, just a little. It isn't fair how he looks so . . . so . . .

"God, that man is walking kryptonite, isn't he?" Cassidy says, tutting as she shakes her head.

I crack my neck turning to look at her. Is she serious?

Cassidy laughs. "I have eyes. And I know you do too. I see how you look at him."

I stutter, exasperated, and cross my arms over my chest. "How I look at him?"

"Cool your jets." Cassidy gestures for me to turn around so she can flip on my mic. "I don't want your husband."

"What? Are you saying I'm *jealous*?" I say it too sharply, too loudly. Loud enough for Kit to look at me. The grin he gives me is devastating. I grip my skirt in my fists to keep my hands from shaking.

"I'm *saying*, Kit's one of the good ones. It's okay to want him. And it's okay for him to know you want him."

She flicks my mic on just in time to catch my mumbled, "The nightmare never ends."

CHAPTER TWENTY

KIT

Andie looks a mess. She's pulled her hair back into a chaotic bun that's now frizzing at the edges. Her skin is flushed and blotchy from kneading dough and managing being on camera while cooking for the last couple hours. She's got marinara on one of her canvas sneakers and flour streaked across the neck of her blouse.

She is without a doubt the most stunning human I've ever seen.

I can't help but smile as she approaches. Her tough exterior cracks for a moment, and she looks me in the eyes as a smile flits across her face too.

Its effect has me unraveling, as if she's found the loose thread she left in my heart ten years ago and gave it a solid tug.

"Hey." Her nose wrinkles as she says it, and that thread in my heart loosens again.

"Hi." I lean on the counter because my knees have suddenly turned to Jell-O. "How was your day?"

"Long." She gives me a flicker of a smile again. "I won't bore you with the gruesome details of the charmeuse catastrophe of twenty twenty-four."

"Was blood drawn?" My eyes fall to her hands.

"No more than usual." She holds her palms up for me to see.

"I told her to use duppioni silk instead, but she won't hear it." Jamie pours a glass of wine and slides it across the counter to me.

"It's too structured." Andie shakes her head. "I need this to *flow.*"

"Are you a designer, too?" I ask Jamie. Andie's hands are still between us, so I take one in both of mine and knead her palm like I did on our honeymoon. Her small intake of air, followed by a shiver and her eyes sliding closed, is enough for me to know I should keep going.

"Never professionally." He waves off the idea. "More of a hobby, really."

"You know, Andie could really use an extra pair of capable hands while she gets ready for Fashion Week," I suggest.

Her eyes fly open and she glares at me, snatching her hand back.

Watching the interaction, Jamie begs off. "I don't have that level of skill."

"I didn't even know that duppioni silk existed until now. You've got more than the standard level of knowledge for producing garments."

Andie's glare is relentless, her jaw taut and nostrils beginning to flare.

"It's nice of you to say that." Jamie nods. "I'm going to—" He gestures vaguely to the hallway Andie emerged from earlier, then steps away, leaving me to her wrath.

She takes a deep breath. "I can't believe you just—"

"Found someone who may be able to help you and pointed it out?" I scoop up my wineglass and take a sip.

"Even if I wanted the help"—she crossed her arms over her chest—"I can't afford to pay him."

I shrug. "I can."

Her jaw drops. "I—You—What the hell is wrong with you?"

"I'm trying to help." I frown into my wineglass.

"Help?" She spits out the word and looks away, working her jaw. When she looks back at me, her eyes are bright with tears threatening to fall. "If you want to help me, maybe you should be here when we're filming."

"I was with my mom, you know that."

"I'm aware." She sniffs as she walks around the kitchen island to look in the oven. "I had a long day."

"So did I."

"And then I had to be here for this cooking class. Alone. While you got to be at home and relax. I'm tired, Kit. If you want to help, then show up so I'm not carrying this"—she waves at the huge studio setup behind us—"all on my own."

The thread in my heart pulls taut, snagging on the rawness in Andie's request. It's not like I don't know being on camera is taking its toll on her. All of us are beginning to crack under the pressure. It's why I don't want cameras invading my mom's privacy when she needs to be focused on healing.

It's not fair of me to offer that protection to Mom and leave Andie to do it alone.

I set my wineglass down with a sigh and follow Andie around the island. When I'm close enough, I ask gently, "If I hug you, are you going to stab me with one of those fancy chef's knives?"

She swipes her palm across her cheek, but I saw the tear before she could hide it. She shakes her head.

I slide my arms around her waist and pull her into me—her back into my chest—and rest my chin on the top of her head. She stiffens for a second, then takes a deep breath and sinks into me. I breathe in, too. She smells like garlic and the soft floral scent in the soap she keeps in the shower.

"That was a lot of words to say you missed me tonight." I give her a squeeze, so she knows I'm kidding. Mostly.

She digs her elbow into my ribs. When I loosen my grip, she turns in my arms, a smirk on her face. "Believe it or not, I did just fine without you."

"You sure about that?" I nod to the lumpy pizza in the oven she's been staring at.

"I wouldn't laugh too much." She flicks one of the buttons on my shirt, and it sends a jolt of electricity straight down to my cock. "Your punishment is to taste it when it's done."

"Punishment?"

She gives me a devious grin. "I made it just for you."

"You didn't poison it, did you?"

She shrugs and lets out a little hum. I feel that in my cock too.

"Poison or no"—I tug on a strand of her hair that's fallen from her topknot—"I missed you too, sweet potato."

She wrinkles her nose and shoves me away with her hands on my chest. But she's smiling. I'll take it.

After the pizzas are out of the oven, Andie watches as I take a bite of hers. The dough is somehow tough and raw at the same time. The marinara is bitter and acidic. I force a smile as I swallow the bite.

"Delicious," I lie, giving her a thumbs up.

She snorts. "Liar."

"The cheese is great," I insist.

"It's no secret I'm not a good cook," she says before taking a sip of wine. "Not the housewife-y type."

"I don't need a housewife." I set the abomination of a pizza slice down and wipe my hands on a napkin. "I just need you, sweet potato."

She tosses her napkin at me and rolls her eyes.

I snatch her hand off the table and begin to massage it the way I know she likes. "Thanks for not poisoning me."

"I can't kill you. Who would give me hand massages?"

"Nice to know you need me for something." We both smile, suddenly light, and she lets me take care of her hands. "And please, never cook for me again."

CHAPTER TWENTY-ONE
ANDIE

Kit only owns three suits: one navy, one charcoal, and one black. To say I'm surprised it's that few would be an understatement. He wears them to work every single day; I just assumed he would own at least a closet's worth. I stare at the suit he's chosen for today hanging on the closet door—it's a classic navy, with a white button-down and a simple red tie.

The pants are wrinkled from the move over here. I sip on my mug of coffee, trying desperately to ignore the cameras over my shoulder. When they said they'd be filming every waking hour, they meant it. They want footage of us at our married best—brushing our teeth and making coffee and generally tiptoeing around each other in the mornings.

At least they're not forcing me to talk to him. He's in the shower, and that would be awkward. For all kinds of reasons.

After the pizza disaster last night, he offered to massage my hands before bed. Selfishly, knowing his day was long too, I took him up on it. My whole body shimmered as he worked lotion into my skin, and I held my breath when he slid my wedding ring back on. It took every ounce of self-control I possessed to *not* climb into his lap and thank him for his effort. This morning, I can't seem to look him in the eye without thinking about it.

And after his confession about what's going on with his mom, I don't have it in me to wall him off. He'd been so close to me, and the buttons on his shirt were so perfectly undone around the notch in his throat. It would have been the easiest thing in the world to kiss him, to take it too far.

That part of our relationship has always worked. And well.

But he said his mom wanted him to apply for the show so she could see him settled before she died. He's been vague about how dire her diagnosis is, but it doesn't matter. His mom wants to see him with a happy wife, and the more time I spend with him, the more I think he wants that life, too. And I robbed him of that option when I said *I do.*

Then he had to go and set the coffee maker to go off this morning. My tablet sat next to my favorite mug on the counter, fully charged.

I don't know what to do with these emotions rising in my throat. All I know is I'm officially on dangerous ground, caring about what happens to Kit and his mom. I'm worried about what will happen to me, too.

I set my coffee on the dresser and flick on my handheld steamer. My skirt needs some attention after the move too. Kit's still in the bathroom when I finish smoothing out the wrinkles in the silk, and my steamer still has plenty of water in it, so I take a few minutes to steam his pants too. They're already hanging up; it's easy enough to move from one garment to the other.

Kit emerges from the bathroom, towel slung low on his hips, shameless in front of the cameras, just as I start on the second pant leg. He pauses when he sees me messing with his clothes, then leans against the wall, a smirk on his face. "Are you ironing my clothes?"

I roll my eyes. "Steaming. They're wrinkled."

"That's very domestic of you." His eyes sparkle with amusement, and he crosses his arms over his chest.

I shoot him a sharp look through a puff of steam. "Why do you only own three suits?"

He shrugs. "I travel for work. Three suits are easy to take with me."

As I reach the hem of his pants, I notice a loose thread. I hand him the steamer and flick open the decorative wooden box on the dresser to retrieve a tiny pair of scissors. This hem has seen better days. Only three suits means he wears them all the time, and if he's had them for years . . . even the most well-made suits have their limits. As far as I can tell, this is a department store basic, not a high-end designer garment.

Almost all of his shirts are beginning to pill around the collars, and every one of them has a loose thread here and there, or a button about to pop off. The man gives new meaning to minimalism. And I mean he *has* to be a minimalist, because if he lives and works at the fucking Colonnade, he can afford a new shirt.

I snip the offending thread from the hem of his pants. "You only have five oxfords."

"What's your point?" He frowns.

I take the steamer from him so I can finish the job. "I just figured a man with your status at work would own more."

He pushes off the wall and maneuvers behind me to drink out of my coffee cup, clutching the towel at his hips with his other hand. "Not all of us can make our own clothes on demand. I have plenty."

I snort my disagreement, but keep my mouth shut. It's not my place to judge how many items of clothing he has. But my side of the closet stuffed full stands in stark contrast to his barren three suits and five dress shirts. I flick off the steamer and turn to face him, setting it down on the dresser. "All done."

The corner of his mouth lifts in a half grin.

"Don't get used to it." I pluck my coffee cup out of his hands and take a sip.

Completely shameless, his back to the cameras, his eyes dip into the V of my robe before skating slowly up my chest to caress my neck before finally meeting mine again. His half grin turns into a full one. "You look beautiful."

Heat rising to my cheeks, I counter, "And you look like you're going to be late."

"But at least my suit will be wrinkle-free." As he slips around me toward his suit, he tugs on my messy bun. Before I can protest, he presses his lips to my cheek. "Thank you."

I almost forget my tablet on the way out the door.

* * *

I'm halfway through pinning a ballroom skirt onto a dress form for one of my Fashion Week designs when I hear my laptop ping with an email. Always when my hands are occupied. I finish the draping, stabbing pins into the form with more force than is strictly necessary. None of it's working anyway. Instead of a ballroom skirt, all I can see in my mind is a towel clinging to Kit's hips.

A ballroom skirt can't capture the intimacy of marriage like that towel can, and suddenly this dress feels so foreign I'm not sure it came from my own mind anymore. My insecurity about being good enough to design my own line rears its ugly head with such force I take in a sharp breath.

Space. I need space.

I already spent the morning procrastinating assembling this dress by filming TikToks of fabric swatches in the sunlight coming in my loft windows. I also filmed a few of my other designs, explaining which silhouette looks best on certain body types. Those videos should last me a week of content at least.

Frowning, I approach my laptop and wake the screen. I groan when I read the subject line: PAST DUE—ATLANTA FASHION WEEK FEE. The email is short and to the point. If I don't pay up by the end of the week, I lose my spot in the tent at Fashion Week.

I planned on paying the fee when Clover Callaway wrote me a large check for the delivery of her dress. As it never came, the fee for my spot at Fashion Week slipped my mind. And now I might lose my spot because a man couldn't keep it in his pants.

The frustration rises in me so quickly, I don't know what to do with it. I pace the room for a few seconds, mumbling every curse I can think of and call the bastard some creative names under my breath.

After all the work I've done on my own—never going into debt, never applying for a business loan, never asking anyone to help me—my dreams are still at the whim of someone I don't even *know*. Someone who will never understand what this means to me, how important it is that I show at Fashion Week.

My swearing gets more colorful as my resentment mingles with the shame I feel at spending so much on materials for Fashion Week, confident nothing could go wrong. I should know better than this. I should be more cautious. I shouldn't have reached so far out of my comfort zone. It was a silly, childish thing to do.

As the *shoulds* reach a fever pitch, profanity isn't enough. I whip around to the dress form and tear the fabric off. The form wobbles at the base as my obscenities get louder, echoing off the walls. Pins scatter on the wood floor as painstakingly cut muslin joins them in a heap. By the time the form is bare, I'm trying to catch my breath.

Someone clears their throat behind me.

I gasp and spin around, smoothing my hair back into my messy bun. My brain short-circuits when I see a man in black pants and a white button-down standing inside my studio holding two large brown paper bags. My hands shaking, I force a smile. "Can I help you?"

"Is this Andrea Dresser Designs?" he asks, eyeing all the bolts of fabric on the far wall.

I clear my throat and nod. "It is."

The man lets out a sigh of relief. "I was worried I had the wrong place."

"Wrong place for what?" I frown as I look him over. Is this one of the grooms from a wedding I designed for? Or a high-profile bride's personal assistant sent to scout out my business and make sure I'm not a liability?

You blew that one, Andie.

"I'm from La Campagne." The French restaurant down the street? He holds up the bags that look damn heavy, bulging at the seams. I gesture for him to place them in the kitchenette as he explains, "This is one of everything we have."

I dare to peek into one of the bags. It's packed to the brim with to-go containers and smells suspiciously like garlic bread. "I didn't order anything."

"Oh, no." He waves it off, and I've definitely missed something. "A Mr. Watson ordered it and told us where to take it. We don't normally do deliveries, but he tipped *really* well."

Something warm tugs inside my chest. I thank the man for his trouble and start unpacking the bags. He was not kidding about there being one of everything. A few salads, two loaves of bread, several entrees, and three desserts in total.

At the bottom of one of the bags is an envelope with my name on it, written in Kit's confident block letters.

I pop it open and pull out the thick card stock with his company letterhead at the top.

It doesn't make up for me missing the class last night, but we'll always have Paris.

A smile pulls at the corners of my mouth. It's not a declaration of love, but it is enough food for a few days.

I tuck all the food I'm not going to eat today into the fridge and stare at the now-bare dress form as I rearrange numbers in my head. Kit doesn't know it, but his large offering today just bought me the slimmest margin of breathing room. If I can stretch these meals out to last a week, I can afford to pay the fee for Fashion Week.

I smile wider at Kit's handwriting as I dig in.

* * *

The next couple of weeks pass by in a blur of dress forms, sketches, and meals sent to my loft to make sure I eat. Suddenly we're halfway through filming, with only four weeks left until D-Day. I told Kit not to get used to it, but I steam his clothes in the morning as a silent thank you for taking care of my hands every night.

He let me sleep in this morning, waking me up with a large mug of coffee on my nightstand. He's already dressed for work.

"I have to go," he whispers, brushing some hair out of my face. Are there cameras here already? "I have a meeting this morning I can't be late for."

His touch is casual but so intimate it sends heat curling down my spine. I'm used to him touching my hands now. This is altogether different and not entirely unwelcome. Bleary-eyed, I roll out of bed, asking him to wait as I straighten my cotton shorts and tank top.

No cameras. Huh.

I feel his gaze on my bare legs as I walk around the bed and duck into the closet. When I emerge, I explain, "If you add a pocket square, it will look like a different suit."

"I don't own any pocket squares." The hint of a smile pulls at his lips.

He looks too good, standing in the morning sunlight that's streaming in through the curtains. Nothing about this is fair. I shake my head to stop my train of thought as it marches down the buttons on his shirt, willing them to open.

"Here." I fold the silk square I retrieved from the closet and tuck it into his breast pocket.

As I pluck the fabric until it lays just right, he asks, "Andie, did you get me pocket squares?"

I roll my eyes. "Of course not. I made you some."

The way his gaze softens makes my cheeks grow warm. I clear my throat and take a step back. "There," I say like it's no big deal. "Looks like you belong in a boardroom."

He tilts his head with an amused look on his face. "It's a meeting with the contractors for the dome. Dress code is safety vests and hardhats."

"Oh." I want to crawl back under the blankets and never come out. "Well. Anyway."

Kit walks to the closet and pokes his head in. His eyes crinkle at the corners when he reaches behind the door and pulls out the skirt I hung up to wear today. He looks between the garment and his chest until I see it.

They're the same fabric. I made his pocket squares out of leftovers from some of the clothes I made for myself. "I'm sorry," I groan, crossing the room and reaching for the fabric I tucked into his pocket. "You can wear another one. Or none at all. It's fine."

He covers his chest with his hand so I can't take the pocket square off him. "The hell I will, sweet potato."

My eyes shoot to his in a glare, and I steel my jaw. I really should be used to the pet name by now.

His half grin is teasing, his eyes warm. "I like that we'll match today."

"I'll wear a different skirt."

I reach for it, but he holds it above my head. The warmth in his eyes turns hot, an open flame for anyone to see. "No, you won't."

My lips part in a silent gasp. That was almost . . . possessive. The heat swirling in my gut and sinking lower tells me I like it. When I narrow my eyes, he says, "Be my good luck charm today. Please. It'll be our secret."

His words are light, nonchalant. But the look in his eyes screams, *you're mine.* My hand shaking as desire curls between my legs, I reach for the skirt. Kit surrenders it. Just when I think he's done, he leans over, close enough that I'm wrapped up in the woodsy scent of his aftershave, and whispers, "Good girl."

He's gone before the wave of heat crashes over me, leaving me hungry and cold as I sit on the edge of our shared bed.

FIRST LOOK AT FOREVER
SEASON THREE
EPISODE SEVEN

PRODUCER:
It seems like you're feeling more comfortable with Kit these days.

ANDIE:
Yes. Well. He works hard to make me feel at ease, I think.

ANDIE:
[frowns]

PRODUCER:
What's on your mind?

ANDIE:
I just . . . hope he isn't giving up too much of himself for me, you know? I want him to be comfortable with me too.

PRODUCER:
Are you starting to care for him?

ANDIE:
I— [blows out a breath] Maybe?

PRODUCER:
Are you going to tell him?

ANDIE:
[chews on her lip] When I know. I don't know.

FIRST LOOK AT FOREVER
SEASON THREE
EPISODE SEVEN

PRODUCER:
You sure do a lot for Andie, don't you?

KIT:
[shrugs] It's small things. Easy things. Isn't that what couples are supposed to do for each other?

PRODUCER:
Does she do anything for you?

KIT:
You've seen her steam my clothes in the morning.

PRODUCER:
Is that it?

KIT:
No. She . . . [runs his hands through his hair] Have you ever watched a TED Talk or had a conversation with a friend that left you so fired up, you knew you could conquer anything?

PRODUCER:
Yeah, I think I know what you mean.

KIT:
Being with Andie is like that. All the time. I can't help but want to do more and be better.

PRODUCER:
It sounds like you have feelings for her.

KIT:
[Smiles.] Maybe I do. That's the whole point of this damn thing, isn't it? [Crew laughs off camera.]

AUGUST

CHAPTER TWENTY-TWO
KIT

It's a beautiful day. Sunny and not too hot yet, dew clinging to the blades of grass and summer flowers. On top of that, we won't have to film until this evening. Cassidy probably has enough footage of us on quiet mornings and cleaning up before bed. I'm so distracted by how nice the day is, I make it all the way to the parking lot before I realize I forgot my fucking headphones.

I let out a silent curse to myself and pause in the sunshine while I debate running without music today or going back upstairs. If I was living alone, I'd run back upstairs, no question. But Andie's up there. In our bed. Maybe in the shower.

After the last few weeks of us acting like a married couple, it feels so natural to touch her. Dangerous. I don't trust myself to go back up there to see her in our bed, looking like a dream come true.

I've been sneaking into work later and later every morning, just to catch Andie in her robe as she steams my clothes. It's not some 1950s fantasy I have—I've made it this long without a woman fussing over my laundry—but it's Andie. In the morning. Undone. Soft. Her smiles when she's like that make me lightheaded.

It's worth every ounce of flak I catch from my bosses for "losing focus." Apparently staring off into space during a meeting, requiring everyone to repeat what they said has me on even thinner ice than showing up late and slipping out the door early to film.

A large semi drives by; the roar of the engine and stench of diesel make me grit my teeth. Fuck it; I'll go back upstairs, and if I'm lucky, she'll still be asleep, and I can sneak out without being tempted to cross the line between us that's looking flimsier by the day.

I head back inside, up the elevator, and pause to take a deep breath before opening the apartment door like it isn't also my home. My headphones are charging on my nightstand, so I tiptoe through the living room and nudge open the bedroom door.

Andie gasps, eyes wide. We both freeze.

My brain short-circuits when I see what she's doing.

Her legs are wide open on the sheets, and she's holding a purple vibrator in one hand. Caught red-handed. She curls her free hand around the T-shirt she's still wearing, her knuckles blanching.

My dick likes that very, very much. I'm only in running shorts, so there's no way Andie's missed it either. Goddammit. These days I've been getting by with fucking my own fist in the shower.

Apparently, she's been helping herself out during my runs.

Adding that knowledge to the image of her morning softness—I am so far gone for this woman. And we are officially on dangerous ground.

Gathering what little is left of my frayed self-control, I drag a hand down my face, turning around, and say with a growl, "I forgot my headphones."

The only response I get is a little "hmph" and the sound of her vibrator turning on. Jesus fucking Christ, there's only so much I can take. "By all means," I grumble, "do continue."

She snorts and I hear a shuffle on the sheets. I nearly jump out of my skin when I feel something soft land on my shoulder. I reach up to grab her panties, still warm from her body and smelling like her. I'm about to come in my shorts. "Are you trying to kill me?"

"I'm trying to get off," she says with her usual amount of snark. "You're the one who barged in here like the building was on fire."

I let out a heavy, shaking sigh. I realize too late I'm standing in front of the dresser. Which has a goddamn mirror on it. My eyes meet hers in the reflection. The sheets are crumpled at her feet, blocking the view I want the most. It doesn't stop my dick from twitching a cheer of encouragement.

"Are you going to leave?" She sounds so removed, aloof. Like she isn't half naked in our bed with a vibrator. With me right the fuck here.

"No." The word rumbles out of my throat before I can think this through.

She rolls her eyes and shifts in the sheets to get comfortable. If she's playing chicken with me, she's really fucking good at it. I actually believe she's going to—

I hold my breath as I watch her position her wand vibrator where she wants it. She lets out a contented sigh, and I nearly black out. I press my hand to the top of the dresser to steady my buckling knees.

The line we drew to keep from touching: absolutely hilarious.

I drag in ragged breaths and try to remember why I came back up to the apartment, and I can't. Then Andie tilts her head back, exposing the soft underside of her throat, and all I can remember is that I desperately want to bite her there.

A swear escapes my mouth in a groan.

Andie sounds remarkably unbothered, if a little breathless, when she asks, "Are you just going to stand there or what?"

I'm going to hell. Maybe I'm already there, and Andie's the devil who brings out the worst in me. All I know is, I'm lowering the waistband of my running shorts and freeing my dick. If she's going to get off being a pain in the ass, so the hell am I.

Her eyes catch mine in the mirror and she smiles a devious smile. "So he's not a perfect gentleman after all."

If she knew all the places in this apartment I'd imagined bending her over and fucking her until she screamed, she wouldn't be saying something like that. I don't dare say that out loud, so all she gets is a grunt as I curl my fingers around my dick and squeeze until my vision blurs around the edges.

I don't miss how her eyes fall to my thighs. She lets out a whimper and shivers on the bed. "I'll make you a deal."

I grunt again. How on earth can she hold a conversation right now?

"Whoever finishes first does the dishes for the next month."

I can't help but let out a puff of laughter. She hates doing the dishes. Hates it. Complains about it every fucking time, like the world is going to end if she has to unload the dishwasher when it's done. I manage to get out a "fine" before she lifts the hem of her T-shirt and my brain sputters to a halt.

I pump my dick as she slowly reveals her stomach, then her ribs, then the glorious underside of her breasts, and finally, her nipples. They're hard and erect and waiting for my mouth. Heat tumbles through me, and I squeeze my eyes shut, slamming my hand on the top of the dresser, clutching her panties so tightly I can't feel my fingers anymore.

Her perfume bottles rattle against each other, making the perfect music to complement her low laughter. I grit my teeth and start fighting back; every time she loads that fucking dishwasher, I want her to think of me and how I could absolutely ruin her for any other man.

In a low voice, I tell her, "I can hear how wet you are."

She lets out a tiny whimper in response. Her vibrator turns up a notch and I smile to myself.

"Tell me," I say as I pump myself once, twice, "is that for me?"

Our eyes lock in the mirror, and for a moment I think she'll tell me to fuck off. Instead, she says, "Like you don't think about me when you fuck your hand."

"I do," I admit with a shudder. "Of course I do."

She lets out a long moan that ends quivering into the silence. A slice of heat slides through my belly and I take in a deep breath. She enjoys the idea that I think about her when I get off.

More than a little breathless, my voice ragged and raw, I tell her, "I think about burying my dick in that pretty pussy of yours. All the time."

She whispers my name, maybe to scold me, but it also sounds a little like, *Yes, please, don't stop.*

My strokes are less controlled now, and pleasure slowly unravels in my spine. "I think about you saying my name, just like that." She groans, and her hips buck against the sheets. "You like the idea of me fucking you, don't you?"

"God, yes." The words are a reluctant whisper as she tosses her head back, eyes closed. Her tits thrust into the air as her back arches. She flicks her vibrator up another speed, and my fist flies over my dick to keep the pace.

"I think about your nails scraping down my back as I fuck you, hard enough that you'll feel me there, even when I'm gone." That admission is too raw, too close to how I feel about her. I clench my jaw as stars pop in my vision.

She's writhing in the sheets now, leading herself up to the edge while I tell her what I want to do with her. The way she's responding is a punch in the solar plexus—she's been thinking about this too. We've both been craving each other, and here we are, all of it within reach and we're still across the room from each other like we might combust if we did touch.

"Christopher," she begs, using my full name, the one no one else uses with me. It's like no time has passed at all.

"Do you remember that night, when everyone else was at the homecoming game?" My legs tremble, heat gathering low in my spine. "When we snuck into the art studio?"

She swears, hips bucking. She remembers. I don't know how either of us could forget. I bent her over one of the tables and buried my face in her pussy until her scream echoed in the empty room. As she came, she knocked over a can with paint brushes in it. I can still hear them clattering to the linoleum floor, the can rattling as it followed.

"I still remember how you taste," I admit, closing my eyes. "How wet you were. How you clenched around my tongue as you came on my face."

Her moans now are louder, punctuated by desperate pants. She's somewhere else. Back in that studio, maybe. After she came on my tongue, she shoved me to the ground and rode me within an inch of my life before I exploded into her like I never came before in my life.

"Do you want to ride me again?" I dare to ask. "Like you did that night?"

"Yes, yes, yes." She thrashes against the sheets, fighting her impending orgasm, and I'm going to win this stupid fucking contest. All at once, she kicks the sheets in the right direction and I can see her glistening pussy, swollen and ready for me, as she says, "I want to come all over your dick."

She opens her eyes and meets my gaze in the mirror.

My orgasm rips through me with such force my thighs slam against the sharp edge of the dresser. I shout her name and barely have time to cover the tip of my dick with her panties as I spill into them, bucking my hips like I want to be spilling into her. My knees buckle as I slam into the dresser, sending perfume bottles toppling over as my orgasm racks on and on and on.

And if this is what it's like coming just *near* her, I might not survive being inside her. I can't fucking breathe.

My only consolation is that she's arching off the bed, shaking as she gasps my name over and over, like I am inside her.

I swear as a second, smaller orgasm rockets through me when I thought I was done. I slouch against the dresser, resting my forehead on the mirror as I catch my breath. Fucking hell.

Andie is an actual fantasy come to life as she trembles through her climax. Just when I think she's done, she arches off the bed again and I chant in a whisper, "One more. Give me one more."

Her shout as she comes again is incoherent, but I tell her, "Yes, God yes, that's fucking beautiful."

She collapses back on the sheets, trying to catch her breath. I swallow the lump of emotion in my throat, tearing my eyes from her listless form on the bed. I don't know what to say.

All I know is the shame rising so quickly, I can't stop it. It's over my head now, drowning me, pulling me out to sea, farther and farther from her every single second. She doesn't speak. The hum of the vibrator finally stops, leaving us in cold, stony silence. Isolated like we hadn't just connected on the most primal level mere moments ago.

My energy is sapped, and I'm not sure I can walk without stumbling. I won't be running today. My phone buzzes in my pocket and the shame rises up to strangle me anew.

I wince, remembering that I have a meeting this morning, and I don't know how much time I just spent in this fantasy. Fuck.

It's just as well. I don't know if I could stop myself from touching her if she decides to steam my clothes this morning.

This feels too real. While we pushed each other to the finish line, we weren't faking it. We were *together*. I don't know how to go backward.

I force myself to stand, head still so light the room tilts a bit. But I manage to move without falling. I walk to the bathroom without looking at Andie on the sheets. I can't stand to see her right now, to add to my humiliation.

Her voice is soft. "Kit."

I pause, afraid to look at her. "I'm sorry."

Andie sighs and the sheets rustle. Before I can back away, she's in front of me in just a T-shirt, her cheeks still flushed from her orgasm. "I wish you weren't."

"No?"

Her fingers rest on my jaw, nudging my face so I'll look her in the eyes. "I'm not sorry. Not when I was worried this side of you was gone."

I frown, unsure of what she means.

She sighs, her fingers falling to my chest. My heart lunges toward them like it's been summoned. "You've been so controlled," she says to my chest, "I was worried I lost you."

"I'm right here," I say gently. "If you want me, all you have to do is ask."

She presses her lips together like she's trying not to say something.

I sigh and press my fingers to the bridge of my nose, closing my eyes.

Her whisper is so small, I almost miss it. "I'm asking."

I open my eyes and meet her gaze. Her eyes are open and honest and hopeful.

"I want you to be comfortable around me. Even when—*especially* when the cameras aren't around." She shifts on her feet.

My phone starts buzzing in my pocket again. I grumble a curse under my breath. "I'm running late. We'll talk later, okay?"

Her hand falls to her side as she breaks our connection. I miss her touch already.

Before she can go, I bow to press my lips to her cheek and whisper, "You look beautiful."

CHAPTER TWENTY-THREE
ANDIE

Cassidy greets me when I pull into Ax Me No Questions—a bar with ax throwing in the back—ready to clip my mic on. She tells me Kit's already inside.

This date has been on our schedule for a while, because apparently watching us go to work and hang out before bed isn't interesting enough. After our *moment* in the bedroom this morning, I haven't been able to think about anything but Kit and how he said my name as he came. Dealing with another one of the show's forced scenarios is not something I'm interested in tonight.

I take a deep breath as I head to the back of the building, where we've been permitted to film with no interference. Kit is already here, as promised, and he's chatting with Dr. Shaw.

I stop short. "Is this a therapy session?"

Cassidy nudges me forward. "It's a date. With a little assistance."

Dr. Shaw perches on a barstool while an extra producer runs a fluffy makeup brush over her obscenely high cheekbones. Kit leans on the tabletop, flashing his charming smile. The one that doesn't reach his eyes. I hate that smile.

"Why don't you take a seat, Andie?" Dr. Shaw says when the producer steps out of frame.

I offer a weak smile and tiptoe over the cords crisscrossing the painted cement floor to join them at the table.

Kit gives me a lopsided grin. "Hey. How was your day?"

I can't tell if he's asking because he was coached to or if he means it, so I only offer the perfunctory, "Good. Thanks."

"I'm just here to check in and see how things are going," Dr. Shaw says from her corner of the room. "To hear how you're adjusting or help you through an argument you two may have had, that sort of thing. You're the only couple that knew each other before the altar, so your journey is a bit different than the others."

Kit clears his throat. "So far, I think we're doing well, considering the circumstances."

"Do you agree, Andie?" Dr. Shaw pins me with a look that sees all. Shit.

"Sure." I lift one of my shoulders. "So, um, why are we here if we're supposed to talk with you?"

Dr. Shaw smiles. "While we're not there for every moment of your marriage, we do see some of the footage, and we noticed something way back on your honeymoon."

"What's that?" Kit wraps his fingers around a pint of beer. Even now, in this room full of people and cameras, I'm thinking about how they wrapped around his—

"You both do better when you're up against a challenge. Working as a team," Dr. Shaw explains.

I blink away the memory of Kit's hands. "So we're here to throw sharp objects across the room?"

"Exactly." Dr. Shaw gestures to the targets on the opposite wall. "Talk while you try something new. I'm here to mediate and offer perspective. Only if you need it, of course."

Kit nods. We walk over to the line where we're supposed to throw axes from and he mumbles, "Weirdest therapy session ever."

I snort, then smack my hand over my mouth.

"See?" Dr. Shaw says from the table behind us. "You're communicating better already."

I force a smile. Kit and I listen to one of the employees explain how to throw an ax and do it safely. I attempt a couple of practice throws, my ax only bouncing off the target and clattering to the ground. Kit, however, was made for this kind of thing. He shrugs off his jacket and tie, unbuttons the top two buttons on his shirt, and rolls his sleeves to his elbows. While his arms are truly magnificent, my mind can only focus on *thighs, thighs, thighs* as he lunges forward to release the ax with a primal grunt.

"There is something I'd like to address," he says when the attendant leaves us to it, snapping me out of my fantasy.

"Okay," I say slowly, gripping the handle of a new ax. Ignoring the way my heart rate picks up, I choke up on the handle, winding up for a throw. "Go for it."

"This morning, we . . ."

"Oh my God!" I shriek, my ax slipping from my hands, not even making it halfway to the target. My cheeks burn with humiliation. I can't believe how we acted in our bedroom this morning, and now Kit wants to talk about it? *Here?* I mean, he did out our previous relationship on day one, so I wouldn't put it past him.

"Andie," Dr. Shaw says soothingly, like she would to a child throwing a tantrum. "Can you please listen to what Kit is saying? I want to make sure you hear him."

I swallow and force myself to face him. Kit frowns, eyes fixed on his hands as he gets his grip on an ax. I shoot daggers at him with my glare. If he so much as mentions a hint of the intimacy we shared this morning, I'll—

"You told me you were worried that side of me was gone." He winds up, then launches the ax toward the target. It sinks in with a satisfying thud. It's not a bullseye, but it's close. He shakes out his arms and looks at me, head tilted in question. "I've been trying all day to figure out what you meant."

Unable to articulate a single thought—my head is still spinning from this morning too—I reach for another ax.

"Andie," Dr. Shaw interjects when I'm silent for too long, fussing with my grip. "What side of him did you mean?"

"Um." I squeeze my eyes shut and search for a way to explain it that won't give away what we did this morning. A tall order when his groans are still echoing in my head. "The side that's . . . less than perfect, I guess."

"Less than perfect," Dr. Shaw echoes.

Kit frowns. "I'm not perfect."

When Dr. Shaw gives me a look, I heave the ax over my shoulder and focus on the target. "You're so controlled and closed off." My words get lost to a grunt as I throw the ax. It's the first one of mine that lands anywhere on the target instead of the floor. I take a deep breath and look at Kit. "Sometimes it feels like you're not even here."

Kit blinks, his jaw going slack. But he has no response.

"It seems like that surprises you," Dr. Shaw says. "Can you tell Andie why?"

"I thought you didn't want me to—" He shakes his head and drags a hand through his hair. He picks up a new ax and tries again. "Andie, any time I try to show you how I feel, it's like you throw a shield up between us."

I clench my jaw tighter.

"You're doing it right now," he says with a chuckle. "Look at how tight you're wound up."

This time, when his ax hits the target, I flinch.

I force myself to unclench my fists.

"Let's take a deep breath together, okay?" Dr. Shaw demonstrates an exaggerated breath for us. Kit and I follow, and I have never felt so ridiculous in public.

The pause in action allows my mind to wander back to how Kit panted after his climax this morning. Warmth spreads from my hands to the rest of my body, tingles chasing it down my spine. I hope this shirt provides my happy nipples with enough coverage in front of the cameras.

Kit walks toward the targets, collecting our axes to bring them back to the line. He grunts when he wedges them out of the target, the muscles in his shoulders rolling underneath his shirt. When he walks back toward me, I look at the ground.

"Kit," Dr. Shaw guides him, "how does it make you feel when Andie puts up that shield?"

He looks me in the eyes, leaning on an ax he props against a barstool. "It makes me feel like you'd rather be anywhere than with me."

"That's not true," I blurt without thinking.

"It's how he feels, Andie."

I give Dr. Shaw a warning glance before returning my attention to Kit. "I really enjoy spending time with you."

Kit huffs out a disbelieving laugh.

"I do," I insist. His stance is too comfortable. Smug. I snatch the ax out from under him, causing him to stumble.

"You put up this wall." He grabs another ax and winds up for a toss. "And it makes me feel like I have to put a wall up too, because you don't want anything to do with how I feel about you."

He heaves the ax at the target and hits the bullseye. My mouth goes dry, and my tongue is heavy. I have no idea what to say.

"How do you feel about her, Kit?"

"I feel . . ." He takes a deep breath, taking the time to meet my eyes. "I really enjoy spending time with you too. You make me happy, Andie. And I want you to know that I'm here with you. You can rely on me."

"I—" I bite back my words, afraid to say them out loud. I reach for an ax, hoping I won't have to reply to that.

"You can say what you're thinking, Andie. This is a safe space." Dr. Shaw spreads her hands in a gesture that says *we're all friends here.* Except we aren't. This is all being filmed and will be picked apart by audiences across the country.

"Ten years ago, you wanted nothing to do with how I felt." I grunt as I release the ax. It hits the target with a satisfying *thunk.* Staring at the handle jutting from the wall, I tell him, "You told me that if I wanted you, all I had to do was ask. So I did."

"You did." He nods, a half grin tugging at the corner of his mouth.

"But then you left." I force myself to look him in the eyes. Dare to let him see how much it hurt to watch him walk away. It's easily the bravest thing I've done this week. "In the middle of our conversation, you left."

"One of my bosses called, and I—" He takes in a sharp breath and grips an ax. He doesn't turn away fast enough, though. It's the first time I've seen this side of him since we got married. Vulnerable. Scared. Even when we were talking about his mom's cancer diagnosis, he wasn't like this.

"I want to be able to trust you. To rely on you." I swallow the bitter taste in my mouth. "But that doesn't happen overnight." And once he has that trust, he can break it in a heartbeat. I know that all too well.

Kit is silent, frowning and focused on his throw. He stares at the target too.

"Andie," Dr. Shaw interjects, "what do you need from Kit moving forward?"

I heft an ax over my shoulder. "Keep showing up. Please."

In our periphery, Cassidy smiles, her hand reaching for Steve's. But he's balancing a camera on his shoulder, so she settles for hooking her hand around his biceps and leaning into him.

Kit waits until I release the ax from my grip before he says, "I can do that."

"Kit, what do you need from Andie?"

He takes his time lining up for his throw. When the ax hits its mark, he finally says, "I don't care if you're upset with me or having a bad day. Talk to me. Let me in."

He turns to meet my eyes, and I dip my chin in a nod. Letting people in has never been my strong suit, but I know I'll look like the villain if I point that out now.

"Good." Dr. Shaw offers a smile, clapping her hands together. "This is good work, you two."

She stands, signaling that this session is officially over.

"You have the targets for another thirty minutes," Cassidy informs us.

Kit smiles, offering me an ax. "What do you say, sweet potato?"

I grip the handle and can't help but smile back. "I've got time."

His smile grows wider.

I lift the ax and focus on the target. "Do me a favor."

"Anything."

"Next time you throw, can you do it real slow so I can enjoy it?"

His laughter mingles with the thud of the ax against the wood of the target.

FIRST LOOK AT FOREVER
SEASON THREE
EPISODE EIGHT

PETRA ASHLING:
Five weeks ago, our couples said "I do." While they've begun to build their own family, they also married into each other's families.

DR. KENNETH LEON:
Meeting each other's families is an important step in our couples' relationships.

DR. LAUREN SHAW:
Family provides a new lens for our couples to view their partners. It can be stressful, but it's necessary to fully understand where each other came from. Especially in a scenario as unconventional as this one, the support of family can determine the long-term success of their marriages.

CHAPTER TWENTY-FOUR
ANDIE

I stand on the sidewalk, squinting through the windows of the restaurant Cassidy told us to be at today. It's new, and they've made sure it was empty for today's dinner with my mom and Jim. I knew this would be part of the show when I signed up—bringing Kit to dinner and letting my mom get a good look at him now that we've been living together.

After our interlude in the bedroom and the farce of a therapy session last week, Kit has been more openly affectionate. I've done my best to let him dismantle the walls that keep me safe, brick by precarious brick. We touch more freely, and we meet eyes across the room more than we used to.

Something has definitely shifted. I just wish I knew what came next.

Maybe we should try archery or something.

Kit brushes his knuckles against the back of my hand. His touch makes me feel like I ate a bag of Pop Rocks, my whole body fizzing. Give it a few minutes, and another flash of a new wedding dress will gallop through my mind. Kit's touch hasn't failed my muse yet.

Despite the work we've been doing, we still haven't slept together. Or gotten each other off again. At all. My whole body is screaming for more, but I don't know how to ask for it.

"I like that dress," he says. Though the cameras aren't pointed our way just yet, our mics are on in case we get into a fight out here or something. Cassidy doesn't want to miss any good material. I glance down at my dress—a structured gray-blue sheath with an asymmetrical neckline—just as Kit says, "It must have taken you forever."

My eyes fly to him as I take in a sharp breath. "How did you know I made it?"

The corner of his mouth lifts into a half grin. Casually, like we do this all the time, he hooks a finger into the fabric at my hip and tugs me closer. "Pockets," he answers. He bows his head to press his lips to my temple and murmurs, "You look beautiful, Andie."

Warmth pools in my belly, spreading out through my fingertips. I breathe him in for a moment and tug on his pocket square. He never wears a suit without one now, even to a relatively casual dinner. With my mom. I swallow the nerves tangling in my throat. "Are you nervous?"

He tugs on my pocket again. "Should I be?"

He doesn't know about my mom's way of taking care of us. He knows I was a mess during her divorce when we were in college, but he doesn't have the context to know why. "How many different languages can you say *bad idea* in?"

Kit presses his lips to the top of my head as he laughs softly. It sends a tingle down my spine. "Maybe three."

"Oh, then it will be fine." For now, curled against him in the middle of an Atlanta sidewalk, the world is still, and I am safe. I fight the urge to purr like a kitten in a warm blanket.

Cassidy finds us in our half embrace and cracks a smile. Probably because she thinks she won't have to lead our conversation tonight. By the end of dinner, I bet she'll wish she had.

As soon as my mom and Jim take a seat, Kit touches me under the table. He absentmindedly traces the hem of my dress just over my knee, back and forth. It's not a sexual touch, just a familiar one. One that says *I need to feel you next to me.*

I never want it to stop.

In contrast to Kit's suit, Jim is in a butter yellow polo shirt that he's tucked into his jeans. It's a quintessential Dad Look, and it stands out in contrast to my mom's designer wrap dress. After shaking Kit's hand with a smile, Jim stretches his arm across the back of my mom's chair.

"Have you been taking care of my daughter, Kit?" My mom wastes zero time getting to the point. Cassidy must be happy dancing behind us.

Kit smiles as plates are set in front of us—we didn't even order first; this must be part of the show. One less thing to interrupt the conversation, I guess. "I try," he says amiably. "But she's been taking care of herself for a long time. She doesn't need me for much."

I bite my tongue to keep from saying something I shouldn't, like how I actually need his touch to create these days. As I place my napkin into my lap, Kit catches my fingers under the table and gives them a quick squeeze before letting me go like nothing happened. My heart leaps against my rib cage.

I take a sip of water to calm myself down, then tell Mom, "Kit's made a habit of sending me takeout every day for lunch."

"You'd forget to eat if I didn't." Kit presses his knee to mine. An anchor in the storm I can feel brewing over the bread basket, even if no one else can see it yet.

"Amazing I've survived all this time without you." I take a bite of warm bread and give him a smirk.

At the same time Kit says, "You can't create when you're hungry," my mom adds her two cents: "You really should stop with the takeout, dear. It's catching up to you."

I clench my jaw and do my best to remember where Mom's advice comes from: years of catching upper-class men who took care of us. It's the only way she knows how to survive.

Kit subtly nudges the hem of my skirt high enough to rest his warm palm just above my knee. Still not a sexual touch. Instead, it's rooting me to the spot, fully present in my body. I take a deep breath and offer him a wavering smile. He gives my knee a squeeze.

I turn my smile on Jim. "I'm sorry," I tell him across the table. "My mom's never told me—what is it you do for a living?"

Usually they're bankers, or my personal favorite, "consultants." The kind of rich white man job that no one can really define. Jim's smile in return is genuine. "Nothing anymore." He cuts up his steak—not one bite at a time, but all at once. "I used to work for the county as a project manager, but some good investments paid off more than I ever expected them to. Between those and the state pension, I was able to retire. Though I still drive for Uber sometimes, near campus."

"I keep trying to get him to stop." My mom chuckles and shakes her head, diamond studs glinting in the lamplight.

"No one told me how boring retirement would be," he defends himself, good-naturedly. "And being near the kids keeps me young." He flashes my mom an affectionate smile, and she returns it, giving his forearm a squeeze.

I push my food around on my plate. Something about this isn't sitting right with me, and I can't put my finger on it. Maybe it's because Jim seems so . . . normal? When a waiter comes to refill our water glasses, he thanks them and tells them the meal is delicious. Jim is *nice*. Genuine. I spin my wedding band on my finger, frowning.

"So, Kit." My mom folds her arms on the table and leans forward like she's talking to her best friend. "What is it you do?"

I curl my hand into a fist underneath the table. The twinkle in Mom's eyes means she's sizing Kit up, gauging whether he's worth keeping. I made the mistake of letting her meet one of the men I dated after college. She gave him the cold shoulder after she discovered he was a teacher. After we broke up, she told me, "He never could have given you the life you deserve." So I try to deflect her with a joke. "Aside from drive me up a wall?"

"I'm good at multitasking." Kit shoots me a look. "I'm a managing architect for a resort company."

His hand is still heavy on my thigh. He must know that if he lets go, I'll run.

"That sounds interesting." Mom sips on her white wine. "How much do you—"

"Mom," I bark loudly enough it startles Kit, his fingers digging into my leg. "Don't." *Do not ask him how much he makes, especially not in front of the cameras.*

"Travel." Mom gives me a look that says I've taken everything the wrong way. "With a job like that, you must travel quite a bit."

Kit flattens his hand and rubs circles over my knee with his thumb. "I do, but I don't see nearly as much of the locations as I'd like to." He punctuates the statement with a tap on the inside of my thigh.

"Andie is very tied to Atlanta, as you probably know." Mom gives him a knowing nod. "Do you own a home here in the city?"

I bite the inside of my cheek to hold back a groan of frustration. I foiled her plan to ask how much he makes, but there are other ways to discern a man's financial worth, my mom always says.

"I don't," Kit admits. "The resorts I work for put me up in their rooms while I'm there."

"Where are you staying now?" Mom won't let it go.

Kit shifts in his seat, perhaps only just now realizing my mom isn't interested in his job so much as his net worth. "Buckhead" is all he gives her.

Mom's eyes light up with the mention of the richest area of Atlanta. Fuck. I clear my throat and attempt to change the direction of this discussion. "We haven't seen you since the wedding." I pick up my silverware and scoop a bite of salmon onto my fork. "What have you two been up to?"

My mom looks to Jim in a silent question. Jim blushes and asks, "Now?"

"It's too exciting." Mom smiles her best smile. "I can't wait until later."

"We don't have to do this in front of the cameras," Jim says gently, without a hint of judgment in his tone.

My eyes dart between them, then to my mom's left hand. No giant rock on her finger. No rings at all. My pulse skyrockets, knowing whatever she's about to tell me isn't going to be *I went shopping the other day and found the perfect pair of shoes.*

"What's too exciting?" Kit asks, bless his heart.

Mom picks up her wineglass and, her voice going up an octave, exclaims, "Jim and I eloped last weekend! Surprise, we're married!"

She snorts. No, that's not quite what she does. She's much too controlled to snort on camera. But she just got dangerously close to laughing like we used to when it was just us living in her car. It's a genuine noise I haven't heard from her in a literal decade.

All the blood drains from my face, trying desperately to keep up with my racing heart. My stomach pitches forward, as if I've just tumbled over the edge of a cliff. It's a long way down.

Kit gives my knee a squeeze and says earnestly, "Congratulations!"

I, however, am frozen in time, unable to say anything at all.

Jim watches me, concern in his kind eyes, but I can't seem to muster the necessary enthusiasm. It's not like I didn't know this was going to happen; I shouldn't be so blindsided. But in the short time I've known Jim, I can tell he's not like the others. He's not slick and calculating, flaunting his wealth with every step. He's wearing a polo shirt tucked into his jeans. Fuck, he drives for Uber because he gets bored in retirement. He doesn't deserve this, what I know is coming next.

I press my lips into a thin smile and lift my wineglass in a half-hearted toast. "Congratulations."

Everyone politely clinks their glasses across the table. I stay seated just long enough to sip my wine and set the glass down with an unsteady hand.

"Excuse me," I say quietly, slipping out of my seat. When I notice a camera following me, I throw over my shoulder, "Just going to the bathroom."

Which isn't a lie. I flick off my mic pack as I lock the door to the trendy bathroom at the back of the restaurant. I rest my shaking hands on the cool porcelain rim of the sink and can't stand to look at myself in the mirror. After only two ragged breaths, there's a soft knock on the door.

Before I can lie and say I'll be out in a minute, my mom's voice comes through the door. "Andie, honey, can we talk?"

I don't want to talk, but I know the cameras are still out there and my mom's mic is probably on. The producers don't need more family drama to splash across the screen. I heave a sigh and unlock the door. My mom complains as I reach around her back to find the switch for her mic.

Cassidy can yell at me later; this conversation is private.

"What?" I demand, crossing my arms over my chest.

"Do you not like Jim?" She tilts her head to study me.

I let out a frustrated noise and bury my face in my hands. "I like Jim just fine, Mom." And it's true. I do like Jim. That's part of the problem. Because knowing my mom's pattern—find a rich man, marry him, divorce him in a few years and take him for all he's worth—I know polo-tucked-into-his-jeans Jim is going to get hurt.

Worse, it's a cruel reminder: I'm doing exactly the same thing with Kit, aren't I? Using him as means to an end?

Kit knowing it's coming doesn't make it any kinder. In my quest to become *not* like my mother, I've done exactly what she would have.

"Are you having problems with Kit?" Mom rests a hand on my shoulder.

I shake my head. I'm not having any problems with Kit. He sends me lunch and does the dishes and wears the pocket squares I made him and sets me on fire with a single glance.

The problem is me.

"You don't have to stay married to him forever." Mom says it so casually. Marriage is a business decision, after all.

I swallow the lump in my throat. I don't have to stay married to him, but I do have to let him go in a few weeks. Here in this tiny bathroom, the weight of it nearly crushes me. "Tell me it's different with Jim."

"Andie," she scolds.

"Tell me," I insist. "Tell me you want it to be different this time."

She's quiet, her eyes meeting mine across the small bathroom. A whole lifetime passes between us in a matter of seconds. This cycle of marriage and divorce—I know she did it to take care of me, of us. I know it's her way of protecting us. But I don't need her to save me anymore. I need to believe there's more out there for her. Maybe for me.

Quietly, my mom gives me her answer: "I can't."

I sniff, unceremoniously wiping my nose on my arm, my heart breaking into another thousand pieces. My phone buzzes in my dress pocket, and as I wake up the screen, I say bitterly, "Well, you don't have to stay married to him forever."

She clears her throat. "I'm going to leave you be."

I nod as another tiny shred of hope in me withers away. "Best wishes to the bride."

She slips out the door as I read the message from Kit on my screen, *Leave your mic in the bathroom and sneak out the kitchen. Call me when you're out back.*

CHAPTER TWENTY-FIVE
KIT

Andie is quiet as I drive through Atlanta's busy streets. When she called me from the alley outside, I told Cassidy I had a work emergency. She was pissed, but I don't care. Anyone who looked could see Andie was crumbling at the dinner table. Steve must know how helpless I feel, because one touch and a murmured exchange with Cassidy saw me on my way, camera-free.

Andie's been working herself to the bone trying to get this fashion line put out to keep her business in the black, and then her mom blindsides her with a marriage announcement of her own at dinner? *On camera?*

My blood simmered under my skin as her mom left the table to talk to her in the bathroom. I barely managed polite chitchat with Jim for a few minutes before my skin began to feel too tight. I had to get out, and I had to take Andie with me.

She didn't question me when I grabbed her hand and pulled her to my SUV, a block away. I don't have a plan beyond getting the hell out, but seeing her like this reminds me of the night she showed up at my door crying over her mom's divorce.

I change lanes so I can turn toward Georgia State. I don't really know what to do, but in my bones, it feels like we need to go back to go forward. I park in a random lot, not caring if I get a ticket, and we both climb out into the humid night air.

Andie closes her eyes and takes a deep breath, turning her face toward the sky. When she looks at me, I nod my head in the direction of a walking path.

Without a word, she slips her hand in mine. We walk for a few moments before she says, "Thanks for breaking us free."

"Any time." The campus is mostly empty since school is out for the summer. It's not long before we find ourselves heading toward the old arts building. Our story started there; it only makes sense, I suppose.

When we make it to the building, Andie gives me a mischievous smile and heads toward one of the side doors. I frown, not sure what she expects to find. It's summer and it's after hours. Every door in this place has to be locked.

She lets out a squeal of delight when the door she tries creaks open. I'll be damned.

As I slip inside, she tells me, "The art students used to find ways to keep the locks jammed, because they never knew when their muse would strike."

The door shuts behind us, and she slips her hand back into mine. I don't question it, too afraid she'll realize her mistake and let me go.

We wander down the hallway as Andie tests a door here and there. She breathes out a triumphant curse when one gives under her push. I'd be a fool not to follow her inside.

It's not the room where we met, but it's close enough. Easels folded and stacked against a far wall, a couple of large tables, and a counter along one wall, where extra supplies live during the semester.

In the privacy of an art studio, I finally get the nerve to ask, "You said a lot happened after I left. Do you want to tell me about it?"

I think she's not going to say anything at all as she runs her hand along the counter. Then she says in a quiet voice, "Well, there was my mom's divorce."

"You were hurt by that, I remember." I slowly walk toward her, needing to be closer. "Have you spoken with your dad since?"

She lets out a puff of laughter and hops up to sit on the counter, demurely crossing her ankles. "Keith isn't my dad."

I lean on the counter next to her and frown.

"I've never met my dad. Honestly, I'm not sure my mom is positive who he is. Keith was husband number three." She looks over at me, her teeth sinking into her lower lip. Her eyes flick down to my chest. "Take off your jacket."

Heat slices through me at the suggestion. I don't argue, slipping out of my suit jacket. Before I can toss it aside, she takes it from me and shuffles the fabric in her lap until she can see the cuff of one of my sleeves. Her fingers pull at a loose thread.

She shifts so she can reach into her dress pocket and pulls out a sewing kit, of all things. I cover my mouth with my hand to hide my smile. Fucking pockets.

"Always prepared, sweet potato?"

"What would you do without me?" She holds a needle between her teeth while she digs for some thread in the same color as my jacket.

"I don't want to find out."

She gives me a look, eyebrows raised. "Noted."

The flicker of a smile that crosses her face won't get her out of this conversation. She was truly *broken* that night she came to me. If Keith was *just* husband number three, I wouldn't have had to hold her against my chest for hours while she cried. "Was Keith important to you as a stepdad?"

Andie threads a needle with the confidence of a seasoned professional, then shakes her head. "Not really. It's just . . . my mom married him, and they were together longer than the others, and I thought maybe she'd found love and happiness and comfort. The things you're supposed to want out of a marriage, you know?"

I slip my hands into my pockets and nod. "I take it she didn't."

"Nope." Andie pops the P and pulls her needle through the cuff of my jacket. "What she found was a man with a flush bank account who didn't have the foresight to ask for a prenup."

She meets my gaze from under thick eyelashes. This view of her is one of the best I've ever witnessed—freckles across her nose, hands at work, eyes asking me a silent question. My hands itch to capture it, somehow. I don't want to pull out my phone and snap a picture—that would ruin the moment—and there's nothing to draw on nearby. So I settle for letting my eyes map her lines and constellations, inking them against my rib cage for safekeeping.

Andie lets out a small sigh and turns her attention back to her work. "Jim is husband number six."

I swallow, fully understanding her mom's inquiries into the nature of my job and where I live.

"You want to know the worst part?" she mutters, placing stitches with a steady hand. "Every time she gets married, I think to myself, maybe this one will be different. Maybe this one will stick." She shakes her head. "She did it to keep us safe the first time. After husband number two left when I was a kid, we lived out of her car for a few months. Keith gave us a home, if nothing else."

Her words are a fist straight to the gut. "I didn't know."

"Of course you didn't," she scoffs, eyes still on her work. "What would you have thought if I told you I was homeless in junior high?"

"That we have more in common than I thought." The words tumble out without my permission. She stops fussing with the jacket and looks at me, her lips parting gently.

I push off the counter and pace in front of her. "Andie, I grew up in a single-wide trailer. I know what it's like to not have anything."

"And your parents?"

"Loved each other very much." When I steal a glance at her, her shoulders have curved inward, and she's staring at my jacket again. My heart rages against my chest—I just told her I had the one thing she never had: a loving family. I can't tell her I left because we had too much love, the loss of it nearly broke us.

So I offer her another piece of me. "Every time I go home to see my mom, all I can think of is how they would stay up after I went to bed. The walls were thin, so I could hear them discussing what they were going to give up this week so they could afford a new jacket for me, or shoes, or breakfast." I rub my jaw with my knuckles and stare at the linoleum floor. "They gave up a lot for me. Sometimes I wonder if they should have."

"It sounds like they loved you." She pauses her work to look me in the eyes.

I shrug. "It's clear your mom loves you, too."

She nods, then finishes the last few stitches in silence before producing the tiniest scissors I've ever seen. "When Keith left, my mom had nowhere to go, and divorce proceedings take a while. So we rented a little apartment together until she could find her next victim. I dropped out of school because I had to work so I could eat. Keith had been paying my tuition, anyway." She sighs and sets my jacket to the side, folding her hands in her lap. "I got hired at a dry cleaner, and the owner's mom taught me how to mend things and do small alterations. When they closed down because they couldn't pay on their business loans, I got work at a bridal shop as a seamstress."

I stop in front of her and meet her gaze. There's my missing piece—how she went from a driven business student to a dress designer. One of life's more humbling moments. And it explains why even her school email address was unreachable at the time.

"You were meant to make dresses," I whisper. "You're incredible at it, you know?"

Her lips tilt into a half-smile. "You've never even seen one in action."

She's right. I saw some half-finished dresses at her studio and poked around her website. "I'd like to," I admit.

She chews on her lip, brows pulling together in thought. "Is that why you only own three suits?" she asks. "You're not used to having much?"

"I—" I want to argue, to say it's just an economical choice. But she's just seen the truth more clearly than anyone. Besides, last week she said she wanted me. Sort of. So I step closer. I place my hands on either side of her hips and look her in the eyes. "I never want to forget where I came from."

The muscles in her throat work, and her gaze falls to my mouth. "Do you think we can ever really move on?"

"Andie." I can't stop myself from saying her name with so much yearning I should be embarrassed. But if she wants me, this is it. The yearning is part of it.

"How can you look at me like that?" she whispers.

"Like what?"

"Like you still—" She clamps her mouth shut and shakes her head. "I've just told you my mom marries to divorce for money, and you know I plan to—"

Something sharp lodges under my ribs at her point. She's going to divorce me for money, too.

"It doesn't have to be this way," I murmur, begging her to see it my way. She can stay with me. I'll help her achieve whatever she wants to. As the idea comes to me, I offer. "You said you needed investors, right? I can do that; I have the means to invest in your company."

The look that crosses her face is painful. She averts her gaze. "Kit, you don't understand."

"Help me understand, Andie. Please." I want nothing more than to *understand*. "I'm on your team, remember?"

"I have to do this on my own." She turns her eyes back to me. Steely determination lights them up. "My mom relies on the graces of whoever will say *I do*. Her life is in their hands, and at their whims. She did the best she could with what she had, but I—I won't do it. I won't leave my life up to anyone but me."

"You know I wouldn't do that to you," I insist, hoping she sees how serious I am.

"Do I?" she asks, determination giving way to something softer. The rawness in her voice reminds me of how we used to be—fearless and fiery and *together*. Until we weren't, and it was my fault. I broke more than her trust that night. She rearranged me on a molecular level, and it seems my leaving did the same thing to her.

"I do think we can move on from the past that shaped us." My voice is stretched thin, and I'm desperate to hold onto this tenuous truce we've reached. "I think we can build the life we want. You can travel with me and make dresses for brides around the world. I can help you build your business, and we can eat dinner together every night. Make a family that doesn't have to worry like we did as kids. I know it feels unimaginable after everything we've been through, but I believe we can do it. Let me help you."

Her voice breaks. "Kit—"

"What do you need from me to know I'm in this with you?"

She runs her finger down the buttons on my shirt, and her lips tilt into a small smile. "You saved me from the horror show that was dinner. It's a good start."

I rest my forehead against hers. "Are we really still at the start?"

She sighs. "I feel like we're getting—"

A door slams in the hall. Shit. If we tripped some sort of silent alarm and the police come searching, we can't stay. It takes everything in me to push off the counter and let her slide to the floor.

She holds out my jacket. "Let's just . . . go home."

CHAPTER TWENTY-SIX

ANDIE

"Where the hell did you two run off to last night?" Jeremy Levine paces our show-furnished living room. He's shorter than I expect him to be, with all the power he yields at Optimax. Apparently, our stunt last night was worth enough to call the executive producer down from on high.

Kit and I sit next to each other on the tiny couch, hands folded in our laps. So close to touching, but not quite.

I think we can move on from the past that shaped us. His words won't leave me. They're too earnest, too full of hope. My stupid heart wants to wrap itself up in them, as if they can protect me from cruel twists of fate. It wants to believe he meant them with his whole heart. Even though I know how this ends, I find myself hoping against all hope that maybe we always were meant for each other. As if such a thing exists.

Kit subtly shifts next to me, just enough so our thighs barely touch. My eyes fall to where the heat of his leg sears into mine. I swallow.

Kit clears his throat. "The cameras got to be too much. We had to get away. I'm sorry for not simply telling that to your crew."

"My crew is under orders to keep filming for the full day," Jeremy fumes. His tie clip glints in the sunlight pouring in the windows as he makes another turn of the room. "They can't put the cameras down, because it's in their contract. Just like it's in your contracts to be fully present while filming."

Kit's leg presses ever so slightly against mine. I clench my hands more tightly together and say as calmly as I can, "Being filmed for that many days a week and that many hours in a day is exhausting."

"You think my crew isn't just as exhausted?" Jeremy bends closer to me, to get in my face.

"Maybe they need a break too." I clench my jaw and stare him down. I made a deal with myself a long time ago that I would never be beholden to a man, and damn it all to hell if I'm going to start now.

"They signed on for this, just like you did." His face turns an alarming shade of red.

"I don't know how you expect us to connect as a couple in any authentic way when—"

"You're not the first couple to ever be on this show!" he booms, and—fuck me—I flinch. Kit's leg presses hard into mine and his hand flies to rest on my knee. "We have been making this show for years now; we know how to match couples and have them connect on camera!"

"Mr. Levine," Kit says in an even tone even I can't decipher.

"And you," he rounds on Kit. "My crew said this was likely your idea."

"We both left." I release my hands to massage my temples. Kit and I were so close to . . . *something* last night, and this blustering man in my living room is giving me a migraine.

"You told my showrunners that you knew each other before." He's in my face again, and it pisses me off. I curl my hands into fists in my lap. "Why should I believe that you're not playing this up for your fifteen minutes of fame?"

"You will not call my wife a liar." Kit's demand booms in the small apartment living space. I bite my lip to hold in my gasp.

A shiver slides down my spine at the dark undercurrent in his calm request. I like it. Maybe too much. It's all raw power and popping sparks of electricity that say *mine*. I shouldn't like it, but my toes curl in my shoes anyway.

Kit wraps my fist in his warm grip. I relax my hand and mesh my fingers with his. He takes a deep breath and asks Jeremy, "How are we supposed to connect when the only time we have is in front of a camera crew?"

"We don't pay you to connect off camera where no one can see what happened between you."

"You don't pay us at all," I bite back. I still have to make money whether or not we're filming, and right now, my designs for Fashion Week are my only hope.

Jeremy turns a shade of red that's almost purple and opens his mouth, presumably to yell in my face again. Kit gives my hand a squeeze. "Mr. Levine, please do not yell in our home."

Jeremy glares at him, then a disgusting grin slides across his face. "You mean the home that the show pays for."

Kit huffs, looking away from the conversation, locking his eyes on the fridge in the kitchen, a tic in his jaw. His hand is an anchor. It's the first time we've touched since holding hands in the Arts building yesterday, and it's sending every piece of armor I put on afterward clattering to the floor.

"We will film you here as much as we need until a story appears," Jeremy says with finality. "The story we tell on the show is about falling in love. In your case, it's about falling in love despite whatever happened before. The longer that takes, the more footage we need. Understand?"

Oh, I understand explicitly. Connect on camera or we'll never be off camera. Kit nods, but refuses to look at him, still.

"You both signed contracts." He straightens his lapels. "If you run off again, I will consider you in breach of those contracts, which means you forfeit rights to any payment for damages the show may give you."

I swallow the knot of anger in my throat, glancing at Kit. He knows I need the money from choosing divorce. We can't afford to be in breach of the show's contract.

"I have a wedding this weekend," I offer. "At the Botanical Gardens." It's my last one for the season, unfortunately. Jeremy looks at me like I'm a child speaking out of turn. Wringing my hands, I make my point. "I can talk to my bride about letting the show film while I work. Kit mentioned he wants to see one of my dresses in action, right?"

"I do," he offers me a smile.

Jeremy's lips curl into that smile again as he nods. "That's an excellent idea, Andie. Thank you."

Kit's jaw tics.

"While we're at it: Kit." Jeremy's voice gets marginally lower and exponentially more threatening. "Part of the contract is at least one day with your family on camera with your new wife."

Kit snaps his focus back to Jeremy, and I swallow a gasp. His eyes are brimming with something dark. It's a look that says *go there and you'll live to regret it.*

Slowly, in a low voice, Kit tells him, "I've told you before: my mother is sick and needs time to recover."

I look at my hands in my lap. Am I never going to meet his mom? She's at the center of everything Kit does, and he wants to withhold us from each other? I bite my lip until it hurts, just to stop the tears pricking the backs of my eyes. It doesn't matter if I meet his mom; that's not why I'm here. My heart rebels by pounding faster, shaking its fists at me in frustration.

Jeremy matches his tone. "I'd believe it more if it came from her directly."

Kit glares at him, curling one hand into a fist in his lap and gripping the arm of the couch with the other. A vein bulges in his temple as he clenches and unclenches his jaw. The two men are locked in a battle of wills, and if I strike a match, this whole room will ignite and take us all down with it.

"Kit," I say softly. Neither of them moves or acknowledges I said a single word. Honestly, I'd be surprised if they remember I'm even here. But Kit is jeopardizing my best shot at my dream. He damn well knows that after last night.

My fingers shake as I rest my hand over his fist. It takes a moment, but he lets out a frustrated sigh and opens his hand to lace his fingers in mine. He rubs his other hand over his mouth as he breaks eye contact with Jeremy.

As he meets my gaze, I say, "We can visit her for dinner, so she doesn't have to worry about going anywhere."

Kit's throat works to swallow. He opens his mouth to speak, then slams it shut again.

I squeeze his hand a bit too hard and say through a stiff jaw, "We can't afford to be in breach of contract, right?"

He closes his eyes and presses his fingers to the bridge of his nose, shaking his head. His shoulders rise and fall with a deep breath before he looks at me again. "No," he agrees, "we can't."

"Then let's do this right." I offer him a shaky smile. "Besides, I'd love to meet your mom."

"Glad to see your wife at least has some sense." Jeremy smirks.

Kit mutters a curse under his breath, then stands, hands on his hips. He's a head taller than Jeremy, and maybe that's the point he's trying to make. Through his teeth, sounding exhausted, he asks, "Are we done here?"

Jeremy narrows his eyes. "Do not touch the mics again. They're expensive equipment and I only want my team handling them. You could have cost us thousands if someone had found that mic pack in the bathroom before my team did."

I snort and roll my eyes. The restaurant was empty specifically because we were filming there. His crew were the only ones who would have found the mic.

"Done." Kit shoves his hands in his pockets and strides toward the front door.

"We need more of you two on camera, together, *trying*," Jeremy says to Kit's retreating form, like I'm not right fucking here.

Kit opens the door and gestures vaguely back toward me. "We'll go to the wedding this weekend, right?"

I punch my heart back down into my chest and nod. If nothing else, we're still a team.

Kit sweeps his arm toward the open door with a pointed look at the executive producer. Undeterred, Jeremy hovers over me. With a smug look on his face, he tells me like he's sharing a secret, "Keep him in line, will you?"

Like Kit isn't his own person with his own wants and needs that have nothing to do with me. Even though I wish some of them did. I stare at a throw pillow on the chair across the room. "Fine."

Kit clears his throat.

"It was nice speaking with you, Mrs. Watson." He offers me the slightest incline of his head.

I hate the way everyone calls me that, like somehow I'm just supposed to give up who I am because of a stupid show and a sham of a marriage. Even if I'm beginning to wish it was real.

Finally taking the hint, Jeremy walks toward the door. I follow, as if I can bodily block him from reentering our apartment and our lives. He exchanges a glare with Kit before making his exit. Kit closes the door behind him with such control, the only sound is the click of the latch.

I'm left in the tiny entryway, with Kit mere inches away. My vision is full of him, and the lines of his shirt begin to blur as tears well in my eyes.

"You're shaking," he mutters under his breath. Before I can deny it, his arms wind around my body and press me into him. I bury my face in his chest as his fingers twine in my hair. He presses his lips to my temple. "You look cooked through, sweet potato."

I make a sound that's half whimper, half laugh. Kit chuckles in response, the sound thrumming its way through me. My voice comes out in a squeak. "Thank you for standing up for me."

His fingers curl against my scalp, and shivers race down my spine. "I knew my wife was a badass; it was amazing to watch it firsthand. But I wasn't going to let you have all the fun."

I laugh, the sound muffled by his chest. He laughs too. After I fill my lungs with him one more time, I pull away. Hands still in my hair, his gaze falls to my lips like he might want to—

His phone buzzes in his pocket and he lets the air in his lungs out on a frustrated groan. His hands slide from me, leaving me cold. "It's going to be one of those days."

I sniff, tugging on the hem of my shirt. Kit checks the caller ID, then looks back at me, his emotions shuttered. I want to smash his phone against the door. Instead, I say weakly, "I'll see you later?"

"Later," he agrees, reaching for his messenger bag. Every night, still, he takes care of my hands. Even though I wish it was more now. I take a couple of steps back to cede the entryway to him. He slips out the door, but as it's almost closed, he pushes it back open, surging toward me.

I gasp as he catches my face in both his hands and presses his forehead to mine. My eyes flutter closed, waiting for the kiss my body's been starved of for too long now. Every cell in my body stills and nothing else matters. Just Kit. And me. Together. On any old weekday morning, like we chose this and each other, instead of being crammed together for entertainment.

I can see the future Kit spoke of last night, where we build the life we want.

But the kiss doesn't come.

All I get is Kit's whispered "You look beautiful" before he leaves me breathless in an empty apartment, staring at the closed door.

CHAPTER TWENTY-SEVEN
KIT

Crickets chirp in the cool night air as I carry my laundry basket down to the apartment complex laundry room. It's late; the cameras left about an hour ago. Andie is drawing in our bedroom upstairs, and we ate dinner together. It's all incredibly domestic and makes the life I told her we could build feel even closer.

"Kit!" Patrick calls to me from a table near the pool. Jamie is with him, his feet propped up on another chair.

I wave and give them a smile. Patrick jerks his head in the way men do that means *come here.*

My shoes scrape against the pool deck as I pivot to join them. I set my laundry basket down on the table next to them and take the last empty chair at their table. Patrick reaches into a small cooler on the ground between them and pulls out a can of cheap beer. He slides it toward me.

I crack the top and get comfortable in my seat. "What are you two up to?"

"Bitching and moaning, mostly." Patrick shrugs. "The spouses are in a mood, so we thought it might be best to give them some space. You?"

"Just laundry." I take a sip of the beer. It hardly tastes like beer, but it's cold and carbonated, and I can't remember the last time I got invited to *hang out* with friends.

"Where's Andie?" Jamie asks.

"She's upstairs. Working."

Patrick lets out a low whistle. "She works a lot."

"She does." I give him a nod. "But so do I. Par for the course."

"All Leslie cares about is work." Jamie rolls his eyes. "No, that's a lie. All he cares about is looking like he has everything together." He pushes his apartment key around on the table. "I don't fit the image."

"That's not true." Patrick reaches over to squeeze Jamie's shoulder. "You're a fantastic human."

"Thanks." Jamie forces a smile. "I just wish Leslie thought I was too."

I lean forward to rest my elbows on the table. "I didn't know you and Leslie were still struggling."

Jamie shakes his head. "It's fine. We have a therapy session soon that may help."

"It's not fine." I clear my throat to dislodge the emotion that's made itself at home there. "I'm sorry I haven't been around much. You both deserve better."

"I appreciate you saying that, man." Patrick raises his beer can in a salute. "We've missed having you around."

"But you're here now," Jamie says. "So tell us how things are going with you and Andie."

I let out a heavy sigh.

"That good, huh?" Patrick laughs.

"I think we're finally getting somewhere." I shrug. "But I'm not sure she knows I'm all in, you know?"

"Have you told her that?" Jamie asks.

I frown, thinking back to our conversation in the art studio. We both revealed things about our past that we hadn't shared the first time around. I told her I could see what our future looked like and that I wanted her there with me. But I never told her how I felt right now, in this moment. "Not in so many words."

"Maybe you should try some new words." Patrick turns his baseball cap backwards on his head. The bro level at the table intensifies.

"I'm afraid if I tell her how I feel, I'll push her away," I admit, turning my beer can on the table. "She's reluctant to trust me. With good reason, I guess."

"What's the good reason?"

I sigh, examining the steam curling up from the hot tub into the night air. "When we dated the first time, she told me she loved me, and I couldn't say it back."

Jamie's eyes bulge and he spits out the sip of beer he just took. "What?"

I nod, confirming it. "We were twenty-one and had no idea what we were doing."

Patrick is quiet for a moment, lost in thought. "You couldn't say it back because you didn't love her or because you were scared?"

"One hundred percent it was because I was afraid." I sip on my beer while I sort out my thoughts. "She obviously took that poorly, and I never got to explain myself because . . ." Emotion rises quickly, and it's all I can do to choke out the words. "My dad died. Suddenly. And I had to go home. By the time I made it back, Andie wanted nothing to do with me."

"That's rough, man." Patrick agrees. "You were both vulnerable and needed each other, and instead you had to go it alone."

I can't believe how succinctly he put that. All I can do is nod. My beer can crinkles under my grip, so I let it go.

"Tell her how you feel about her," Jamie tells me. "Maybe it's what she needs to get closer, you know? To know she's not alone in feeling it too."

I tap my fingers on the table and look between Patrick and Jamie. They're both looking at me like they're worried about how I'm doing. What a concept. My constant travel for work doesn't exactly help me foster these kinds of relationships. I never realized how important they might actually be. "I need to hang out with you guys more often."

"Yes, you do." Patrick tilts his beer can in my direction with a smirk.

"Why are you down here, then?" I ask, leaning back in my chair, glad to be out of the hot seat for a moment.

He shrugs. "Kendra got overwhelmed with . . . all of it. She asked for some time alone. I am happy to oblige."

I raise an eyebrow. "You're not worried she doesn't want to spend time with you?"

"Nope." He sips on his beer. "I know what I bring to the table, and so does she. Trust me, her wanting a little alone time is not a reflection of me as a husband, or of her as a wife. Sometimes shit just gets to be too much, man. I'll be here when she needs me."

I nod. He makes way too much sense sometimes.

We finish our beers in amiable silence, listening to the breeze shimmy through the trees and the hum of the pool filter.

"Okay." Patrick is the one to break the silence. "Here's what's gonna happen—we're all going to go back up to our apartments. Jamie, you need to tell Leslie how he makes you feel when he tells you to be more serious. Kit, you're going to tell Andie you're all in. With those exact words. And I'm going to tell Kendra I love her, and I'm here when she's ready to talk."

Our chairs scrape across the patio as we stand. Patrick and Jamie head home, and I grab my laundry to finish what I started. We're headed to that wedding this weekend. Maybe it's time I use the romantic atmosphere to my advantage.

CHAPTER TWENTY-EIGHT
KIT

Andie's eyes are fixed on the bride's dress as she dances for the first time with the man who is now her husband. I'm glad I got to see one of her dresses in action. The photos on her website are beautiful, and the fabric draped on dress forms in her loft are intriguing, but if I wasn't here to witness this, I'd have missed how different the dresses are when they *move*. My work is static; buildings don't sway in a slight breeze or wrap around someone's body like they're a part of it. Andie's consideration for movement is nothing short of genius.

And if I wasn't here tonight, I'd have missed the awed whispers of wedding guests as the bride walked by. Even now, as I sit at a table near the back of a tent with Andie, some guests at the bar are talking about how it sparkles in the light.

Andie's fingers tap on her thigh to the rhythm of "The Way You Look Tonight," and she tips a sip of water into her mouth. As the bride and groom spin on the dance floor, utterly enchanted with each other, I can't help but think about how Andie and I did this mere weeks ago. We've gotten so close to something more than a marriage for show a few times now.

Steve and Cassidy lurk in the wings. I catch Steve's eye, and he gives me a thumbs-up.

Before Cassidy mic'd us upon arrival, I asked him, "You said she hated you at first; what turned the tide?"

Steve smiled, watching as Cassidy fussed over where to hide the mic in Andie's bodice. "I was there every day, man. The good ones and the bad. *Especially* the bad ones. When I finally told her how I felt, she couldn't deny it anymore."

"It?" I raised a brow.

He shrugged. "That we had something worth fighting for."

Now, beneath the fairy lights of someone else's declaration of everlasting love, the mic pack weighs heavy on my waistband under my coat. I'm done waiting.

I'm done hoping we'll find the right moment, that suddenly all the pieces will fall into place. Much like my work, you can't argue with the laws of physics. There's no point. Instead, you find a way to work *with* them. Andie and I already have our foundation built; it's time for us to work with it instead of against it.

We're at a beautiful wedding in Atlanta's Botanical Gardens, string lights through branches absolutely everywhere the eye can see, and a fountain is lit up just outside the tent. It's time to make our moment happen instead of holding back.

My fingers brush the small of Andie's back through the silk of her dress—one she most definitely made herself. She looks over her shoulder, her eyelashes gilded in gold from the string lights around the centerpiece.

Fuck it—I lean forward and rest my chin on her opposite shoulder. She stiffens for a split second before leaning in, her chest rising and falling against her bodice. "What are you doing?" she murmurs, her eyes back on the bride and groom.

"Enjoying the party." My hand slips around her waist. "Everyone is fascinated by the dress."

She offers me some neutral information about it, something she'd probably tell any bride who asked. "It took the better part of a year to get that neckline right."

A low hum comes from my chest. "It's beautiful."

"Just like your thighs." Her lips curl into a smile. I smile when she tilts her head so her temple presses to mine. A small gesture of thanks, of trust, of giving in.

The groom twirls the bride, her gown glittering in the light. I curl my fingers against the fabric of Andie's dress. "Can you believe we did that six weeks ago?"

"No," she whispers. "Sometimes it doesn't feel real."

A low chuckle vibrates through me. "It all feels real to me."

Andie tears her eyes from the newly married couple on the dance floor, pinning me with a look so raw my heart aches. Her gaze falls to my mouth.

Aside from our wedding day, and despite our clash in the bedroom a couple of weeks ago, we still haven't kissed. Not since we were too young to know how much it would mean.

"Would it really be so bad to care about each other?" My eyes rove over her face, tracing her freckles in the low, romantic lighting.

Her lips part to answer, but the music ends, and the crowd around us applauds. Moment over.

Andie primly clears her throat and joins in the applause.

So do I, but my arms wrap around her waist to clap my hands in front of her belly. We're not done talking about this, and I'm not letting go until we are.

As the applause fades, I whisper against the shell of her ear, "Come dance with me."

Her answer is low and breathy. "I'm working."

I can't help the way my lips curl into a smile. So fucking stubborn. "It's a wedding. There's supposed to be dancing." Besides, I know Heidi is running around here somewhere—the last time I saw her she was stuffing a canapé into her mouth before swiping furiously at her tablet. If something goes wrong with the dress, she'll alert Andie.

I'm about to remind Andie what the executive producer said about needing us to cooperate when she sighs. "Fine."

It's a small victory, but I'll take what I can get. I stand and offer her my hand. She takes it and doesn't even complain when I lead her away from the dance floor, toward the tent's exit. We stop next to the sparkling fountain, and I ignore the shuffle nearby as Cassidy and Steve line us up in frame.

Instead, I place one hand on Andie's waist and offer her the other. She steps into my dance frame just as the next song cues up inside the tent. "I promise I won't trip over my own feet this time."

"That makes one of us," she quips, her fingers tightening on my shoulder.

A few bars into the song, I take the plunge. "Andie, I'm done pretending."

Her eyes go wide and dart over my shoulder toward Cassidy and Steve. Her voice is stretched thin as she echoes, "Done pretending."

"Yes." I pull her in closer, so our hips are pressed together and the small of her back arches around my hand. "I'm done pretending I don't have feelings for you when every time you look at me, I'm yours."

"Oh." It's a whisper, lost in the water cascading off the fountain, but her lips form a perfect O just before her eyes soften.

"I've been holding back." My pulse bounds, putting it all on the line. "I don't want to scare you or push you, but I don't want you to wonder where I am in this. I know you've been hurt before, and that it's hard to trust me. But I have feelings for you. Real ones. I'm all in. It's something *my wife* should know, don't you think?"

"Kit," she says my name on a sigh. "We've only been doing this for a few weeks."

"It feels longer than that, doesn't it?" I counter, my fingers digging into the flesh on her hips. I force myself to relax. "Can you really tell me you don't feel this—what's between us—too?"

My eyes fall to her throat as she swallows. Her hand curls more tightly around mine. When I meet her gaze again, she admits, "I'm scared."

"Of what?" My voice is softer. Gentle. I don't know if Steve's equipment can pick it up, and I don't fucking care. "Me?"

She shakes her head and lets out a frustrated noise. Her hand releases mine, and before my heart can drop, she moves it to my neck, stepping closer. "Not you, no."

I take in a slow breath, knowing I have to tread carefully if I want to keep her close. "You jumped off a platform in the rainforest just to prove to me you wouldn't let your fear of heights stop you."

"Well, I *really* wanted that pencil." Her lips curve into a shy grin, and her fingers brush the hair at my nape.

I smile in return, warmth flourishing in my chest—we have inside jokes again. That has to count for something. "What are you afraid of, Andie?"

She's quiet, chewing on her lip, for what feels like an eternity. When I think she's locked me out, she finally says, "I'm afraid of getting lost. In you, in this. Losing sight of what matters to me."

It's the most honest she's been with me on camera, and the layers beneath what she's said go so deep, the only ones who have a hope of understanding are the two of us.

"It's so easy to get wrapped up in this." Her eyes reflect the fountain's lights back at me. "In the idea of true love and a happily ever after. In you."

"In me?"

She dips her chin into a nod. "You're easy to get lost in, Mr. Watson."

My lips pull into a frown. I don't particularly like the idea of Andie getting lost in anyone but herself. "Is that your way of letting me down easy?"

She lets out a puff of laughter, her fingers flitting over my pocket square—one that she made, of course. "The opposite, actually. It's my way of saying I think I'm already in over my head."

My heart launches at my rib cage, and I take in a slow breath to stay calm. "Is that a good thing or a bad thing?"

"Depends on whether or not you'll catch me as I'm falling." She meets my eyes in the dark, and I see everything in her gaze. Our past, our present, our future, if we're brave enough to reach for it.

"I'll catch you. I'll get you a helmet, if it'll help you take the leap." My lips tug into a half grin. "We're not in a dance studio, so we should be able to stick the landing."

She laughs, her body humming beneath my hands. This is the lightest I've felt in ages. I pull her in close, so our bodies are flush with each other. She stands on her tiptoes and rests her chin on my shoulder, her arms linked tightly around my neck. I feel her breath all the way through me, and I know the feeling. I've wanted to hold her like this, to be held like this, for years now.

"I'm glad it was you, that day at the altar." I play with a strand of hair that's made its way loose from the tidy knot at the back of her head.

She slides her hands to my chest, curling her fingers around my lapels, and arches her back so she can look me in the eyes. I hook my fingers into her bodice where it meets her bare shoulder blades, holding on for dear life. She licks her lips, a little line appearing between her brows. "I need you to promise me something."

"Anything." My answer is quick off my tongue; I've been waiting a lifetime to pledge allegiance to her.

"I'm already in over my head," she reiterates, running her thumbs over my lapels. "Promise you won't let me get lost."

I swallow. I'm not sure if that was an honest request to be her compass in the dark, or if it was a subtle reminder that she couldn't afford to lose herself because she still needs to divorce me in a couple of weeks. And I can't ask for clarification with the camera hovering nearby. For now, I settle for my honest answer. "I'll keep you safe."

It must be enough, because she pulls on my lapels until I bring my face close to hers. Our lips a hair's breadth apart, I whisper another truth. "You look beautiful."

Her response lights me up—her lips press to mine with a hardness that betrays her desperation. I slide a hand to her neck, using my thumb to tilt her jaw, and open my mouth to soften the kiss. It's an offering that she takes readily, opening to me in return.

She asked me to keep her from getting lost, but I'm not sure how I'm supposed to do that when I'm hopelessly upside down. All I know is the clash of our teeth and the slide of our tongues and the breathy whimper she lets free when I gently bite her upper lip. She slips her fingers beneath my coat, her fingernails biting into my chest through my shirt.

I grip the back edge of her bodice in a fist, my knuckles digging into the flesh over her spine. We're teetering on the edge of something so good it hurts, and I can't bring myself to stop. Our mouths crash together again, not caring that we're in public, or that she's working, or that there's a camera nearby, ready and willing to blast every piece of this moment on TV.

We've finally broken through whatever stupid wall was in our way, and we're getting somewhere.

Thank God.

CHAPTER TWENTY-NINE

ANDIE

When I see my reflection in the bathroom mirror, I let out a groan of frustration. I dig in my clutch for the small tube of concealer and the powder compact I always carry to weddings, knowing they won't be up to the task in front of them. Kit absolutely ravaged me out by the fountain. All's fair, I suppose, because I hadn't shown him any mercy either.

My body buzzes like I had too much champagne, even though I haven't had a drop of alcohol all night. My lips are swollen, lipstick kissed right off them. My chin and cheeks are red and flushed from being shamelessly smashed against Kit's face while Cassidy and Steve filmed *everything.*

I'm desperately patting concealer onto my chin when Heidi pushes open the bathroom door and stares at me. A mischievous grin crosses her face. She crosses her arms and leans against the counter. "Well, that explains why your husband looks so flustered."

"Don't call him that," I mumble. This concealer is only making me look white as a ghost, the pink of my skin still peeking through. "Is there something wrong with the dress?"

"All is well." She gives me a look from my toes to my face. "Making out at a wedding; I never thought I'd see the day."

"Shut up." I cap my concealer and toss it in my bag with a little too much force. The whole clutch teeters on the edge of the counter before tumbling off.

When I bend to scoop it off the ground, Heidi lets out a laugh. "Holy shit." She scoots around to look at my back. "You two really went for it."

I turn around and look over my shoulder into the mirror. Fuck. Kit's fingers left marks on my skin where he held onto me like I was his lifeline. I groan and bury my face in my hands, utterly humiliated. I'm supposed to be here in a professional capacity, and I got lost in Kit—his hands, his mouth, his words.

I'll keep you safe.

"Relax." Heidi rests her hands on my shoulders. She turns me back toward the mirror to assess the mess Kit made of my face. "With the way they were eye-fucking during the ceremony, the maid of honor and best man are probably against one of these fairy trees right now. Nobody noticed whatever you were up to."

She grips my chin and turns my face this way and that in the light. Determining the damage is something she can work with, she pops open her bag and pulls out a travel pack of makeup wipes. I take a deep breath and savor the coolness of the wipe as she works.

"He says he has feelings for me," I whisper, still terrified of the truth.

"Is that such a bad thing?" Heidi asks the same question Kit did earlier.

I close my eyes when she asks me to, and she begins wiping away my minimal amount of eyeliner and mascara. "It is when I'm supposed to divorce him in two weeks. I don't want to hurt him."

Heidi hums in a way that says she understands. "You don't want to hurt him," she repeats, switching to my other eye. "Because hurting him would hurt you."

"Yes, because I—"

Oh no. My eyes pop open to see Heidi's lips stretch into a smug grin.

"I hate you." I cross my arms over my chest. She got to the bottom of that too quickly; it's not fair. Has it been that obvious to everyone but me?

Heidi wipes away the last of my makeup and tosses the wipe into the trash. As she digs through her bag, she says, "Okay, let's talk this through. He has feelings for you, and you have feelings for him."

As much as I hate that she's right, I give her a firm nod.

She squirts some tinted moisturizer onto her fingers, then begins to smooth it over my face. "If you don't divorce him, what happens?"

"I lose out on the money I need to keep my business afloat until I can find investors," I repeat mechanically. None of this is new information.

"What about a business loan?"

"No," I say firmly. I saw what happened to the dry cleaner I worked for when they couldn't make ends meet. Down went their business and, in turn, their whole lives. "Not an option."

"What about Fashion Week?" she asks calmly, moving on to a tube of mascara. "I thought that was the whole point of you showing."

"It's not a guarantee." As much as I believe in the dresses I'm making, it doesn't mean anyone else will find value in them.

"Blink," Heidi demands. I obey. "Would it be so bad to continue making custom dresses for a while?"

I bite the inside of my cheek. "I need room to breathe," I say. "I don't have that now. One bad review on a bridal website could ruin me."

Heidi nods her understanding. She pulls out a tube of petal pink lipstick and smudges some onto my cheeks, keeping her silence.

"He offered to invest in my business," I say quietly, remembering how earnest Kit sounded that night. Like he would give anything to make my dreams come true.

"Why don't you take him up on it?" Heidi goes to work on my lips, smoothing the petal pink over them too.

I use it as an excuse to not answer. Kit could up and leave me—just like last time—and take the future of my business with him. More than that, though, it would mean answering to him, letting him in on my decisions. Everything I built on my own wouldn't be *mine* anymore. It would be Clover Callaway's cheating fiancé redux.

But now that Kit is all in, I don't know if I can pull the trigger on divorce either.

Hurt him, hurt myself, stay stuck. None of my options look great at this point.

"Andie," Heidi interrupts my spiraling thoughts. "Would it really be so bad to have someone on your side?"

"This wasn't supposed to happen."

I move to bury my face in my hands again, and Heidi grips my forearms, shaking her head. "Nope, you'll ruin your makeup."

I heave a sigh, slouching forward. "I'm so tired."

"Take the night off." Heidi shrugs. "Crystal can handle any dress emergencies, and everyone's too tipsy to notice a bead loose anyway."

"No." I shake my head. "I mean, I'm tired of this show and trying to protect myself from whatever the hell is happening with Kit."

"So let him in." Heidi says it like it's the easiest thing in the world. "He's told you he cares about you; you care about him. Why not just see where it goes?"

"I—" I plan to list all the reasons I can't do this. Kit will leave, just like the last time. Only this time, I know it will be because he decided it's too much work to be with me. I'm too afraid, too distant. But if I give in, I know I'll crave him like the air in my lungs. I wasn't kidding when I told him it would be so easy to get lost in him.

Heidi pats my elbow, just like she does when she's done giving a bride a pep talk. "If you both have feelings for each other, and you're both clearly ready to jump each other's bones, just do it. Forget about what comes next for a second. You have a man who is obsessed with you—as he damn well should be—and you want to be with him. So do that. Be with him."

I deadpan, "Are you giving me permission to sleep with my husband?"

Heidi rolls her eyes. "I'm *saying* . . . you've been operating in survival mode for too long. Maybe it's time to enjoy what you worked so hard for."

CHAPTER THIRTY
KIT

I'm surprised when Andie returns from the restroom, slipping her hand into mine as she whispers, "Let's get out of here."

Steve and Cassidy barely keep up on the way to the parking lot.

I'm flabbergasted when Andie tells me to drive us to her loft, and utterly blown away when she kisses me against my SUV, only pulling away when the production van screeches into the parking lot.

She pulls me toward the building, ignoring Cassidy's pleas for us to slow down. We're breathless when they catch us at the door to her loft. Andie tugs her microphone cord out of her dress, flashing Cassidy a smile. "Sorry, no cameras unless Optimax has an after dark channel."

"Can we at least get a shot of you closing the door?"

My whole body buzzes with what I know is on the other side of that door. My mic makes a satisfying pop when I pull it free from my collar. "Do it fast." I hand the mic pack to Cassidy. "If I don't get her alone in thirty seconds, we'll all regret it."

Andie laughs, adding her mic pack to mine in Cassidy's arms. She unlocks the door and pushes it open.

I wrap my arm around her waist, stepping closer. My body is completely blocking hers from view at this point. I look over my shoulder to tell Steve, "Here's your shot in three . . . two . . . one."

Andie trips over her long skirts as we tumble through the door. She loses her balance with a squeal, and I try to catch her, but it's too late. Gravity yanks us down toward the floor. I land on top of her with a grunt, then kick the door closed behind us.

"Okay, well, good night!" Steve yells through the door. I snort out a laugh, burying my face in Andie's neck while we wait for their footsteps to retreat.

I breathe her in, groaning. One dance and one kiss have made me a madman, desperate for more of her. She giggles underneath me, like we're young and free and happy again. Like nothing bad ever happened between us, and I can't help but press my lips to her skin. I let loose another low groan at the taste of her skin.

She sighs under my kiss, whispering, "Dress. Off. Please."

I'm too happy to help. I find the zipper at the back of her dress, undoing the hook at the top. But in my haste, I jam the zipper only a couple of inches down her back. A swear escapes me, and Andie laughs.

"I helped you put this thing on, how hard can it be to get it off?" I tug at the zipper one more time, hoping it will let loose.

"Get off," she says with a smile.

Reluctantly I let her out from under me. With a deep breath, I shake my suit jacket off and untie my tie, my eyes on the sway of her hips as she kicks off her heels and walks farther into her studio. We didn't bother with any lights when we came in, but the loft is bathed in moonlight pouring in the wall of windows, Atlanta's city lights twinkling against the night sky.

Andie glances over her shoulder, lashes lowered, lips open ever so slightly. Silhouetted by moonlight, she's the sexiest thing I've ever laid eyes on. The madman inside me roars. I get up and prowl after her. She smiles, scurrying away from me.

I pick up my pace, and her fumbling steps tangling in her skirts are no match for my long strides. She's in my arms in seconds. I crush her to me so I can feel the rise and fall of her breasts through her bodice. Breathing heavily, she reaches blindly behind her, knocking over a cup of beads that clatter to the ground, sparkling in the moonlight. My lips are on her neck again when her fingers curl around a large pair of fabric shears.

I lift my head to kiss the corner of her mouth where I've already smeared her lipstick. "You're not going to murder me, are you?"

She turns into my kiss, opening her mouth to let me in. Our tongues slide along each other in a dance that mimics what we did for the cameras less than an hour ago. It's lighting all of me up, and I tremble.

When she pulls away, both of us panting like we're desperate for more, she holds the scissors between us and raises a brow. "Cut me out of this thing."

I gulp, my eyes falling to her dress. I can't see much of it with her crushed to me like this, but I can't bring myself to let her go for even a moment. She hooks her free arm around my neck and arches her back, pulling her chest away from mine.

Okay, I take it back. This moment, with her offering herself to me, where I can see the shadow of her racing pulse in her neck in the moonlight, hips pressed to mine—this is the sexiest thing I've ever seen in my life. My heart rails against my rib cage.

I manage to pry one of my arms loose, but only because my fingers trace the neckline of her bodice over her breasts. A smile tugs at my lips as goose bumps raise on her skin. My own breathing ragged, I gently hook my first finger inside her bodice in the valley between her breasts. "I can't cut you out of this."

"Why not?" She frowns.

I duck around the scissors to capture her lips in a kiss. When we're both breathless with it, I break the kiss, pressing my forehead to hers, scissors still between us. "You made this dress," I murmur. "I can't ruin it."

Her lips part in surprise, and the hand she's clutching the scissors in falls to her side, her knuckles still white around the blades. "It's not one of mine."

Liar. I let out a snort of laughter. One day she'll realize I see her better than she thinks I do.

"This line, here?" I dare to reach out, my finger gently following a seam that goes from her ribs underneath her arm and arcs under her breast before diving down to her navel. She lets me do it. "And this beadwork, here?" My other hand moves to trace the delicate beading along the neckline of her bodice. "This color? And the hidden pockets?"

I slide one arm around her waist again and take a deep breath, rocking her gently with me like we're dancing again. Her eyes sparkle with tears, and it pulls at my heart.

"Andie," I say with a soft smile, "this dress could only be one of your designs."

The muscles in her throat ripple in the moonlight. She lets out a deep breath and brings her free hand to my chest, trembling. She presses her palm over my heartbeat and looks me in the eyes.

"I don't care," she whispers. "I want you to do it."

My breath catches in my throat. She wants me to do it. She trusts me to do it. I can't believe she's just . . . handing this to me. Maybe she finally understands. Maybe she finally knows how much I feel for her in my bones.

I slide my hand down her bare arm, loving the goose bumps that rise on her skin in response. Slowly, I curl my fingers around her wrist, pausing to feel her pulse. It races like mine. She's inviting me to remove her armor; she's got to be terrified. Nobody gets this close to her. Nobody.

I move my fingers to the handle on the scissors and she loosens her grip on them so I can slide the blades free of her hand. "Touch me," I tell her as I nuzzle into her neck, breathing her in.

Her now empty hand moves to my jaw. She lifts my head to kiss me. I give in to her silent demands for more, more, more.

Harder, faster, more.

We're both breathless and groaning by the time I have the sense to break the kiss. She licks her lips like she wants to capture every last taste of me there. I reluctantly let go of her waist so I can hook a finger in her bodice again, to pull it away from her skin.

I move slowly so she has time to stop me if she's changed her mind, placing the blades of the shears against her sternum facing downward. She shivers, eyelids falling closed, tilting her head back.

She's giving herself to me, and I feel like my entire world just quaked underneath our feet. "I can stop," I whisper in the dark, my eyes on the rise and fall of her breasts around the blades of the scissors.

"Don't stop," is her breathy reply.

I open the blades ever so slightly, trapping the neckline of the bodice between them. I pause, still terrified to ruin one of her dresses. I know how much time she spends on them. I know how they're her heart and soul on display for anyone who knows enough to simply look.

I know it's just fabric and beads and thread, but destroying it feels sacrilegious. Like I'm shredding the pieces of her I love. It's the opposite of what I came here to do.

She's begging you to do it.

Eyes still closed, she gives me a slight nod of her head. Green light. Hand trembling, I press the blades closed. The crisp sound of metal slicing fabric rings through the deathly quiet loft, and Andie gasps.

I still, waiting for her to pull away. To change her mind. To run.

Her eyes flutter open, and she meets my gaze. I must look maniacal—so turned on I can't see straight, and so fucking terrified at the same time.

She doesn't run. Instead, she uses both of her hands to begin unbuttoning my shirt, her lips gently parted.

I open the scissors and move them downward. Another slice of fabric comes as she's halfway down my shirt.

Our breathing is the only other sound in the world. I'm mesmerized by this moment. It's like seeing one of my blueprints rise from the ground, in three dimensions. Everything is precarious and I question every equation and line until suddenly it's done. A testament to a leap of faith and an appreciation of art.

The scissors' blades glint in the moonlight as I keep working my way down the bodice, inch by glorious inch. Andie's fingers curl around my open plackets, and in one breathless look, she asks a silent question.

She knows how careful I am with my clothing, how little of it I have. She's asking for my consent to break me free. To remove my armor, just like I'm removing hers.

I let out a low noise of approval.

She rips my shirt open. My buttons join the beads on the floor, and I know I'll never find them. I don't care. I'll buy another shirt. I'll ask her to embroider her name on the tag, *Property Of.*

Her hands explore my bare chest, nails scraping my skin and threading through the hair there. I'm so hard, my vision blurs around the edges. I don't trust myself with sharp objects at the moment, so I toss the scissors on the floor. They sound like gunfire, scattering beads and buttons on impact. Andie doesn't flinch.

I trace the deep V I've cut into her neckline, her skin hot and smooth under my touch. I need to see more of it. Mimicking her motions, I grip the loose edges of the bodice in my fists and meet her eyes.

"Do it," she whispers in the dark.

I gather every last reserve of control I have and tear her dress wide open. She gasps and licks her lips.

I let the fabric fall from my hands. It sags for a moment before the weight of the bodice slips over her hips, the skirt billowing out as her dress falls to the floor. Some beads roll across the floorboards, caught in the dress's downfall.

Andie's not wearing a bra. Jesus. She's only in a lace thong, her dress around her ankles.

This. *This* is definitely the sexiest thing I will ever be lucky enough to lay eyes on in my lifetime.

And I'm still wearing pants.

What the hell am I doing?

I roll my ruined shirt off my shoulders. "If you think my thighs are great, you should see you right now."

Andie's fingers fly to my belt. "Shut up." She's got my pants on the floor in record time, and I wrap both my arms around her, skin on skin, crushing her to me with a hot kiss and a groan.

Her hands are everywhere, her nails sinking into the muscles in my back with a delicious bite. *More.*

Crazed, I lower us both to the floor, spreading her dress over the mess of beads on the floor, too impatient to make it to the bed upstairs.

She trembles as my hands slide to her thighs, tugging that lace thong down, down, and away. I push her legs open. Wider. Wider still.

I lower myself to the ground in front of her. The seams of her dress bite into my stomach as I settle in, licking my lips. "Hold on tight."

CHAPTER THIRTY-ONE
ANDIE

The boning on my dress underneath me digs into my elbows as I prop myself up to watch Kit work, the muscles in his shoulders rolling in the moonlight.

His eyes glitter with something magical, like just the sight of me bare before him has him transported to another plain of existence.

I want this delicious tension to swell until it shatters, leaving us both completely wrecked in its wake. Kit's thumbs brush the insides of my thighs, and all the air leaves my lungs in one trembling sigh. It morphs into a frustrated curse as he does it again, closer to where I want him.

Where I need him.

I've been avoiding the thought that I need him anywhere, for any reason. But that's a lie. It's always been a lie. Right now, my insides ache with a gaping chasm of emptiness. It's been empty for so fucking long, I've forgotten what it feels like to be filled up.

Kit swipes his tongue over my center, his breath skimming over my skin. My hips buck off the floor, reaching for him after he's pulled away. Before I can force myself to relax, to hide my desperation, his thumb is on my clit, and I see stars.

My head falls back as a groan claws out of my chest, and I know Kit can see it. How afraid I am, how small I feel, how empty I've been these past years without him. And he's split me wide open, just like he ripped my bodice with his bare hands. There's no hiding from him. There never has been.

"You taste exactly the same." His voice drapes over my skin like mulberry silk. Pure luxury. "I never stopped being hungry for it."

"Please." The word slips from my lips without my permission. It's high-pitched and trembling and *needy*.

His thumb slides between my folds, slick with arousal, not penetrating, but with the kind of urgent pressure that makes me crave all of him. "Andie, I need to hear you say it."

"Say what?" My voice cracks, and I throw an arm over my eyes, embarrassed by what he's reduced me to in a matter of seconds. But I gave him permission, didn't I? Handing him those scissors with the silent plea, *Let me loose, let me breathe, let me* be.

His thumb makes its path through my folds again as he says in a low voice, dark with promise, "The truth."

I tremble, and a bead skitters across the floor. It's another piece of the flimsy fortress around my heart falling away. The words are heavy on my tongue, and I'm so tired of holding them in. But I'm terrified to hear them in the space between us. Afraid of the havoc they'll wreak if I let them go, where I can't control them anymore.

I swallow with a whimper.

"Look at me when you say it," he says, the edge of command in his voice sending a crackle through my veins.

Goddamn him and his silent dare—he knows I can't say no. I grit my teeth and meet his gaze. I expect to find a challenge, a sharpness to his expression.

I want it. I want the antagonism I need to tear into him, to take what I need right now, without regret. I want us to fight each other for release until neither of us can move.

Kit clearly has other plans.

His eyes have gone soft, a line appearing between his brows. His whisper hangs in the silence like a promise. "It's just you and me, Andie. Tell me the truth."

Tears hot behind my eyes, I curl my hands into fists at my sides, bracing for impact. I open my mouth so the words pour out in an urgent whisper. "I need you, Kit. Please."

"Good girl." The glitter in his eyes returns, but he only allows me a glimpse of it before he seals his mouth over my core and closes his eyes with a groan. I can't help the cry that escapes me as I fall back on the hard floor.

It's been so long, but Kit remembers everything. Like he cataloged every single place on my body and how it needs to be touched. His lips and tongue work at a furious pace, the stubble on his cheeks rasping against my thighs.

My hands scramble for purchase on the wood floor as pleasure uncoils deep in my belly.

Kit lifts my legs over his shoulders. His hands climb up my stomach to pin me to the floor.

I whisper a curse into the dark, sparks heating up my insides in bursts of sensation. A preview of the main event. The way he's got me pinned down means there's nothing for me to do but surrender to him. It's what he's wanted this whole time, isn't it? To give myself over to him, pliant and wanting?

And it feels so good, I do.

I slide one hand into his hair and curl the other around the leg of the nearby drafting table, holding on for dear life. Kit's fingers scrape the underside of my ribs, like he's searching for my bleeding heart. His mouth never stops, never gives me a moment to catch my breath.

My climax crashes into me so suddenly I cry out. My voice goes hoarse as my body tenses. My free hand slams to the restored wooden floor and my spine arches right into his waiting hands, like he's got my heart on a string. I can pretend he doesn't affect me all I want; the truth is, he's one hell of a puppet master, and I'm his to play with. Heat unfurls between my legs and crackles through my limbs. I shake and shake and pant through the orgasm, equal parts pleasure and ache, still not full enough.

I lift my head to see what the hell he did to make me feel like *that*, and the look in his eyes is pure sin. His eyes crinkle at the corners as his tongue softens its strokes over my clit. The bastard is mighty pleased with himself for that, isn't he?

I melt into the floor, unable to fault him for it. The room spins, so I squeeze my eyes shut. "I hate you."

"I know, sweet potato." Kit's mouth moves up my stomach as he emerges from between my legs. He takes a detour to lave each of my breasts, sucking my nipples into his mouth before letting them go with a soft pop. I'm trembling with need again by the time he runs his tongue along the underside of my jaw.

"I don't have a condom with me," he says, voice taut with longing and disappointment. "Didn't think I'd get this lucky."

His hips settle between mine, the weight of him alone making that chasm in me feel wider, gnawing with hunger. He's not playing fair. I don't care. Tilting my hips to cradle his length against me, I admit, "I'm on birth control, and I'm safe. You?"

"I'm safe too." He props himself up on his elbows, his chest rising and falling with shaking breaths. He shifts to cradle my head in his hands, forcing me to look him in the eyes.

Damn him. For all my wishes to keep this sex as impersonal and distant as I can, just to keep my fool of a heart safe, Kit's intent on keeping us linked. We're both connected to a live cable, and when we touch the track, there is only go, go, *go*.

"Andie," he says in a low voice, "we don't have to do this. I'll stop."

The tears from earlier are back, climbing up my throat. I can't let him see them, so I crush my lips to his in a desperate kiss.

He kisses me back with a hunger that knocks the wind out of me and thrusts his hips in time with his tongue.

Time to take some control back, to shield myself before I completely fall apart in his arms. "Stop and I'll never forgive you."

He enters my body like he never left. We hold our breaths as he fills me so slowly, I could scream in frustration. "God, you're so—"

He smirks. "Amazing? Perfect? Everything you dreamed of?"

"I waited a decade for this, and you want to take your time?" I hook a leg around his hips and pull him in.

"Jesus, Andie." He grunts, squeezing his eyes closed. "You can't just do that."

"I already did." I sink my nails into his shoulders.

"You'll pay for it." He draws out and slams into me.

"*Yes.*" I'm not sure how long it's been since I've had sex, but I know it's been ten years since I've had sex *like this*. Our sex has always run the gamut, from slow and lazy to fast and furious, but it was always, always more than our bodies speaking to each other.

Sex with Kit has always been an earth-shattering *event*.

I can't dwell on it, or I'll drown. So I roll my hips, and we are so utterly fucked. We have never, ever done this without a condom, and it feels so otherworldly, I'm already coming undone.

Kit drives into me, mouth set into a determined line. On a mission.

I tilt my hips an inch forward, two inches back, but no matter what, the emptiness inside me still yawns wide open. An itch I can't scratch, even with nothing at all between us.

I let out a frustrated groan, and Kit grips my thigh to his side, holding me still.

"Kit," I warn, my hands curling into fists on his back.

"Who are you fighting, Andie?" he asks gently. More gently than his taut muscles would lead me to believe is possible in a moment like this.

It's all it takes for me to break. My sides heave with a sob. "I'm sorry, I can't—" I bury my face in my hands.

"I'm not fighting," he whispers, his lips on my neck. "Don't fight."

"What does that even mean?" I mumble, and he smiles. How the hell can he be smiling right now?

"Let me in." He captures my lips in a kiss. "Tell me what you need. Let me help you get there."

I move a hand to his chest, fingernails biting into his skin.

"What do you need? Time?" he asks through gritted teeth.

"No, I need—" I shake my head, utterly embarrassed by my own shyness. "Can I get on top?"

His lips pull into a grin as he plants a hand on either side of my head. I whimper when he pushes off me, but he doesn't go far. After he settles with his back against one of the windows, he beckons. “Come here.”

I follow, straddle his hips, and guide him into me. When I bottom out, we both roll our heads back and groan. There it is, the piece of me I was worried I'd never be able to reach. He's so deep I can feel his pulse like it's mine. I kiss him slowly, my tongue moving in time with my hips as I ride him.

He reaches his hand between us, and I break the kiss on a sob, burying my face in his neck. His fingers sink into the flesh of my ass as he adjusts our angle, groaning when he finds it.

Soon our skin is smacking, echoing in the silence of the loft. I press my hands against the cool glass on either side of his head, bracing for every stroke as I inch closer to the edge.

With a grunt, Kit plants his feet on the hardwood floor and thrusts into me, harder and deeper than I've ever felt. I let my control collapse around me as Kit drives out all the pain I've held for the last ten years.

“Kit,” I gasp. “Kit, I'm going to—”

He presses his lips into my hair. “I know. Let go. I've got you.”

I shatter around him with a shout that echoes in the loft. Kit doesn't stop his steady rhythm, my pleasure streaking with pain. When he finally lets go, he buries his face in my neck with a groan that rattles through my aching bones.

We're slick with sweat and arousal, throbbing with pain and pleasure. I'm dizzy, absolutely untethered from my body as I come down, resting my forehead against the glass, my breath fogging Atlanta's skyline.

I make an attempt at levity. “Nice to know those thighs aren't just for aesthetics.”

He wraps his arms around me, pulling my body snug against his so his laugh shimmies through me too. I sink into the feeling of safety.

We don't speak at all as we clean up and stumble upstairs and into my bed. As I'm draped over his naked chest, sleep pulling me downward, I pretend I don't hear Kit say, “I'm still in love with you, Andie Dresser.”

FIRST LOOK AT FOREVER
SEASON THREE
EPISODE TEN

PRODUCER:
You and Andie seem to have grown closer after the wedding you went to.

KIT:
[smiling] Huh. Do we?

PRODUCER:
Have you been physically intimate yet?

KIT:
[grins]

FIRST LOOK AT FOREVER
SEASON THREE
EPISODE TEN

ANDIE:
[eyes wide] Are you asking me if we've had sex?!

PRODUCER:
Yes. Have you been physically intimate with your husband?

ANDIE:
[long pause]
I don't want to talk about it.

SEPTEMBER

CHAPTER THIRTY-TWO
KIT

"Sorry, what's the timeline on the glass installation on the west quadrant?" I ask for probably the third time in the last hour. Joe's answered me every time, but my mind has been somewhere else. Namely, in bed with Andie, every second the cameras weren't hounding us over the weekend. I shiver like her fingers are dancing down my spine right now, under the hot Atlanta summer sun.

"I'll email you the timeline," Joe says, completely unaware of just how far away I am at the moment. "You can take a look when you've got more time."

I give him a grateful smile, then bury my face in my hands, knocking my hardhat off my forehead in the process. Mistake. Every time I close my eyes, I see Andie against the window in her loft, riding me until we both came. How she tossed her head back as she clenched around me, letting out a cry like I'd either broken her or saved her. Maybe both.

"Mr. Watson," one of the hotel employees calls my name from the pathway to the dome. "Someone's here to see you."

I look up from the blueprints I'm pretending to focus on. My breath freezes in my lungs—Andie is a vision standing among the greenery.

She's in her typical work attire: a flowing skirt that hits her mid-calf and a simple blouse with three little buttons at the neck.

Despite the fact that Steve and Cassidy are right behind her, I can't help the smile spreading across my face. My heart swells about three sizes larger in my chest. She smiles back as I approach. "Did we have plans today?"

She wrinkles her nose and shakes her head. "You left before I was up this morning. I thought maybe you'd have time for lunch?"

I check my watch; it's close enough to lunchtime, and it's not like I would ever turn down a chance to spend time with Andie, even if it means dealing with the cameras. They spent the weekend following us to the grocery store and making us play a stupid card game where the suit we drew informed the "secrets" we told each other.

"I always have time for you," I tell her honestly. "Do you want to see the dome before we head back inside?"

She nods eagerly, and I smile so hard it hurts. We stop at a workbench outside the dome, where I outfit her with a hardhat and a safety vest to match my own.

"I think helmets are your look." I tap on the brim of the hardhat.

She flips me off, and I laugh as we walk deeper into the dome.

As I explain how I designed the triangular panels two-thirds of the way up to open and close with an innovative hydraulic system to help keep the temperature inside the dome perfect year-round, I definitely don't check out the sway of her hips as she examines my work up close.

"What do you think?" I ask, hands on my hips, as we stop at the far edge of the dome. It's quieter here, construction on this end is mostly finished.

"It's beautiful." She runs her fingers along one of the soldered points where several triangles meet. "But I've always thought that."

I tilt my head in question, my brows drawing together.

She waves it off with a smile. "Heidi showed me the drawings months ago; they plan on doing a lot of weddings here, so they reached out to event planners in the city for advertising." She chews on her lip as her eyes meet mine. "Something about it felt familiar to me, and when you told me you were an architect working for the resort, well . . ."

I let out a puff of laughter. "I didn't know I was trying to impress you before we even met at the altar."

She sighs, looking at the web of metal arching overhead. "I keep thinking I should have known it was yours earlier. It really is beautiful, Kit. I designed a dress inspired by it after I saw the drawings."

"I'd like to see that." I give her a warm smile, amazed at how our souls knew where to find each other this whole time, even when we were adrift. Anchors in the storm.

"There you are!" A booming voice shatters our quiet corner of the dome. I turn to see one of the Colonnade's bigwigs marching my way. He's as wide as he is tall, and he's forgone the safety gear, wearing a suit that likely costs more than all my clothing combined. His face is red from the heat and presumably the walk from the main building, and he mops the sweat off his forehead with a handkerchief he pulls from his pocket. Diamond cufflinks sparkle in the sunlight.

He swats his way past Steve, giving him serious side-eye. I doubt he'll sign the release for Cassidy, either.

I greet him with a firm handshake. "What brings you out here today, Clyde?"

"Big Boss Hammersmith just called to talk about the Montalcino build." Clyde's gaze slides to Andie, then back to the camera. Alarm bells go off in my head.

I clear my throat and gesture to her. "This is Andie. My wife." She looks at me *fondly* when I say it, and I know my stupid grin matches the one on her face. "Steve and Cassidy are here filming . . . a documentary."

Clyde looks between us and blinks. "I didn't know you were married."

I scratch the back of my neck, searching for the right answer. "It's new."

I'm still in love with you, Andie Dresser.

None of this is new. It's so old it's embedded in my bones and inked under my skin. Andie has always been it for me. The difference is now she's finally starting to let me in, to see it too.

As though he's already forgotten Andie's here, Clyde sets his gaze on me. "Hammersmith won't be happy to hear you've gone and settled down."

I frown. "What does it matter?"

"He's still annoyed that you chose to take this job." Clyde smacks me on the shoulder.

Ah, fuck. It's not like I'd planned on keeping my nuptials a secret forever, but I've never had any priorities other than the company since I was hired. It made the big bosses feel safer picking me to lead projects, knowing I'd be at their beck and call without anything holding me back. It meant a level of financial security younger me could only have dreamed of. It meant I could take care of Mom, even if I was far away.

"I guess Collins is fucking up in Montalcino."

And I know where this is going. I cross my arms over my chest and widen my stance. It takes everything in me not to step in front of Andie as a shield. "I have to be here." I shake my head. "My mom is—"

Clyde brushes the thought aside with a flick of his ring-heavy hand. "You know how Hammersmith is. He wants the best, and you are the best."

I rub my hand over my jaw with a sigh, suddenly exhausted. For years I've been the Colonnade's yes man. It's always been something I've been more than happy to be. But today, it feels heavy across my shoulders. I can't bring myself to look at Andie, but my body screams for her to touch me, to ground me, to let me know she's here.

"Like I said, I just got off the phone with him." Clyde's voice is too loud; he's standing feet away and yelling like we're in a crowded train station. "Collins is fucking up, and he wants you to fix it. You didn't hear it from me, but there's a C-suite job in it for you."

I clench my jaw as I look at the dome I've been working on. It's the closest to home I've been—knowing my mom is an hour's drive away. Patrick and Jamie invited me to watch a game next week. And now I know how Andie saw me in the lines of this structure before ever knowing I was in Atlanta. It all feels a lot like roots twining their way through the soil under my feet.

Clyde turns to Andie and says with a slick grin, "You'd like to live in Italy for a while, wouldn't you?"

Goddammit.

"Clyde." My tone is low, a threat lying in wait. When Clyde returns his attention to me, I say, "If Hammersmith wants me to fix it, he can come ask me himself."

I don't doubt he will, either. But it should at least buy me some time. Time to convince Andie how I feel. Time to make sure I wouldn't jeopardize my job with a rash decision. Time to finish filming this damn show, whose clock is up in less than two weeks now.

"If you don't mind"—I reach for Andie's hand, twining my fingers in hers—"we were going to eat lunch. I'll catch up with you later."

Clyde chuckles like I'm a fool but leaves us to it. Cassidy runs after him, so she can get her release signed. Steve stays with us, though.

I lead Andie out of the dome, shedding our hardhats and safety vests as we depart. Her silence scares me. As we walk, I explain, "Montalcino is a centuries-old estate."

"You've seen it?" she asks, her eyes on the ground. A little line appears between her brows.

I sigh, wishing I hadn't been the cause of it. "They asked me to go after Paris, but I turned them down for Atlanta." Remembering my mom's advice to let Andie in, I add, "They weren't thrilled with my choice."

"So, are you going to go to Italy?" she asks. Her voice is small and distant and I fucking hate it. I could strangle Clyde for having that conversation in front of her.

With a frustrated groan, I run my hands through my hair. A C-suite position would set me up for life, financially. It's a level of security I still crave after all this time. Unable to look at her when I say it, I frown at an oak tree nearby. "I don't know."

Andie stares at her feet. When I think the silence might kill me, she mumbles, "You didn't even tell them you were married."

I utter a curse under my breath, directed at Clyde. We need to be alone. My hand finds hers, and I tug her off the path toward that oak.

"I'm not dressed for a hike," she complains. Good. At least she's talking. Steve is fumbling to get through the brush, thank God.

I pull her around the trunk of the tree and pin her against it, a hand on either side of her head. She gasps, but her hands find my stomach, hot through the worn fabric of my Henley. They make me heavy, ready to settle into our spot against the tree instead of itching to get away. Our mics are still on, but after Clyde refuses to sign a release, I doubt much of this encounter will be usable anyway.

"I didn't tell them I was married," I echo her earlier sentiment. "Of course I didn't. It was for a reality TV show my mom coerced me into signing up for. And my bride has been insistent on locking me out."

"That was six weeks ago," she counters. "A lot's changed since then."

I study her face, searching for a cutting remark she hasn't said out loud. Nothing. Her eyes are clear and locked on mine, her lips gently parted. Soft and open. She meant that. Warmth unfurls in my chest, cascading down my body, and let out the air in my lungs in a heavy breath.

Fool that I am, my eyes fall to her chest, where I can clearly see her nipples tightening under her shirt. I bow my forehead to hers and let out a soft groan. One of my hands falls to her hip, needing to feel how close she is. How real this all is.

"This job," I explain, "it pays well. It allows me to take care of my mom. Anything she needs. The downside is that I'm not here for her, physically, when she needs help. Then they announced a Colonnade here in Atlanta, and I thought my problems were solved. But my boss almost didn't grant me the transfer. I had to threaten to quit."

Andie's small intake of air nearly kills me. I wince.

"Now Clyde is going to tell him that I've gotten married and settled down." My hand squeezes her hip before sliding to her waist. "Andie, I grew up with nothing. I've fought incredibly hard to be where I am now. I've given up a lot along the way."

"I know," she murmurs. Of course she does. If anyone understands the desperation of moving past their circumstances, it's her.

"In the past, if they told me to relocate to Italy, I'd be on a plane tomorrow." I'm being honest, saying things out loud I've never dared think about before. My fingers find the hem of her shirt and tug gently, sliding the fabric between them. "You're right—a lot of things have changed in six weeks."

I ignore Steve crashing through the brush by the tree.

My hand moves to Andie's jaw, my thumb brushing her lower lip. Her eyes stay locked on mine. We're closer now than we were six weeks ago—she'd have never let me touch her like this weeks ago—but I still feel like I'm reaching for her in the dark. "Say something, please," I beg.

She swallows, and my thumb follows the knot in her throat as it works its way down. Her eyelids fall closed, and she gives her head a small shake. With seemingly a herculean effort, she says quietly, "You know I'd never ask you to stay."

All the air in my lungs escapes in a rush, my head light. It feels a lot like a goodbye. I wince. "Don't say that. You have every right to ask me to stay."

Her lower lip quivers and she looks away. "I know what this job means to you." She shrugs. "I know you wouldn't ask me to give up my business, either."

I curl my fingers into the bark on the tree, savoring the rough bite into my flesh. She thinks a lot of me, to say she knows I wouldn't ask that of her. I'm not sure I have it in me to be so selfless, not now that we've found each other.

With a heavy sigh, I say, "It's all hypotheticals at this point. Let's just . . . have lunch."

Andie clears her throat primly. "I just remembered—I have a client meeting at one, and I have to leave now to make it on time. Maybe next time?"

She doesn't have a client meeting, and she hasn't had one for a while. It's why she's so worried about the money from the show. "Andie, please. Stay in this with me."

Her eyes grow wider, making her look remarkably like a scared animal I've just backed into a corner.

"Please," I beg. "Talk to me."

"I will." She presses her fingers into my chest, her eyes on my throat. "As soon as I even know what to say." Her eyes find mine. "It just hit me that you travel for work, and I—"

"I've told you I travel for work." My voice pulls taut, ready to snap at a single ounce more pressure.

"You did," she agrees.

Before I can make my case—that I'll still be at her beck and call, that I'll take care of her even if we're a world away—she presses her lips to mine. It's a slow and gentle kiss, with her opening to me, offering herself up. The only thing that gives her desperation away is how she clutches my shirt in her fists. I wish it did more to soothe the anxiety climbing up my throat.

"I just need some time to process," she whispers.

"Process." I run a thumb along her jaw. "We don't have to talk about it right now. But you came to have lunch with me. Let's have lunch."

Her eyes soften.

"I know you're hungry." I can't keep the edge of desperation out of my own voice as I try to lighten this conversation up. "And I really don't want to deal with your grumpy ass later because you forgot to eat."

She takes a deep breath, and I watch the rise and fall of her chest. She wants to run, I can tell. But she's the bravest person I know, so she stays. "Okay," she agrees. "Lunch. And I do *not* get grumpy when I'm hungry."

"Sure you don't, sweet potato." I smile as she slips from under my arms. She tosses me a hesitant smile over her shoulder when she finds her way back to the path to the resort. I force myself to take air into my lungs and follow.

I'm not sure how I could bear to be away from her for months at a time, maybe flying her out occasionally to visit. I'm sure I know someone who's involved with the fashion scene in Milan; that could be a draw for Andie to join me in Italy and I—

"Hypotheticals," I mutter to myself as I catch up with her, then pick up her hand.

We pause for Steve to catch up before heading to the restaurant.

The reality of my job is that I will eventually have to leave Atlanta. I've always known that. I told Andie I travel for work; she knows I'll have to leave too. I've been taking care of my mom from afar for a long time now. I just need to show Andie I can do the same—be there for her even when I can't be nearby.

CHAPTER THIRTY-THREE

ANDIE

I completely forgot we're having dinner with Kit's mom tonight. When I arrive home to him and the crew waiting for me, my head is a jumbled mess. Somewhere between my foolish decision to visit Kit at work and an afternoon buried in my own work, I can barely focus on putting one foot in front of the other.

Not how I wanted to meet Kit's mom, truthfully. She's so important to him, and now that we're all in, tonight matters. I'm supposed to be poised and pulled together and the kind of wife that would make Kit proud.

Instead, I can't bring myself to have even a sliver of decent conversation with Kit on the drive. He can't seem to find our normal push and pull, either. So I just throw glances at the GoPro Cassidy fastened to the passenger-side corner of the cab in Kit's SUV, to film us while we're on our way.

By the time we pull into a dirt driveway beside a robin's-egg blue single-wide, my heart is in my throat. Kit loves his mom; everything he does has her at the center of it. She's fighting cancer, and he's holding it all together.

She wants him to find a wife and settle down, and tonight she'll be meeting me. Someone who, mere weeks ago, signed on to marry her son because there's divorce money in it. Hands shaking, I unbuckle my seat belt.

I climb out of the car and take a deep breath. The sky is a Bob Ross painting come to life in oranges, pinks, and purples. Crickets serenade the stars before they've even shown themselves.

Cassidy and Steve greet us, clipping on our mics.

"Any words of advice?" I ask Cassidy over my shoulder while she works.

She laughs. "Not really. Meeting parents is always a mess."

"Oh, good." I tap my foot nervously on the packed dirt driveway.

She gestures for me to turn around, then makes sure the mic is secure beneath my shirt. "Think of it as a challenge. You're good at those."

I swallow the knot in my throat. This isn't like jumping off a platform in the jungle or winning a game of Jenga or throwing axes. This is an important piece of Kit I don't want to risk breaking.

He stares at the front door, a frown on his face. I wish he'd tell me it will be fine, that his mom will love me. But he doesn't.

Released from Cassidy's custody, I walk around the car. "It's beautiful out here."

When Kit doesn't reply, I touch his arm. "You okay?" I ask quietly.

He shakes his head like he's trying to rid himself of a particularly clingy thought, then explains. "It's the first time my mom has been on camera. She was too sick for all the pre-wedding interviews. I'm just . . . nervous."

"About what she'll do on camera?" If my mom is any example, we're in for a wild ride tonight.

"Not like that." He reaches for my hand. "She thinks I'm overprotective. Maybe I am, I don't know. It's weird letting outsiders into our lives."

I lean into him, lacing our fingers together. "Tell me about it."

He smiles down at me, and maybe tonight will be just fine.

Cassidy hops up the wooden steps to the front door and knocks.

When the door swings open, I try to get a glimpse of the woman Kit cares so deeply about. To no avail. Cassidy slips in the door with a smile, closing it behind her so I still have no idea what I'm walking into.

As Steve is hoisting his camera up onto his shoulder, I decide to wave my proverbial white flag. "I'm a little nervous to meet your mom," I admit with a shaky smile.

Kit takes in a deep breath and lets it out in a short sigh as he thrusts his fingers into his hair. "Ready to take the leap, sweet potato?"

I force a smile. "Promise to catch me?"

"Always." He gives my hand a squeeze.

Cassidy emerges from the trailer and tells us it's go time. We wait for her signal, then take the slow march to the front door. The wooden steps look relatively new, even though the platform wobbles a little with all of us trampling on it.

By the time the front door swings open, I'm lightheaded. Kit's holding my hand so tightly my fingers ache, but the woman inside beams. She's about my height, with curling white hair. She's in a house dress with a bright pattern, reading glasses hanging around her neck on a dragonfly chain.

"It's so good to finally meet you," she says, stepping aside to let us all in. Before I know what's happening, she pulls me into a hug. Her grip is much stronger than all of Kit's mentions of her would have me believe. I hug her back, resting my shaking hands on her shoulders. Then she lets me go and holds me at arm's length to look at me.

She looks like the kind of mom who would be checking to see if my hips are wide enough to bear children, and if my body can handle years of household chores. I swallow the knot of disappointment in my throat—I'd make a terrible housewife. Kit is always chasing me down to make sure I've eaten something since breakfast.

"This is Andie," Kit says when the camera crew has shuffled in and made themselves at home in the cramped space. "Andie, this is my mom."

"It's nice to finally meet you, Mrs. Watson." I nod my head in her direction and hold out my hand, even though she's already embraced me like family.

She waves off the gesture with a smile. "Please, call me Maureen."

I give her a shaky smile, my heart pumping faster.

Maureen mumbles something about having to check on dinner and shuffles slowly toward the kitchen. Kit watches her walking with a frown. I know that look. That's his *You shouldn't be pushing yourself so hard* look. I'm glad to know it's not just me he does that to.

My phone buzzes in my pocket, and I dig it out. It's from Cassidy. *Why don't you ask Kit for a tour?*

Normally, I find a way to dodge Cassidy's line of questioning. But I'm just not feeling clever tonight, so I turn to Kit. "Can you give me the grand tour?"

He shakes his head and huffs out a laugh. Holding his hands out to the room, he says darkly, "This is it."

It's small, of course; as a single-wide trailer, it would be. Everything is clean, and even the books stacked on random flat surfaces seem to have some level of order to them. On the whole, it's a cozy space. Unpretentious.

The carpet in the living room is older, and the linoleum in the kitchen is peeling back from the Pepto Bismol pink cabinets. The walls are papered with a floral pattern that looks like it walked out of 1992. The dark green sofa and reddish-brown recliner in the living room are clearly well lived in. Hanging above it is a photo of a younger Kit, his mom, and a man who must be his dad, based on the resemblance. He never mentions his dad; I assumed he wasn't around, but Kit has to be a teenager in this photo.

Clearing my throat, I look down a narrow hallway and ask, "Is that your childhood bedroom?"

Maureen, of course, hears me ask, because she's only a couple of feet away even though she's technically in the kitchen. "It is," she says before Kit has the chance to answer.

"Can I take a look?"

"Of course, honey." Maureen moves to one of the cabinets over the sink. "Make yourself at home."

When I look at Kit, he only lets out a heavy sigh. His only sign of consent is a small sweep of his arm indicating I should lead the way.

The floors creak under my feet as I wander down the short hallway. It makes a bit of a bottleneck, so Steve is lodged in the doorway, Cassidy and an extra sound guy stuck behind him, standing on their tiptoes to make sure they're not missing anything important.

The room has almost nothing in it. There's a twin-size bed and a small dresser that looks like it hopped out of the eighties. On the wall closest to the door, there's a small closet.

"I see you got rid of the Spiderman sheets." I try for a lighthearted joke, even though my heart is tearing in two, remembering what he told me about the conversations he heard his parents have late at night.

I don't feel sorry for Kit, not like that. Sure, this place is small, but it feels like more of a home than I ever had. I can't remember my mom ever telling me to make myself at home. Even in our own home. We were always visitors, passing through on borrowed time. When Kit doesn't bother to acknowledge my comment, I sit down on the edge of the bed, and the mattress springs squeal.

I ask carefully, because I truly want to know, "Did you like growing up here?" Maureen seems warm and loving, and he had all this outdoor space to run around as a boy.

Finally, the flicker of a smile crosses his lips. "Yeah," he replies. "We made it good."

It's my turn to frown. I open my mouth to ask about his dad—I know just how touchy a subject that can be—but don't get the chance.

Cassidy says from behind Steve, "Kit, can you sit on the bed with Andie? It's hard for us to see you both from here."

Kit's jaw tics, but he relents. The mattress sinks next to me, and it takes all my willpower to keep from leaning right into him.

Gently, I tell him, "Thank you for inviting me to dinner tonight."

His lips twitch in a flicker of a smile. "My mom would have murdered me if I didn't."

"Ah, so the force feeding is a family trait." I nudge him with my elbow.

He rolls his eyes. "I'm plagued with stubborn women."

I press my hand to my chest in mock offense. "I thought you found my stubbornness charming."

"More than that." He smiles for real this time, his eyes crinkling at the corners. "But we don't need to scandalize the crew tonight."

Before I can sink into the liquid heat in his eyes, Maureen calls us back out to the table for dinner.

* * *

After a meal filled with shallow questions about what I do for a living and how odd it was to get married on TV, Kit collects our plates while I help Maureen to the living room. She catches me looking at the family photo above the sofa.

"He takes after his father," Maureen says with a smile. "In more than just looks."

"He doesn't talk about his dad at all." Honestly, by the way Kit speaks about his family, it's like his dad doesn't exist.

Maureen shakes her head and picks up another photo from the end table. It's a candid: Kit's dad and his mom sitting in lawn chairs in front of the trailer, laughing. She runs her finger along the metal frame. "Neither of us do." Her smile cracks under pressure. "It's been a decade now, but it all feels fresh most of the time."

"Were they close?" I murmur, a far corner of my mind whirring to life. All this time I assumed Kit had rushed home purely to protect his mom.

"They were. Kit wouldn't be who he is without Harry being so involved." Maureen nods. "He passed very suddenly. There was no way for us to prepare or adjust. One day he was here and happy, and the next he was gone."

I swallow the lump forming in my throat. I want to ask more, but it feels like we've crossed into sacred ground, and I don't want to disturb it.

Kit's voice startles me. "Twenty fourteen was a hard year."

He leans against the doorway between the kitchen and the living room, hands shoved into his jeans pockets. His brown eyes are deep with an aching I can't touch, and a small crease forms in his forehead.

After a beat of silence, he joins us in the living room, taking a seat on the recliner in the corner. He bows forward, his elbows on his knees, and clasps his hands together. My gaze falls to his wedding band and my heart lurches.

"Dad passed in November," Kit says in a calm, quiet voice.

"I remember." Tears build behind my eyes and I shake my head. All I can think of is that chilly night we'd warmed each other in bed. The night I told him I loved him. The morning I woke, and he was gone.

Maureen reaches for Kit, squeezing his forearm. Kit rests one of his hands over hers. "Kit came home from school, and we made it through together."

Kit shakes his head and makes a frustrated noise. "I left you," he says to his mom, voice pulled taut.

Maureen shakes her head. "I forgave you for that a long time ago."

Kit gives his mom's hand another squeeze, then his eyes meet mine. He clears his throat and tells me, "My grief was too heavy. I thought maybe if I ran fast enough, it couldn't catch me."

Something hot and sharp digs under my diaphragm, and I press a hand to my stomach to feel my breath. I remember the voice mail I left him when he disappeared. After a week of waiting to hear from him, I finally broke. Every edge of me was jagged and raw and aching with his absence, and I needed to purge. So I called. When he didn't answer, I left a voice mail telling him things I'd have never told him had I known why he left.

Then he came back, trying to reach me. I was so damn stubborn, so concerned with how he hurt me, when I should have seen how deeply he was hurting too.

I can still feel the pain he left me with like it was yesterday, but the anger I feel rising to the surface now is different. I want to pound on his chest and shake him and demand he tell me why he wouldn't just let me be there for him. Why not call me sooner? I'd have been there for him. Didn't he trust me? Wasn't I enough?

Kit's eyes find mine, and he holds my gaze. There's a whole conversation in that look, one I wish he hadn't waited ten years to have.

VOICE MAILBOX OF CHRISTOPHER WATSON
NOVEMBER 19, 2014

Hi. It's me. [sniff]

I don't know where you are and I—

[sigh]

Missing you hurts, and I just wish you'd call and tell me you were okay. But you can't even give me that. Do I mean that little to you?

I can't believe I gave you everything and you just . . . you took it with you. That piece of me is gone, and you can't even tell me where you took it. It feels like you were just some fever dream my brain made up. I should have known better. No one can be as perfect as that.

I thought I loved you, but how can I love someone who just leaves me while I'm sleeping? How do you love a ghost?

I hate you for this. Maybe one day I won't, but right now . . .

[sniff]

If you come back, I don't want to know about it. I don't want to see you or hear from you. Leave me alone.

I guess this is—this is goodbye.

I hope you're happier where you are. Without me.

CHAPTER THIRTY-FOUR

KIT

Andie is quiet on the drive back to Midtown. Even now, when Cassidy and Steve are long gone, when the camera is miles away, Andie still doesn't speak.

I follow her to the apartment from our parking garage, not sure how to break the silence.

Jamie and Leslie save us the trouble, all but crashing into us on the stairs. They're giggling, holding hands. Andie and I exchange surprised looks, eyebrows raised.

"Sorry, sorry!" Jamie whirls around to put up his hands in apology.

Leslie is smiling as wide as I've ever seen him. "We're off to have some fun."

Jamie tucks into Leslie's arms and kisses him on the cheek. Leslie's blush grows deeper.

Andie smiles too. "Have a great time."

"Oh, we will," Jamie promises as he tugs Leslie to their car.

"They look happy," Andie says wistfully, watching them go. "I'm glad."

"Must be the magical therapy session Jamie was talking about the other day." I shrug. "Good for them."

Andie keeps a small smile on her face on the way to the apartment, but it's full of pain. Her eyes say it all.

Now she knows—why I left without a word, how we were both in pain we didn't know how to express. It should feel lighter. I always thought if she understood what my dad's death did to me, it would feel like a revelation. Instead, the heaviness of the night weighs me down, my vertebrae grinding together as we walk through the door.

Andie kicks off her shoes and drops her bag on the bench by the door, then beelines for the kitchen. I hang up my messenger bag and remove my shoes too, unsure of what's coming—a storm or quiet so loud it drowns out everything else.

When I finally have the courage to join her, she's pouring wine. Two glasses. Some of the pressure building in my chest dissipates.

She picks up her glass and takes a sip, closing her eyes. I follow suit, watching her for a sign of . . . anything at all. She's been so quiet; I don't have a clue what's going on inside her head.

When her eyes meet mine, she says, "Why didn't you tell me?"

"I did." I shrug. "You wouldn't let me in the door."

She winces, looking down at our feet on the linoleum. "You left me in the middle of the night after I told you I loved you and you couldn't say it back. What else was I supposed to do?"

I want to give her the same answers I've been giving myself for the better part of a decade: I was in shock, it happened so fast, I forgot my laptop, my phone bill was delinquent, and I couldn't turn it back on. When I returned, she'd blocked me on every social media platform, and her school email didn't exist anymore. I finally found her, and her roommate stood guard when I wanted to fall into her so I could fall apart again. All the words get gummed up in my throat, and they won't come out. I swallow some wine.

Finally, I tell her the truth. "If I kept saying it out loud—that my dad was gone, the person who wanted so much more for me—that would make it real. And it couldn't be real, Andie. It couldn't be."

She blinks. Sniffs. Shifts on her feet. "I'm so used to not knowing my own father, I just assumed . . . If I'd have known how much he meant to you, I'd have never—" Her voice breaks, and she wipes a tear off her cheek with the heel of her hand.

The voice mail. She'd have never left me that voice mail. "I didn't tell you. How could you have known?"

"I should have *felt* something," she says, her cheeks splotching with pink. She curls her free hand to a fist at her side. "Even then, it felt like you were some missing piece of me that fit into a forgotten corner of my heart. I should have been able to feel it when that piece of my heart broke."

Her words startle me. She never spoke of how she felt for me then. The only evidence I have of her feelings were days and nights of laughter twining around my heart like our limbs wound in bed. And that one whispered confession before it all fell apart—*I love you*.

All I can think of is the qualifier in her confession: *even then*. Which means we still have a chance now, don't we?

At my silence, she says, "I never even told you what you meant to me. I'm sorry I didn't make you feel like you could tell me those things."

"Andie," I scold gently. "I knew how you felt. You did tell me."

She keeps going, pacing the small kitchen like she didn't hear me at all. "I'd have waited for you. If I'd known, I'd have waited. But I was selfish, because selfishness is how I've survived, you know? But I could have waited. I could have done better."

I sigh and set my wine aside. On Andie's next turn of the kitchen, I hook my finger into her skirt pocket and tug her back to me. Her hands shake when I pluck her wineglass from them. Quietly, I tell her, "You'd have been waiting a long time."

She rests her trembling hands on my chest, balling them into fists. "I could have done it, but I was too focused on myself and didn't stop to think that maybe you needed me."

I can't help the half grin tugging at my lips as I let my hand settle into the curve at the small of her back. "Andie, it's not your fault. I didn't tell you what was happening. You were right to be upset."

"Broken." She fiddles with one of the buttons on my shirt. "I was broken when you left."

My familiar friend guilt returns, a knife driving between my ribs, angled at the soft organ that always caused so much trouble. "I'm sorry.

I was in no place to be the man you needed back then. It's my fault you—"

"It's not your fault." Her voice is louder and firm. Leaving no room for debate as her eyes find mine. "Kit, you lost your father. Your life was upside down. How could it be your fault?"

"I hurt you," I croak, my arm tensing around her.

"You were hurting." The look in her eyes is pure salvation. I'll drown in it if I look long enough. It's a promise blanketed in hope. I can be selfish. I can wrap myself in her offering. But it will mean costing her the money she needs. This ache behind my ribs is new, different—to love someone so fiercely and still be so far away.

Her fingers trail along my jaw, then play at my throat. I swallow. I should tell her how I feel, how I lost her once and I might not survive if I lose her again. How I want to support her dreams, but I don't want her haunting mine with what-ifs when this is over.

"We're here now," I whisper, even though there's no one else around to hear. It's not the whole truth, but it's the truth. This moment could stretch on forever, or it could just be for a few more days. But right now, we're together, and it's ours.

Andie must feel it too, because she stands on tiptoes to press her lips to mine. The kiss turns desperate, our bodies crushed together as our tongues tangle.

And if I tell her with my body all the ways I love her, if I hold her through her release, her cries mingling with my own, if we strip down to nothing between us, holding each other in the fluorescent light of this rented kitchen . . . is it enough? Can I let it be enough when she walks away for good?

CHAPTER THIRTY-FIVE
ANDIE

My designs are mocking me.

Eating cold leftovers from the takeout Kit sent a few days ago, I stand in my sweatpants and hole-y Georgia State hoodie, worried I'm a complete fraud.

Twelve of my eighteen dresses for Fashion Week are lined up on dress forms, bathed in light from the wall of windows in my loft.

Since I don't have another wedding to worry about, I at least have plenty of time to stare at my creations and hate them bitterly. I spent so many hours pulling them together, and here in the sunlight, they all feel monstrously wrong.

Nothing about these dresses feels new or special or even *good* anymore.

Perhaps if I wasn't thinking about dinner with Kit's mom so much, I'd feel better about them. Worse, we still haven't talked about the possibility of him going to Italy.

I want to scream at him for his silence, his absence, even though he's been in bed with me every night since. That's what killed me slowly the last time—the sudden disappearance of the Kit I gave my whole self to.

I should have just stayed in my studio for lunch that day. If I had, I wouldn't know any of this: how it feels to finally have let him in only to hear that he's leaving. Which should be what I want, since I *need* to divorce him in two weeks, but now that he's been in every corner of my body and soul, I know how much the emptiness will hurt when he goes.

I know it's not the same as last time, but this isn't what I want. If we're together, I want to be together, not in different hemispheres.

I don't want him in half measures.

Worse, I understand him—I won't give up the business I've worked so hard for, either. Giving it up to gallivant around the world at the whims of Kit's company, solely reliant on him for everything, isn't an option. He knows that. And it's not like I can have some sort of traveling studio. Dress forms and bolts of fabric don't exactly travel well.

I can't believe I'm searching for ways to meet him in the middle when he won't even consider staying without me begging him. What a goddamn mess.

"Oh, I love that one," a voice says behind me. I whirl around, stunned to see any sort of visitors here.

Heidi snorts a laugh at my surprise. "This is Andie Dresser," she tells the statuesque Black woman in a smart suit beside her. "She's one of Atlanta's best up-and-coming dress designers."

"Up-and-coming?" The woman strides over to the third dress from the right to examine it up close. "As in, not too many people know about her yet?"

I shoot Heidi a look that says, *Who the hell does she think* she *is?*

"Andie, this is Odette Thorne."

My eyes go wide. "As in, the woman marrying—"

"Yes." Heidi nods. She gives me a slow smile. "She's looking for someone to design her wedding dress."

I whisper fiercely, "Why didn't you tell me you were coming?"

"I called you three times and texted you twice," she whispers back.

I stab my plastic fork into my cold lo mein and stuff my tongue into my cheek. Of all the days for me to not change out of my pajamas. Every gossip column in the world was abuzz with Odette's engagement to a country music megastar who shall not be named. At least not here. Privacy is one of my business pillars. It has to be if I'm aiming to work with higher-profile brides.

"I've never seen a neckline like this." Odette glances at me, her umber skin luminous in the sunlight. "It's genius."

I eye the dress; just moments ago it was laughing at my incompetence as a designer.

"Is this one making it into the show at Fashion Week?" Heidi asks me a leading question.

"Oh. Right." I set my takeout container aside, ignoring that I'm in pajamas, and tell Odette, "I'm finalizing my lineup. There's six more half-constructed over there."

I open my mouth to suggest we take a look at those too, when two voices interrupt.

"Oh, those windows are gorgeous. This must be a source of inspiration."

"The floors are clearly restored; she's got an eye for history."

We all turn to see who's walked into my studio. I leave the door open during the day so brides and vendors can find me—or for Heidi to spring high-profile brides on me at the last minute, apparently.

There are two women in business attire eyeing my space. The one in red-framed glasses eyes the corner of my loft taken over by bolts of fabric. She opens up the leather portfolio she has clutched to her chest and scribbles something down as she tells the other one, "We could definitely use some shelves to display the bolts of fabric. Organize by color?"

"Nuh-uh," the other woman shakes her head. She's Black, wearing a great pair of high-waisted pants in a stunning magenta. "Organize by type of fabric."

Panic stirs in my guts. "Excuse me. Can I help you?"

"Oh, sorry," Red Glasses says with a smile. "I'm Catarina, and this is Ruby."

When they don't continue their introductions, the frustration I've fought all day rises to the surface. I tamp it down with a polite smile. These women are young, maybe just out of school. "I'm Andie, and this is a private studio."

"Love those pants," Odette tells Ruby over my shoulder. I don't disagree, but if they even so much as ask for an autograph, I won't be selling a dress to Odette. Or any other elite bride, when word gets out. I breathe in through my nose to remain calm.

"If you don't mind me asking," I say, my fists clenching at my sides in an attempt to keep my temper on a tether, "what are you doing?"

"We're here to help." Ruby reaches into her bag. She presents a résumé on cardstock as she closes the space between us. "I graduated just last month from Georgia Tech. I double majored in fashion design and business administration. Last October, I interned with the board for Atlanta Fashion Week, and I spent a summer in New York with Lila Bennett."

"Love her designs," Odette sighs behind me.

"Same. They're poetry in motion."

Before I can get a handle on the situation, Catarina presents me with her résumé too. "I also graduated from Georgia Tech, with a degree in information systems and graphic design. I've spent the last few years working at the corporate level with DigiTech and Bonnie Mae Industries, restructuring their databases and redesigning everything from letterheads to their customer-facing websites and apps."

"This is all very impressive"—I set the resumes aside—"but I don't understand why you're here."

"Fashion Week," Ruby says, matter-of-fact.

When I blink, still not sure what she's talking about, Catarina adds, "Jamie told us to meet him here."

Jamie? I slowly shake my head. "I don't—"

Heavy footsteps enter my loft behind them, and my stomach ties itself in a knot to see Jamie strolling in, Cassidy and Steve on his heels. Camera on and aimed at me. I step in front of Odette, as if my faded reindeer flannel pants will hide who she is and why she's here.

Fuck, fuck, and triple fuck.

As calmly as I can, I say through my teeth, "What are you doing here? I don't remember any filming at my office on the docket today." I'd have remembered. Cassidy would have given me timetables and met me earlier to strap on my mic.

Odette swears behind me. The blood rushes out of my face. I spin to face her, my hands up, palms facing outward in a placating gesture, like I'm soothing a wild animal. "I'm so sorry; let me figure this out." I face Cassidy and tell her, "I absolutely did not approve filming at my studio today."

"Jeremy's orders," Cassidy says wearily. She shrugs like it's out of her hands. "And Kit said it would be a good day for you. No appointments on your calendar."

Jamie at least has the decency to look embarrassed, holding his hands up, palms out. "I'm sorry, Andie. Kit said you still needed help, so I came with reinforcements."

I close my eyes and press a hand to my forehead. "Goddammit, Kit."

Odette's voice comes from behind me. "Heidi said you worked alone."

"I do." I turn to her with a grimace. She's going to fire me for this invasion of privacy, I just know it. And I don't even work for her yet. I mourn the income from a dress that will be featured in magazines all over the country. For Kit to jeopardize this is just—

"I've always thought you should hire an assistant," Heidi says. Very unhelpfully, I might add. I glare at her.

Before this can go any further, I tell Cassidy and Steve, "I need you to turn the camera off and leave. Please."

"Andie, you know we need to—"

I hold a hand up in a gesture that says *STOP*. "If Jeremy has a problem with it, he can pay me a visit later. My client's privacy comes first, so you need to go."

"What's all this about?" Odette asks before Cassidy can get a word in.

My head is spinning in ten different directions, and I can't stop it. I take a deep breath, hoping the bile climbing up my throat doesn't try to make an escape.

I bite the inside of my cheek until I'm sure I won't burst into tears. My answer to Odette is as shaky as my smile. "It's ridiculous, but there's a reality show filming in town and—"

"*First Look at Forever*??" Catarina squeaks over my shoulder. Her eyes almost bug out of her head, and Steve and Jamie give her sheepish smiles and small waves. "I applied to be on their production team, but no one even looked at my résumé. Oh, wow. They found you a match?"

My lips press together in a tight smile, and how the hell did I wind up explaining my personal life to Odette Thorne and two complete strangers? "They sure did."

The interlopers squeal with delight, and Odette pushes for more. "Do you think they got it right? I've heard the success rate for the show is pretty incredible. You're not going to stop designing dresses, are you?"

I look to Heidi for help, but she's just as stunned as I am. Jamie's look is all apology and sympathy. It's not his fault Kit set him up to fail.

All at once, the suggestion that I would give up what I've built simply because I'm married breaks me. My voice is loud enough to echo in the studio. "He's a man who thinks he can walk into my life and turn everything upside down. He told me his mom wants him to fall in love and settle down and thinks that it's his *job* to fix all my problems, even though they're not problems, I'm just *busy* running the *business* that I *built* with my own two hands. And there's cameras *everywhere* looking for a love story when all I want to do right now is ask him how he can even consider leaving when we're so close to something so perfect it hurts!"

The room falls silent. I swallow the gut-wrenching feeling of having said too much. I never speak of my personal life with a client. Not like this. I *never* complain about running my business, lest anyone think I'm ungrateful for what I have. I have always worked myself to the bone. I have always been tired, sacrificing sleep and other luxuries to keep things going. I have always worked through lunch and sewn dresses until my fingers bleed. I have never been close to falling apart.

But a few weeks with Kit seems to be my undoing.

I take a deep breath and force a wan smile. "I'm sorry." Turning to Cassidy, I say, "I'm not going to ask you again. I take my clients' privacy seriously."

The word *client* sits bitterly on my tongue. I know Odette won't want to sign with me after this, anyway.

Cassidy sighs. She caught me ranting on camera already. "Talking heads later, before your date," she reminds me.

Cool, great. We'll pick this moment apart on camera. As long as she leaves. I give her a firm nod. She taps Steve on the shoulder, and I watch as they leave. I refuse to look away from the door until I hear the elevator close behind them.

"It sounds like a lot to take on." Catarina nods, solemnly.

"It's not easy," Jamie agrees. "For any of us."

"Catarina, Ruby. Jamie." I sigh, my shoulders slouching as I feel exhaustion wrapping around me like a wet velvet cloak. "I'm sorry you came all this way, but I can't afford to bring anyone on right now."

The three of them look at each other, having a silent conversation, punctuated with tilted heads and nods. Jamie delivers the news as gently as he can. "He's already paid all of us for a thirty-day introductory period. To get you through Fashion Week."

"Oh my God." The words are lost as I bury my face in my hands, tears welling too hot and fast. I can't stop them. My shoulders heave and I only barely manage to muffle a sob as I shake my head.

A warm hand falls on my back as Heidi's voice floats gently behind me. "Andie, I get emails from you at two in the morning."

I sniff, insisting through my hands, "I work best late at night."

"On invoices?"

The room is quiet while I pull myself together. I can't do this here, not with an audience. I'm so humiliated I want to melt into the floor. I'm supposed to have it all together. I'm supposed to create a flawless experience for brides, and here I am, breaking down about my own goddamn marriage.

Kit's going to leave. Nothing I say will stop him. That's why he sent me all this help. He wants to make sure I'm taken care of while he's gone, just like his mom. I'll be well kept and here for him whenever he deigns to visit me.

I'm sure my eyes are rimmed with red as I turn to Odette. "I'm sorry. I'm not having the best day."

Ruby steps forward and speaks in a soothing voice. "I'm sorry to have bothered you at an inconvenient time, but if I may?" She gestures to Odette.

Defeated, I shrug. "It's up to her."

Odette gives me one last look of pure pity, then says to Ruby, "Let's hear it."

Ruby gently nudges me to the side, and I look on, numb, as she begins asking Odette about her ideal wedding dress. Questions I should have asked her myself but couldn't seem to pull it together long enough to do. Heidi takes notes on her tablet as they talk, too.

Before long, Odette turns to me, her mouth in a firm line. "You've given me a lot to think about. Thanks for your time."

I can only nod as Heidi and Odette depart. Catarina and Ruby are already compiling notes and swiping through photos on their phones.

Jamie gives me a hug before they leave, too.

I want to cry anew. These two women Jamie brought are more qualified than I am to do my own damn job. And Kit paid them all, thinking it would, what, make me feel better? Help me get more sleep, or something?

All I feel is inadequate. These two women have impressive degrees and experience. The only things on my résumé are a year at a dry cleaner and another at a chain bridal store as a seamstress. I'm self-taught at everything from hemlines to spreadsheets.

What a perfect cherry on top of this shit sundae. For the first time in a long time, I feel in my gut how easy it is for all of this to be stolen from me. By someone else, who said he'd be my partner at the altar. This is why marriage was never on my list.

And Kit can go to hell.

CHAPTER THIRTY-SIX

KIT

I'm going through employee reviews when I get the call. It's my least favorite part of the job—rating employees like an app on a phone—so my phone buzzing across my desk is a welcome distraction. After dinner with my mom and the conversation with Andie afterward, I hoped to feel surer about decision day. It's only a few days away now, and I thought surely I'd know my answer.

Or rather, surely I'd know Andie's answer by now. She hasn't said she's changed her mind about the divorce money. She hasn't told me she wants to stick it out and see what we can be. She hasn't told me that she loves me. Nothing like that. Even after I told her I was all in.

Hell, she knows I may be jetting off to Italy for work and won't even ask me to stay. I thought, with everything we've uncovered, we'd be farther along than this.

All we have is a couple of weeks of nights in bed together and a handful of experiences from the show stitched together with the thread of our first crash and burn.

I hope it's enough.

"Hi, Lisa." I answer my phone because I never ignore a call from Mom's home nurse and sink heavily into the expensive leather chair at my desk. The penthouse is even emptier than it used to be, with my sparse belongings nestled in a closet beside Andie's. "Did I forget to pick up a prescription again?"

"Kit." Lisa's voice is firmness wrapped in crackling cellophane. It puts me on edge. "Your mother fell while trying to dust the tops of the cabinets this morning."

I bolt upright, the employee reviews blurring in front of me. "What? She can't reach the tops of the cabinets."

"If she's on a stool, she can." Lisa is so calm, my skin prickles with the anticipation of a storm.

"She wouldn't be so—"

"I found her when I got here thirty minutes ago. She was disoriented and in severe pain."

My vision begins to narrow, growing dark at the edges. My voice cracks. "Is she—?"

Lisa seems to understand my fractured attempt at information gathering. "I called an ambulance. They're taking her to Emory."

"Thank you." I hang up before Lisa can tell me any more. I'm already spiraling. My hand shakes, so I toss my phone onto my desk and stare at it. The dark screen reflects the ridiculous luxury of my surroundings back at me.

I knew I should have taken Mom out of that trailer. I should have brought her here and kept her close. She was so stubborn, though, and I didn't want to make the one parent I had left angry, so she stayed. No matter what I offered her, she insisted on living there.

"What's the point of living if I can't do it on my terms?" she asked me the last time I suggested an assisted living facility.

At this point I've lost track of how many times I've offered her more than what she has, and she refuses every one of my attempts. Emotions are swelling in my chest so quickly I'm not sure how I'm going to keep breathing. I'm pissed and I'm scared and I'm hurt and I feel so, so small.

I need to *do* something. To run. So I stand, snap my laptop shut, and stride out the door to meet Mom at Emory.

* * *

Mom is dwarfed by the large hospital bed. She's hooked up to monitors, beeping in a chorus around her. I'm not sure what any of them mean, but the cacophony is enough to put me on edge. The doctors have been by, as well as the nurses, and they've all explained to me that she broke her hip when she fell. Nothing else. Her brain is fine.

It's a simple enough procedure to fix it, and they're booking her for surgery first thing in the morning tomorrow. It would be tonight, but with her cancer diagnosis and course of treatment, they want to make sure everything is in order.

So that leaves me sitting by her bed as she dozes off, holding her hand in mine. The IV is taped haphazardly over her hand, and I run my thumb over the tape edges as if that will bring any more order to the scenario. My foot taps relentlessly against the linoleum floor. Running while my world screeches to a halt.

We talked for a while after she was admitted to the hospital. She was in pain, but once she had some morphine on board, she was back to being stubborn. I asked her what she was thinking, and she replied she was bored and might as well clean.

I was so furious with her, my jaw began to ache with how hard I clenched it. Didn't she understand? I've already lost my dad. I can't lose her too. I can't.

Now, her eyes heavy, she gives my hand a squeeze.

"Where's Andie?" she asks, her voice a mere rasp among the machines.

"She'll be filming soon," I mumble.

My mother, however, sees right through me. "She doesn't know you're here."

"She'll understand," I say out loud, willing myself to truly believe it. "I'll call her once you're settled."

"If I get any more settled, I'll be dead." Mom pins me with a knowing look.

"Mom." My voice breaks under the stress and tears well hot behind my eyes. "Don't joke about that. Please."

She squeezes my hand. "I'm okay, Kit. Good as new in no time. The doctors all said so."

"For your hip." I wipe a tear off my cheek with the palm of my hand. "We're going to have them check everything again. Twice."

"We don't need to do that."

I bury my face in my hands, trying to keep the last pieces of my sanity intact. "Plagued by stubborn women."

"I'm not the only one who's stubborn," she counters. "You got it from me, you know."

"Mom," I scold, suddenly exhausted. I don't have the energy or the heart to tell her that I think Andie is still leaving. That I tried my hardest, but it's not enough. Andie can't find it in her to love me, not like she used to.

Mom tuts. "She'd be here if she knew."

"You don't know that," I mutter to my feet. She knew about my dad's death and still wouldn't let me in the fucking door.

"I do."

"You met her *once*. For about three hours."

"I can tell by the way she looks at you." Mom shifts in bed, then winces. She sees me stand, ready to call a nurse in, and waves it off. "I'm fine, Kit. Sit back down. Call your wife."

I fall back into the uncomfortable hospital chair and frown. When did I become everyone else's nuisance? Andie doesn't want my help, and my mom doesn't either.

When I look at my feet, I notice a scuff on my shoe. All I can think about is rubbing it away, making it perfect again. I want to explain to my mom that Andie may look at me like she's . . . I don't know, thinking of caring about me. But that's not a prize. Andie cares deeply about everything; it's why she's so careful about who and what she lets in. It doesn't make me special.

She may *look* at me like she cares, but for the first time I'm wondering if the looks are enough. If the nights in bed are enough. Not for her, but for me. I've been willing to take any scrap of attention she can give me. But here in a hospital room with my mom, I realize how close I am to losing her, and all of Andie's looks wouldn't be enough to keep me afloat. I need more than that. I need her trust, her time, her love. Openly and unabashedly. I don't want to spend the rest of my life tiptoeing around what I really want to say, how deeply I really feel.

When the chair creaks as I stand to get my cell phone from my bag, my mom says, "Thank Christ. You had me thinking I raised an absolute nincompoop."

CHAPTER THIRTY-SEVEN
ANDIE

I take in the small art studio as Cassidy clips a mic pack on me. Kit was gone this morning when I woke up, but he left a little gold envelope taped to the coffee maker. Inside was a note saying to meet him here for a date after work. He chose it, the note said, because the producers wanted to film us doing something we used to enjoy, the first time we dated.

As it is, I'm ready to rip him a new one for sending assistants *and* cameras to my loft like he owned the place. I called him three times to have this out before we were on camera tonight, and he ignored every single one.

So here I am, in an art studio in Midtown, wedged between a hip coffee shop and some sort of cottage-core boutique. Kit isn't here yet. It's fine. He has a longer drive in this shitty traffic. He'll be here soon.

A man in gauchos and Birkenstocks floats toward us. And when I say float, I mean he clearly just finished meditating and manifesting world peace or something, because his facial features are so serene and his graying long hair flows behind him.

"Welcome," he says with a smile. His voice is gentle. "I'm Dash, the owner of Inner Self Art Studio."

I shake his hand and fumble through a greeting.

"Are we ready to create from within today?" he asks, cupping my hand in both of his. He leans forward eagerly, like my answer matters.

I look over my shoulder toward Cassidy. "Shouldn't we wait for Kit?"

Cassidy looks at her watch, her mouth smoothing into a thin line. Then she shakes her head. "We only have the studio for a couple of hours. Let's get started, and he can catch up when he gets here."

Dash waves a tiny remote, and pulsating, lax music with no lyrics throbs through some hidden speakers. He turns to me with a smile.

My phone rings in my purse. Dash winces. I'm totally ruining his vibe, but I feel it in my bones. Something is wrong.

I gasp when I see who's calling. "Kit," I say his name with a relieved sigh. "Where are you?"

"I'm at Emory." He sounds exhausted, his voice heavy and hoarse.

"Are you okay?" I look over my shoulder at Cassidy, who's frowning.

"I'm okay." Kit sighs. "I'm okay. But Andie, my mom, she . . . she fell."

"Oh no."

"The doctors say she only broke her hip, but—"

"I'm coming." I throw my purse over my shoulder and turn to walk out the door we just entered.

"No." Kit says loudly. Firmly. "Don't."

I stop in my tracks. My voice breaks. "What?"

"Andie," he says like he's explaining it to a child, "you need to stay and film or your chance at that money is shot. Remember what the executive producer said?"

"Yes, but I—"

"We'll be okay." He swallows. "I'm here and I'm taking care of her. I'll stay the night, so I won't be home."

"Kit," I plead.

"I'll see you soon, okay?"

He hangs up before I can argue. He won't even let me tell him that the show doesn't matter if he needs me. I stare at the phone in my hand, stunned by his coldness.

"Is everything okay?" Cassidy asks gently.

"No." I begin tugging on my mic cord, unwinding it from my blouse. "I have to go."

Cassidy rushes over and grabs my hands in hers. "Andie, this is our last chance to film before we hit the mandatory separation period."

I sniff and shift on my feet. "That's nice, but I don't care."

"What's wrong?"

"Kit needs me right now." My voice rises an octave. "I can't be here when he needs me."

She frowns.

Dash steps closer with a hum. "Now let's all just take a deep breath."

I glare at him. "A deep breath won't change the fact that Kit's mom is in the hospital and she's already sick and . . . I need to go."

Steve turns off the camera and rests a hand on Cassidy's shoulder. "It's an emergency. Jeremy will have to deal."

I give her a pleading look. She sighs and helps me undo the mic. As I walk out the door, she yells after me, "Let us know how everyone's doing, okay?"

I give her a thumbs-up and run to my car.

* * *

The hospital is a fluorescent-lit maze, and my tunnel vision looking for Kit isn't helping me find Maureen any faster. I take a deep breath and pause in the hallway. I squint at the signs on the wall telling me which unit is which way, and they all feel indecipherable—a jumble of letters and numbers that mean nothing to me.

"Can I help you?" A nurse carrying her dinner from the cafeteria stops when she sees me struggling.

I press a hand to my forehead. "I'm looking for Maureen Watson."

"Do you know which unit she's in?"

"I'm not sure." My shoulders slump.

"How do you know Ms. Watson?"

I swallow. "I'm her . . . daughter-in-law. My husband called me to tell me she was here after she broke her hip and—"

The nurse pulls out her phone and begins texting.

"I'm sorry," I say, my voice breaking. "I'm not normally like this. I'll just . . . figure it out."

The nurse shakes her head. "Nuh-uh. Follow me."

I can't keep up with her brisk pace as she winds around the hallways to a set of double doors. She uses her badge to open them and walks me to the unit desk. "I found Mrs. Watson's daughter-in-law in the hallway. I'm sure she'd feel a lot better if she could be with her for a bit."

The young man smiles gently at me. "Of course. She just ordered her dinner, and I'm sure she'd love some company. I have some sandwiches and sodas in the fridge if you'd like to eat too?"

I nod, tears welling hot in my eyes. "That would be perfect, thank you."

The man walks me down the hallway and knocks on the doorframe to a patient room. "Mrs. Watson? I have someone here who would like to see you."

She looks at me and her face breaks into a smile. "Andie. I'm so glad you came."

I timidly walk into the room, looking in the corners for Kit.

"He's not here." Maureen shifts up to sitting in her bed with a wince. "He went to grab some things from home."

"Oh." I force a smile. He did say he was going to spend the night. "Good, I guess."

"Take a seat and tell me what you've been up to."

With shaking hands, I pull one of the vinyl chairs over to her bedside. "We were about to start filming when Kit called, or I'd have been here sooner."

"You're right on time." Maureen nods her chin toward the door, where someone in a black chef coat is bringing in a tray to set on the table beside her bed. The man who helped me earlier returns with a sandwich and soda for me. Never in my life have I been so grateful for PB&J and a Coke.

Maureen and I chat over our food about how my plans for Fashion Week are coming, and I ask her about the book she's reading. I'm laughing at how the hero thought he could get rid of the heroine by telling her to shoot him if she didn't like what he had to say—then she *did*—when I hear a familiar voice behind me.

"Andie. I didn't expect you to be here."

"Of course she came." Maureen waves off the suggestion that I wouldn't have come. Maybe she can talk some sense into her son.

I flash Kit a smile, hoping if he sees that Maureen is fine with this, he should be too. "We've just been having dinner and catching up. I've got some sandwich left if you're hungry."

He sets his messenger bag down on a chair in the corner of the room. "I'm not hungry."

"Is that coffee going to be enough for the night?" I eye the paper cup in his hand.

"I'll be fine." He sets the coffee down too. "Andie, can I talk to you for a minute? Privately."

"Oh." I put down my sandwich on the table I'm sharing with Maureen. "I'll be back."

She waves us out the door. "Take your time."

Once we're both in the hallway, Kit drags his hands through his hair. "What are you doing here?"

I cross my arms over my chest. "Your mom is in the hospital. Of course I'm here."

"I told you not to come." The words grit out lower and angrier than I expect. He balls his hands into fists at his sides.

I frown, unsure why he's this angry. "You sound upset."

"I am upset." He shifts on his feet. "Did you at least stay to film?"

"No." My brows draw together. I echo what Steve said to get Cassidy to let me go. "This is an emergency. There's no way I could film instead of being here with you."

"Dammit, Andie." He drags his hands down his face and turns away. His shoulders rise and fall with a deep breath before he faces me again. "We could be in breach of contract for this."

I nod. "I know."

"Then why did you come here?" he demands, his voice stretched thin with desperation.

"Gee, I don't know, Kit." I throw my arms out in frustration. How unbelievably dense is this man? "Maybe because you needed me. Maybe because I care about your mom, too."

"I told you I had it handled." He says it through his teeth. Now I'm angry too.

"Right." I pace on the linoleum, heat rising in my cheeks. "You handle everything. You hire a home nurse for your mom, and you offer Jamie money to help me because I can't afford to pay him."

"You need the help," he insists, hands on his hips. "I can pay him. It's a win-win."

"It's *not* a win-win." I whirl around to glare at him. "Aside from the fact that I explicitly told you I didn't want your help with my business, did it occur to you what you're doing to us?"

His eyebrows shoot up. "Us?"

"Me and your mom." I wave an arm back at Maureen's room.

"What am I doing, Andie?" His voice is loud enough that a couple of heads turn toward us as we argue. That's nothing new. We've had an audience with the camera crew for long enough to be numb to it. "Please, enlighten me."

"You're setting yourself up to run away again." I set my jaw to stop the tears pricking the corners of my eyes. "You say you're making sure we're taken care of here while you're away. But really, you can't face being here when things get hard and scary. I'm not going to let you do that this time."

"You won't *let* me?" He takes a step closer to me, his arms crossed over his chest.

"No." I lift my chin to look him in the eyes. "You say you're here and staying and that it all feels real, but I know you're ready to take that position in Italy."

"I'm not leaving you. Come with me."

Lie. I shake my head. "You know I can't do that. My business—my life—is here in Atlanta. Don't you see? Your mom and I don't need to be *taken care of.* We take care of ourselves just fine. We want you to be here. With us."

"Don't pretend you know what my mom needs from me," he growls.

"Fine." I sigh, my shoulders slouching. He's trying to loom over me when I wish he'd just hold me. When did we stop being on the same team? "I want you to be here with *me.*"

"I'm right here." He says it with enough vitriol that something in me curls up to protect itself.

I swallow, fighting back. Jamie and Leslie had the tough conversations and came out okay. I can be brave here too. "I knew that walking away from filming today was a risk. But you and your mom are more important than the show. And you still told me not to come. You're keeping me at an arm's length even now."

He scoffs. "Don't act like this is somehow altruistic of you."

"Goddammit, Kit." I press my hand to my forehead. "I'm trying to show you I love you."

"You're not even in this for love!"

I reel back with a wince. Wounded. I suck in a breath of air, but all I can feel is the fear that he's walking away, threatening to suffocate me.

"You're not even in this at all," I fire back. More heads turn our direction. "You're not married to me, you're married to your damn *job*. You're going to leave, no matter what I do. No matter what I tell you I need."

"Did you suddenly change your mind about decision day?" he asks, pinning me with his glare.

I hold it, searching for his heart in there, anywhere. I don't know how else I can explain that I'm stuck. If we still choose to divorce, I can get the money I need. It might already be moot since I walked away from filming today, because I already decided that Kit mattered more to me than the damn money. But even if we choose to stay married, he's going to leave. I've told him I need him here, and he's not even entertaining that as an option. It's a full-soul ache that I can't escape.

"I don't know." I wipe a tear off my cheek and take another step back. "Tell your mom I had to go." I turn on my heel and walk toward the exit before the signs become too blurry for me to find my way again.

CHAPTER THIRTY-EIGHT

KIT

"How's your mom doing?" Cassidy asks me as I sit on the uncomfortable couch in our tiny apartment living room. She's at least kind enough to ask it before my mic is on and the camera is rolling.

"She'll be okay." I sip on my coffee. Mom got out of surgery around nine this morning. I stuck around until they moved her back to her room on the floor. The only reason I'm not still at the hospital is because I had to film a talking head about what I'm thinking of as we go into our mandatory separation period before decision day.

Forty-eight hours to clear my head. I don't know if I should be grateful or full of regret. After my fight with Andie yesterday and a shit night of sleep in a hospital chair, I'm lucky I can sit upright and put my shirt on the right way.

Petra and Dr. Leon join me after their makeup artist is done making them look bright and fresh and awake. Cameras are set up to capture different angles, their cords tangled on the floor at my feet.

The cameras all whir to life, and I'm definitely not ready for this. Petra opens her mouth to speak when the apartment door swings open, crashing against the wall. All heads turn to witness Andie in sweatpants and a T-shirt three sizes too big. She looks like I feel—bags under her eyes, hair askew, like she's not sure how the hell she got here.

"Kit, listen, I'm sorry I—" She stops abruptly as her eyes bounce around the scene. Who's here. What we're doing.

The apartment door squeals closed in the silence. She clears her throat and stands up a little straighter. "Sorry to interrupt. I need to speak with Kit. It'll just take a minute."

I look into my coffee cup, a frown pulling on my lips.

"Andie"—Cassidy rests her hands on Andie's shoulders—"you can't be here right now."

"But Kit and I need to—"

Cassidy shakes her head. "Decision day is in forty-eight hours. This is the part of the show where you can't contact each other until the big day. Kit will stay here and you'll stay in your loft, yeah?"

She looks at the floor, silent.

"It gives you both time to reflect on your marriage. Alone."

"I don't want—" Andie's voice breaks. A tear falls from the corner of her eye. She hastily wipes it away. "Cassidy, please, I need to talk to him."

"The show—"

"I don't give a damn about the show!" Her declaration ricochets off the walls of the entryway. Her shoulders rise and fall with a deep breath. She looks me in the eyes. "This is more important."

"You'll have a chance to talk on decision day," Cassidy says, holding the apartment door open.

Andie looks at me again. "Kit, please."

I don't know what else there is to say to each other at this point. She wants me to stay in Atlanta. She knows I can't. Not if I'm going to take care of my mom the way she needs me to.

Andie said she loves me, but when I asked her point blank about decision day, she couldn't admit she wanted to stay with me. What's left to say?

Quietly, I tell her, "You should go."

The noise that leaves her can only be described as a squeak. Her face is sheet white as Cassidy ushers her into the hallway. My heart sinks to the floorboards, and the air in my lungs comes out in a whoosh.

At Dr. Leon's questioning look, I say, "We had a bit of a disagreement last night. Time apart might help."

He nods knowingly. Both he and Petra shift in their seats before getting down to business, asking their probing questions I don't have answers for.

CHAPTER THIRTY-NINE
ANDIE

I'm not exactly sure how I ended up here, standing outside the door to Maureen's hospital room. After Kit dismissed me from our apartment after I begged him to buck the show and talk to me, Cassidy led me to my car, reminding me that I'm not allowed to contact Kit. At all. No texts. No phone calls. No emails. No goddamn carrier pigeons, either.

But he's busy at the apartment filming, and my sleep-deprived brain led me here.

"Hey, Andie," the man from yesterday—he's a nurse, his name tag says Cody—smiles as he greets me. "It's good to see you back."

"Yeah." I choke on the word, wringing my purse strap in my hands.

"Let me know if you need anything, okay?"

"I will." I force a smile as he heads down the hall. Because I don't want another nurse to recognize me, I knock on the doorframe to Maureen's room.

She looks at me, and a smile nearly splits her face in two. I don't deserve it. She clicks off the TV. "Andie! How are you?"

I shrug and pull up a chair. "How are *you*? How's your hip?"

"I had a rod put in it." She pats the offending hip. "Hurts like hell right now, but they assure me it will be good as new in a few weeks."

"Good." I nod, swallowing the emotion I can't keep from rising in my throat.

"What's eating you?" Maureen asks, her brows furrowing.

I sniff and wipe my nose with my sweatshirt sleeve. "I probably shouldn't be here, but I wanted to see you and make sure you were okay." It's partially true, at least.

"I know you and Kit fought last night." She rests her hand on mine.

"You do?"

"Even if he hadn't come in here sulking, the nurses gossip like it's what they're paid for." She offers me a smile.

"I'm sorry." I can't look her in the eye. "I shouldn't have left without saying goodbye last night. I was just . . . overwhelmed, and Kit didn't want me here."

She shakes her head. "An utter nincompoop."

That makes me smile. "He can be, definitely."

"If you don't mind me asking," Maureen shifts in bed to face me, "what did you two fight about?"

I chew on my lip, unsure how to explain that I originally signed up for the show for money. That Kit thought I should be filming to preserve my shot at it. That I think he matters more than the money, but he won't listen to me. I'm not sure how to do that, so I ask, "Did he ever tell you we dated before? In college?"

"Truly?" Maureen's eyebrows shoot up.

I nod. "It was only a few months, and we broke up, but I was surprised to see him at the altar. How could this man who left me all those years ago be my perfect match, you know?"

"Left you?"

"We were dating right before . . . right before Harry passed." I look at our hands overlapping—mine rough and calloused, hers pale and fragile. "One night, I told him that I loved him. He couldn't say it back. And we were young, you know? I was really hurt that he didn't feel the same way I did. I shut him out. Then he left to be with you. I thought he was just . . . putting distance between us."

Maureen nods and pats my hand gently. Like a mother would. It brings tears to my eyes. I wipe one away with my sleeve. Voice thick, I tell her, "Last night I told him I loved him, and he . . . he couldn't say it back. Again."

"Sweetheart." Maureen stretches to grab me a tissue from the table next to her hospital bed. She hands it to me, then pushes some hair out of my face. Her hand is warm and gentle. Safe. "He may not have been able to say it, but I know he loves you."

I shake my head. "He can't." If he did, he wouldn't still be itching to leave. He wouldn't have told me to keep filming yesterday and to stay away from the hospital. He wouldn't have sent me away this morning.

"I saw you two together," she insists. When I say nothing in return, she sighs deeply. "How much has he told you about how he grew up?"

I shrug. "He told me you didn't have much as a family."

"We didn't." Maureen looks over my shoulder, thinking for a moment. "I'm afraid that Kit somehow got it into his head that love only means sacrifice."

"What do you mean?" I wipe my nose with my sleeve again, despite the tissue Maureen provided.

"We gave up a lot for him." She looks me in the eyes. "For each other. It's how we loved each other when we had very little. One Christmas when he was about ten, he said he didn't want any presents for himself. He wanted me and Harry to have something nice instead."

I can't help but smile. "That sounds like him."

"After Harry passed, he doubled down and worked so damn hard."

I nod. "He was always studying. Always pushing."

"He worked so hard to build this life that meant we never had to worry about money." Maureen sighs. "But what I think he missed is: the money doesn't matter if you can't enjoy the life you have. I'd hoped he learned that growing up, but instead he feels responsible. For everyone. All the time."

My lips tug into a half grin. "He does. He's protective of you. He thinks I need to be taken care of or I'll starve, or something. Like I haven't survived somehow without him this long."

"I don't think it's about survival." Maureen purses her lips. "I think he doesn't want us to struggle. He wants us to thrive. He wants to share all that he's built but doesn't know how."

I frown. “I asked him to stay in Atlanta. I told him I wouldn’t, but I did.”

“What did he say to that?” She squeezes my hand.

I look at the floor. “He asked me to come to Italy with him for his next assignment.”

“You own your own business, don’t you?”

I nod. “I can’t leave. My life is here. And you’re here, too. I thought he’d—” I can’t help the sob that bursts from me. I bury my face in my hands while Maureen strokes my hair, gently shushing me like she would a child. “Now we can’t talk to each other until decision day, and I need him to know I love him. Even though he couldn’t say it back, I love him.”

“Kit’s always done things the hard way.” Maureen soothes. “But he’ll make the right decision in the end. He always does.”

FIRST LOOK AT FOREVER
SEASON THREE
EPISODE SIXTEEN

PRODUCER:
Are you excited to see Andie today?

KIT:
Apprehensive, yes.

PRODUCER:
You had a few days to think about your final decision.

KIT:
[frowning] I did.

PRODUCER:
And where did you land?

KIT:
[sighs] I wish I could talk to her before we go into that room.

PRODUCER:
You know we can't allow that. It's not the format of the show.

KIT:
[nods, looking at the ground]

PRODUCER:
If she was here right now, what would you say to her?

KIT:
[voice breaks, looks into camera] I'm sorry. That's all. Just . . . I'm sorry.

PRODUCER:
What are you sorry for?

KIT:
Can we just go in and do this?

CHAPTER FORTY
KIT

Decision day.

The crew got seventeen different shots of me getting out of the hired car they had drive me up the length of the country club driveway.

My hands shake as Cassidy tells me to enter through the glass French doors, shake hands with Dr. Shaw, Dr. Leon, and Petra, before sitting down on the couch next to Andie. They peppered me with questions before I went in, about how I'm feeling, if I'll say yes or no. But I won't have to give my final answer until we're asked. Together. On camera.

I'm sick to my stomach as I tug on my lapels, careful not to obscure the pocket square I'm wearing—one Andie made me.

Andie also made that dress. I know, not because it's been in our shared closet for eight weeks (it has), or because I discreetly checked all her dresses to see which ones she made herself (I did). No. I know because it's exactly like her: airtight seams and a pattern that makes it look like armor across her chest, even though it's a delicate pink and undoubtedly soft fabric.

Then there's the hidden pockets at the hips. If I didn't know to look for them, they'd remain her secret.

I love and hate that I can spot her own designs a mile off. It means I'll never be able to look at a dress on a woman the same way.

Dr. Leon adjusts his own lapels for the camera while Petra waits for the cue to begin the conversation. Andie sits close enough to touch, and still a world away. I haven't spoken to her since our fight the other night. For the last forty-eight hours my mind replayed her desperate plea as she tried to get to me: *I don't give a damn about the show!*

My eyes slide to her hands, hoping I can get a glimpse of the state of them, to see how much she's thrown herself into her work. If she's taking care of herself without me to bother her about it. I swallow when I realize I can't tell.

I should have told her how much I love her hands—how capable they are.

"You two are the surprise of the season," Petra begins, gesturing to us both. "You dated once before and then got married, sight unseen. How did it feel that day at the altar?"

"Like I was falling, with no safety net." I offer a small smile.

Andie studies me for a moment. "Sounds like you should have brought a helmet."

That makes everyone chuckle, including me. I rub my jaw with my fingers, unsure what to say.

"What about you, Andie?" Dr. Shaw asks, her hands folded neatly on her lap.

I hold my breath while Andie ponders for a few seconds. Finally, she says, "A nightmare."

The hosts exchange dramatic looks that I'm sure will look great spliced together on TV.

Andie sighs and explains, "This man who left me after I told him I loved him all those years ago was supposed to be my perfect match? How humiliating."

The hosts smile amiably as she waves away the idea.

"But then"—she turns her eyes on me—"I got to know him for who he is now. We had fun and we found our rhythm again. The nightmare morphed into a bit of a fever dream. It's still hard to believe it's all real."

I give her the slightest nod of acknowledgment, unsure what to say.

"Andie," Petra says, a smile pulling at her lips, "is there anything you'd like to say to Kit before we get started?"

She looks at her hands in her lap and takes a deep breath. When she looks into my eyes, I'm crumbling. She's got to be able to see it. She knows me better than anyone. She always did.

"Kit," she says softly, like a caress. "There's a lot I could say, but mostly I want to thank you for taking care of me."

She swallows and holds my gaze.

The corner of my mouth tugs into a small smile, just for her. The cameras weren't around when we did it, but most every night, I took care of her hands, bandaged any new pricks in her fingertips, and toward the end, before we fought, I kissed away the ache of the day's work before bed.

"Kit," Petra cuts into my thoughts, "what about Andie? Is there anything you'd like to say to her?"

My mouth goes dry even though I knew they were going to ask this. We were briefed on it yesterday. The words I want to say simply won't come. I want to tell her she's beautiful, that the years away from me have been good for her. That I'm sorry I was so cold in the beginning. That I wish we had more time.

But most of all, I want to apologize for not being what she needs. I had two days to sit alone with the truth: If I've given all I can and it's not enough, nothing ever will be, as much as I wish it could be.

I simply frown and shake my head. None of it's good enough, and I don't want to say any of it in front of an audience.

Andie shrinks beside me, pulling away ever so slightly.

"Over the past eight weeks," Dr. Shaw says, "you've been through a lot together, without even knowing who you were going to marry. You took a leap of faith that day, and another one every day since."

Petra nods sagely, as if this part isn't scripted. "You had your first look at forever eight weeks ago and spent these eight weeks exploring what the future could look like. Now it's time to make a decision." She turns to Andie, her expression growing serious. I can already see how they'll layer this under dramatic music for TV. "Andie, do you want to continue this marriage?"

She licks her lips and looks at her hands again, smoothing them over her skirt. The one she designed for herself and made for herself, without anyone's help.

My pulse kicks up a notch, and I hold my breath. If she says yes, I have no hope of saying no.

Her lips pull into a frown, and she tangles her fingers together, clenching them so tightly her knuckles blanch. Her chest rises and falls with a deep breath. The silence stretches on so long and so taut, I'm afraid I'm going to snap clean in two waiting for her answer.

I'm frozen in time as she meets my gaze, so soft and open I'm not sure how to hold it.

Something inside me breaks. Not shattering and splintering like glass, but a slow fissure under duress finally gives way.

I close my eyes and turn away from her. When I open them, the hosts are smiling. Like they know something I don't.

But the answer is in Andie's hesitation. She still doesn't think I can be who she needs. I can love her ferociously from Italy and it won't be enough. She knows I won't give up my job, and I know she won't ask me to choose between her and taking care of my mom.

If she says yes, we'll hate each other soon. I can't bear the thought.

If she says no, I won't survive it.

My vision goes gray around the edges. I don't turn to Andie. If I look at the hope in her eyes, I'll fall apart. I won't be strong enough to do it. So I level my gaze on Dr. Shaw. "I think we should divorce."

The tiny gasp that escapes Andie feels like a sledgehammer straight to my ribs. I can't breathe. My hands are shaking, so I rest them on my knees.

It's the only answer. In time, she'll understand it was our only way out. I won't doom her to a life with me when I know I'm not enough for her. I won't give up the life I've built between who I am and who I used to be. This will break my mom's heart, but at least I can say I tried.

"I think it's safe to say that decision comes as a surprise to everyone." Petra tries to smooth over the brutal truth that just escaped my lips. "Can you tell us how you came to that conclusion?"

Andie sniffs.

Fuck.

I bow my head and close my eyes, forcing my lungs to take in air. It hurts. It physically hurts to do this. But I have to.

I walked into this thinking I could make everything right with Andie. That we could finally choose to be together. We were meant for each other.

Then we broke through all the bullshit keeping us apart only to find we would never cede the lives we built without each other. It's not the first time this morning I wish I hadn't been so stupid when we were younger.

Andie's become more beautiful, stronger, more incredible than I could have ever imagined. The Andie in my dreams doesn't hold a candle to the one sitting next to me. She asked me to keep showing up. I tried, and it wasn't enough.

I lift my head and meet Petra's eyes. "I wasn't the man she needed ten years ago, and I'm still not. I'm sorry."

Andie gasps again. Then, before they can ask her how she feels or what she's thinking, she stands. Her voice is thick with tears as she tells no one in particular, "I'm sorry, I—are we done? I can't—breathe and I don't want—I can't be here. I'm sorry."

She slips away, but not before I hear her muffle a sob as she opens the door behind us.

I don't want to talk to the hosts. Every fiber of my being wants to chase after her. But I give Andie time to escape. Time to run. Let her be the one who leaves me behind this time. Even though I was the one to end it. Again. Without explaining myself fully. Just leaving her to suffer through it. Alone.

Fuck me.

It's better this way.

I stand slowly, calmly. In a smooth voice, I tell our hosts, "Again, I'm sorry."

Before they can ask me to elaborate now that she's not here, I look to the producers in the wings. "Can you please remove my mic?" I've fulfilled my obligation to the show contract, and I'm done. I can't stand here trying to maintain the outward chill of a cold-hearted bastard while I'm falling apart inside.

I want to drown my sorrows in expensive liquor in the privacy of my own apartment and not worry about how bad I'll hurt tomorrow. It doesn't matter. I deserve it. Hell, I'd have punched any bastard who treated Andie like I just did. Giving myself a hangover I may never recover from sounds like a good alternative punishment since I can't clock myself in the jaw.

But this sharp, temporary pain will be easier in the long run. It will be easier than slowly watching the light go out of Andie's eyes as she realizes she has me in name, but not in truth. Better to hurt now than to give either of us the false hope that we can change who we are to make this work.

FIRST LOOK AT FOREVER
SEASON THREE
EPISODE SIXTEEN

PRODUCER:
I think it's safe to say Kit surprised everyone today.

ANDIE:
[nods, sniffling]

PRODUCER:
He didn't wait to hear your answer. Do you know why?

ANDIE:
[wipes her eyes and shakes her head]

PRODUCER:
Can you tell me how you're feeling?

ANDIE:
[voice breaking] I feel so small. I gave him everything I could, and it wasn't . . . it wasn't enough. I walked in thinking maybe more time would have fixed it, but now I don't know. I don't know, I don't know.

ANDIE:
[cries, covering her face with her hands]

ANDIE:
[through her hands] I want to hate him. I want to be mad, but I can't find it anywhere in me. He was so . . . so . . .

ANDIE
[muffled sob] Please, just let me go. This hurts too much.

CHAPTER FORTY-ONE
ANDIE

If you asked me how many brides I've seen break down in the course of my career, the answer would be: as many dresses as I design.

I just never expected to be one of them.

I'm not sure how I got to Heidi's office without getting into a wreck. The plush cream faux fur rugs greet me as I stumble in the door, my vision blurring in front of me. Tears rising in my eyes make the chandelier in the lobby look like it's twinkling. It lends itself to the idea that this must all be a dream. A bad one, but a dream nonetheless.

Kit spent eight weeks trying to win my trust, to take care of me, to prove he could be what I needed. Then before I could tell him I wanted to keep trying, he opted out. Quit. Left me.

After I told him I loved him.

Again.

My whole body aches like my limbs are being stretched in different directions. It's bone-deep and heavy. I worry I'll sink right through this carpet.

Praying for numbness to arrive soon, I ignore the receptionist asking me how she can help. I stagger past her desk and down a hallway to Heidi's door. It's all I can do to lift my hand and knock. But when I do, my wedding ring glints in the pendant lighting overhead.

Tears threatening to break free, I try desperately to pull the ring off. Heidi swings open her office door only to see me grunting as I tug at my stuck wedding ring, tears ruining my mascara. I sniff and my voice breaks. "I can't get it off."

Her eyes soften. I'm not a hysterical bride. I'm her best friend, and she's mine. She pulls me into the room and closes the door behind us. She wraps me into a hug with one arm, then uses her free hand to pick up the phone and let her receptionist know to hold her calls and cancel her afternoon appointments.

I feel like a child, my rib cage creaking with sobs too big for my body. I'm stronger than this. I'm more than this. I hate Kit for leaving me like this. Again.

Heidi guides me to one of the cushy armchairs in a small seating area she keeps in her office. Heavy sample books are on the modern coffee table, one open to tablecloth options, and another open to centerpieces. I can't look at them; they remind me of too much.

Right now, I can't fathom ever setting foot in a ballroom again. Not when this gaping wound in my chest wants to swallow me whole.

Heidi gives me a furry pillow to hold, pours me a glass of water, then wedges off my heels, tossing them aside. After scooting a box of tissues closer to me, she takes her seat in the other armchair, primly crossing her legs and folding her hands in her lap.

I don't want to guess how many times she's had to do this—calm the hysterical woman who showed up at her door—but she's probably the best at it, just like she is with everything else she does.

"So," she says quietly, calmly. "Decision day."

I nod, squeezing my furry pillow tightly to my chest.

"What happened?" Heidi asks, not a hint of judgment in her voice. She'd probably make a great therapist.

I swallow, then croak, "He didn't even let me answer."

Heidi studies me for a moment, then asks gently, "What was the question?"

"If I wanted to stay married to him." I grab a wad of tissues with a clumsy fist. "I was going to say yes. I was going to tell him I wanted to try, because I—" I shake my head, a new wave of tears letting loose. "I love him. I wasn't supposed to love him."

"I take it his answer wasn't what you wanted to hear."

I crumple in my chair, bending forward at the waist, wishing I could sink into the upholstery and never return. "He wants to divorce, and it's not like last time but it *hurts*, and I don't know what to do. I'm so stupid."

Heidi tilts her head while I catch my breath through a round of sobs. When I pause to wipe the snot away from my nose, she says, "You're not stupid."

I sigh, slouching over the pillow still protectively clutched to my stomach. "I already loved and lost him once, and I thought somehow it would be easier this time. How is that not the dumbest thing you ever heard?"

Heidi doesn't flinch. She simply watches me shred a tissue. When I think the silence will stretch on forever, she picks up her cell phone. Her voice falls into a comfortable murmur as my pulse pounds in my head. "Kimber? Yeah. Will you order from that place on Third, the one with that lemon butter chicken? Order enough for an army, and get something for yourself, too."

I bow my head, smashing my wet tissues against my face, as a new wave of humiliation crashes over my head.

Before this stupid show and this sham of a marriage, I always prided myself on my ability to keep going. To push through when things were hard. And to do it on my own.

Then Kit showed up with that disarming smile and his pet names and his insistent need to *help*. Letting him in was so natural. His touch lit me up, and he sent me lunch every day because he always said I couldn't create if I wasn't fed. He coaxed me into bed at a decent hour more nights than I care to admit.

Here Heidi was, canceling her day for me, ordering us food, and settling in for the long haul. The pride I had in never needing anyone's help was a house of cards. Staring at the wreckage, I've never felt so powerless.

"Am I really that much of a mess?" I ask as she sets her phone aside. "That everyone has to take care of me, or I'll spiral into nothingness?"

"Honey, no," Heidi says with a frown. Her brow wrinkles with concern as she begins pulling pins from her smooth French twist. "You just lived through eight weeks of being *on* all the goddamn time only for him to stomp on your heart and drag it through that perfectly manicured country club grass."

"That's a visual," I mumble as I take a sip of water.

Heidi kicks off her shoes and shakes out of her sharp blazer. "Now." She tucks her feet under her on the chair. "Tell me everything."

* * *

I spend the next hour spilling my guts to my best friend. Heidi gasps in all the right places as I reveal how we faked it for the cameras. Until it wasn't fake anymore. The food arrives just as I finish telling her about the fight I had with him a few days ago in the hospital hallway.

Heidi moves the sample books off the coffee table so we can use it to eat. We're quiet while we break open the to-go boxes. Heidi wanders over to the fancy file cabinet she has in the corner. It's got a hidden mini-fridge we've enjoyed a bubbly water from, from time to time. She comes back with a bottle of vodka, glass frosted over from the cold.

She shrugs as she sits on the floor next to the coffee table. "Desperate times."

I give her a fraction of a smile. It's all I can muster.

After we shove a few bites of food into our mouths, she asks, "You made him pocket squares?"

I roll my eyes. "It's not that big of a deal. I had the fabric lying around and he needed them, so I whipped some together."

Heidi nods, making a noise I can only describe as sarcastic, if that's possible.

"What?" I mumble around a piece of chicken.

Heidi stabs at a stack of lettuce drenched in chipotle ranch and shrugs. "I've been friends with you for years, and I've never so much as gotten a handmade handkerchief from you."

She shoves a forkful of salad into her mouth while I stare blankly. She's not wrong. I've never made her a scarf or a simple skirt or anything. She never asked. But neither had Kit, had he? My shoulders curl forward with defeat. "I'm a bad person, aren't I?"

"Of course not," Heidi scoffs as she repositions her legs on the plush carpet. "You know what you want, and you're focused on the endgame."

"I'm selfish," I mutter to a piece of chicken on the tines of my fork. "I kept reminding Kit that I needed the divorce money. Like that was all that mattered to me."

Heidi shrugs. "It's why you did the show in the first place. I think it was brave of you to be so honest with him."

"Really?"

She nods. "And it says a lot about him that he didn't get petty about it."

I swallow. Kit had never tried to undermine my mission. He offered an alternative, sure. But he never made me feel bad about my work or the time I spent on it. "Is it stupid that I kept waiting for him to just say the right thing, and I could get past all my reasons for saying no?"

"What was the right thing for him to say?" She tilts her head in question, fiddling with a piece of plastic wrap from a to-go container.

I stare at the bottle of vodka on the table, condensation slipping down the smooth glass sides and pooling at the base. Somehow, I still believe that if Kit said the right words in the right order, he'd loosen this knot still lodged in my chest. If he could just say them, I could let go of how afraid I was of loving him.

He apologized for leaving me the first time. He supported my ambition to the point of vetting assistants for me, of offering to be an investor himself. He sent me lunch because he knew I'd forget to eat if he didn't. He noticed which of my dresses I made, always searching for the hidden pockets. And the night we decided to give in, he showed his hand—he knew every intricacy of my work.

I'm afraid of how deeply he knows *me*.

And perhaps the biggest fear of all: What if nothing he said would make it right? At least his brutal silence was something I was comfortable with, even if I drowned in it.

I whisper my reply. "I don't know."

CHAPTER FORTY-TWO
ANDIE

The closet in our tiny apartment feels so much emptier with Kit's three suits missing. I don't know what law of physics makes it feel this way, but I hate it. I sniff to hold back another wave of tears as I pull more of my own clothes off the rack and teeter into the bedroom.

"How are you doing?" Kendra asks as she sits on the end of the bed. When the rest of the cast heard about what happened on decision day, my phone wouldn't stop ringing. None of them wanted the dirty details. They all wanted to make sure I was okay.

"Trying to pull myself together." I shove my clothes into my suitcase with an unseemly grunt. For the first time in a long time, there are no cameras to perform for.

Leslie leans in the doorway, his normally perfectly styled blond hair a mess, like he dropped everything to be here for me. "Have you heard from him since D-Day?"

I shake my head. "I don't expect to. He's very good at disappearing."

"Patrick's tried to reach him," Kendra offers. "But he hasn't heard back."

"I'm not surprised," I mumble. They let me finish emptying the closet in silence. I don't know what else there is to say.

I zip up my suitcase. Before I can move it myself, Leslie takes over, heaving it off the bed and wheeling it out into the living room. I follow, wiping my nose with my sleeve.

"What do you think?" I ask Jamie, who's at the small dining table, poring over my designs and schedule in preparation for Fashion Week.

He looks up with a mischievous grin. "It'll be a lot of work, but I'm in if you are."

"No going back now." I return the fist bump he offers, and it makes me smile too. After returning to my work a couple of days ago, I realized I had too much on my plate to do alone. Jamie was thrilled to get the phone call, eager to get back to his own creative work, too.

Kendra resumes packing up the few items in the kitchen that weren't show-provided. She plucks Kit's drawing off the fridge. "Do you want to keep this?"

"I shouldn't." I walk over to join her and take the drawing from her. "But I can't bring myself to get rid of it." It reminds me of such a gentle, happy time. And I'm realizing I need more of those. I *deserve* that kind of comfort and safety in my life.

There's a soft knock on the door. When I yell for them to come in, Cassidy and Steve enter. She's carrying two trays of coffee orders from the shop down the street. "I heard you were all here."

"Patrick's on a firehouse shift." Kendra shrugs. "He'd be here if he could."

"How are you, Andie?" Cassidy asks as Steve hands out the coffees.

I fold Kit's drawing and tuck it into my skirt pocket. "I'm a mess, honestly."

"One hundred percent understandable," Cassidy nods, her curls bobbing without headphones to get in the way. She looks more rested than I've ever seen her.

"I'll be okay," I shrug, "with time." It took me the better part of a decade to get over Kit the last time. I'm worried this time may ruin me for life. But I don't want any of these people to know that. Not when they're all so happy with how their own lives turned out.

"You're going to turn your pain into art and take over the world." Jamie stands and wraps me in a firm hug.

Leslie joins in, hugging us both. Soon Kendra and Cassidy are part of the pile. Steve gives me a huge grin and wraps his arms around us all.

"I know we're not here to make friends," I sniff, "but I'm really glad I met all of you."

"Maybe the real prize was the friendship we found along the way," Jamie says in a sing-song voice, his cheek pressed against mine.

Everyone groans collectively before squeezing tighter. When we finally break apart, I feel a little lighter. A small piece of my heart snaps back into place, and I smile. We hold our plastic coffee cups up in a toast to the journey of a lifetime. And when I fall asleep in an empty bed in my loft that night, I feel a little less alone.

OCTOBER

CHAPTER FORTY-THREE
KIT

"Have you heard from the doctors yet?" I ask Mom as I bring her another cup of coffee in the living room. I've been crashing at her place for the last couple of weeks because I can't stand to go back to that giant empty suite at the Colonnade. My left hand already feels too light without the wedding band on it.

I still have it, of course.

It sits on my nightstand in my childhood bedroom, wrapped in one of Andie's pocket squares, mocking me.

Mom shakes her head as she takes the mug from me. "Some mail came for you."

I let the change in subject go and follow her gesture to the cream, calligraphed envelope on the dining table. Despite not living at home for over a decade, I always list it as my permanent place of residence. I figure I'll change it when I finally have a place of my own, even though that's not in my near future.

There's no return address. I pop open the flap at the top.

All the air in my lungs whooshes out when I read more calligraphy on cardstock. It requests my presence at Atlanta Fashion Week. Scrawled on the bottom in Andie's harried handwriting is the message: *I don't know the perfect words, but perhaps I can show you.*

"What is it?" Mom asks with a grunt.

When I see she's trying to get up to investigate for herself, I return to the living room, envelope clutched in my hand. "An invitation to a business event," I tell her. It's not exactly a lie, but it's definitely not the truth.

I take a seat in the recliner in the corner and toss the invite on top of the divorce papers I received a few days ago, collecting dust on the side table. I don't know what to do with them. When I got to the first page Andie had already signed, it felt like a fist to the gut. It had only been a couple weeks. Her signature was confident and straightforward on the page, ready to be done with me and our relationship.

I can't blame her. It's not like I gave her an option or left the door open for further communication or . . . any of it. With a frustrated sigh, I turn my attention to a short stack of romance novels. I nudge the one on top with my index finger.

I clear my throat. "I'm sorry I couldn't make things work with Andie."

"Why are you sorry?" She calmly takes a sip of coffee.

I sigh. "Because you want to see me settled, and I can't seem to make that happen."

Mom chuckles. She shakes her head and asks me with a smile, "Did you want it to work for yourself, too? Or just for me?"

I scratch the stubble appearing on my jaw after a few days without shaving. I've been calling in to work while I lick my wounds, so I haven't been pulling myself together like I normally do. Hell, I'm still in sweatpants and a T-shirt and it's almost noon. Patrick invited me out for a beer with Jamie, but I don't know if I can fake a smile, even for them.

Had I wanted it to work for myself? I want to say yes, but I'm not sure that's true. I went into it thinking I could give Mom some peace of mind. Then my wife was Andie, and I thought I could make it right after hurting her all those years ago. I spent our eight weeks trying to show her all the ways I could be a good husband.

Quietly, I answer, "I'm not sure."

"What do you mean, you're not sure?"

"I mean . . ." I look at the romance novels on the table. "I originally signed up for you, and then I spent eight weeks trying to be perfect. For her."

Mom tilts her head in question. "Did she expect you to be perfect?"

I frown, rubbing the spot on my finger where my wedding band used to be. Over the past eight weeks, Andie asked me for a lot of things. But none of them were about being perfect. She asked me to stop trying to solve her problems. She asked me to do the dishes because she hated doing them. She asked me to let her in and tell her how I felt. She asked me to let her be there with me in the hospital.

I love you feels so simple now. Why couldn't I bring myself to say it back to her in the hospital?

"No," I finally say. "She didn't. I think I put that expectation on myself."

"Kit." Mom scoots across the couch so she can rest a motherly hand on my knee. "I'm not sure where you've gotten the idea that you have to be everything to everyone, including yourself."

I swallow. "You gave up so much of your life to raise me, and Andie gave up so much of hers to be on the show and be married to me." I'm still not sure we're eligible for the "damages" listed in the contract, especially after Andie left filming to be with me in the hospital. That's her dream of saving her business, potentially gone.

"It sounds like you feel *guilty* for taking up our time."

Honestly? I do. But I don't know how to voice it.

"Honey," Mom squeezes my arm, "did it ever occur to you that I *chose* to have you?"

I know that. I've always known that. My parents were so young when they had me. Mom chose my dad over being left in her family will. Which is yet another layer to my guilt. "Don't you think you could have had a better life without me? If you hadn't married Dad?"

Mom grunts. "You're not hearing me. I chose to have you, just like I *chose* to love your father."

I meet her gaze. She says she chose it all, but I never thought about choosing to love somebody. I thought it was something that happened organically. That you were born into it or felt the connection and just fell into it. That there was no choice in the matter. None of the love in my life felt like a choice.

"The life you think I gave up to have you?" Mom smacks her hand against her own knee in frustration. "It was my choice to let it go. I was happy to do it. I *chose* to be happy."

"Even though we both . . . left you?" I choke on the words. Dad slipped away in front of our eyes, and then I ran to avoid the memory of walls closing in. To avoid *her* because I couldn't look at her in pain without my lungs collapsing. Leaving was the only way I could breathe again.

"We can't control everything." She sips on her coffee. "It hurt like hell when your father died. It still does. But we chose to love each other every day, even when it was hard. I can't find it in me to wish I'd chosen differently."

I swallow and stare at a spot on the carpet.

She nudges me with her fuzzy slipper. "And you came back."

"Did I, though?" My voice catches. "I took a job that keeps me away from you most of the year because it pays well. So I can take care of you."

"I thought you took your job because you like it." She sets her coffee mug aside.

I frown. I can't remember the last time I thought about whether I *like* my job. I like that it allows me to support her. I like that I can pretend, if I'm halfway across the world, that I don't miss this single-wide trailer and the memories it holds.

But as I think of boarding a plane to Italy, I'm so weary of it all. The running, the pretending, the constant battle between my heart and my head. The life that showed me how to breathe again now threatens to suffocate me. I rub my palm across my forehead to ease the ache spreading beneath my skull.

Mom shakes her head. "You can stop using me as an excuse, Kit."

My instinct is to argue, to circle the same point I made when I came home in the spring. That I do enough for me. But I can't convince myself anymore. I only nod, staring at my hands.

After another long silence, she tells me, "I liked Andie. I thought she'd be good for you."

"I'm sorry I couldn't make it work, Mom."

"For me?"

"For me." My voice breaks, and I clear my throat in an attempt to shake it. I drag my hands down my face and let out a heavy sigh. I feel like I'm on the edge of a breakthrough; I'm just not sure I want to know what the other side looks like.

"You care about her." It's a statement, not a question.

I swallow the lump in my throat and admit with a croak, "I do. But I'm a complication her life can't afford."

Mom's question is gentle. "Who decided that? You, or her?"

I look at the divorce papers on the table. Her signature on the documents is decisive, isn't it? "It doesn't matter. It's over now."

"Forgive me for saying, Kit, but it doesn't seem like you want it to be."

"I don't think it's my choice anymore." I drag my hands through my hair. "I fucked it up."

"Did she tell you that?"

"Her signature on those divorce papers tells me that."

"She chose to divorce you?"

I swallow. Because no. No, she didn't. I'll never know what her choice was.

And I walked away because I will never be the man she needs. I can't face it.

"Kit," Mom says firmly, "did she choose to divorce you?"

I clear my throat and admit the truth. "No. I'm the one that opted out."

Mom rolls her eyes dramatically. "Why would you go and do something like that?"

"Because I was never going to be what she needs, Mom. I'm too . . . difficult to love. With my job and my need to take care of everyone even though I can't be in the same room with them."

"Have you not been listening to a damn thing I just told you?" She smacks me on the leg. "She *chose* to be on the show, and she *chose* to marry you. She *chose* to show up at the hospital when you needed her. I don't care what you think she needs; she showed you that what she wants is *you*." Another smack on my leg. "And you walked away because—what?—that isn't what you think love should look like?"

"I should be able to love her without hurting her."

"Oh, Kit." She shakes her head. "Do you know how many times you hurt me growing up? Too many to count. Loving someone doesn't mean you won't hurt them. It means you'll stay even when you get it wrong."

You know I won't ask you to stay. Andie's words come back to me, her image framed against the bark of an oak tree. She knew I would leave, knew I would do this, and she told me she loved me anyway.

"You've never hurt me," I murmur.

"That's a lie." Mom shakes her head. "Aside from all the times you were angry with me growing up, for whatever reason, I can tell I hurt you by not being . . . present, myself, after your dad died. And yet here you are, still talking to me. Forgiving me for my misstep. *Choosing* to let it go and love me still."

"That's different."

"Is it?"

I frown. It *is* different, right? I think of the day we fought at the hospital. Andie was furious with me. For a lot of reasons.

But all the same, she let me in. She told me all the ways she was upset with me. Then she told me she wanted to be there for me when I needed her. She let me into her bed and into her body and into her heart. Because I asked. She chose to do it. Even after I hurt her.

"Do you love her?" Mom's words interrupt my thoughts.

"Yes." The word escapes my lips before I can stop it. I love her. Fiercely. I can't love her perfectly, but I can love her with all of me.

"And she wanted to stay in the marriage?"

I swallow, gripping my knees so tightly my knuckles blanch. "I don't know. I didn't let her answer."

Mom throws her hands up in frustration. "Then what the hell are you doing slouching around my house?"

"I thought it was my house, too."

"That was before you got married." She says it with a smile. "It's time to build your own home now."

I shake my head slowly. "She signed the divorce papers. She's done."

"Why don't you let her choose what she wants instead of rejecting yourself for her? Why? Because you think you're not good enough for her?" Mom looks at the papers on the table too.

"I'm not." I shake my head. I am definitely not good enough for Andie. Not after this.

"Her choice to make, Kit. You are so easy to love; I can't imagine she doesn't. Face it. Let her choose you."

Our eyes meet, and I swallow as hope blossoms in my chest for the first time in weeks. If Mom is right about choosing to love someone, do I dare hope that Andie might still choose me? Even after I hurt her again?

I don't want to spend my life hurting her. But I remember her falling apart at the dinner with her mom after she announced another marriage. Andie didn't need another person to come in and out of her life. She needed someone who would stay, even when things got a little rocky. All I've done so far is leave.

Do I even deserve to ask for her forgiveness this time?

"You do." Mom nods, because apparently, I said that last bit out loud. "You always deserve love and respect, and that includes forgiveness."

I chew on my cheek while I mull it over. My big boss Hammersmith is in town this week. It might be time to have a difficult conversation about my future with the Colonnade. For once, what I need isn't their security and giant paychecks.

"Don't sit here and wallow, wishing you could have done it differently." Mom insists. "Do it differently, and give her the choice to keep loving you, just like you've chosen to love her even now, after you've seen her signature on the divorce papers."

CHAPTER FORTY-FOUR

KIT

"Did you seriously think we wouldn't find out you were on a *reality show*?" Hammersmith paces in the living room of my suite at the Colonnade. He called me in after I'd been dodging all responsibility at work for the last two weeks. His slicked-back dark hair shines under the recessed lighting, his mustache twitching with annoyance.

"I wasn't hiding it." I shrug. "Not really. I just didn't think it would matter since I didn't miss work at all."

"You went on a whole-ass *vacation*." He tosses a glare my way and keeps pacing. "You brought cameras on our property. They tried to get Clyde to sign a release form to be on TV."

"He didn't have to sign it," I offer, refusing to let Hammersmith get under my skin. "And the trip wasn't on the company's dime." I've worked for this company for five years, always at their beck and call, going to the literal ends of the earth whenever I was asked.

I've taken two weeks to be miserable and away from it all. I'm allowed to do that.

"He didn't sign it!" Hammersmith pauses and shoves his hands into his pockets, looking down on me in my seat on the buttery leather couch. "And I hear you got married, too."

"That point is moot." I scratch at the stubble on my jaw in an effort to keep myself from breaking down in front of Hammersmith. I'm still working out a plan to get Andie back, but it's illegal for them to fire me just because I got married.

"Things didn't work out with your reality TV wife?" Hammersmith barks out a laugh. "Who could have seen that coming?"

I frown, staring at the modern marble coffee table. Andie and I were so close to having it all, and I blew it up because I was . . . afraid. Not of her, not really. I was afraid that keeping her would mean giving up this life I've built. But what is the point of building all of it and working this damn hard if I can't enjoy what I've *earned*?

"Regardless of the show"—I lean forward and rest my elbows on my knees—"my mom is here, and she's still going through treatment for breast cancer. I have friends here. A home."

Hammersmith narrows his eyes. "What are you saying?"

"I'm asking to work from Atlanta." I shrug. "I can travel to different locations for check-ins, but I want to live here. Settle down."

"What's gotten into you?" Hammersmith examines me like a specimen under a microscope.

"Things change. I've changed." I tug on the cuffs of my suit jacket. It suddenly feels too small, too structured. "And you owe me, Hammersmith. I got you the Paris property. And the one in Sydney."

He takes a deep breath. "After all the bullshit you've put us through the last few months—forcing the transfer, the reality show, dodging all our efforts to reach you the last couple of weeks—wouldn't you say *you* owe *us*?"

I run my hands through my hair. "What do you have in mind?"

"You, on a plane to Montalcino, tomorrow." He holds his hands out, palms up, like he's offering me the deal of a lifetime.

"And if I say no?" I raise my brows in question.

"Then you're just not a good fit for our company." He glowers from his spot above me.

It's doing nothing but remind me of all the hoops I've jumped through for this company. All the late night phone calls I answered. All the flights I ran to catch and the problems I worked through the weekend to solve. All the holidays I missed with my mom. The fight with Andie in the hospital hallway, where she asked me to stay and I was too afraid to let go of the security this job provided me. So afraid to lose my financial safety net, I may have lost the best thing to ever walk into my life. Permanently.

"Well." I slap my hands on my thighs. "That decides it, then."

I stand and button my suit jacket.

"I knew you'd make the right choice, son." Hammersmith smacks me on the shoulder. "Sarah has your flight information."

"Tell her to forward it to Clyde." I hold out my hand for him to shake. "I'm not going."

Hammersmith pauses, then laughs. A deep belly laugh that ends in a wheeze. "That's good. That's very good. I almost believed you for a second."

"Believe it." I shrug, digging the keycard to the penthouse out of my pocket. I smack it on the coffee table. "Consider this my resignation. Effective immediately."

"There is nothing worth blowing up your career with us for," Hammersmith blusters, hot on my heels as I make for the door.

"That's where you're wrong." I open the door. "I appreciate everything you've done for me. All that you've taught me. All the opportunities to see the world and grow my skill set. But I'm at a point in my life where no amount of money or promise of promotion is enough, not when I can't enjoy the life it affords me."

"You walk out that door and you will never work with the Colonnade again!" His shout echoes in the marble entryway.

I don't flinch, instead setting my jaw. "That's a risk I'm willing to take."

He glares at me, eyes bulging, face turning so red it's almost purple. I've never seen him so angry. And I've never seen him look so small.

I reach my hand out as a peace offering. "Thank you for everything. But it's time for me to go."

I wait for him to take it, but he never does. I let out a sigh, give him a nod, and say, "Goodbye, Hammersmith. Best of luck."

As the elevator doors close behind me, I can't help but smile. The man reflected by the elevator door is not afraid of what will come next. He can handle it. He's happy. Bold. *Free.*

CHAPTER FORTY-FIVE
ANDIE

"Okay," I say on another turn of my studio, "tell me where we are."

It's early in the morning, with five days to go until I show at Fashion Week. The pressure is on. The coffee in my hand and the sun spilling through my wall of windows do nothing to calm my crackling nerves.

"Dresses two, seven, thirteen, and eighteen were finished and bagged up yesterday," Ruby informs me, swiping at her tablet.

Kit was right about me needing help, and he'd already paid for some. After Jamie reviewed my plans and said he was in, he came with reinforcements, bringing Ruby and Catarina along with him. I have an actual *team*, and while it comes with new stresses, it does mean I can delegate.

"That means dresses one through ten are done, completely." Catarina crosses off a couple of lines in her notebook. "I have a lineup of models coming through tomorrow, and you can make your final choices."

"This has to be perfect," I say for the thousandth time this week. Jamie nods knowingly from one of the dress forms, where he's working on completing the beading on a bodice.

Ruby and Catarina don't comment on my neuroses. They've seen enough of it by now to know it has nothing to do with them; they do some goddamn amazing work. They keep their heads down and their focus sharp. I love them for it. Where did Jamie find them?

"We'll be done in plenty of time for you to make your appointment this afternoon," Catarina keeps going.

He's not here to see it, but I imagine Kit would be proud I squeezed in some time for self-care in the days leading up to the main event. In addition to going to bed by ten every night, I've been building in time for myself during the day. Yesterday, I had my hair done. Tonight, it's a manicure. Maybe one day I'll be able to erase his touch from my skin.

My heart throbs with the thought of him. Everything is so raw, still. Even now, I look at the windows and think of him begging me to let him in, to let him know what I need. I wish I'd been better at expressing it that night, or even by our fight before decision day.

Maybe he'd have chosen to stay if I had.

Yesterday, Optimax emailed saying they would cut me a check for damages as soon as a copy of the divorce papers was returned to them. But only with both signatures. Kit hasn't signed. Or at least, he hasn't done me a solid and sent the document to the show's lawyers. It's one last, tenuous connection to him, and I'm not sure how I feel about it.

My eyes fall to his drawing on hotel paper; I taped it to my drafting table after we moved out of our tiny apartment, and I can't bring myself to remove it.

"Hey," Jamie acknowledges me when I walk over to observe his work. It's perfect. Because of course it is.

"Hi." I force a smile. "Have I told you today that you're a lifesaver?"

He laughs as he pulls his thread taut. "Only twice."

I chew on my lip as he threads another bead and tacks it to the bodice.

"You okay?" he asks gently.

"Stressed," I admit. That's another change I've made since Kit left. I don't tell people I'm fine when I'm clearly not.

Jamie raises an eyebrow. "Just about Fashion Week?"

"No." I grab a metal stool from a few feet away and take a seat next to him. "Have you heard from Kit?"

He offers a kind smile. "We've tried to reach him. He's texted back, so I know he's alive, but no, we haven't talked."

I let out a sigh and tap my fingers against my mug. It's too much to ask for him to reach out after I sent him an invitation to Fashion Week, right?

"I'm sorry, Andie." Jamie shakes his head. "I really thought you two were going to make it. We all did."

I shrug and try to keep my voice from breaking. "Me too."

Catarina waves a small envelope from across the room. "This came for you."

Desperate as I am for some word from Kit, I practically run across the studio and snatch it from her fingers. She doesn't flinch, but she does smile. I hope I can afford to keep her on after the time Kit already paid for runs out.

There's no return address. I rip open the envelope and pull out the contents. It's a note card from a hotel in the Florida Keys and a glossy photo of my mom and Jim. They're swimming in a lagoon in life vests, smiling while they pet a dolphin who's poking his snout out of the water.

I've never seen my mom swimming. It's such a stupid thought to have now, but growing up, bathing suits were worn to be seen, to draw attention to the best parts of her body. Not for actually swimming.

Frowning, I look at the notecard. It's one sentence scrawled in my mom's handwriting: *It's different this time.*

Tears nip at the corners of my eyes, and I take in a deep breath, only for it to get snagged in my throat. A tear falls and I wipe it away with the heel of my hand.

The knot in my chest I wished Kit could untangle just loosened another degree. Every seam I stitched together for this line has been doing the work too. I've been digging my raw fingertips into the mass of fear and teasing out the truth, little by little. Maybe one day I'll have solved it completely.

I sniff and read the note again, running my fingers over the words. "It's different this time."

"Hmm?" Ruby looks up from her tablet. "Did you say something?"

I shake my head, clearing my throat. "No. Nothing. Except—"

Both women and Jamie look at me expectantly.

Clutching the note and the picture to my chest, I ask them all, "Would it be crazy to attempt just one more design?"

CHAPTER FORTY-SIX

KIT

This tent is crowded. I pull the cardstock invitation from my breast pocket and stare at it again.

It's been a week since I accepted a job with Mason Architecture here in Atlanta and moved into their cozy library office in a restored craftsman home. I trace over Andie's handwritten note at the bottom of the invitation.

It's not a confession of love or an offer of forgiveness, but it's enough. There was no way in hell I was going to miss this day. So I put on a suit for the first time since my conversation with Hammersmith—the one she'd fixed the cuff on, and the first pocket square she gave me—and showed up ready to offer her everything I can think of.

I locate my seat only to find it buttressed on either side by Leslie and Patrick. Kendra sits on Patrick's other side, beaming. When I sit, Patrick smacks me on the back. "Damn, I'm glad you showed, man."

"Wouldn't miss it." I shake Leslie's hand. After I take in Patrick's *Miami Vice*–style suit, I tell him, "You look good."

"Kendra picked it out." He smiles sheepishly.

"Where's Jamie?" I ask Leslie.

"Backstage." He gestures in that direction. "He's been working with Andie for the last few weeks."

At my frown, Patrick tells me, "We've been *trying* to talk to you, but you won't come out from under that rock you ran to."

Just as the lights lower, I say, "Next week. We'll hang out for real."

My heart pounds against my rib cage and I hold my breath, waiting for what's next.

Music starts up—a steady, throbbing beat coming from speakers mounted on the stage. A projector casts a spinning kaleidoscope of flowers on the stage.

The first model emerges in a structured dress. The bodice flares out at the model's waist into a curved, voluminous skirt. When the model walks, the fabric shimmers in the lights, and I'm not quite sure how Andie pulled off the effect. It all looks a bit like armor—a chest plate to protect a soft heart beneath it, a Spartan shield formation forms the skirt—and it doesn't take me long to understand. Geometric. Triangles.

The dome in the gardens at the Colonnade.

I swallow the lump in my throat, waiting for what's next.

It's structured, too, but Andie's taken the triangle panels from the first bodice and opened them to make a sort of vest worn over a simpler gown. The bodice has a spray of rose gold beads arching over the model's hip and curling up toward her navel. The fabric of this skirt is softer, too, moving a bit more with the model's walk around the runway.

With the next dress, the outer shell is gone. It's a simpler silhouette, with a skirt that appears liquid under the stage lights. I itch to run it through my fingers to see if it feels as cool and refreshing as it looks.

Each dress flows more naturally than the one that came before it. It's a carefully crafted narrative of a bride coming undone. When the tenth dress emerges with a plunging neckline and beaded bodice, my mind is back in Andie's studio, making her mine.

She let me in. She begged me to break down her walls, and I did. But I didn't think I'd have to offer my own heart up on a platter to keep her doors open. It's terrifying, but I'm ready to do it now. No running this time, I've made sure of that.

I can only hope she chooses me.

The final dress is a slip of a thing, hardly any form to it at all. The model's shoulders are bare, with nothing holding up the bodice, and with no visible fastenings. I'm not exactly sure how Andie got the ethereal, loose shape to stay on the model without falling off. It looks like some kind of magic as the skirt flows into a short train on the runway. The crowd around me oohs and ahs as the model struts by.

As the parade of models comes out in their dresses again, in a line, I hold my breath. Andie emerges arm-in-arm with the final model, beaming.

I gasp when I see it. She's carrying a bouquet and wearing the dress she wore on *our* wedding day, except she's modified it. The most jarring change is the color: it's a bright crimson. But she also shortened the length on the skirt to her knees. When she's close enough, I can see how the edges of the dress are raw—she left it unfinished, messy, even going so far as to undo the beading around the neckline as it scoops over her breasts—I find myself standing, my legs propelling me toward the back of the stage.

No running away. It's time.

CHAPTER FORTY-SEVEN

ANDIE

If backstage is chaos, this side of the curtain is *loud*. There's applause coming from all sides, and I try to hold it together as I march down the runway with my models. In my designs.

Holy shit, they're applauding my designs.

All at once, I remember why the hell I'm even doing this: to land some investors and take these designs across the country. Buoyed by the applause coming from the audience, it's the first time I realize I might actually accomplish what I set out to do.

Back at the beginning of the runway, I turn to give the audience a little bow as I attempt not to bawl in relief. Through the haze of the spotlight, right off stage left, in the crowd, I glance at the seat I reserved, hoping against all hope it was the right thing to do. To put my heart on the line one last time.

While Patrick, Kendra, and Leslie are giving me a standing ovation, Kit's reserved chair is empty.

It feels like a punch in the stomach. I force myself to stand an inch taller, spine rigid. I will not break down.

He left. After saying he wanted to divorce me. Then he basically fell off the face of the earth, just like the last time. It was silly to hope he'd show.

And dammit, I'll be okay. I have to be. Even though that knot in my chest is pulling tighter with every breath.

I should know better than this, better than to hold out hope. It was only luck that I'd ever seen him again after the first time he walked away. If it had been up to him, he probably wouldn't have chosen to see me again.

As I return backstage, the applause here is even louder, punctuated with whoops and hollers. Jamie is up on the scaffolding, telling everyone to head to the dressing area and hang up their dresses. In the flurry of commotion, Catarina pulls me aside. "I've got someone who wants to speak with you. About investing in your line."

"What?" I snap my head in her direction. "Already?"

Catarina nods, beaming. "They have a small conference room inside. It's the last door on the left. He's waiting when you're ready."

I swallow, giving her a nod. Without thinking, I pull her and Ruby into a bear hug and tell them tearfully, "Thank you so much, both of you. You made this silly dream of mine come true and I—"

My voice cuts out when they both squeeze me tightly. "Best show of my life!" Ruby sounds like she means it.

"Go meet your guy." Catarina nudges me toward an exit. "You've earned this moment, Andie. Take it."

I wipe the tears off my face as I swallow the lump in my throat, riding the wave of catharsis to the conference room inside the main building.

I open the door to find a man in a bespoke suit with his back to me. He's holding a stack of paperwork. My heart lurches in my chest when he turns around, a half grin hooking the corner of his pretty mouth.

My knees very nearly give out, because it's the same view and the same look he gave me almost four months ago, walking down the aisle in my very own wedding dress—the one I'm still wearing—to start the beginning of a truly transformative experience.

Kit.

He came. And he's wearing one of my pocket squares.

I give him a shaky smile, too afraid to guess at what it means that he's here. "Hey, stranger."

He turns to fully face me, eyes tracing a path from my toes to my face. It feels like his hands all over me again. "Hey," he offers with a wistful smile. "You look beautiful."

Tears prick the backs of my eyes again. "You always tell me that."

"It's always true." We stand on opposite ends of the room, afraid to get closer.

The way he's looking at me right now, his eyes soft with hope and apology, something clicks in my brain.

He's always, always told me I look beautiful. Every time I saw him. From our kiss at the altar to every day after. Because there it is, the perfect thing for him to say: *You look beautiful.*

It was right there, the whole time.

I can't believe it took me this long to figure it out.

I take in a sharp breath. "Kit, when you say I look beautiful, what is it you're really trying to say?"

"How I feel." He lets out a huff of laughter and takes a step closer.

It's all the invitation I need—my feet hurry across the room as I give in to the pull humming between us. Kit's here, and he wants to talk, and that must mean—

My eyes fall to the stack of paper next to him on the small table. I stare at the letterhead, frozen.

These are the divorce papers I sent to him weeks ago. And on top of them, there's a check for a hundred thousand dollars. One of the official kinds, from a bank. Which means this move was premeditated. He came in here ready to hand me divorce papers and a pile of money.

He takes a deep breath. "I want to invest in Andrea Dresser Designs. Silently. I don't want a say in what you do."

I roll my tongue in my mouth, trying to absorb the bitter taste of disappointment. How dare he do this on the best damn night of my life? I thought for a split second he was here to . . . I don't know . . . ask for forgiveness? To tell me he made a mistake?

But my vision blurs as I close my eyes and slowly shake my head.

Despite all of this, I still love him. My heart is still reaching for him through my rib cage. And my mind knows we can still work it out, if we do this our way.

I take one more deep breath and open my eyes, ignoring the screaming in my chest as I simply stare at the divorce papers like a ticking time bomb. Now or never, I suppose.

CHAPTER FORTY-EIGHT

KIT

Andie stares at the divorce papers I brought with me, and time stops.

She sniffs and swipes a tear away from her eye. "I don't want your money, Kit."

Shit. I swallow. She doesn't want any piece of me, not even something so impersonal as a check from my accountant. This isn't how this is supposed to go. We've barely said two words to each other, and I'm already fucking it up.

"I'm sorry," I blurt out. "We never talked about decision day, and I—"

"That was your choice." Her hand curls into a fist at her side. She closes her eyes, takes a deep breath, then says, "Kit, I . . . I've missed you."

Her voice breaks, and it nearly bowls me over.

She doesn't give me any time to recover, dropping her hands to her sides and holding them open, palms facing out in a gesture of surrender. "I'm sorry for how I treated you on the show."

I clench my jaw, holding my breath. Afraid of what's happening.

Her eyes are open and honest and glassy with tears as she meets mine. "You were so kind to me, making sure I was taken care of in ways I haven't even thought of. And I didn't appreciate any of it. I'm sorry."

"Andie." Her name is a gentle plea coming from my lips. She shouldn't be sorry. I was the one who left.

"You said you couldn't be the man I wanted." She speaks a little louder, more sure of herself. "I made you believe that. And you're so goddamn selfless, you left. So I could get what I needed."

The words claw up my throat, desperate for her to hear them. "Please, I—"

"I never got to tell you," she says, voice wavering. She clenches her jaw and looks me in the eye, so I know she means what comes next. "You made me so *happy* every day we were together. Even when we were fighting. You were always on my side, fighting *for* me, not against me, and I've never had that. I didn't know how to accept love so selfless, so I let you think I didn't need it."

The backs of my eyes grow hot, tears forming.

"I love you, Kit." Her voice breaks again, and she looks away. "I want you to live a life that makes you happy, and if that doesn't include me, I—"

"Andie." I shake my head.

"No, it's fine." She sniffs, reaching for the divorce papers. "I'll just . . . make sure everything's in order and let you go."

I stand frozen in time as she begins thumbing through the document on the table. Her hands shake with each turn of the page, and my heart sinks a little lower. I'm not sure how we got here, her thinking I actually want to leave.

Suddenly, she stops, her eyes laser focused on the page. Her lips twist into a frown, and she frantically flips a few more pages. She stops once more, this time letting out a gasp.

"You didn't sign," she whispers.

I run a hand through my hair and take the plunge. "Of course I didn't sign."

Her hands tremble. She lets go of the divorce papers and presses her palms to the tabletop, bracing for impact. "Why not?"

"Since the day we got stuck in the front row in that damn art class, you've been it for me. I didn't want to leave back then, and it killed me to walk away on decision day. The only way I'll sign those papers is if you tell me—right now—that's what you really want."

Her whisper is nearly swallowed by the distance between us. "What?"

"I never told you much about my life before I met you, and that's my fault. But I need you to know that I have loved you in the only way

I knew how." My voice breaks, tears threatening to spill over. I bury the heels of my hands in my eye sockets and take a deep breath. "It wasn't until marrying you and learning you all over again that I finally understood that what I thought love was . . . was all wrong. I thought you needed some fairy-tale perfect prince to solve your problems and make sure you never knew what it was like to not have something you wanted."

"No." She shakes her head, new tears forming in her eyes. She steps closer, close enough to slide her hands down my lapels. "I don't need you to solve my problems for me."

"I know that now," I whisper. My hands are shaking at my sides, and I don't know what to do with them. I'm afraid to touch her in case she disappears like a mirage. "You needed one thing from me—you needed me to stay. When we were fighting, looking at the end of everything we built, you needed me to show you I would always be there. And I left. Again. Worse—I sent you away."

She's nodding as her chin quivers.

"I'm sorry, Andie." My voice shatters, and it's all I can do to reach for her. "I'm so sorry I left. I love you so much; I couldn't stand to think I failed you." I wrap my arms around her waist and crush her into me. She buries her face in my chest and sobs. Through my own tears, heart aching, I say, "I know I broke your trust. I know you have no reason to believe me, but I have loved every single day we spent together. Even when we were fucking it up."

One of her sobs comes out as a laugh against my chest.

"Let's start over." I stroke her hair. "If you still don't want me to invest in your company, we can sign the divorce papers and get you the money. Then let's . . . date. Let's be together like normal people. I found a firm in Atlanta to work for, and I found a house in Decatur I'd like to get your opinion on. I'm not going anywhere. I want to date you for as long as it takes to build that trust back, because I love you and I want you to know I'm here. I'm always going to be here, no matter how rough this gets. Just . . . will you be my girlfriend again, Andie?"

She shakes her head against my chest, curling her fingers around my lapels. My heart breaks all over again. She uses her fists to put some distance between us, then gives my lapels one final tug. Her answer is quiet, but final. "No."

Her lips pull into a sorrowful frown as her eyes wander over me. It feels like she's memorizing me before saying goodbye. I can't breathe for the pain of it.

"I don't want your money, and I don't want to be your girlfriend." She swallows after she says it, like it was bitter on her tongue.

My hands fall away from her body, preparing to let her walk out of here, because there's no world in which I keep her.

"After all this"—she gestures weakly to the walls of the room—"there's only one thing I want from you." She takes a step to the side so she can scoop the divorce papers off the table.

"What do you need me to do?" I ask, terrified her answer to that question is *go.* I'll give her any goddamn thing she wants, but I'm not sure I can leave on my own volition. My feet are rooted to the spot, and I'm suspended in time.

She holds the divorce papers between us. I swallow, unable to stop my racing heart. Her whisper is a gunshot in the silence.

"Stay."

My lungs seize, and I'm afraid to break the fragile quiet between us in this room.

Her eyes search mine for the longest minute of my life. She's the one to break the silence with a trembling plea. "Kit, just . . . stay. Be my husband. Let me be your wife. We have been downright *awful* at this marriage thing, but I don't want to start over. I love what we have, and I wouldn't change any of it. So . . . stay. Please."

I blink, unable to tell if I'm hallucinating. Andie is asking me to stay married to her? After I failed her over and over, she still wants . . . *me*?

She chose me.

"Kit," she whispers, shaking the papers between us. "Say something."

I let out the air in my lungs and say with a laugh, "My mom is going to be so insufferable when she finds out she was right."

"About what?"

"You."

She tilts her head in question. "What about me?"

Like those words broke the space-time continuum, I startle into motion. I take the papers from her and toss them to the side haphazardly, closing the space between us as she gasps. She melts into me as I pull her so close I can feel her heartbeat in tandem with mine.

"Burn that damn document. You're perfect." I tangle my fingers in her hair and drag her lips to meet mine. "I'll stay." I steal her gasp with a kiss. "I love you; I'll stay." I repeat the words between kisses, over and over, until we're breathless with it.

She drags her thumb along my bottom lip. "You bought a house?"

"Not yet." I wince. "I wanted to make sure it was something you like . . . I mean, you don't have to move in, or anything, if you—"

"Of course I do." She smiles. "We're married. And someone has to make sure I eat."

I laugh.

"One more thing." She presses her forehead to mine. "Or . . . two more things."

"Anything," I agree without knowing the details, running my thumb along her jaw, awed by even this small piece of her.

"I'm not changing my name," she says with finality.

I can't help but smile when I shake my head. "I'd never ask you to, Andie. Besides, your name is a *brand* now."

She smiles, biting her lip. I take the invitation to pull her close and kiss her again.

"And the second thing?"

She has a twinkle in her eyes as she tells me, "I'm keeping that pencil."

My laugh echoes in the small room. I lift her off the ground and kiss her hard on the mouth. "Keep it. I'll buy you ten more."

She shakes her head. "I love that one because it's yours."

I raise a brow.

"And maybe because it's the one I drew all the dresses in my show with." At my laughter, she says, "It's a *really* nice pencil, Kit."

We're mid-kiss when there's a knock on the door. It swings open before we can answer. The same assistant who helped get me to Andie today stands in the doorway, open-mouthed. "Sorry, I—"

"It's okay." Andie giggles. Reluctantly, I set her down. She's still working tonight, as much as I'd love to whisk her away for some more *private* reconciliation time. "What's going on?"

"Um." The assistant steps aside and gestures to the women in the doorway behind her, "This is Molly Birmingham from Down the Aisle Bridal, with—"

"Odette Thorne," Andie says, eyes going wide. Quickly she smooths her hair, and as she walks around me, I straighten her skirt. If these women are important enough for Andie to know them by name, she'll want to look her best.

Molly and Odette step into the room and eye the divorce papers scattered on the ground like it's the last day of school in a summer musical. When Odette returns her gaze to Andie with a raised brow, Andie shrugs. "We—that is, Kit—I mean—"

I step forward and offer my hand. "Kit Watson." I shake both their hands. "Andie's *husband*."

Andie blushes but holds her head high as she offers a handshake as well. Odette gives Andie a mischievous grin. "I can see where you get the inspiration for your designs." She tilts her head toward me, and I can't help but smile.

"Yes," Andie agrees solemnly. "He's a *big* help, if you know what I mean."

"You'll have to tell me all about it over coffee," Molly says. "Next week? Ms. Thorne alerted me to your talent, and I'd like to discuss a potential partnership."

Odette holds a perfectly manicured finger up as if to tell us to hold on a moment. "*After* you agree to design my gown, of course."

"Of course." Andie nods. "I'll get you on the schedule right away."

Her fingers curl around mine, and she squeezes. I squeeze back, my chest swelling with pride. She did it. Andie fucking *did it*.

"Next week is perfect," Andie says smoothly. She looks to her assistant. "Catarina, will you make sure Ms. Birmingham has my number so we can pick a time? And block out the next custom dress slot for Ms. Thorne."

Catarina nods, already pulling out her phone. As Molly turns to give her information, I whisper in Andie's ear, "You are everything, Ms. Dresser."

"Oh my God!" Kendra squeals from the doorway, and soon we're crushed in a cast group hug. All of us still married.

It seems the matchmakers got it right.

ONE YEAR LATER

EPILOGUE
ANDIE

"Jamie and Leslie, one year later!" Petra gestures for the crowd beyond the soundstage to cheer. They do, including whooping and howling. It makes me smile. Jamie and Leslie have just finished talking about how they adopted a Bernese mountain dog puppy named Couscous.

When the crowd calms down, Petra gives everyone a sly smile. "Speaking of happily ever afters, let's talk to one of *First Look at Forever*'s favorite couples!"

The crowd roars once more as Kit and I walk onto the soundstage set up to look like some kind of modern pink and semi-cozy living room. All the seating is angled toward the cameras, and everyone is perched on the edge of their chairs, dressed to the nines.

Kit keeps his hand on the small of my back all the way across the stage, and he even reminds me to wave and smile at the crowd. I let out a breath when we plop down on the pink sofa on stage left.

The show aired a full nine months after we filmed, and this reunion episode is live. I've avoided all cameras, save my cell phone for the occasional TikTok, since we stopped filming. I feel like a toddler learning to walk all over again.

"Welcome." Petra smiles at us, the glitter on her cheekbones sparkling in the spotlights.

"It's good to be here," Kit says smoothly, tugging on the lapels of his jacket. He's wearing a pocket square I made him—yellow silk. He wore it because it matches the golden underlay of my dress—a one-shoulder number with a snug bodice and my signature flowy skirt overlaid with golden metallic organza, including hidden pockets, of course.

"Now, on decision day, Kit"—Petra glances at the branded notecards in her hands, then pins him with a glare—"you decided to divorce."

He nods. "I did."

"You never really explained why." Petra leans forward, resting her chin on her fist.

Kit clears his throat and leans on the arm of the sofa. "There were a lot of reasons, but the biggest one was that I felt I was never going to be the man Andie needed. So it felt easier to let her go."

"Andie," Petra turns her pout at me. "You seemed so upset after Kit gave his answer."

"I was." I agree. "I had fallen in love with him. Again. And he decided to walk away."

Petra nods, her brows drawing together.

I take a deep breath and say, "You see, we both gave in to what scared us."

"We did." Kit rests a hand on my knee and squeezes. "And it was the biggest mistake I've ever made."

Petra smiles.

Kit looks at me. "Andie was the one who was willing to put her heart on the line, and she invited me to see her show at Atlanta Fashion Week."

"So, the question everyone wants to ask is"—Petra looks between us—"are you together now?"

I smile at Kit. He squeezes my knee again. "Yes," I say. "We are."

The crowd gets loud, cheering us on.

When it quiets down, Kit looks at Petra. "Thankfully, we realized our mistake before it was too late. We never signed our divorce papers."

The crowd applauds. I smile, blinking into the stage lights.

When the applause settles, Petra says, "On that note, we have some photos from your vow renewal a few weeks ago." She gives the crowd a sly look. "Would you like to see them?"

The crowd cheers, and the first photo of Kit and me at the altar for the second time flashes across the projector screen behind Petra. The cheers melt into *awwwws*.

We're standing, hand in hand, in the garden of the home we bought together in Decatur. Heidi was the officiant, with tears in her eyes the whole time.

Looking at these pictures on the projector, I'm suddenly so glad we decided to do it again. I'll never forget seeing Kit waiting for me the first time, back when we had no idea what we were in for. The heart-stopping terror teetering on the edge of pure elation is a heady mix that I will always, always associate with him.

But the second time, I got to drink everything in, because I knew what I was walking into.

Petra says, "Andie, did you design your own dress?"

"I did." I smile at the picture of us. "It was the only option."

After several arguments with Kit, I finally relented and, instead of working on my dress into all the wee hours of the morning, I blocked out the time I would have used on a dress for a client to use on myself.

A lot of things have changed about our relationship this go-around, but his relentless insistence that I was worth the time and attention I gave to others was one thing that hadn't. It never wavered, and a year later, there were split seconds in which I began to find myself believing I was worth it too.

So, during daylight hours, I designed and constructed my own dress. It was relatively simple compared to a lot of the dresses I send down the aisle. There's no intricate beading or scalloped hems or even a small train. Instead, the magic is in the construction. The panels of the corset are a pale taupe, while I covered the boning in pure white, so you could see the amount of construction that went into it. Normally, I make a point of hiding everything that holds the dress together. The more mysterious the inner workings, the more magical it looks. At least to the untrained eye.

But it didn't even feel like a choice when I sat down to design my own dress. I didn't want to hide a thing. The structure—something that isn't necessarily glamorous—is out there for everyone to see. The real work behind the dress is on full display, and it's exactly the statement I want to make.

"She was stunning," Kit interjects. "She's always gorgeous, but my poor heart wasn't prepared for her in this dress."

I roll my eyes at him.

"I mean it." He reaches for my hand and squeezes. "I'll remember how you looked walking toward me for the rest of my life."

"You cleaned up well, yourself," I tease. He wore a simple black suit and crisp white button-down. A basic black tie around his neck. A pocket square made of the same taupe as in my dress. What the photo doesn't show is that I also embroidered the buttons on his shirt to all contain a small white flower.

"Speaking of," Petra smirks at both of us. "Andie, your appreciation for Kit's . . . physique has become an internet meme."

"I am aware, yes." Since the show aired, I haven't been able to go a single day without being tagged in one of them. Once, someone even stopped us on the street mimicking my obsession with Kit's thighs.

Petra looks at the screen. "Let's look back at those moments."

I bury my face in my hands as a montage plays of every time I mentioned Kit's thighs. In between are gratuitous shots of his legs, just for fun. For a while, a mashup of me saying "thighs, thighs, thighs" was a trending sound on TikTok. I used it to advertise a dress I designed with a high slit up the left thigh.

Kit laughs beside me while I continue to blush furiously. The crowd's laughter sounds genuine, at the very least.

Finally, the montage ends, and Petra asks, "Are his thighs still amazing?"

"That's a great question," I tease. I gesture for Kit to stand up.

He waves it off, but the crowd only gets louder.

When Jamie cheers from across the stage, Kit takes a dramatic breath, then stands up for inspection.

The crowd cheers him on as he walks across the stage, posing at intervals, feeding into the applause. Of course, I take the time to enjoy the show too. Kit's thighs really are a work of fucking art, and I make sure to enjoy them daily. In a fitted suit, he looks absolutely delicious, and I'm already thinking about how to reward him for this display when we get home.

When he finally sits back down, waving off the crowd's audible disappointment, Petra gestures to the next photo on the screen. "Tonight isn't the first reunion for season three, is it?"

The picture she's pulled up is one of all of us at our vow renewal—Kendra riding piggyback on Patrick, who put on his baseball cap with his suit; Jamie and Leslie in a salsa pose with serious faces; Kit and me, laughing so hard our ribs ached. Cassidy and Steve lounge in chairs in front of all of us, wearing Wayfarer sunglasses and playing it cool.

I smile every time I look at it. It reminds me of the journey we took together.

"I'm so grateful we got to have everyone with us." I press a hand to my chest and look across the soundstage at the other couples. My heart has grown to fit all of them in there. I wouldn't be where I am without them.

After meeting with investors, I was able to bring Jamie on full-time. Catarina designed an entire five-year plan for my business, which now included manufactured dresses in bridal salons across the South. According to her charts and graphs, we were on track to expand to the Northeast later this year. Ruby oversaw most of the design decisions for those dresses. I designed them, of course, but with manufacturing came modifications to balance cost and profit. Ruby had more knowledge in that arena, and after a year working with her, I trust her taste implicitly. She knew how to swap a more expensive fabric for a less pricey one without sacrificing the integrity of the dress.

I still spent time making dresses for demanding brides, but I cut my calendar by a third and upped my prices. Kit, Catarina, and Jamie teamed up to convince me that was not only feasible, but absolutely necessary as my business grew. It also allowed me more room to take the classes I needed to finish my business degree.

Truly, there are many days I cannot believe this is my life. That I built. Not without help, I learned, but it's mine, nonetheless.

"And Kit," Petra guides the conversation, "we all want to know—how is your mom doing?"

Kit beams. "As of last month, she's cancer-free!"

The crowd screams their excitement along with the rest of the cast. Petra waves to a photo of us at our vow renewal with Maureen, my mom, and Jim.

"It sounds like you two have it all figured out." Petra beams.

"Hardly." I wave it off with a snort.

"Yeah, we're still screwing up most of the time." Kit reaches over to give my hand a squeeze.

I give him a fond smile, and suddenly we're the only ones in the room. "I wouldn't have it any other way."

Kit's eyes crinkle at the corners, his smile so wide it has to hurt. "Me neither, sweet potato."

Petra has to yell over the crowd's cheers. "And that's a wrap on *First Look at Forever*, Season Three! Join us next season to see if our matchmakers can get it right again!"

But my eyes are still on Kit, and he hasn't looked away from me. In front of the whole world—or at least the people watching the reunion live—he kisses me, and time stops. While this life feels like a dream made for TV, our love is very, very real.

ACKNOWLEDGMENTS

While it's true that writing is solitary and often isolating, it's also true that none of us do it alone. Help comes in all forms and from all corners of my life.

Kaitlyn Katsoupis, thank you for seeing the potential in my work and continuing to fight like hell behind the scenes to get my words into the world. The kind of work you do is magic. Holly Ingraham, thank you for taking a chance on my book based solely on a tweet. Your guidance has made this book better than I ever could have made it on my own.

Amanda Wilson and Michelle Cruz, your endless support has my endless gratitude. You've both been with me for many manuscripts before this one, and I hope many more to come. *Not You Again* may not have existed without you. Your meme drops, your encouraging words, your commiserating, your inside jokes. The ups and downs of creative work—and life—are much easier to endure with you both on my side.

Tobie Carter, I'm so glad KissPitch brought us together. Your GIF game is unmatched and your heart is bigger than any I've ever witnessed. It truly holds me together on my worst days. There are big things coming for you; I feel it in my bones.

To Livy Hart and Ava Watson, the very first readers of this book, thank you for loving the whole mess. Without your enthusiasm and demand for more pages, I don't know how I would have reached The

End. Cass Scotka, I'm so glad you spoke up about your desire to read this book before it even fully existed. Your guidance and margin screaming never went amiss.

To my beta readers—Kate Robb, Katherine Olson, and Julie Cassidy. I will never stop being grateful for how generous you were with your time and advice. (Julie, I can never get a Taylor Swift Easter egg past you!) You all helped shape this story in ways big and small, and I hope you see your mark in these pages.

I'm forever grateful to the romance writers of SF2.0. The way we cheer each other on and pick each other up when we stumble is beautiful to watch. Ellie Palmer, Mallory Marlowe, and Dallas Rose, your positivity as *Not You Again* was finally released into the world was an absolute game changer. Jen Devon and Kathryn Ferrer, your kind words and excitement for this book buoyed me when doubts threatened to drown me. I hope you never underestimate the power of a simple "just checking in."

Desirée Niccoli, I'm so fortunate to call you a friend. Your stories transport me to another place entirely, and I'm so grateful you let me read your words. Your support in this industry is worth more than I can say. Vik Francis, I've loved working with you on your own book. I also want to thank you for encouraging me to fall into a low-stakes, completely for me creative hobby. Thanks to you, I'll ride the waves of publishing, charting my course with a fountain pen and ink.

Laya Brusi and Sarah T. Dubb, thank you for your listening ears and your encouragement. They make all the difference. To my Alcove Press siblings Noreen Mughees and Mae Bennett, I'm so glad I don't have to go on this journey alone!

A special thanks to the team at Alcove Press: Dulce Botello, Mikaela Bender, Mia Bertrand, Stephanie Manova, Megan Matti, Rebecca Nelson, Thaisheemarie Fantauzzi Pérez, Doug White, and Matt Martz.

Corina and Danika, having you nearby is a gift. When I said I wanted to write romance, neither of you batted an eye. You've only ever cheered me on and asked to read what I've been working on, and I can't overestimate how much that means to me. I'm looking forward to many more poetry readings, sleepovers, and bad movie nights.

Last but certainly not least, Mr. Pierce. Our story began twenty-four years ago, and I would be lying if I said parts of this book weren't inspired by you. Throughout the years, you've supported every wild decision I've made, and through every twist and turn life throws at us, you've been by my side, an unwavering pillar of support. You've also been a soft place for me to land, and that is worth more than you'll ever know. Here's to many more years of laughter, friendship, romance, parenting, travel, growth, learning, and love.

To anyone who feels like they have to carry the weight of the world on their shoulders all alone, please look around and see who's waiting in the wings to swoop in and help. All you need to do is ask.